Alms

Alms

A NOVEL

Cynthia Macdonald

PENGUIN
CANADA

PENGUIN CANADA
Penguin Group (Canada), a division of Pearson Penguin Canada Inc.,
10 Alcorn Avenue, Toronto, Ontario M4V 3B2

Penguin Group (U.K.), 80 Strand, London WC2R 0RL, England
Penguin Group (U.S.), 375 Hudson Street, New York, New York 10014, U.S.A.
Penguin Group (Australia) Inc., 250 Camberwell Road, Camberwell, Victoria 3124, Australia
Penguin Group (Ireland), 25 St. Stephen's Green, Dublin 2, Ireland
Penguin Books India (P) Ltd, 11, Community Centre, Panchsheel Park,
New Delhi – 110 017, India
Penguin Group (New Zealand), cnr Rosedale and Airborne Roads, Albany, Auckland 1310,
New Zealand
Penguin Books (South Africa) (Pty) Ltd, 24 Sturdee Avenue, Rosebank 2196, South Africa

Penguin Group, Registered Offices: 80 Strand, London WC2R 0RL, England

First published 2003

1 2 3 4 5 6 7 8 9 10   (FR)

Manufactured in Canada.

NATIONAL LIBRARY OF CANADA CATALOGUING IN PUBLICATION

Macdonald, Cynthia, 1963–
Alms / Cynthia Macdonald.

ISBN 0-14-301379-3

I. Title.

PS8575.D625A44   2003   C811'.6   C2003-903078-4
PR9199.4.M428A44 2003

Visit the Penguin Group (Canada) website at **www.penguin.ca**

for Russell

"I have my standards, and some day I hope to live up to them."
—GROUCHO MARX

CLIFFORD KEARNEY WAS THIRTEEN the day he climbed on board sin and made himself its captain.

He'd stolen six bucks from his sister Rosemarie and made his way down to the Exhibition; bought himself three hot dogs, scoped the girls in shorts, then set off on foot for the ferry. The first thing he saw at the marina was a man telling the bowline of a shiny new sailboat that it was a cocksucker.

The bowline's problem was that it refused to be untied with one hand, and one hand was all the man had to offer it right then, since every square inch of his other one was clamped round a sloshing highball. "Kid," he barked— seemingly at Clifford, though the black sunglasses made it hard to tell.

"Me?" the boy asked.

"Yeah. Mustard face. Y'any good with knots?"

The man wore tartan Bermudas with black socks. On his head was a dingy old Panama with a perfect round hole in it,

1

carved, Clifford fancied, by a bullet. The man didn't look like the boat's owner and perhaps he wasn't.

Clifford wiped the mustard from his mouth and clambered aboard, thrilled by his sudden escape from reliable land onto the lake's precarious bob. He knew squat about knots but this one was a cinch for anyone with two hands and a minimum of booze in his blood and he untied it handily.

"Well, Jack be nimble!" the man cried. He shot the rest of his old-fashioned overboard and fired up a cigar. "Come on underneath, Chip, we'll fix you a cocktail."

It was only noon by Clifford's shoplifted watch but he shrugged and followed the man down below deck into a tiny cabin. Its gloom was a perfect showcase for the El Dorado glint of a bar such as the boy had never seen: bottles of every shape holding liquids of every colour and not one of them near full. The man decanted some dark purple glop into a crystal snifter, called Clifford "Chip" again, and gave it to him.

Clifford did not know why the man kept calling him Chip and the crappy drink hurt his teeth. He thought he might be more of a whisky man and was about to take his leave, but then something long and brown stirred on the small couch.

A mischievous wind rocked the boat and pitched him toward the stirring thing. He fell on the ground and it—she—took sudden shape before him: leg, hip, waist, breast, all encased snugly in skin softer than the leather of the chairs, cooler than the marble on the bar. Scented with coconut and gardenia.

"Oh," she said, upright now and all parts in place. She had a hand on her hip, its talons ablaze with orange paint.

Clifford got up, righted himself, and took the woman's place on the couch, the better to revel in her slick topography. How did this dilapidated coot land a prize like this?

The man thrust out his hand. "Lloyd L. Llewellyn is my name. Seven *L*'s. Most *L*'s of any name in Canada. What's yours?"

"Clifford," said Clifford. "Only one *L*."

"Whadderya studying in school, Chip?"

The boy set his snifter down, kept his eyes on the woman. "Uh—the usual. Math and that."

She picked up her robe and stretched into it with a series of feline elasticisms, then brushed something imaginary off her shoulder and click-clacked out of the cabin, oblivious to the boy's tortured watch.

The old man yawed about this and that under the fog of his cigar and Clifford stopped listening to him, squinting out the tiny window for a dart of arm or false eyelash. Didn't add up, he thought. This old fossil had no class and fewer looks but check what he had to show for it—a bar full of bottles, a sweeeeet boat, and one heart attack of a girlfriend. Maybe he was worth listening to.

"Whadderya thinking about studying, then?"

Clifford took another sip of the glop and choked it down. "Well," he mumbled. "Well." He didn't exactly know what the question meant but figured it had something to do with adulthood. And adulthood, as it concerned him, was already pretty much mapped out.

"I was thinking," he said, shy. He didn't want the woman to hear. It might hurt his chances with her, if any should come up.

"Thinking what, Chip?"

Clifford relaxed into the vinyl upholstery and jiggled his drink.

"Never mind," he said. "It'd never happen anyways."

*T*HE DEATH OF MARTINE CRAYTHORN'S CAREER was hard at hand. Clayton—she never called him Mr. Pine—had always been somewhat indifferent to her, but over the past week indifference had turned into contempt. When he greeted her in the morning, she could practically see his breath.

The author of *Attitude!* magazine's "Good Scouts" column was due for certain erasure and within hours, too. It was Friday, and all of her copy for next month's issue was written, edited, off to the printer. There was really nothing left for her to do but to wait until after lunch.

Martine had no appetite, but picked up a paper bag from under her desk anyway. She spread a linen napkin before her and placed three celery sticks on the left side of the napkin, close enough to touch each other. The carrot sticks she put in the middle, two inches beside the celery. The hard-boiled egg went last, beside the carrots on the right. Three servings out of her daily allotment of ten: she inscribed this fact in the little notebook she always carried with her, then started eating the food, three bites to a stick and four for the egg.

Business reporter. She had always loved the bitter aluminum taste of those words in her mouth. In practice the job was thuddingly dull, but she didn't mind. It was easy and it gave her time to do the daily crossword. She'd known Clayton since childhood—*Attitude!* was propped up and paid for by his wealthy father—and felt she could get away with anything, but this, apparently, was not the case.

At a quarter to two, Clayton leaned out of his office.

"Martine—would you mind coming in here for a minute?"

He gave her a look that was both doleful and terrified, and asked her to take the seat across from him. He cleared his throat and began. "Happily," he said, "we're looking at a budget surplus heading into eighty-eight. Less happily, it means we'll be having to make some changes."

It was an execution with a plastic knife; it was going to last minutes instead of seconds, and each one of those minutes would be crammed with rancid business euphemisms which, instead of softening the blow, would only deepen and sharpen it. Martine sat up straight with her long white hands folded still on her lap and her unscuffed pumps folded grace-fully beneath her. She was the staff member with the neatest desk, the straightest teeth, and the best posture. But none of these things would save her now.

Clayton finally sat down and dickered with his desk calen-dar for a minute. Martine noted that one of his green contact lenses had floated several microns off course, revealing a watery grey iris the colour of prison food.

"It's about Good Scouts," he said. "And I think you know what I'm going to say."

Good Scouts had been Martine's idea. Each month she took it upon herself to delve into the decency of the business community, profiling its finer members: the T-shirt manufacturer who made regular free shipments to community sports teams, for example, or the hair salon owner who gave free makeovers to underprivileged teens. Her first column was about Clayton's younger brother Jeremy, owner of Young Canadian Home Reno and Repair. It was a tricky one to start with since Martine had had a long, if hopelessly tepid, romantic association with him dating from late childhood, so in her article she'd fudged the fact that, although he hired high school students to work for him (Jeremy: "that counts as good!"), he paid them half the minimum wage and permitted them no more than fifteen minutes for lunch. Nonetheless, Good Scouts was as close as the thin, underread *Attitude!* got to virtue, and virtue was Martine's business — or had been, at one time.

"Saint Martine," the Pines called her: the little girl who didn't have to be dragged to mass but walked there of her own accord, the one who used to sit in their den leafing through the *Encyclopedia of the Saints,* who organized back-yard games of "communion" using ripple chips instead of hosts. That was a long time ago, though, and Clayton had probably forgotten.

"There might be an award in that," he'd said, when she first proposed the column to him. "No ads, but we could get some kind of award. Is that what you were thinking?"

"Yes," she'd replied quietly, embarrassed to let him think anything else.

Yet in spite of the distance she'd travelled from sainthood, Martine clung tenuously to the illusion. At age twenty-three she was no longer any better than other women; indeed she often suspected herself of having become far worse, no match, at any rate, for a good four of the seven deadlies. She knew that Good Scouts was only a tinfoil halo. But it was the last remnant of what she had once thought of as herself.

On the subway home she revisited the evisceration Clayton had performed on her. It turned out that one of the Scouts wasn't so *good* after all. He'd been Martine's favourite, too, the property developer who donated free office space to struggling artists. Pompadoured, French-cuffed, flamboyant, and Martine definitely suspected something when he poured them both Rob Roys in his office at eleven o'clock in the morning. But she was enjoying herself too much to care.

The struggling artists turned out to be filmmakers. And the film . . . Martine replayed the image of Clayton sliding the videocassette toward her, sheathed in its bright pink box, a box which bore the awful words that would seal her fate forever: *Raw Sewage 2.*

"Wow," she said, "what could that—"

Clayton stopped her. "Let's not even think about what this film might be about, Martine. Let's not even let our minds go one inch in that direction."

Martine went to pick up the box but thought better of it. "But these people look so . . . *normal,*" she said. The man and woman in the picture were smiling, sitting on a couch, dressed tastefully, casually—it was like a family photograph, a pair of cousins relaxing after Thanksgiving dinner.

"Well, then you pop it in your VCR, Martine, if that's the kind of thing you're into." He rubbed his prematurely craggy brow. "God. If it were only porn, I could probably keep you on. But if my dad finds out about this, he'll kill me."

She slumped against the subway pole, remembering the scene. The developer had been the one to call her up, after all, sensed something about her, lured her there as a kindred spirit. One more Rob Roy, she thought, and I might have ended up starring in—what, *Septic Tank Hank*? The dismissal itself wasn't killing her, no; if she'd been fired on a point of honour, she could have held her head high. It was the implied reproach to her character. When the other *Attitude!* employees had their handwriting analyses returned to them, they'd giggled. Not Martine.

"The struggle for letter verticality indicates inflexibility, self-absorption. Middle zone letters are narrowed, meaning the conscience is powerful . . . but covering strokes in the upper zone tend to cancel its unusually strong demands."

The report went on to say that Martine had a trait commonly found in anti-social personalities. Something called the "felon's claw," marked by a certain angularity in the way she wrote her *f*'s.

"But it's just a tool," Clayton had reassured her. "We don't set too much stock by it." That night in bed Jeremy Pine told Martine that his brother's own report had been even more damning, hence the exercise's just-a-toolness, and lucky for her, because that way he couldn't take anyone else's too seriously. But *she* couldn't let it go. Felon? Felon! Look, wasn't she . . . well, there had to be some proof against it, wasn't there? I mean, she was taking her half-brother to the zoo tomorrow, wasn't she? Wasn't that something?

Martine arrived home to find her mother sitting in the solarium with a bottle of Zinfandel on the table beside her, smoking a menthol and looking out into the garden. From behind her hair was glamorously whorled, black, giving no hint as to the grievous slashes and runnels on what was once a beautiful face. She had on her rose silk peignoir and did not turn around.

"How was work?" she asked. It was only five after four.

"Fine," Martine said. Her mother had often taken to spending her afternoons this way for three months now, ever since her second husband left: looking out at the garden, smoking, drinking. Some days there would be a dish of grapes beside her, or a little bottle of pills. The house was so intensely clean that any glass or vial or bowl on the round breakfast table looked ceremonial and foreign.

"You won't forget the Fandango, tomorrow," Louise said.

But of course Martine had forgotten it, and now found herself committed to both the zoo outing and to pouring mimosas at the hospital foundation's Summer Park Fandango, and this, all this *bullshit,* when all she wanted to do was think about herself. And her future, whatever that was going to be. But Louise was partly responsible for phoning and air-kissing the fundraiser into being, and in that state Martine found it especially hard to refuse her; Louise had always been a bit fragile, though never more so than in the past three months, in the wake of her marriage to a stepfather

10

Martine had always found laughable and not someone whose leaving should sadden anyone. But it saddened Louise, and drove her most afternoons to the solarium or to her large white bed, and Martine felt that even the smallest extra disappointment might produce uncaulkable cracks in the poor woman's mind. Awful as she felt, she couldn't skip out on the Fandango. And she sure as hell couldn't let on she'd been fired.

"Of course," she said, removing her shoes and letting her own dark hair fall free from the tight chignon in which she kept it by day. "But can I bring Obike?"

Louise turned around. She'd never liked Obike, or more properly the idea of him. For three years after his birth, she would only refer to him as "the creature."

"Obike? But why? This isn't a party for children, *minou.*"

"You said there'd be fire-eaters."

"Yes, but . . ."

Louise put out her cigarette and shrunk into the gigantic peignoir, which made Martine wince. *Should have checked the size when I bought it—but it was 4:59 on Christmas Eve!* More felony, she supposed. And how to prevent herself from committing even more now? There was no saying, "See, I told Dad," since the word "Dad" would instantly translate to "husband," which would then send Louise into weepy contemplations of the two she'd had: snarling meanies, the second one interested only in her money, the first interested only in his female graduate students—one of whom he'd left her for, an arrangement that was later to result in Obike. Even to have brought up the boy's name was wrong, Martine knew.

11

"I won't bring him," she vowed, though getting out of it would be tough. "I won't bring him, Mama," she repeated, as if the repetition itself would free her. Louise smiled weakly and turned back toward the garden.

But as Martine ascended the stairs that evening, she ably divined the complete wimping-out that would surely take place the next day, when her father and half-brother showed up at the door, all frisky about the zoo.

When the next day came, and one o'clock and the pair of them with it, Martine congratulated herself on her perspicacity. They were painfully eager, as she'd predicted. Wearing matching golf shirts—she'd got that one right, too. And her caving in took place at the exact moment she'd forecasted it would.

"The zoo," she said. "What a nice day for it, too."

"We've been reading about the tigers, haven't we?" Professor Craythorn cried, with a hearty clomp to his young son's back. If you asked Martine what she thought of her father, she would not have been able to tell you. She had no opinion, only a kind of rudimentary neurological response: a feeling that he was so hale, direct, and devouring that she would never be able to refuse him anything. But then, he'd never asked for much.

"I'm looking forward to it," she said, glad that her mother had already left. She invited her brother in and listened to him prattle while she searched the front-hall closet for her cape.

"Six o'clock?" asked Professor Craythorn.

"Six o'clock," croaked Martine.

"Aren't you going to be hot in that cape? It's boiling out," Obike offered brightly, after they'd watched their father leave. Martine ignored him. "We have to see the tigers first," he continued. "I thought I might see some in Ghana when we go there, but Daddy says they only live in Asia."

"You're going to Africa?" she said, alarmed. "With our father? When?"

"In the spring, to help put in some pipes or something."

"Oh." She smiled tightly. Her agronomist father had never so much as taken her to the drug store for a lollipop, let alone on one of his many African trips. She got the Fulani blankets, sure, and little carved zebras or *mbiras* from the market, which she'd play with for five minutes, then throw away. Stuff—she never lacked for stuff. What she'd rather have had was her father.

"You know, Obike," she said, "I really don't feel like going to the zoo today. There's actually a party I'd rather go to instead."

"A party?" the little boy asked.

"Yeah," she spat vengefully. "A *party*."

It was a beautiful summer Saturday. They got off the subway and walked close enough to the action to see the fire-eaters, the ladies in pink and yellow chiffon, the Villanueva Quintet, and the tuxedoed waiters from Satay by the Lake. But then Martine stopped at the park's edge, pausing on the curb.

"Are we going?" Obike asked tetchily. He was under-standably grumpy about the zoo and it was the first thing he'd said in fifteen minutes.

"I don't know," Martine replied. She watched Mott Colterblake, urologist and family friend, capering across the turf with a mimosa in his hand. He was an exhaustively aggressive character and Martine had never quite learned to deal with him, not even the least, most fleeting instance of him. There was dreadful Jane Pine, too, high heels viciously piercing the park's turf, and at least five or six other people Martine didn't feel she could tolerate today.

Timid little mouse, isn't she?

This was the general line on Martine, and for many years no one thought much of it—except the then-vivacious and graceful Louise, who'd once tried to derail the affliction by signing her only child up for modelling classes. But they didn't help at all, and past a person's fourteenth year, shyness is rarely excusable. Past fourteen is when the quiet start being tagged as strange or stuck-up, two adjectives graven like tattoos on the adolescent Martine, especially since she carried herself so proudly: bad posture, at least, might have inspired pity. She took questions that would ordinarily have inspired paragraphs of jolly reply from the other Moore Park girls—"How was Neuchâtel?"—and alchemized them into lead—"Fine, thank you." A dance of suspicion ensued among the neighbours. Even Martine's shiny dark hair and fine features plunged in value. Without charm, she was nothing more than a cheap figurine, something more for the cabinet than the mantel. *That Craythorn girl . . . she's never really come out of her shell, has she? What do you think could be the matter?*

She tried to fix the shyness. She had no choice. Her people were the late-century rich, back-patters and horse-laughers.

They didn't understand silence. They were her compatriots and she had no others; stay quiet and she would have to live without work or love. So when she came of age, entered university, and was forced to declare a major, she chose communications. But it didn't work. The stuck-uppedness stuck. She could not and never would communicate.

She had tried and now, bereft of a career, the trying felt over. Great warnings and denunciations staggered around inside her trying to find an exit sign. *Repent, Mott Colterblake!*

"Come on, kid," she said gently. "Let's take you home."

On the way back, Obike looked truly miserable. "We were supposed to go to the zoo," he said after a while. "You're going to get your name crossed off the list." It was a problem, he was right. It wasn't a question of where they hadn't gone, but of where they almost had. Professor Craythorn wouldn't want Obike exposed to his first wife's crowd, lest he be infected by a BMW virus or Louis Vuitton spirochete, and thus end up a soul-dead business reporter like his older sister. Obike was strictly protected from anyone who would vote Conservative via an index of approved playmates and play destinations, which was posted by Martine's stepmother on a bulletin board in their tiny downtown kitchen.

The list was silly, but she was still as scared as her brother was. Of what, though? Why couldn't she say? The Professor scared you and that was that. Martine often thought that if he weren't so busy doing the right thing—starting up agricultural cooperatives in Africa, firing off angry letters about apartheid, manning the bullhorn at rallies devoted to the cessation of cruise-missile testing—that he could start a cult. He had the touch. It was a power Martine had always admired. But as she looked at Obike now she wondered whether admiration was really the proper attitude. She wanted to place a hand on the boy's shoulder, but didn't. They hadn't touched since he was a toddler, and it would be strange now.

"You're going to get fired," said Obike. "You won't get your money for today."

"It's okay," Martine reassured him. "I . . . have another job, anyway."

"What do you do?"

"I write articles. About business people."

When Obike was a baby Martine used to wish he resembled her more. That way, she thought, she might have felt the easy sibling connection so present and obvious in the large Pine brood, with their identical straw-coloured heads and pug noses. But to wish away the baby's coffee-coloured skin was so patently immoral that she never let anyone know she was doing it. He was so unlike her anyway; so comfortable in the world, and at such a young age, too.

"What are business people?"

"Business people," replied Martine, "are two-headed monsters with scales. They carry square cardboard bags full of poisons. They carve mean letters to people with knives, then strangle them with the striped ropes they wear around their necks. Didn't your dad ever tell you that?"

"No."

"He used to tell me," she said as the subway exploded into the station. "*All* the time."

Alms

Obike bounded up the steps to the tiny apartment where his father and mother lived. He had actually been born there— "On purpose!" Louise had hissed to Martine. Rumours abounded that Abeni had made soup from the placenta, or planted it outside in a neighbourhood park, but Martine refused to believe them.

She followed him slowly, as if walking a plank. When they passed the Professor's newspapers, ostentatiously bundled and ready for the recycling depot, the pit in her stomach felt colder still.

Goodness was once rote habit for her, too, the way some girls take up the piccolo or collect little pink pigs. A habit abetted by the private Catholic schools of her youth, where she had only been placed so that Louise could keep up with the Pines, whose mother regularly preached the importance of hot-lunch programs and early social networking (the uniforms were *darling,* too). You only needed one Catholic parent to qualify and that would sort of be Louise. The Professor had no time for religion, or any institution for that matter—he'd once filled out his tax return in Roman numerals and got himself audited within an inch of his life. Religion, he felt, was definitely the opiate of the masses: the adorable, if incredibly stupid, masses.

But Martine took to Catholicism with disturbing gusto. At school, she helped the nuns organize the Christmas food hampers and always brought extra wax beans and creamed corn, oblivious to the disgust of her classmates. She would pray at her desk instead of doing what was asked of her, until the teachers got tired of it and told her to knock it off. She wouldn't. She spent her days praying and dreaming, doodling pictures of skeletal African children in her work-books.

Martine was fascinated by these children, the kind you saw on television or in magazine ads; she called them "porepeople." The Professor obviously had a thing for them too, regularly jetting to Dahomey or Togo with bags of millet to scatter at their feet. These unfortunates lurked everywhere at Catholic school: on posters in the hallway, in class discussions, in biblical parables—they were everywhere but in the seat next to Martine, and their very absence was most appealing to a quiet child like her. When people were there, they obtruded. They asked questions and expected answers. But the flat poster-faces of the poor made no sound whatsoever, for which Martine was grateful.

In any case, they seemed to have no voices with which to make sound, only eyes, eyes that were greater, darker, and rounder than any she'd ever faced. With their dark skin and jutting stomachs they were fascinatingly alien, and Martine was drawn to them; she believed the jutting to be natural, not an effect of malnutrition. She knew her father wouldn't keep tearing off in their service for no reason at all. He always came home from each trip changed, his face haunted by whatever it was he'd seen. What new secrets lay behind his eyes? she wondered. How she longed to go with him!

One day she asked him to take her, while he was packing for yet another trip. He shook his head. "There aren't any amusement parks where I'm going," he said. "There aren't any movie theatres playing *Chitty Chitty Bang Bang*."

Martine felt that he was growing to dislike her and didn't know why. She only hit on it years later: when he looked at the straight back and sleek ponytail, he saw only the noxious, coin-shaped genes of heiress Louise. Martine would never win with him, but she kept trying anyway.

"I want to buy this kid," she said to Louise one afternoon, dropping a Save the Children flyer on the hall table. "Gimme ten dollars so I can send away for her."

Children like this were "starving," which, Martine believed, was hardly the worst thing that could happen to you. "I'm starving," she'd heard Sharon Colterblake say to Louise many times after tennis. "I'm absolutely going to *die* I'm so hungry." It was an easy problem to fix: all you had to do was eat. Right?

The Professor greeted them at the door, nattily dressed as always. He was like Martine that way: sartorially ruthless, knife pleats in the jeans at all times, a sworn enemy of the frayed cuff and hanging button. His clothes were inexpensive, but invariably held in the highest regard.

"You're back a little early, aren't you?" he asked, but it wasn't a question.

"The zoo was closed," Obike muttered as he scuttled toward the kitchen.

The Professor stared after him for a tormenting few seconds before turning to his daughter. "Closed?" he intoned coldly, knowing it wasn't so.

"No," Martine blurted, realizing he'd discover the truth in the end. "I just had this thing I had to do, and I forgot. So, we did that instead."

Abeni poked her head out of the kitchen. "Hey, did you have a good time?"

Martine grunted that they had. She always played it cool here, feeling that any friendliness toward Abeni would equal disloyalty to Louise.

The Professor ushered his daughter into the room and motioned toward the couch. "So what was this thing," he asked, "this thing that was so important."

Martine's gaze fixed on a flyer sitting on the coffee table. Electric pink, the same colour as her mother's favourite lipstick. WE NEED TUTORS, it said. Everything else in this apartment was earth-coloured: all the furniture, carvings, hangings; the paint on the walls, the clothes of the inhabitants. Had there been a dishwasher, or a television, they would have been that way, too. So the flyer really stood out and she could not take her eyes off it.

"It was a party," she said. "A benefit that Mom was putting on, for the hospital, to raise money for their HIV Primary Care Clinic, and stuff."

"Hmph," he said. "Who was at this . . . party?"

"Well, you know . . . the Colterblakes and . . . the Pines . . ."

"Jesus Christ."

"But it's okay, you know. Because we didn't go."

"What do you mean, you didn't go? You just said you did."

"I know, but. We sort of went and we sort of didn't."

The Professor sat back, folded his arms across his muscular farmer's chest, and stared. He looked weary. His babysitter had not delivered.

"I don't know why you think a nine-year-old child would find a hospital party of any interest, anyway."

"But, Dad—" Martine countered, "*HIV!*"

The Professor leaned forward. "Excuse me?"

Martine thought she could mollify him with mention of a just cause. He was normally a sucker for such things, no question of that. He really never took a break from serving mankind, not even on statutory holidays.

She remembered the last Christmas they had together, when she was eight years old. She'd spent the morning tearing gilt wrap from so many boxes that by ten o'clock she was fairly drowning in loot—dresses, jewellery, gloves, dolls—most of it from Louise but quite a bit, too, from her Berthiaume grandparents in Montreal. The Professor just sat watching her, refusing to open any presents, looking at his watch. He declined pancakes, too. After breakfast, he ordered his daughter to put on her best new outfit and get in the car.

"Where are we going?" she asked.

"Just to the children's hospital," he said. "So you can see the other side of Christmas."

They took an elevator to the long-term care ward and joined a small group of carolers, some of whom seemed to know him. The group made its way to a sort of large play-room where a number of boys and girls in their pyjamas were gathered around a large plastic tree opening their presents. Some were Martine's age, thin and bald; she realized with horror that this might be their last Christmas, and it was a matter of simple torture for her to croak out the carols.

On the drive home she asked her father, "Daddy, could— could that ever happen to me?"

The Professor paused before he spoke. "Probably not," he said airily, strangely in the Christmas spirit now. "But you never know. Life takes strange turns sometimes."

With that remark, all the coloured lights in the passing bushes seemed to grow dim; Christmas was done. Martine went home and sat nauseated before her jumble of new dolls and blouses, her ached-for Spirograph set. She couldn't eat any of her turkey or plum pudding.

So it was natural for her to assume, years later, that her father would back off when told of the righting of a wrong, even a wrong righted with chamber music and fire-eating mimes. But he just shook his bearded head again. *"HIV,"* he said. "I am not even going to ask you what you mean by that."

Martine might have pointed out that, in accordance with twenty-year-old folkways, he never gave a rat's butt where she was at any given point in her childhood, and that for him to take the moral high ground now in the matter of childcare was really something. These gruelling little couch post-mortems after her twice-monthly outings with Obike represented the only private time they ever had together. Ah, well. The only thing was to keep reading the pamphlet, its gay pink a balm in the middle of all the earth tones. WE NEED TUTORS. GLENSTONE PUBLIC LIBRARY.

"All right, Martine," her father said, rising heavily from the couch. Her very presence seemed to exhaust him. "You'll get around to taking him some other time, I guess." Then he walked to the kitchen, and the second his stocking foot hit the kitchen tile Martine heard him brighten: "Hey, hey, fella! I haven't seen you all day!"

She sat for a minute, listening to the Craythorn family play happily in the kitchen: Papa Bear, Mama Bear, Baby Bear. Like a dark-haired Goldilocks, she had blundered into someone else's home. She put on her cape and let herself out.

*L*OUISE WAS ASLEEP by the time Martine got back to Moore Park. It was five-thirty. She took her pumps off and crept up the stairs. No sound but the heavy thwack of the grandfather clock in the downstairs hall. That and the vacuum were the only things one ever heard in this vastly underpopulated house.

Martine's bedroom hadn't changed since she was seven years old. There was the vanity with its heart-shaped seat, its contents arranged before the mirror: perfume atomizer, Mémère Berthiaume's silver brush and comb set, the jewellery box which, when opened, revealed a plastic ballerina who pirouetted to the tune of "Lara's Theme." The mauve bedspread was eerily smooth; credit Emelda, the long-time housekeeper, woman of talent and mystery. Yellow throw pillows lay still and perfect underneath the brass bedstead. Louise had tried to argue Martine into a canopy but she wouldn't hear of it, too girly, and she'd also rejected pink bedding and rose-patterned wallpaper. Mauve was the compromise, though Martine insisted on calling it purple. Louise won the flowered wallpaper argument, too, yet Martine satisfied herself that the golden nosegays were righteously bright, with angry black pistils.

"Martini?" Louise was not quite asleep. Martine sat frozen on the bed, trying to hold off going in to her. She knew that her mother only wanted a hug and there would be no talk of her absence at the Fandango. Louise never liked a fight.

Martine rose and walked down to the darkened master bedroom. She crept through a vale of air freshener to where her mother lay, then wrapped her in her arms. She might have liked hugs had she not been forced to dispense them with metronomic regularity, overhot silken hugs that trained their choked recipient to resist most any kind of touch at all. She was a good daughter, though. She never stopped hugging first, but she did count the seconds, which always numbered from eight to ten.

"I'm sorry, Mama. For not showing up, and . . ."

"It's all right, *minou*. Did you have supper?" The great moist eyes stayed shut. She spoke slowly, as if her jaw needed oil.

"I will," Martine lied. She'd snuck two mimosas at the Fandango and then promptly lost her appetite.

Louise closed her eyes again and said that was *lovely,* and from the way she said it, it was extra lovely, liquidly, languidly lovely. Then she drifted back to sleep again.

Martine watched her for a minute in the dark. For some time she'd wanted to leave this house, never more so than today. But if she did, who would take care of Louise? Sure,

Sharon Colterblake and Jane Pine could take her to lunch; Emelda could iron her dresses and launder her nylons; men might come for a while, but probably wouldn't stay that long. Who would there be to love her?

But then, Martine winced, I'm probably not the best person for the job either. She held her mother's hand and marvelled at its softness, the tender insistence of its small knuckles. I hurt her, too, I can't help it. It's as if she asks for it.

She pushed the hand away gently, replaced the pill bottle in the medicine cabinet, and picked up the empty glass and wine bottle.

If I stay, she thought, I'll only hurt her more.

She took the glass and bottle down to the kitchen. There was a note on the fridge: "Jeremy called."

Through the solarium window she could see the great Pine home, dark windows shrouded in ivy. Only a few years ago all those windows were lit, giving onto hallways that were crowded with clattering teenagers. It was an irresistibly attractive house for Martine, whose own house was childless, petless, rank with the stench of divorce.

When she was growing up, the Pines ruled Garland Avenue—it was their Hyannisport. As children, they were always commandeering it for family football games or fixing their palms in the new cement of freshly poured sidewalks. Later, when Pine girls pawed their boyfriends in the street and Pine boys blared Motorhead from their bedroom windows, you just had to take it. They were the Pines. Calling the police would be unthinkable.

The door to their massive house was always open and it was easy and attractive for only children like Martine to fancy herself one of them, though she hadn't a fraction of their boldness and was physically so dissimilar, small and dark instead of brawny and blond. They took her in anyway— though of course they took everyone in. Louise had set up a beautiful playroom for her daughter in the basement, complete with an easel, a pink piano, several life-sized stuffed bears, and a beautiful porcelain doll collection. But the little girl felt adrift there and it went unused. She far preferred the lively ramble of the Pine house and did whatever she pleased there, wandering around and helping herself to books and toys, snooping around Cathy's room and marvelling at the length of the chain Monica had made from chewing-gum wrappers.

Even at seven years old, though, Martine was appalled by the messiness of these rooms; those in her own house were burnished and mausoleum-still, the kind of rooms where a used sock on the carpet might as well have been a dog's corpse. Wandering through Cathy's lair, it was hard for Martine to resist picking up a 45 or a teddy bear or a pair of panties, behaviour that also became automatic in the other girls' bedrooms. The Pines mocked her for it.

"I guess you expect us to pay you," sniffed Joanna. "But my mom already pays Merlinda and Fettie and Daisy. So if you want to clean, you'll just have to do it volunteer."

Martine didn't know what "volunteer" meant and was afraid to ask. She thought it must be something dangerous or shameful—it had to be, coming from salacious junior-high Joanna. She tried it out at dinner to see if she would get in trouble.

"Pass the volunteer milk," she said.

"'The volunteer milk?'" asked Louise, a slight smile playing at her frosted lips. But pass it she did, without comment. This hardly reassured Martine, however. Her mother wouldn't be *au courant* as far as the new swear words were concerned. The little girl worried the rest of the evening away. Volunteer, volunteer . . . looking it up in the dictionary would be of no use if it were a new schoolyard locution. She tried to sleep on it. And finally, just as she was falling asleep, the idea stabbed her in her little mauve bed, with a simplicity that made her feel stupid for not having come to it before: *volunteer* means *without underwear*. She stopped cleaning their rooms after that.

Joanna Pine hated her, anyway. In those days Jane Pine seemed to favour Martine over her own daughters, with her little ankle socks and kilts, her hair always brushed back and caught in a ponytail. "Oh, Joey, look at her little locket! Did your mother give you that, dear?"

"It's from my pépère," Martine explained. "For my confirmation."

"Isn't it *darling*. Joey, you have some lovely confirmation jewellery, too, don't you? What about that charm bracelet from Auntie Pat?" But Joanna didn't really hear her mother; she sat before her on the stairs in a crocheted halter top and patchwork jeans, completely wreathed in pot smoke. "And take that blasted cigarette into your room," Jane cried, waving the cloud away. "It stinks to high heaven!"

"It's not a cigarette, Mother," said Joanna dully.

"Of course it's a *cigarette*," Jane blatted. "Do you think I was born yesterday?"

If Martine had a favourite Pine in those days, it was Jeremy. He was the funniest, and startlingly handsome, too. They were in the same class, but while she earned high marks without effort, he was always on the verge of failing. She could see him trying, bent hard over the work and trying to force sense out of the sums and stories they were required to learn. Sadistic teachers made a particular point of calling on him so he could model his defects for the class, and every day he slumped a little lower in his chair.

In the end it was too much for Martine; she felt sick with pity and decided to muff an arithmetic test to show solidarity with him. She just wrote down any old thing, not even looking at the questions, and with some triumph was later able to slide her paper over to his, a proud red *F* astride its miserable answers. He barely smiled, but she knew he was pleased. So she did it again and again, and by report card time they were true confederates, the worst students in their class.

All this worried Louise, of course. "You do know that Jeremy Pine once dropped his younger brother off the Scarborough Bluffs," she cautioned.

"He didn't drop him—they stopped him in time."

"Well, it's the thought that counts. But why? Why him, Martini? Is it just because he's an underdog? Someday you'll realize that the underdog is usually the underdog for a reason."

In fact, Martine spent a lot of time in those days sitting at the top of the great main staircase while Jeremy practised for the Bluffs by pitching poor Elliott down the stairs. Over and over he did this, without any comment from Elliott, since the younger boy, like Martine, was no talker. Elliott just took it, weirdly, rolled down and flopped to a stop, then staggered back up the stairs for more. "That is just so mean," Martine admonished after a week or so of watching this game. "You're going to break his arm or something." But her protests were half-hearted. It secretly fascinated her to watch that big, pink porpoise of a boy dropping in aching increments, punishing each cool green-carpeted stair with his bulk. Then back up he came, always, without a word. Every time. Which had to mean, Martine figured, that Elliott liked it. Didn't he?

One day, to their surprise, Jeremy and Martine found themselves necking in the laundry room. They were fourteen years old. Thereafter he was her boyfriend, sort of. At least, she'd never had any other. But the relationship was a desultory botch from the start. There was never any real physical chemistry between them, for one thing, but Martine, with her hatred of loose ends (and her vestigial pity for him), kept grinding on with it through the years, vowing to leave as soon as the eventual sex and conversation were up and running. Jeremy, though, was like a radio station she couldn't quite tune into; the static and fuzz persisted, the knob kept falling off.

He never ended up noticing these things himself. Perhaps he wasn't that bright after all. Last year, in fact, he'd asked her to marry him.

"Let's get hitched," he rasped one night, irritated, as if frustrated about leaving something on the bus.

"Is that a proposal?" Martine choked. It could have been. She'd had never had one before; they might all be like that in real life.

"A pro—come on man, nobody does that stuff any more. Let's just get married."

Cynthia Macdonald

She stared at him, then burst out laughing. It wasn't a very romantic thing to do, but he just scoffed and turned off the light.

She lay beside him, one hand against the machine-made slope of his latissimus dorsi. She knew he wasn't sleeping either. I never should have failed that math test, she thought. Who knows where I might be now?

She stared hard at the note on the fridge, willing it to read something else. *Jeremy didn't call* would have been nice. Or maybe: *Jeremy never called. You never met Jeremy.*

Had the last been true, she would never have had to hold her nose and write of the penultimate Pine's "gumption" and "moxie"; of his "can-do attitude" and his "little staff that could." She would never have had to sit for fifteen minutes thinking up alternative ways to say "blond" (it was a long article, in which the other Pines made cameo appearances: Monica was "fair-haired," Joanna "gold-plaited," and Jeremy ended up resembling "a young George Peppard"). She would not have to meet him tomorrow, go back to his condo, refuse his offer of melon liqueur, undo her blouse and bun, and lie like a crushed squirrel beneath the talentless press of his big Pine body. Her life would have been Pineless, and maybe the better for it.

She picked the note off the fridge, crumpled it up, and went to bed.

*M*ARTINE WOKE UP Monday morning to the Saharan vastness of nothing to do. Even the city's sidewalks did not need her, as they were being trod even this minute by many other, more purposeful feet.

If she were to leave this house, she would need a job, but what? She decided to figure it out while cleaning her room, which was, of course, already clean. There was the closet, though.

She got up, put on her robe, and started hacking around beneath the racks of pendant black skirts, pants, and blouses. There was a bicycle pump in there for some reason, and four unsigned yearbooks. There was also a rolled-up Persian carpet that Louise hadn't found a place for in the house. And there was the shoebox.

The Bible and the Kelly Centre photograph were still there, as well as an old rosary and Martine's worst report cards; her marks had never really recovered after her self-imposed trip down south to Jeremy. All the letters her father had written her from Africa were in there, too, letters that only revealed how little he knew of what she'd become: he wrote to a pink phantom back then, to Cordelia instead of Goneril, but there'd been love in them or something very like it. Her own letters back, many of which she hadn't sent but had kept, were generally terse and studded with small homilies.

September 14, 1972

Dear Daddy,

I have decided that when I grow up I will be a nun in Biafra or a backup singer for Cat Stevens, whichever need is greatest. Cat Stevens is a GREAT guy his music crossed the British ocean to touch all of us. I love his song "Peace Train." I could do the ee-ah-oo-ah part if not needed for Biafra.

Hard to believe this was written by the same hand that won second prize in the city-wide Lenten Literary Contest only three years later:

*She lingers in a doorway on summer's hottest day
Her tiny face lined with bleakest dismay*

The poem was autobiographical, but the specially convened adjudicators from the Catholic school board didn't know that, of course. They were understandably deceived by the poem's title: "Rosita of Peru." They gave Martine a paperback copy of the New Testament, which disappointed her; it seemed so flimsy, hardly up to the magnitude of her achievement. But then she had very high standards for prizes, and nothing visible or tangible would have satisfied. The best prize would be a feeling: a feeling she constantly chased but couldn't quite nail.

She took out the Kelly Centre photograph and fingered it. There she was, the star of the show, with an actual smile on her face.

The photograph started on its road to being taken when an administrator from the centre had come to speak to Martine's homeroom class one day. She was looking for volunteers to work with the children in residence, who suffered from a variety of physical disabilities. The place was just across the street, and children were invited to help out on their lunch hours.

Martine raised her hand forthrightly, and saw with some relief that she was the only one. Goodness was her property, and she wasn't about to have somebody else steal it from her.

"What are you doing? They got blind kids there," hissed Jeremy, sitting behind her. "And kids who drool and there's even some our age in diapers. It's a House of Horrors. You'll regret it, man." She frowned at him while the teacher wrote her name down.

But when the appointed day came, she simply couldn't do it. She crossed the street and stood before the door, unable to enter. She realized that when her beloved unfortunates were loosed from poems and posters, when they took on another dimension and expected Martine to watch them, talk to them, and—gasp—touch them, they lost their appeal. Handicapped children were certainly no less than other human beings, but they *were* human beings, instead of abstract concepts, and therein lay the problem. She stood in front of the door for five minutes, reasoning that if someone opened the door, she'd walk in. But no one did.

Later, when her embarrassed teacher demanded an explanation for her absence, she pleaded sickness. But the lie needled her through the months that followed, and after a very long while she decided to do something about it.

She settled on the idea of a bottle drive, which was a favourite fundraising tactic of the Girl Guides and local bantam hockey team. She spent a week picking through her neighbours' garbage cans in search of glass bottles. She pressed Louise into driving her around, which Louise could do, since in those days she spent relatively little time in bed and the solarium hadn't been built yet. But her mother's approval was grudging and abashed. She didn't exactly savour the picture of her daughter turning into her ex-husband.

Martine ended up filling the trunk of Louise's Mercedes several times over. She took the bottles to a recycling depot, cashed them in, and handed over the money to the Kelly Centre. She then phoned the neighbourhood paper and told them what she'd done.

A reporter took notes and wrote an article. LOCAL GIRL RAISES MONEY FOR CHARITY went the headline. Above the story was a grainy photo of Martine shaking hands with the lady from the Kelly Centre. The young philanthropist looked concerned but radiant, and Louise had bought her a new polyester pantsuit for the occasion. The principal put a commendation on the intercom. Kids wheeled around and stared at her in class, and she preened. It was totally cool. A moral jackpot. Her part-time candystriper job had nothing on it. It was like being the star act on "Kiddies on Kamera," or winning the Miss Canada contest. It was her moment in the sun, and she yearned for others.

The phone grangled several miles away in her mother's bedroom, but even though it was right beside Louise's bed it didn't wake her. Martine knew this from Emelda's shrill serenade at the bottom of the stairs. "Mrs. Craythorn? Mrs. Craythorn? MRS. CRAY—ah, forget about it."

I can't stay here this morning, thought Martine.

She put the shoebox back in the closet. It was then she remembered the pink flyer at her father's house: WE NEED TUTORS. She had made a thorough study of it in the time she spent avoiding his bored glare. READING, WRITING, AND MATHEMATICS, it said, and GLENSTONE PUBLIC LIBRARY, and READING ACTION COMMITTEE, and MONDAY. Monday— as in, today? That might be a gig, and a virtuous one too. That might be just the antidote to *Raw Sewage 2*. It didn't expressly mention porepeople, but you knew they had to be part of the deal. Of course, if the Professor and Abeni were also part of the deal, that would wreck things. But Martine decided to gamble on their being busy with other good works.

She sprang out of bed and made for the telephone. The library lady said that the orientation started at eleven o'clock.

The address may as well have been on Mars, and her journey would be labyrinthine and long. But—porepeople!

She'd have to dress down for the literacy job, but not so down that she'd look like one of the clients. It was a tricky balance. In jeans and a T-shirt she'd blend nicely; *clean* versions thereof would mark her as helper instead of helped.

Emelda was standing over the stove yattering about her husband's ulcer while Louise sat, awake now and vaguely listening, puffing on another menthol. When her only-begotten entered the kitchen she broke into a warm smile and looked to be fixing for a hug. This Martine avoided with a quick detour to the fridge. She opened it and cased the humming lit shelves for juice, but none was immediately apparent. Not that there wasn't plenty there: leftover pork roast, mashed potatoes, ginger ale, a jeroboam of homogenized milk, single-serving puddings, peaches, low-cal whip topping, cucumbers, red Jell-O, enough sauces and condiments to stock a ship. Then the back of the fridge, where lurked neglected franks 'n' beans, a taco salvaged from an election party in 1974, wizened hunks of onion and tomato, and a box of baking soda to aerate the whole. The fridge sagged under the weight of the freezer, full as it was of Eskimo pies and chicken cutlets, shoestring fries and bags of frozen succotash. Then the cupboards, oh, the cupboards: dried beans and spices, food colorants and powdered soups, giant paper satchels of sugar and flour and cereal—nine, ten boxes of it, some nutritious and some not so, everything from Shredded Wheats to Choco-Berry Puffs—and cans: Numbo-Ghetti, Bing cherries, creamed corn. An entire shelf reserved for Berthiaume soup, which came to them gratis, Louise's father having founded the company. For two people, a full harvest—the best, the most, from field, factory, and slaughterhouse. But all she wanted was orange juice, and there wasn't any there.

"Sit, Martina," snapped Emelda. "How you want your eggs?"

"No eggs," she grumbled back, "*thank* you."

There were Scandinavian cutlery and plates on the sunroom's dining table, a yellow woven tablecloth, and a pot of chrysanthemums in the centre, as well as butter and jam on chunky little plates. Breakfast had long been a kind of sado-masochistic minuet in this particular kitchen. Every day Martine pleaded for nothing but juice, which was usually given her, but Emelda always cooked her something hot and plentiful to go along with it, something she knew would go uneaten and get scraped into the trash. The fighting about it had long stopped. Years back, Louise had the vigour for it and exercised it nightly.

"There are children starving in India, Martine, who would be very grateful for that lamb chop."

"I know, Mother. That's the *point*."

Sometimes the poor woman could only clutch her head between her hands and weep. Such a hard daughter she had; a cold steel rod with hair. "Honestly . . . do you think if you don't eat dinner tonight, it's going to make a difference? Who will notice besides me? Couldn't you just be a vegetarian or something?"

In Martine's childhood, before Professor Craythorn moved out, he would often tuck her in at bedtime and tell her, not of Tigger and Sleeping Beauty, but of Biafra and Bangladesh. Countless millions suffer from malnutrition, he

Cynthia Macdonald

said. A small fraction of the world's people eat half of all food produced. Every few seconds in the world a child dies of hunger. When he moved downtown, he left behind a child electric with guilt; a set of tangled wires her exhausted mother was powerless to unravel.

*M*ARTINE GOT ON A BUS, then a subway, then a streetcar, and soon she found herself standing in front of the Glenstone Library. TRAINING SESSION INSIDE, a sign in the window proclaimed.

The windowless room she entered was full of other aspiring teachers. In the middle of them all, a pretty redhead phosphoresced quietly in the corner.

It was Carolyn Colterblake, daughter of the odious Mott and Sharon. Carolyn: eater of ham sandwiches, drinker of homogenized milk, provincial champion in the four hundred and eight hundred metres!

Actually, "pretty" was probably a better descriptor of Martine: petite, with her economical face and its neatly carved features. She often thought of herself as too small for real beauty, though, on nodding terms with disappearance, a state nurtured by her bizarre diet. In another era she might have won points for her delicacy, and that she didn't now rarely concerned her. But seeing broad fluid Carolyn sitting there, her hair jouncing, her teeth big and wet, she was gripped for a moment by cheerleader envy.

Martine went and sat down beside her. She wore a name tag that said: HI, MY NAME IS CAROLYN. Her complexion looked freshly polymerized and tinted by some benevolent dollmaker. "Martine Craythorn! Oh my God."

Martine greeted her stiffly and sat down. Carolyn was the one Louise always compared her to, as in: "I hear Carolyn got top marks at the Kiwanis Festival" (when Martine had not even entered), or, "Didn't Carolyn look lovely at grad-uation!" (while Martine wore a severe black sheath and rejected the idea of eyeshadow). Why, why the hell was Carolyn here? Her parents were bad people, "Christian as pigs" in her late Mémère Berthiaume's phrase, so what angle could she possibly be working? And really, Martine thought nastily, who between the two of them had earned the right to give—to whom would it come more naturally? She slouched in her chair and arrived despondently at the answer: the one holding the gifts, of course. And that was Carolyn.

To cheer herself up, Martine thought back to the time that Jeremy had sent Sharon Colterblake to the hospital. Their mothers all belonged to the same gourmet club, and one evening he had laced their zabaglione with acid he'd bought from some guy at the Eaton Centre. This sent the ladies home in a right state, including Carolyn's mother, who'd been taken to the emergency room screaming about the knitting rabbits that were darting across her vision. Jeremy was grounded for a week.

"So what are you doing now?" Carolyn asked.

"Well—this. I'm doing this."

"No, but I mean besides. Are you still with that magazine?"

Oh, that the ceiling fan would fall on her, Martine thought. She sat up even straighter than usual and folded white hands on her lap. "No. No, that's over for me now. I'm not doing anything like that ever again."

"Oh . . ." Carolyn replied with a weak smile, uncomfortable with the drama.

"But don't let me bore you with my problems," Martine breezed. "You—you're studying psychology, I hear."

"I am," Carolyn said proudly. The fan did not fall on her but blew hair onto her lips; three shining strands fluttered into her lip gloss and she pushed them away. "Masters in clinical psych, actually. I've been pretty busy at this clinic downtown, doing some counselling work. With teenage girls. So I'm glad this is only weekends."

"Only on weekends?" Martine sputtered.

"God, I hope so. I mean it's not like they're paying us."

"Oh? How much *are* they paying us?" Martine asked, feigning calm. But the session was starting.

First, they all had to introduce themselves and say what they did, a suitably gruesome exercise insofar as Martine was the only one who had nothing to tell them on that score. Then the leader switched off the lights and on came a film about a little South American jungle dweller named Pito. It was one of those ancient, spotted prints with a wobbly soundtrack, a film so old that its makers were no doubt unanimously dead.

Pito the Fisherboy featured a happy twelve-year-old submitting with suspicious cheer to a band of aggressively white visitors who've travelled the Amazon by raft to school him in the art of reading Dick and Jane books, to what end Martine could not figure. So he could expand his *opportunities,* she guessed, so he could become a doctor, or a teacher, or a thrice-divorced producer of television commercials, or at the very least be able to alphabetize a spice rack.

But where did reading ever get me? she thought. Maybe it was much more useful to thread nets and fend off piranhas with your elbows, and that, in the end, was the film's conclusion, too; it ultimately wearied of its condescending premise and floated back down the river with its khaki-clad tutors. *Though I've beat you and I've flayed you, by the living God that made you, you're a better man than I am, Gunga Din!*

In fact, the thought occurred to Martine that they had all been lured under false pretences to an *anti-*reading seminar, some kind of Pol Pot rig-up where they would all be sent to South American islands to do authentic work among authentic folk. This idea was reinforced within five minutes, when the seminar leader started leading the class in actual calisthenics, such as Martine had heard workers were hourly forced to do in repressive totalitarian regimes.

In the middle of a deep knee bend, Carolyn looked up — her knees bent much deeper than Martine's — and said, "It's volunteer."

Martine remembered the night she had learned the proper definition of that word. Louise was in front of the floor-length mirror in her bedroom, testing a succession of necklaces against the gown she planned on wearing to an upcoming ball. "Why don't you wear your favourite?" suggested Martine. "The one with the diamonds and the blue things."

"Sapphires," answered Louise, who seemed to be inclining toward a string of chunky yellow beads, an old gift from one of the Professor's trips. "Oh, it would just be a waste to take that out. Nobody will see me anyway. I'll be sitting at a table in the back—that's where they put the volunteers."

In the back: that's where they put the volunteers. Without underwear was a sufficiently disgraceful idea, Martine thought, but without pay, that was worse. It meant your work wasn't worth anything. It was true that she didn't strictly *need* money from this tutoring job. If she wanted to leave home, there were savings bonds she could cash in, as well as surplus from an educational fund that was hers to spend. A loan from Pépère wasn't out of the question either. But it was the principle that mattered here. Why should the *Attitude!* job pay her, when ennobling work such as this did not? It was just like the world to load bond traders down with all the money, when the ones who actually improved things—women, mostly—had their succor mainlined and unrewarded. Sure, she could earn some token stipend as a teacher or social worker, but then she'd have to follow dull grey rules prescribed by others. No, she would set this right. She was going to help, and somehow— maybe not now, but in the end—she was going to earn a decent living doing it. It would be nothing less than an act of revolution.

Martine's student was named Joe. He was in his mid-twenties, worked in a dead-end job at a meat-packing plant, and was looking for something better. In his spare time he was an amateur boxer; in fact, but for a few small details, he was an exact replica of the character played by Sylvester Stallone in the *Rocky* films.

They met on a sunny Saturday in the dingy basement of a library near Joe's house. Martine fished her Grade One copies of *Farm Friends* and *The Funny Sunny Bunny* out of a plastic bag and set them before him.

He grimaced at the books and asked, "You got the *Sun*? I only like the *Sun*."

Martine flinched. "No, I don't care for the *Sun* myself."

"*Sun*'s the only good paper. Has the best pictures."

She informed him in a bristling whisper that he'd find a whole new world open to him if he learned how to read books. He picked up the copy of *Farm Friends* and stared at it a minute. "You're right. I've always wanted to read this."

She was socially helpless against the sarcasm, unsure of how to field it. Ignoring it in favour of her prepared speech seemed the best choice. "Before we start, Joe," she told him, "I think you should know that while I may be a terrific reader, school wasn't a total picnic for me either. You might be surprised to know that I failed the odd course, too." Of course, I *meant* to, she told herself, I didn't *have* to . . . But by high school, academic mediocrity had become so much a part of Martine Craythorn's life that she could not remember a time when things had been any different. Could I have done any better? she asked herself. No, actually. I don't think I could have.

Joe was perplexed. "I ain't never failed no course," he said.

She was astonished; anger vanquished her self-pity. How could he be illiterate and not . . . while she, perfectly intelligent, but (looking back on it now) somewhat lazy and inclined to daydream, always with one eye out the window, looking for the big chance beyond gerunds and fractions, looking for the large work, the real work of the world—very lazy, actually, but how could she fail and not he?

"You must have, though."

He crossed his arms. "No, ma'am. But I'm not completely comfortable that *you* did. You're supposed to be my teacher." He saw her blanch. She seemed on the precipice of tears, so he placed his big hand over hers. "Hey. Hey. It's okay. I'm sure you're still as smart as anybody."

Joe and Martine were the same age, born six months apart. As the weeks wore on there would be nothing at all in the way of sexual tension between them: Martine sensed without pride that it may have been because they were both shameful subscribers to the idea that the man should teach and the woman should learn. It turned out that Joe could read at a grade-school level, and always checked the sports scores. "But I got a little trouble with the job applications," he averred, firing up another in a line of illicit smokes. "And I gotta get outta this plant because it's making me nuts, man. Coming home from work covered in blood—you try it, it's no fun."

Of course, Martine no longer knew what it was like to come home from work. "Just out of curiosity," she poked, "how much do you make right now?"

"Me? Seventeen."

"Seventeen—as in, dollars an hour?"

"Yeah," he said, disgusted at the pittance. "Can you believe it? Like this job you have, how much you make?"

"Er," said Martine.

"Like thirty, thirty-five?"

"Gosh, silent *e* is a tough one. Maybe we should look at some exercises for next week."

They dawdled a bit over the books and then both decided they'd rather be drinking coffee in the restaurant across the street, where they found themselves an hour later, trading life stories. Joe lived with his parents, two brothers, and what sounded like a profoundly nasty grandmother, whom Martine judged to be the behavioural and physical equivalent of Rocky's bulldog. "Don't call my house, man," he said. "If a girl calls for me, I don't hear the end of it." But what he really wanted to discuss was cash and earnings. It was a subject he wouldn't let go.

"No, really, you must make a lot for teaching, eh? Come on. Come on." He smiled broadly, his moustache hair spreading like a well-used push broom. "I won't tell the tax people."

"Okay, look," Martine mumbled, fiddling with her watch strap. "Okay. Okay, I make—okay, I make nothing."

"Nothing?" His moustache contracted in confusion. He wasn't used to the word. It depressed him and he sat a while staring at his wadded napkin. Then he called for the bill and made a flamboyant offer to pay it.

Martine shivered, then willed herself to a violent stop. Cold pride broadened her narrow shoulders. "The fact that you're *paying* nothing for the lessons," she said as she watched him take his wallet out, "should have given you a clue I was *making* nothing for teaching them."

"I know, but I thought it was a trial offer, like Columbia Records or something." Joe frowned. "I gotta say I don't feel too happy with this."

"I can see."

"I mean, you're getting something out of it, right? You're a student teacher and you're just practising, right?"

"No. I mean, who knows, I might teach, but I don't . . . I don't know why I'm doing this." Why was she doing this?

"I don't think I like you earning nothing. You think I'm a charity case or something?

"Well . . . yeah."

He was stunned.

"Doing it for free," he muttered. "Maybe it's because you—which grade was it that you failed?"

Her eyes darkened. "It wasn't a whole grade," she said tinily. "It was just a course or two."

"Sorry, sorry," he said. "But anyway, do they have any teachers you can pay for? Because I gotta learn how to fill those applications, you know. I gotta get out of that job. It's killing me."

"No . . . I think they're all pretty much like me." Martine thought of Carolyn Colterblake's student and how he'd probably be able to speed-read *Great Expectations* after one lesson. But Joe went on. "I don't pay anything when I go to the doctor, either, and the doctor still gets paid," he mused, picking at his teeth with a credit card. "Let me pay you. You'll do better if I pay you and so will I."

"I don't think I—"

"Come on. You're too young and pretty to be some stinky old volunteer lady. A little skinny for me, but you know, some people might think so. So let me pay. I'm good for it."

Martine smiled shyly. After all, it was what she had wanted in the first place. "Okay."

47

"Good. Now how much will you charge me?"

Martine squirmed. She had no expenses, but still. "Five bucks an hour?"

"Hey, you're not walking your neighbour's dog here. Take some pride in your work. Come on. Charge me anything. I'm good for it."

"Seven?"

He rolled his eyes. "Seven. Tellin' ya, Fats, you better marry a rich guy. Otherwise, I don't like your chances. Seven it is."

They met on Saturdays for two hours each time. After the first three weeks Joe raised Martine's salary to eleven-fifty an hour and bought her yet more coffee. He added pizza, too, and at his urging she always submitted to a few altruistic bites. In truth, buying and eating pizza was all they ever got done and poor Joe could not really be said to be progressing on the literary front.

He also fixed her broken Walkman, unknotted her confirmation locket, and gave her the following advice about Jeremy Pine: "Dump the jerk."

"Why?"

"Guy puts interior paint on the outside of people's houses. Happened to my sister. He did a deck for her last summer and now it makes the rest of her place look haunted."

In a sense, bad stories about Jeremy struck Martine as being the worst stories of all—in spite of their differences, they'd known each other so long it was as if they were the same person. And anyway, he was Jeremy—little punk Jeremy with the pug nose, and in that respect every black mark and petty crime, every shady business move or late-night drug run could not really be taken seriously.

It was true that if you looked past Jeremy's current self-made, booth-tanned, blow-dried state, you'd find a certified bad kid. But wasn't that all the more reason to admire what he'd become? After all, his brother Elliott had only survived the Bluffs episode to become a true reprobate: he'd actually been in *jail*. Next to Elliott, Jeremy had actually made good.

Martine had always been a little wary of her boyfriend, though. He'd supplied her with numbers for her article about him that were so grossly inflated, they might themselves have been responsible for her soul's expiration. The night she wrote, for public consumption, that Young Canadian's customer base was six times larger than it actually was: surely grounds for an express ticket to Purgatory, if not the Big Kiln itself. The limp, slimy fax containing this detail sat on her desk for a day or so before she called him about it. She didn't address the numbers directly, however. What she said was: "Jeremy? Can you start wearing a condom?"

He raged predictably. "Why? I don't have any diseases! I don't have any diseases! Anyway, wearing one of those things is like . . ."

"Reading a great poem in translation?" Martine offered.

"Yeah," he agreed with enthusiasm, even though all poems were the same to him, translated or otherwise. He wouldn't wear one, and since then they had not really had sex any more; the sex, rather, had them. After the last obligatory impalement she lay uncomfortably against the stone expanse of his chest trying to sleep, but she'd picked too hard a pillow. This was when he'd asked her to marry him for the second time.

"No," she said. "And please don't ask again."

He took the rejection quietly, though neither of them slept. An hour later, his back turned to her, he started to whisper stories he clearly hoped might hurt her, stories of other girl-friends he might have had over the years, who might have been more receptive to his kindness. But the stories had no effect on her, and in these dying days of their entanglement even her pity for him vanished.

But back to Joe, for whom no pity was possible, not when the reverse was far more appropriate. The situation was really starting to bother her by the time he landed a job in the Parks and Recreation Department that paid twenty-five dollars an hour. Martine, of course, remained unemployed.

"So thanks for teaching me to read," he said.

"I taught you how to read two words—*name* and *address*. And you already knew them anyway."

"Yeah, well, that's all you really gotta know, it looks like. Don't worry. I'm sure something will come up for you, too." They said goodbye with an awkward little hug at the bus stop.

Martine went back home and spent the next couple of days trying to craft a resumé with the help of an old typewriter her father had once used to fire off caustic letters to *The Globe and Mail*. The final result pleased her, as it seemed her relative lack of job and educational experience was more than offset by a wide variety of hobbies and interests: skiing, sailing, horseback riding, ballet, pottery, highland dancing, playing the oboe, candlemaking.

Highland dancing would be the dealmaker, she told herself.

Of course she was a lapsed practitioner of these things, though they had all come as naturally to her as breathing (except the oboe, a phallus even more disobedient than that appended to Jeremy Pine). But while she was mulling over the epic transcription she'd made of her life, the phone rang. It was the intake coordinator from the Reading Action Committee, wondering if Martine might somehow find a moment in her schedule to get her *ass* down there right away.

The lady received Martine with all the sternness a person wearing cork-soled sandals could convey. "So," she said, sorting through files on her desk, "you must be related to Abeni Craythorn somehow."

"No," Martine lurched in all-too evident horror. "No, no. God, no. Well, I mean, she's my father's wife, but that's—"

"Abeni and I are good friends," said the lady. Her thick brown bangs were streaked with grey and her room smelled like the Professor, like the air at his ban-the-bomb rallies. Eau de mung bean, Martine thought. "We've done quite a bit of committee work together."

"Oh."

"Well, why don't I just get right to it then. It's come to our attention that you've been charging your student for his reading lessons."

"Charging—it was his idea!" Martine gasped, forgetting her natural intimidation. "He wouldn't do it unless he paid me!" She collected and composed herself, then continued her defence through clenched teeth. "He said he didn't want to be a charity case."

"He called our office specifically to recommend that we compensate our instructors along the lines of your arrangement with him." The woman had an obtrusive white cyst between her eyes that appeared to expand as she angered. "I told him that was not our policy and that, unfortunately, you had abused his trust."

"Maybe he's right," Martine said, growing quietly livid. "Maybe you should pay your teachers."

"Are you joking? We can barely afford the rent on this place."

"I was a good teacher," Martine said, eyes darting about the depressing little room. "I provided as good a service as . . ."

"Now there, well there, that's the other thing I wanted to talk about. He told me he can still barely read. He said all you two did down there was smoke cigarettes, eat pizza, and tell Helen Keller jokes, whatever those are."

"That's not true," retorted Martine.

"Are you accusing your pupil of *lying*?"

Unused to confrontation, Martine was afraid the lady would lash at her, hurt her. She backed off and looked down. "It's just," she bleated, "I don't smoke."

"Look," said the lady. "There are lots of volunteer teachers in the world. There are volunteer doctors, too, and even pro bono lawyers. If a job doesn't lend itself to volunteerism, it really isn't worth anything to the world, is it? You've never heard of a volunteer banker, have you?" They sat in silence, shooting each other rivalrous frowns, like cats on a stoop. "When you do a job for money," said the intake lady, "the money becomes the most important part."

To which Martine replied, with dripping dolour: "Then you tell me what I'm supposed to live on. Just tell me that."

The lady sat back and fixed a smirk on Martine's Moore Park fingernails, which were paint-free but perfect: ten little marks of Cain. "Well," she said sarcastically, "I'm sure you'll manage."

They won't let me in, thought Martine. They never will, no matter what I do. I'm a target: the princess in the tower, who sleeps under the fur of endangered animals, who dines off fat grapes dropped into her by slaves. I cannot change teams.

The lady picked up a green pencil, tapped the desk, and made a pouting motion with her lips. "Tell me, Martine, why did you want this job in the first place? What were you looking to get out of it?"

"I—I wanted to help people," Martine said. It was the spirit in which she'd come there. But then she saw Carolyn at the orientation . . . and they made her do *calisthenics* . . . and after a half-hour, she was already thinking of some way to undermine the whole thing. Which she had. The sandalled lady obviously saw through her and prattled on, only too eager to suppress all hope.

"Well, if you want to help people, you could work in a restaurant. Downtown? Wouldn't you like that? You could clear very good tips at some of the better places. Your father's a professor, I'm sure he could set you up."

Martine coloured and drew sharp fingernails in toward her palms.

"Anyway," the woman continued, "we'd like you to repay what he gave you. You don't have to do it all at once, but of course it really would be the right thing to do."

Here it was again, somebody telling her what the right thing was but not why. Martine had a sudden urge to press her thumb against the lady's cyst, really really hard, until it popped all over her paperwork. "I have one question," she said in a low voice. "Did he have a good time? Joe?"

"Well, yes," answered the lady. "In fact, he seemed to think it was quite amusing that he still can't read. But we're not here to show people a good time. I specifically asked him whether his experience had been productive, and that's when he told me about the Helen Keller jokes. A good time is hardly going to help him get where he needs to go, is it?"

Martine stared at her blankly.

"Well, anyway. If you could give him the money back, I'm sure he could use it. This week, if possible."

But the defrocked tutor just sat, still as ever, and within seconds the intake lady grew perceptibly restless, rustling in her chair and tugging at her fingers. Sitting still like that was an old Professor trick and Martine was proud of herself for employing it. You just had to outsit folks, outstare them, and before long they'd bend to your bidding.

"Joe wanted to give me that money," she said. "When people want to give . . . well, we should all be gracious enough to take it. I mean, that's what I think."

The lady sighed, her brow stippled with scorn. "I see," she said, though she clearly didn't. "Goodbye then, Martine. My best to Abeni."

As she left, Martine turned to the woman and said, "He doesn't need the money anyway, you know." But walking down the corridor, thinking she'd had the last word, she heard her tormentor call out words she would have to take with her into what was left of the day:

"And who are *you* to say what he needs?"

*M*ARTINE STOOD in the Reading Action Committee vestibule and scanned its bulletin board righteously. I deserved that damn money, she told herself. I deserved every penny, and now it's time to make more. There were a jumble of flyers and notecards on it, with several jobs posted: Project Coordinator, Survey Assistant, Outreach Associate. None of these titles meant anything to her, but they all looked like they paid. Then she noticed a small white card in the corner of the board. SECRETARY WANTED, it said, for west-end social services agency. Secretary. At least she knew what that meant.

It meant, for one thing, an air-conditioned subway ride to the west end of the city. In the August heat, even short walks were roasting the doggedly black-caped Martine to a turn. Over the past few days she had often longed for a lamb's lick of cool air on her forearms, but had resisted cafés and movie theatres: they would interfere with all the earning and helping she'd made it her business to do. And how much nobler it was, how much closer to the porepeople it brought her, to stoke her discomfort inside her black clothing and outside the temples of relaxation.

The Helping Hands drop-in centre was not air-conditioned, but it was extremely clean. The linoleum squeaked beneath Martine's running shoes. Turquoise plastic stacking chairs were arranged in a perfect semicircle in front of an ugly wooden magazine rack, home to a variety of publications spaced a perfect half-inch apart. A sofa in the corner was battered but smelled of Scotchguard. In fact, various cleaning products duelled for olfactory supremacy in here— the walls were redolent with Fantastik, while Liquid Kleen wafted from the bathroom, and a canister of Skrub Powder sat just behind the counter.

A strapping blonde woman strode up to the front desk and ushered Martine into her office. "I was just in the middle of my lunch," said the woman, who introduced herself as Claudia. "I hope you don't mind. Geez, it's hot." Lunch was a giant ceramic bowl of what looked like lawn clippings, which Claudia forked back with unseemly greed. Martine took this as a cue to extract her own lunch: a Kit Kat chocolate bar. "I know it's a Nestlé product," she said, heading Claudia off at the pass.

Martine remembered from intermittent tussles with her father that if you at least showed you knew about the breast-feeding mothers and the John Birch Society and whatever else was the problem with eating the thing certain people didn't want you to eat, they would leave you alone after a minute. It was funny: her mother was always trying to get her to eat, but her father's way was quite the opposite. Boycott-mad, he'd been known to swipe California grapes right from her small hands—"Give me that. Jesus, I can't believe your mother buys these damn things"—while pouring Louise's South African wine down the kitchen sink. But this chocolate bar was Martine's fourth serving of the day and she hated anyone interfering with her plans.

She'd developed the serving routine years ago, as a way of satisfying Louise that she was eating properly. Born a gluttonous, passionate eater, Martine's appetite dwindled as childhood wore on. She could never rejoice at the sight of a groaning table; it only symbolized wretched excess in all things. She ate less after the Professor moved out, then, when Louise remarried, even less than that. Louise's new husband was a former television actor and he also happened to be the author of a staggeringly unpopular weight-loss book, the tenets of which neither he nor Louise appeared strong enough to follow. They were forever breaking their own rules and sneaking bits of triple-crème cheese or little hunks of chocolate, and sometimes they would even lick chicken grease from each other's fingers at a restaurant table, which would mortify the teenaged Martine and elevate her growing hatred of weak, rich, and sensual people. Of which she was not one: she decided to develop her own dietary method and to throw her rigid adherence to it in their well-stuffed faces. Ten servings a day, and what the servings were didn't matter. A bag of oranges would do, but so would a grape—all food was the same to her by this point in her life, exasperating and hateful. The only rule attached to the serving routine was that you had to write each instalment down in a notebook, in case you lost track.

Claudia explained that Helping Hands was a drop-in centre that provided information on pregnancy and birth control, job-seeking skills, tenants' rights, welfare, and domestic violence. They did not provide food as such but set out coffee and cookies every weekday at precisely 2 p.m. The coffee and cookies would be Martine's responsibility, in addition to which she would type and stuff envelopes, maintain client files, and figure out how to use the word processor. Some kindly donor had bequeathed this last item to the centre but the staff members who could type were a little wary of it, fearing the damage it would do to their reproductive systems. But since the five-dollar-a-month mothering of a pamphlet photo was the closest Martine saw herself getting to parenthood, she volunteered to sun herself in the machine's amber glow.

To impress Claudia, Martine trotted out her connections to Professor Craythorn, respected aid worker and agronomist, and to the Reading Action Committee. She hoped she could land the job before Claudia took a mind to check references and quite fortunately this is what happened: they must have been desperate. Claudia told Martine she could start immediately, and the money would even be enough to pay rent— should she ever someday have to pay it.

An hour later, as she scooped coffee into the giant percolator, Martine noticed a huge piece of red bristol board posted on the wall. It proclaimed the house rules in a martial black script:

Alms

At Helping Hands we:

1. Do not litter.
2. Observe basic rules of cleanliness and hygiene.
3. Do not ask staff for money, credit, subway tokens, etc.
4. Ask for help when needed.
5. Notify staff of necessities with regard to bathroom cleanliness, etc.
6. Respect limits as to snacks and drinks.
7. Keep hands and objects to ourselves.

She privately mused that Rule Five was sort of funny in light of Rule Four, and that the etceteras did not lend themselves to obvious understanding. There was something delightfully arcane about the last one, too. Didn't these people know anything about sharing?

Martine loved rules, as long as she was the one making them. She loved systems, columns, calculations, and ledgers. One of the chief advantages of earning money, or even of losing it, was the sensuous rise and fall and left-right hipsway of its representative signs, its numbers and decimals, its dollars and cents. After she was given a bank book and five dollars for her seventh birthday, she charted the accumulation of interest avidly; but at the end of the year, only eleven cents the richer, she grew as bored with money as she was becoming with food.

The second Martine finished arranging the Fudgikremes and Golden Shorties just so on the platters, the first customer came in. She was a tired, stringy young woman pulling three small children behind her in a wagon. "Hi, Corinne," yelled

Claudia from the back room. Corinne didn't answer. Two of the children sprang from the wagon and made for the magazine rack, the integrity of which was soon destroyed. "Uh," said Martine. "Uh, I don't think you should . . ." Corinne seemed not to notice and tended to the third urchin, an inconsolable baby. Not sure of what to do, Martine buried herself in more Fudgikreme arrangement; soon after, the eldest of the children emerged from the bathroom wailing: "Mom! Gross! Brianna did a poo on the floor!"

Corinne turned around, exhausted, having projected herself into some alternative ether where the baby wasn't screaming and the three-year-old hadn't shat on the linoleum. She scooted her daughter into the washroom to clean her up while Martine discreetly held her nose and turned away. No sooner had this happened than the executive director of Helping Hands was right there with bleach, a mop, and latex gloves, expertly scooping up the mess. And as Martine watched him, she realized with a halt in her breath who he was.

His name was Flavio Vargas and he'd been a high school classmate at St. Joachim's. His father was some kind of Allendist and they'd come to Canada after the coup. From the second she first noticed him in the halls, he struck Martine as, perhaps, "loudly" Chilean; not "quietly" Chilean, as Sharon Colterblake had once described a colleague of the Professor's while analyzing a dinner party: "A lovely man, you know, not the kind who's always going on about the doings in the soccer stadium." Flavio's most exciting feature was his bold, unapologetic friendlessness, but his deeply tanned skin and thick head of black hair were also drawing cards. He carried an old blue bookbag wherever he went and Martine wondered what was in it. Most compelling, as far as she was concerned, was the way he wore his clothes: the grey St. Joachim's gabardines stretched so stunningly tight you could make out the year on a quarter in his back pocket, the blazer a good size too small and so close to painted on that the principal had to intervene and donate another to him. He couldn't buy it himself; he was only there on a Christian Assistance Scholarship, a fact related by Jeremy, who had taken instant and disdainful notice of the boy.

One day Martine was studying by herself in the cafeteria. She noticed Flavio roving from table to table, asking each group of students a question. He looked like he was selling something. Martine sat in mesmerized thrall to the cling of his trousers, watching him tote his achingly perfect butt around the room. Finally he got to her.

"Good book," he said, tapping her copy of *Down and Out in Paris and London*.

"It's all right," she replied, trying not to look at his crotch. The book was actually pretty dull: the poor folks within weren't Sara Crewe, or the Tree Grows in Brooklyn Girl. No rescue looked to attend them, no great clothes, good food, or handsome young men.

"Are you a socialist?" asked Flavio. *Sochalist* was the way his accent had him say it.

"No," she snapped reflexively. The *Professor* was a socialist. She was . . . whatever a socialist was not.

"Then . . . are you a Christian?"

"Of course!" She went to Catholic school, didn't she? She collected for the food hampers, didn't she?

"You can't be a Christian without being a socialist."

"Yes, you can," she asserted, spine stiffening.

"No, you can't. Jesus wanted to help the poor, not himself. Read."

He took a dog-eared paperback of the New Testament out of his bookbag and showed her a number of underlined passages. It was the exact same book she'd won for writing "Rosita of Peru," with the difference that hers had been promptly stuck in a closet, whereas his had been thumbed and thumbed again in the way the good Lord would have wished. She cramped with jealousy: had he been a winner in the Lenten Literary Contest, too? She had only won second prize in the city. Obviously someone was first, but was she looking at him? My God, he *was* Rosita of Peru! She scanned the pages. There they were, to be sure, the line about the meek inheriting the earth, and the one about it being easier for a camel to fit in the eye of a needle than for a rich man to enter the kingdom of heaven. All the greatest hits, and all so gratingly Professorial in tone; she had never really thought about them.

"And now abideth faith, hope, charity, these three," read Flavio. "But the greatest of these is charity."

"I thought it was love."

"Excuse me?"

"Love. The greatest of these is love."

He leaned over the table to speak more privately to her. "Oh. Yes, that is how they put it. In the newer editions. But when they say 'love,' they really mean 'charity.'"

She stared at the tiny crucifix around his neck, which emboldened her. She knew it never came off, even when everything else did. She spoke to the hypnotizing dangle of it, to the warm throat behind it. "Well, if they don't really mean love," she said softly, "then maybe I don't want to be a Christian after all."

He smiled and drew himself up. The crucifix came to a stop below his collarbone. "Ah. Maybe you don't," he said. He didn't seem to mind much, though. He smiled mysteriously, returned the Bible to his blue bookbag, and moved on to another table.

She'd gone to first base with Jeremy Pine in Grade Seven. Then second, then third, then down a lot of interesting little paths on the way home, though never home itself. And now, bored and tired of rug burn, they were "taking a break." Though for two kids who frankly disliked each other, they could never quite manage to part company. They were always lolling together in the hallway at school, simmering with mutual irritation. "Look at those goddamn sideburns," Jeremy would stage-whisper when Flavio walked by. "Who does that guy think he is, Bobby Goldsboro?"

Martine scoffed. "I think that's a hopelessly racist remark. People wear their hair differently in Chile."

"Well, they should send the CIA down there to hold a style clinic. Anyway, you're just saying that because he's got the hots for you. He looks at you like you were a big juicy enchilada."

"He does not." But Martine both hoped and feared this was true. Flavio fascinated her, but he was also invading her monopolies on solitude and righteousness; when he played a cassette of Victor Jara's folk songs for her history class, complete with the tale of the musician's torture and murder, she was furious. Upstaged—by a foreigner, no less.

But Jeremy was right. Flavio would sometimes try to catch her eye in the cafeteria and she would pretend to be lost in her book. He would never actually follow her down the hall, stop at her locker, or call to her, but she felt his eyes on her just the same. He seemed to be planning some kind of confederacy with her and she vowed to resist.

The day after the Jara thing he approached her once again in the cafeteria. Oh, now he wants to gloat, she thought. Just because their history teacher called his sob story "deeply effective."

"Excuse me," he said. "But was it you who did that thing, with the bottles? You're the one who raised money for the Kelly Centre, no? I was there on Saturday—I do a little volunteer work on the weekends. Anyway, I saw your picture on the wall."

Oh, Christ, Martine sighed to herself. She had lately taken to wearing the great felt cape and now drew it around her. Look how easy it is for him, she thought. To just walk up and talk to people he doesn't know. To march into the Kelly Centre and get down to work. He was the person she wanted to be, should have been; it burned. She returned to her book and prayed for him to go away, but he didn't.

"That was a good idea," he continued. "Can I ask—how much money did you raise?"

"One hundred and twelve dollars."

"Hmm. Not bad, though you might have cleared more with newspapers as well as bottles. It was just bottles, yes?"

"Yes." Why hadn't she thought of newspapers?

"I'd like to do something like that."

"Well," she sniffed, "it's more difficult than you think."

"I'm sure," he said, with a taunting Cheshire grin. "I'm sure it's very difficult."

Then he disappeared. Prick, she thought.

But how beautiful he was! She would sometimes watch him leave school, imagining the brown expanse of his back beneath the blazer and seasonally mandated pullover; she wanted to climb into his bookbag so her entire body could bang softly against his hip, all the way home.

He approached her again one day as she walked to the bus stop. "You don't have to wear that cape all the time, you know," he said. "You could take it off in school at least. Don't the teachers get mad at you?"

She had a sudden, savage impulse to grab his hand into the cape and onto her right breast, to turn the heat up on this miniature cold war, but she held her breath and the impulse died. You do not invite Lucifer into your clothes. "Some of us believe in modesty," she said, with a trace of flirtatious mockery. "I think you might find something about it in your Bible."

He smiled. "But I thought you weren't a Christian."

"I am," she said, "when it suits me."

"Well, why don't you come home with me, hmm?" he asked, with a new seriousness about the eyes. "Come to my house and . . . well, we will see if this is one of those times."

She froze, wondered whether she'd been played and had. There was nothing awkward in his request; he too easily saw how much she wanted him to make it. Damn his confidence! She thought about launching into a lecture about the way we do things in this country, but she knew that three words into such a speech he'd win for all time, that he'd shrug and march home brave and true while she stood at the bus stop kicking at her own xenophobic bum. "No, thank you," she said quietly, then continued walking.

"Wait." He ran up behind and almost ran into her; feeling him so close she shivered with pleasure. "I'm sorry, I did not mean . . . Come, I live just down there. We'll talk about your book you are reading."

She turned around and accompanied him up the street, drawn by a force much stronger than faith, hope, and charity put together. Odd, she thought, that he should live so close to school, when she had to endure the daily hardship of both a bus and subway ride to get there.

But when they reached the house she was stilled by the patchy clay lawn and aluminum siding. She had never been to a house like this. "Come," he said again. They walked into the front room, which was one of the only rooms. It was tidy but almost completely bare.

Flavio divined Martine's thoughts. "My parents won't buy anything big," he shrugged. "They still think they're going back home."

The empty room smelled strange, as if the fumes from too many complicated casseroles were embedded in the dulled broadloom. Martine stood close to Flavio and shut her eyes, that the thrillingly fresh scent of his skin might vanquish the terror she had of this emptiness. The curtains were orange, horribly so. There was a jigsaw puzzle on the wall: an alpine vista of some twenty thousand pieces. "My father," Flavio said softly. "He does them in his spare time." That he should be proud of this! Martine looked on the sad suggestion of art and wondered if he really was.

But she then realized that she was standing close enough behind him that the merest jostle would spirit her lips into his lovely black hair; and he, aware of her breath, knew it; everything he was excused this desolate house, but still. He was on Christian Assistance. There were only a few other kids like that and their uniforms never fit. But Flavio wore his perfectly, it seemed to her now, and as he turned around she closed her eyes against the touch of it on her cape, the cape he opened with hands that went straight to her pulsing waist. She ached as the hands continued around her back and brought her to him, as close as she could possibly be, given the layering of blazers, cape, shirts, sweaters, brassiere, and crucifix, and as those hands somehow found their way under these and onto her skin she reeled and shuddered against him. He had to grip her against the fall. It was beyond delicious; it was far too much.

He guided her gently onto the couch and tried to quell her shaking by placing three warm fingers just under the waistband of her skirt, but this only made her tremble all the more. "Shh," he said. "It's okay. It's okay." But Martine was far too frenzied for "okay." Nobody in the history of wanting had ever wanted so much and no good end could come of it.

His hands were practised, smooth. He unbuttoned and unhooked her with such finesse the clothes seemed to melt away. His fingers transgressed the waistband further and went down into her panties; at the same time he ran his tongue slowly down her collarbone toward a shocked nipple. But orgasm, which came surprisingly soon, hardly relieved her; within seconds she found herself clawing at his sweater and pants, a brainless, graceless animal, all lust and no skill.

While she scratched at his fly with half-paralyzed fingers, he caught her wrist. "It's okay," he said again. "Take it easy."

"'Take it easy?'" she cried, still shaking. "Now?"

"Well—yes. Just sit back. Shhh, relax."

Relax? Was he *insane*?

"But I want to make you happy," she croaked. "Let me. I'm begging you. Please—I swear I'll do anything for you. Anything." She had little practical training in these matters, as he seemed to. She was a virgin, technically, but also a trouper: ever eager to kill the flowery abstraction of teenage fantasy in favour of painful, frictive, hot, messy reality. She went for his fly again and got close enough to feel that he was in fact interested. Yet his face remained a model of perfect control. He took her wrist again and held it. "Calm down," he said again.

She quickly realized that it was no use. Rage! What kind of teenager was this, what kind of boy—what kind of . . . *Latin*? Rage, shame. She had shown him the most secret part of herself and he would not return the favour. All I want, she thought as she sat up and tried to rehook and rebutton herself, all I want out of life is to make others happy—and look where it gets me! She threw her cape on and ran for the door, under a torrent of Flavio's softly accented protestations.

That puzzle, she told herself, hobbling down the street, not quite done up. That puzzle was glued to the wall. That was a boy who lived in a house where a *puzzle is glued to a wall*. What, some demon within her yelled, put you in love with such a boy, anyway? Love, was that what it was? Who knew? Even in the Bible, it didn't mean what it said.

She smoothed her hair and revisited the scene at the bus stop. It was then that a horrible thought struck her. Maybe he hadn't meant for her to actually *stop;* that he, as per his words, just wanted her to *go slowly.* It was all going fine and she had probably wrecked it. But this idea put ice in her spine and she could not indulge it. She vowed to forget about it, and him, forever.

Martine avoided Flavio at school the next day, and the next, and the next. Time passed. At first he seemed properly perplexed, even trying at one point to take her by the elbow, but too gently for capture. She always got away from him, running into classrooms or toward fleeing buses, places where she might escape the still-gorgeous terror of his presence. When he'd pull up a chair across from her in the cafeteria, she'd make her excuses and leave.

Then, one spring day as Martine was leaving school, she saw a fight taking place in the distance. She could just make out the flapping blond head of Jeremy's younger brother, Elliott, the one who'd nearly been dropped off the Bluffs. Elliott had since gone to psychological seed and was even now on probation for one petty crime or another—and here he was, the star of some illegal ruckus not meant for female eyes, the great victim of which, it seemed, was Flavio Vargas.

He was on the ground, stomach down, clutching at his head and weathering another boy's kicks. There were two, maybe three more boys over him. Martine did not want to know about it and could not watch. She was frightened by the scene, but mostly she felt disappointment with Flavio for not being able to defend himself, for landing on the asphalt like a scared puppy and submitting to the wrath of such cretinous thugs. Before, his solitude looked arrogantly and sexily chosen, but without the power to make his own choices he was suddenly unattractive to her. She ran away and tried to forget about that scene, too; and when he showed up at school the next day with an angry red cheek, she turned away from him once again.

But something happened over the summer. In September he came back changed. Astonishingly, he started wearing an athletic jacket in the school colours and even turned up on the football team. The bookbag disappeared and so did the cafeteria tours. He developed friends. She even saw him shooting the breeze with one of his assailants, and sometimes he'd stroll the halls with his arm around a girl, one of the school's prettiest.

It was all awful, to Martine's eyes, and it only made Jeremy step up his sneering. Ever since Elliott had been suspended for his part in the beating, Jeremy had styled himself a defender of bigots everywhere, and though Martine tried to avoid his company she couldn't help the sideswipes and comments made by her former playmate and sometime boyfriend. Jeremy was always there, after all—the bad part of her conscience, hanging around beside her when she got her books out of her locker, dawdling around at the bus stop, sitting next to her at lunch. "Nice *jacket*," he'd say, hooting at Flavio as he passed through the parking lot with his beefy new pals. "Stop it!" she snapped. But her righteousness rang hollow to Jeremy, too. It hardly went any way toward scraping Flavio off the football team and into the folds of her cape where he might, once, have found solace. "Come," he'd said, and would never say again.

And now, all this time later, here he was. The Executive Director. He rose from his labour and caught sight of Martine. He peeled off the gloves, threw them in the garbage, and set to washing his hands. "You," he said quietly. "But without that silly cape."

Martine blushed and wilted; the place was filling up, too, with the sorts of people she'd seen but never talked with, and by God, weren't they trying to talk to her. "Hot!" said a wizened man with filthy glasses and a cane, who picked up a Styrofoam cup and tried to squeeze in between her and the coffee maker as she flinched from him. "Better mix us some iced tea or we'll all fry like pizzas." It was a parade of the lame, the halt, and the blind, and Flavio seemed perfectly at home in it. He signalled Martine to follow him to the back. Along the way he took time to dispense crisp words of welcome to a walleyed man carrying a Madonna record, and to the fearfully apologetic Corinne.

Martine followed her boss into his small, faintly cluttered office. His social work diploma was on the wall, as were several newspaper clippings in which he featured; he had evidently been involved in a number of saintly concerns since high school — shelters, soup kitchens, cleanup campaigns, and protests. A football trophy sat atop a filing cabinet. On his desk, Martine caught a flash of framed snapshot: Flavio with some radiantly generic girl. They both held parasolled cocktails up to the camera and looked happy, happy. Martine turned violently away from the picture.

Flavio bade her sit and sank heartily into the wheeled chair behind his desk. "So. We meet again." His clothing was loose and comfortable, a T-shirt and faded jeans, nothing too small about it any more, though the little crucifix still glinted about his throat. He looked at a thumbnail and started picking at it a bit while rearranging papers on his desk. "I suppose Claudia has told you what to do?"

He wore that strange mocking smile while he spoke but betrayed no real interest in what had happened to her in the four years since he had last seen her. He had probably not thought of her at all. Whereas she . . . she'd studied his language in northern Spain that summer, then over time forgot both him and Spanish. Or the Spanish, anyway. There were, buried in those years, two fleeting, nameless lovers she had taken on breaks from Jeremy, whom she now realized had been nothing more than attempts to retrieve Flavio. The brown of his gaze, the lassitude of his vowels; to detect these even faintly was to fall, if only for a night. But it never worked. She only ever got the exact opposite of what she wanted. Hence Jeremy.

When Flavio left goodness for football, Martine had the field to herself again, just as she'd wanted. But it was a cold and lonely market niche, and one he appeared to have reclaimed.

He recited the Helping Hands mission statement to her. He was earnest about it and a little bored; nothing of that afternoon they'd spent together remained in his voice. She started to ask him a question, but was stopped by the electronic moo of his phone. He took the call, which seemed important— another Executive Director, perhaps—and told her: "I've got to take this."

As she rose to leave, she realized that his accent had all but disappeared.

Alms

Claudia set up a cubicle for her and put her right to work interviewing the clients about their files. There was to be no more Flavio for the day: he would be in meetings, Claudia explained. It was as though he inhabited some penthouse six floors above in which Martine, as some sort of signing bonus, had been privileged to spend five minutes.

*T*HE JOB PROVED SPECTACULARLY UNCOMFORTABLE from the start. She didn't warm at all to them, "the clients," nor they to her. "Used to work at the Humpty Dumpty plant, but they laid me off, right," said a red-faced man with cookie crumbs in his beard. "They got all these machines doing the job now. But I'm gonna go back and see if there's something I can't do about it."

"Why would you want to?" Martine said, incredulous.

"Excuse me?"

"They don't need you when they have a machine. Why don't you apply where you're needed?"

The man laughed so hard at this you would never know he had four hungry children at home. And on that note, Martine felt like saying—but didn't—well, why all these children anyway? Why was it that every woman between the ages of twenty and fifty came in here towing an obligatory

74

cargo of streetrats behind her when they plainly couldn't support . . . But she didn't say it. She tried not even to think it. Giving air to such thoughts was the custom back home, a local variation on dwarf-tossing or cockfighting; a gay, sneering review of pain that wasn't yours.

She didn't say much here, actually. For one thing, she had trouble with the argot.

"I need a fuckin' oil change!" a client walked in bellowing one afternoon. He was wearing a ripped trench coat, wing tips, a dress shirt. He was clean shaven, but his pomaded hair sproinged rebelliously about his scalp. He looked like a psychotic accountant, which is probably what he was. "I haven't dropped a load in weeks. Gimme a blow job, miss."

"A blow job?" Martine fluttered.

"You heard."

"I don't think that will be possible. This is an advocacy centre."

I don't think that will be possible?

Another time, to another man, she said, "Have a good weekend."

"Good weekend?" he hacked. "As if! I'm about to get thrown out of my apartment—and you're telling me to have a good weekend?"

Her response: "Try not to let it bother you." Such was the prissy little line she always took in these situations. She found herself trotting out all the crisp phrasettes that made life in the city seem so polite, so unlike a place where anything bad would ever happen, and she dispensed enough take cares and have a nice days and buh-byes to float a cruise ship. She'd seen enough bank tellers and salesladies in her day to think that was what you did at work, if you were female and thrown daily into superficial commerce with strangers. She knew this wasn't that kind of job but hadn't learned the language for any other. "I wouldn't worry about it," she soothed a young man after he told her he'd never been so low in his life.

He'd been cradling his face in his hands, but this made him look up. "You wouldn't worry about it," he repeated, and she instantly realized how stupid she'd sounded. But she hated this kind of sarcasm; she hated all the reminders of her impotence the clients always tossed her.

Every day, for example, they'd bring her math and economics problems more thorny than any she'd confronted in school. "So I have three hundred and twenty-six dollars, eh?" went a middle-aged woman in a hairnet, thinking aloud. "Rent's two hundred. About twenty-five bucks a week left for food if you pay your phone and toilet paper—I won't give up my phone. I could do meat last week, but only because there was a sale. I got some nice beets sixty cents the bunch this week, but how many of those can you eat?"

"I—I don't know," Martine said. "I don't know how many beets you can eat," although that wasn't really the woman's question. Sixty cents, was that reasonable? How much did lettuce cost? Cheese? Cherries? She'd never paid any attention to sales: if things were on sale, she figured there had to be something wrong with them.

On another occasion a pretty, young woman in a sundress came in carrying a baby. She was accompanied by an intense, slightly built man in blue jeans. He hung behind her as she sat down, then hovered over her as she began to speak. "I'm staying here for a half-hour, all right, Jerry?" she said, frustrated. "I'll be home soon." Finally the man backed off and left. "He's just checking up," the pretty woman explained, rolling her eyes, one of which was bruised. Martine stared stupidly at the black eye and talked with the woman for ten minutes about where she might find donated furniture and cheap cooking implements.

"But it has to be a good couch," said the woman, "because, you know, my boyfriend'll be pissed if all the stuffing is coming out of it or whatever."

"I know," Martine replied, skittering away from real talk, when she had the number for a women's shelter in her desk right there, too. But she was far too frightened to broach the subject. Anyhow, the guy was so small, she thought. It couldn't be . . . she probably bumped into a cupboard. Or a door. "We'll find you a good couch," she said cleanly, then sent the woman on her way.

She preferred the word processor to the people, loved it, in fact, and thus quickly managed to transmute the bulky, handwritten client files into a series of tidy printed sheets. This act of clerical derring-do had everyone in awe.

"Flavio's very impressed with what you did," Claudia told her. "He wanted you to know."

Martine was so thrilled by the citation that she didn't even care about its being lobbed second-hand. She rode this gossamer strand of happiness into the day's first interview.

The client was a well-groomed young man. Unlike the others, he had no bag, nor jacket, nor battered wallet on him. He looked like a graduate student who'd been called away from the library for a second. He propped his elbows on the table and held his face in his hands. "I can't believe I'm here," he said.

But Martine felt too good to hear him. She was huge with helpfulness today; she loved the poreperson and sensed he must love her, too. Shy? Not any more. She was in her element now. "There are a number of services available to you here," she trilled, sucking the admiration from him. "We provide information on tenants' rights, welfare assistance, food access . . ." Oh, she purred, I am the flame of a candle in the darkness of this man's life. Others live for themselves, but not I. It was a Kelly Centre high.

"Now, then," she said. "What would you say is your principal source of income?"

But the man wasn't listening. He just shook his head and looked down at his hands and feet to make sure that it was really him seeking charity and not someone else. "I just really," he droned, "can't believe I'm doing this." A half-minute passed, and he didn't answer about the income, and he didn't seem to care at all about all the great services and the information, or even the Fudgikremes.

And then it hit Martine: the man didn't love her. He didn't even seem to know she was there. He had other things on his mind. And that lady in the corner didn't love her either; and the man with the cane, he didn't even know her name.

And so, having salved all the pain she could, she returned reluctantly to earth.

At the end of the day, after the streetcar and the subway and the bus back to her mother's house in tree-lined Moore Park, Martine sat on her mauve-and-yellow bed and wondered about what she was doing at Helping Hands. Her purpose, she feared, was largely ornamental. She was getting good at smiling. At saying "please" and "thank you." At not butting in. And at being cute, with her trim little figure and glossy ponytail. But it was hardly enough.

It was then her thoughts would turn to Jeremy Pine, a good-looking guy who deployed the silkiest of Moore Park manners as he coated people's houses in soda pop—at least she wasn't him!

He'd called and called after she was fired from *Attitude!* She usually let the answering machine get it, but one day she forgot and blundered into contact with him.

"So," he said. "What are you doing these days?"

Martine was shocked. Was he . . . *worried* about her? Loving concern was hardly his usual modus operandi. It made her squirm, actually, and to harden herself against the discomfort she launched straight into the tale Joe had told her, about how the boys from Young Canadian Reno had turned his sister's back deck into something out of *The Amityville Horror.*

"You believe some illiterate guy over me?" Jeremy demanded. "You would. *You* would. But stupid people aren't any smarter than smart ones, you know." He argued on, but he wasn't arguing to keep her any more. He was arguing to win. "Cut me a break, would you, Martine? I give a guarantee on my work—did you ever stop to think it might be some other company? *I* never got a complaint."

He had a point, but he was a Pine. She wouldn't budge. Over the phone she could imagine him hanging his head, from which a golden forelock surely drooped, heavy with gel.

"But all this is lost on you, isn't it? You want me to be the bad guy and you won't stop until I am." There was a silence on the line.

"See you around," she said.

The next day she went to work and was forced to confront a problem client, a certified violator of Rules One through Five, all at the same time. Martine and Claudia drew straws to see who would have to eject him: a very tall man in a flowing red wig, wearing flowered Capri pants and heels. He was carrying an open purse full of screws and bolts. Martine got the nod. She went and gave him a little tap.

"Excuse me, sir. Ma'am. Uh . . ."

"Ahem," replied the man. "And I told her the baby isn't mine. The baby has blue eyes. Oh, sure, and I don't think I'm going to have a little baby with blue eyes. I don't think so! I don't think SO!"

"Sir, if you wouldn't mind." She was quaking, as she did a lot these days. The old Martine, the one who snapped and sniffed and took nothing from anyone, had gone, leaving in its place the hollow husk of a samaritan. "This is an advocacy centre." Why did she keep saying that? What the hell was an advocacy centre?

"But what I did say? You go back there!" the man yelled, wheeling on her. "You go back there where you came from and don't bother me no more. It's not mine, do you HEAR ME?"

He stamped his foot and several screws flew onto the floor. Martine was about to make for the phone to page Flavio, but he walked in before she got there, confident and direct as the situation demanded. He slipped an arm around the client's waist. "It's all right, Sheena," he said gently. "I know the baby's yours."

"It isn't. Isn't. Is not," Sheena said, cooling a little.

"But who else could it belong to?" Flavio led him/her to the door, whispering all the while. "It looks exactly like you. It's a beautiful baby. It has your nose, doesn't it? Go home and take a look. Go home to your baby now." Sheena took a tissue from his/her bra and began weeping silently, before tottering inelegantly out the door.

Flavio turned on his heel and made quickly for his office, clearly uninterested in any comment on the affair. Then he stopped and stared at Martine.

"Your cape," he said. "You're not wearing it."

It was true—but then, he'd already told her she wasn't wearing it, the last time they'd talked. Had he forgotten that they'd talked? Or remembered, but forgotten what she was wearing? My God, she remembered everything about him from that little chat: the exact fade of his jeans, his T-shirt clean enough to be new, the black leather belt with its scratched brass buckle, the crucifix that might as well have sported *her* wracked and hanging form.

He was looking at her now, in her T-shirt and long black skirt, but in the same way he'd looked at the word processor after she got it running properly: she was like a memo with no typos in it, something you might place a check mark beside. "You look nice," he said, taking the whole of her in with bureaucratic gravity. Then he was gone.

She only saw him every few days after that. He seemed always to be in meetings, but the odd time he'd drop in to straighten some mess out, get back in touch with the little people. Everyone knew him—hey, Flavio! Afternoon, Mr. Vargas! Flavio, I got a cut on my finger. Gotta minute, Flavio?—and everyone loved him, everyone.

Martine lived for such visits. But she hated him, too, and much of her hatred consisted in her incapacity to vault over or even approach his level of comfort with this awful place. Sharing a personal grape boycott at home with the Professor had been easy, and so had earning her public-service badge in Brownies. But here in the trenches things were decidedly harder. As soon as she filled the condom basket, the same joker would walk in and empty it, stuffing all of them into his pocket for personal use; he knew Wednesday was when the rubbers came in. "Uh . . ." said Martine. She said "uh" a lot here. "What do you mean, *'uh'*?" the guy retorted after the first time, and then said, "It's not like *you're* going to be using them."

It was true: she had always thought of herself as pert, petite, neat of feature, and well proportioned, but lately the ponytail drooped, her eyes had sunk, and the servings in the ten-servings game were growing smaller; she was losing weight, although she'd sometimes put on mascara if she knew for sure that Flavio was going to be in the office. Yes, she had once had prettiness to give people, and now perhaps not even that.

But while she could handle her own physical turpitude, that of others repelled her. There was the time a man came in with a terrible weeping sore on the side of his face, crusty and red around the edges and dripping yellow within. Martine tried to hide her disgust as she took information from him but could not. She gagged audibly, in fact. "Sorry," said the man.

She remembered learning, in catechism class, the story of St. Catherine of Siena, who overcame her revulsion at the sight of an invalid's wounds by drinking a cup of his pus. No, Martine thought, shaking her head. I could never be a saint.

The man with the weeping sore on his face said that he had lately been working as a bellman at a big hotel downtown, one Martine knew well. "But they fired me because of my skin. I wasn't getting too many tips by the end."

Martine asked if they couldn't have found him something else out of public view, but the man hadn't asked and they certainly hadn't offered.

"Naw. I love that damn hotel, though. You know it? It's the best-looking hotel you ever saw." He looked around him at the scrubbed linoleum and institutional walls. "They've got red velvet wallpaper. When you're in that hotel you always feel rich, even if you're only making five bucks an hour."

Martine agreed with him. She knew the place. It was a huge, exhaust-stained hotel downtown that had once enjoyed fame as the "Emerald of the Empire." You could tell it had fallen on hard times from the sag of the heavy gold drapery in its windows. Still, Queen Elizabeth always stayed there; the hotel was so old, *both* Queen Elizabeths had probably stayed there. "Hey, you should try and get a job there," the bellman said suddenly.

"Me?"

"Yeah. It's a lot classier than this place. They always need chambermaids and stuff. You'd like it. Actually," he said, leaning forward, "you don't seem too happy here."

True, that. Saving humanity one person at a time was proving rougher than she'd thought. Maybe there was no point to it, maybe it couldn't be done. Maybe it was like trying to mine a coal seam with a teaspoon.

The weather turned colder and Martine wore the cape full-time, even indoors. One late September afternoon she found herself at reception, answering the phone and welcoming clients, a set of menial duties that all staff members, save Flavio, had to perform from time to time. An attractive black man wandered in. He carried a lawyer's litigation bag and wore a cashmere scarf under his brushed charcoal topcoat. Martine thought he must be an inspector of some sort.

"Parlez-vous français?" he asked.

Martine, of course, had a French-Canadian mother, but the Professor had found his wife and daughter's early exchanges in that language to be so conspiratorial he forced them to stop speaking it when he was around, and eventually they stopped speaking it altogether. Martine couldn't really communicate with the man but did manage to divine that he was a journalist, recently in from Zaire. He handed her his card, which identified him as one Didier Thako. *"Vous voulez des* cookies?" she managed. *"Du* café?" The man took a sidelong glance at the cookie table, where the Parker women—a loud mother/daughter set—were tussling profanely over the last fig newton. He declined, visibly shaken by the scene. Martine watched him measuring the cookie-sullying filth under all those fingernails. He was a refugee, still in that silver fortnight between honoured professional and parking-lot attendant; and he couldn't believe that this was now his life. *"Je comprends,"* she told him. Then the phone rang.

The voice on the other end was bright, familiar, female. It requested Flavio. It was told that Flavio was in a meeting.

"Of course. Well, just tell him that Carolyn called and I'll be home about seven-fifteen? I'll be at the library until then." Martine replaced the receiver with a gelid hand.

Carolyn. Colterblake. A *Protestant,* for Christ's sake! When he should be with his own kind, she seethed, he should be with . . . well, me! Why not me? I've gotten over your weird little house, Martine raged inwardly. I've gotten over you stealing my thunder in the goodness department, and you getting the shit kicked out of yourself. The thing is, I haven't gotten over *you.* Argh, Carolyn Colterblake. God, if he could only see past the psychology degree and the track and field trophies, into her past, into the long-ago day she sat braiding Martine's hair on the mauve-and-yellow bed—if he could see that, would he return the phone call?

"Is your dad going to marry her?" Carolyn had asked. They were eleven at the time.

"Who?"

"That coloured lady."

"Abeni? Why would he marry her? That's his cleaning lady."

"No it's not," said lubricious, vicious Carolyn before getting off the bed and going home to Mommy and Daddy and everything fine. "My mom says it's his girlfriend and they're going to get married."

Thus spake Flavio's girlfriend—the one in the photograph on his desk, so standardly magazine-attractive that Martine hadn't even recognized her. But it was just perfect, wasn't it? It just stood to reason. It killed everything that made mascara worth wearing, that made this job worth having. She wrote down the message on a pink slip and stuffed it in Flavio's crowded in-box. Then she wrapped the cape around her and walked past Didier Thako, toward the door, unsure of what her next move would be. *"Bonne chance, monsieur,"* she said gruffly. *"Bonne chance* with everything."

*H*ER MOTHER WAS IN BED when Martine got home. It wasn't even six-thirty. But when Louise heard the great door opening downstairs, she roused herself and tottered to the top of the stairs like a broken swan in a white nightgown.

"My hip," she explained groggily. "My damn trick hip. It's acting up again."

"Oh, Mama, why don't you see a doctor?" Martine asked, as she always did when the subject of this blasted hip came up. But the doctors, Louise always sighed, couldn't do anything; hers was the trickiest hip imaginable, one whose ways were not described in textbooks.

Martine thought of calling the doctor herself, but it wasn't really her business. Her business, she figured, was to submit to all the hugging, put a little butterscotch in the narrative of her days, and serve it up to her mother in a way that might comfort her.

Tonight, though, she was in a rotten mood and reverted to her old crabbiness. "I quit," she said, gobbling her ninth serving, a banana (her eighth had been a Fudgikreme). "But it was a stupid job anyway." She took the notebook and miniature pencil out of her purse and scribbled *banana* while Louise turned away so as not to see it. "They were morons, Mother, the people who ran it. The clients were . . . oh, I don't know. The clients were okay, I guess."

But Louise wasn't really listening. She was staring dreamily at the jasmine plant beside her bed, fingering its sharp-pointed leaves.

Martine had been thinking more and more about moving out. But how could she do it, with this solitary, fragile "mother" to care for? Paradoxically, though, even as Louise was making her most rapid ascent yet to the apex of sickness and somnolence, Martine found herself resolving hourly to get away as soon as she could. When she saw Louise like this—bone-white and drained, with wads of tissue on the night table, her black curls splayed like rotted kelp on the pillow—all she could think was: downtown? Or uptown? Downtown, she decided. Farther away.

Money was a problem, she thought proudly. She loved the idea of money being a problem: it gave her the right to commiserate with others who suffered similarly. But her salary wasn't terrible, and she did have some savings, and of course the twenty dollars from her childhood bank account. Then there was the trust money, and savings bonds—but how could it be arranged without her mother falling apart?

There was a letter by the jasmine plant and Louise held it out to Martine. "This came today."

Alms

The letter was addressed to Mack Donovan, the would-be weight-loss tycoon. Martine unfolded the letter warily. If it was for Donovan, it had to be bad news.

He was a handsome if lumpy Haligonian who had gone to Hollywood to seek his fortune as an actor in bad television shows. In most respects he had the goods for it: Murdo Brownrigg was a six-footer with thick ash-coloured hair and striking green eyes. But once he took off his shirt he was strictly Señor Pillsbury, chubbiness being a scrag-end of his youth he had never quite managed to kill. His thighs rounded forth like Easter hams; and in the wrong pants you could see them and what lay atop them, a caboose, keester, hinie, whatever you would, beach-toy bouncy and begging to be poked with a pin. Yes, from the chest down the whole body was problematic in serial television terms, with the butt engendering the deepest sorrow of all. A big butt was a chick problem. A paunch would have been more manly, he felt. He tried all the diets: Weight Watchers, Atkin, Pritikin, even the draconian Last Chance method which was known to actually kill followers whose livers and hearts could not withstand the battery of near starvation it demanded. But he did not die. His bottom just got bigger. He tried eating nothing but grapefruit for a week and nothing but eggs for two: so what. Sure, all the diets worked for a couple of weeks, but then the giant can came back with interest. He consulted doctors, buddies at the gym. No help whatsoever.

In spite of his avoirdupois, Murdo Brownrigg got a job—and a really good one, a pilot with ABC entitled "Tonto, Bates, and Wilhelm." Who were, of course, cops. Brownrigg, whose name was now Mack Donovan, was cast as the hunk, Bates. As the hunk his mandate was to lure the ladies away from other TV hunks, kick the living crap out of Travolta and Estrada and David Soul, they with their tight little dinner-roll bums packed in designer jeans. Ha! He'd show them. Especially Soul—what the hell was he thinking with that four-dollar hairweave? And Estrada—what was he, five-two? The Canadian named Murdo Brownrigg would show them all; for in his stead now strode Mack Donovan as Don Bates, and the works on a plate were due him: record contract, movies of the week, "Battle of the Network Stars." Except that for the latter, he'd have to take his shirt off . . .

They only had a few weeks to serve up thirteen episodes and he had to lose the weight in a hurry. The lunch break killed him: looking over at Dan McCrae as Cam Wilhelm, snacking down on Bavarian doughnuts and spaghetti bolognese as per instructions from the director—because he was the fat guy, the jolly guy, the guy that kept fucking up and had to be rescued by sage Don Bates and sager Todd Flores as Chase Runningblood, a.k.a. Tonto. Sometimes Donovan thought he should just give it up and let himself spread like McCrae, really try larding up the waist so the butt would look comparatively small. He'd get work, after all. There was never a shortage of fat funny guy roles to go around. But he sensed that McCrae must be miserable, maybe even laughed at and denied the dignity of human sexual life. He guessed that food and more particularly drink were his only consolations, that early death by depression or obesity would be his lot—and he *knew* the fictional Cam Wilhelm was a moron who brought increasing dishonour to the Los Angeles Police

Department with each passing episode. Of course he did. He was fat!

Donovan couldn't let himself go full DeLuise anyway. He was too good-looking otherwise; and one of the worst things an actor (or indeed most people) had to deal with was the state of being a little this and a little that, fat here but skinny there, beautiful eyes but a huge nose, that sort of thing. It made having a sense of one's own identity difficult. It stopped you achingly short of being called attractive. So one day he just said this: Fuck it. He started eating what he wanted, though was too guilty to eat an entire serving of what he wanted, a feeling that translated to half an eclair with lunch, a few sips of milkshake at dinner. He'd always atone for such dereliction by washing the vice down with virtue in the form of a few Brussels sprouts or a stick of celery. Since the sprouts didn't completely nullify the guilt, he'd chase his meal with a few vitamin E pills and pinch of something ridiculous or poisonous but so unpleasing as to bear the promise of health—marjoram, grated burdock, taproot of wild parsnip.

And wouldn't you know it, he started losing weight. Two pounds one week, four more the next. It was uncanny, though likely attributable to that quasi-Buddhist idea about watched pots never boiling. But Donovan really believed he was on to something with the sprouts and the vitamins and the free-jazz herbal mixtures. He devised a couple of daily menus, photocopied them, then tacked them onto the bulletin board at the gym. Over the menus was the imperative in bold black marker: TELL ME IF THIS ISN'T THE BEST DIET YOU'VE EVER TRIED. He added his telephone number and was, within two weeks, deluged with fully three personal testimonials that matched his own. Because of the Dan Bates gig, he'd met a number of ladies, too, and he plied them with the diet—courteously, though, only offering it to those who had complained about their weight in the first place. When Lisa Doray lost ten pounds he hit the jackpot. She was a no-hard-feelings one-week stand but also the star of NBC's "Li'l Critters" and a good person to know. She put him in touch with a health food grocer who started mixing and selling his "vitamagic" packets in the stores, along with the diet printouts. People paid like crazy, too.

He had to come up with a name for his diet. His first choice was Perfect End, but the grocer said that sounded too much like Last Chance and it would never sell, not after all the deaths. He then thought the Brentwood Diet had a nice ring, but that it sounded too much like the Beverly Hills Diet and how could he follow in the footsteps of its author, a woman who claimed in her book that "eating a balanced meal is like wearing two different skirts at the same time"?

The diet's name ultimately derived from what it did, or seemed to do. The legumes and vitamins, of course, appeared to counteract the negative fat-depositing effects of the Hershey bars and whatever other crud you might include in your meal: hence, Counteraction. CounterACTION! The dynamism of *action;* the culinary connotations of *counter*. It was the very thing.

ABC didn't order up any further episodes of "Tonto, Bates and Wilhelm," but no matter. Mack Donovan would wait for the phone to ring no more! He was on a roll now, with a publisher interested, too. The subsequent book, entitled *Mack*

Alms

Donovan's CounterACTION! was a modest success—it featured Donovan on the cover, mouth open, demonically happy, holding a bunch of grapes in one hand and a plate of pie in the other. But only a modest success. After all, it was 136 pages long, and most of these were title pages or epigraphs. He didn't know how to cook so he couldn't really invent recipes or anything. He didn't really have too much to tell anybody, truth be told. And then a strange thing happened. Diet theory inverted itself. With the advent of nouvelle cuisine, it was the skeletal who were encouraged to deny themselves food; the overweight were cajoled everywhere to stuff themselves. "Eat as much as you want!" "Why deny yourself?" "Sin!" His gym buddies and dwindling supply of girlfriends started toting around another paperback, one featuring a face much less attractive than his own. It was called the Scarsdale Nutritional Program and was written by an actual doctor, a bald and very thin doctor. Fuck! What had modern medicine ever done for Mack Donovan, ex-manatee? This scrawny doctor weasel didn't know what it was like to be fat! "Use your good sense," the book admonished. "But if *you* had good sense," Donovan exclaimed to a horrified 110-pound date (and Scarsdale adherent) just prior to her stalking out of a restaurant, "you wouldn't be so fat in the first place!" He did so much to get the world off Scarsdale that when the doctor was shot to death a little while later, Donovan even considered himself a suspect. He collected unflattering pictures of himself to include in the next edition of *Mack Donovan's CounterACTION!,* pictures, for example, of his buttocks straining against the confines of a lycra bathing suit, the idea being that he was a real guy to whom fatness had happened and not just some cardiologist with a comb-over.

There would, however, be no further print runs. So he took his pictures back to Canada, where he enjoyed some income through telephone sales, and where his netherlands were kept just slim enough to afford him regular work as the dad in a series of commercials for cough syrup.

Night after night he would sit with a bag of Fritos, planning how to grab the holy grail of diet stardom. A television show? Out of his reach. There were no Lisa Dorays in Toronto and those there were would have nothing to do with him. Door to door? Possible, but, he reasoned, Mrs. X won't be too flattered when she opens the door to a complete stranger bearing the message that she could stand to lose fifteen pounds (he always meant to chase the Fritos with celery during these brainstorming sessions but usually fell asleep before he got there). A spa? A spa would be the answer. That Pritikin bastard was raking it in hand over fist by having society matrons submit uncomplainingly to his regime. They just stuffed back all his grub without even thinking about it, not when those potatoes were just chucked in like hiccups between the yoga, tennis, and facials. If Donovan could only get a captive audience like that to bolt down his admittedly odd meal suggestions, all glory would be his.

He sniffed around and found out about a small facility an hour's drive from the city. It had been operating for about a year and was owned by an ex-fashion model by the name of Sharon Colterblake. She had once been a James Bond–girl type, your basic strawberry blonde with full lips and slave-girl eyes and a body that was appropriately peaked and valleyed, though the times might have called for more slenderness than she could furnish. In any case, it was a body not just good enough for bra ads but for entire bra packages. For years, though, she'd been abusing this commodity with white wine, cigarettes, Valium, and Bundt cake, to the point where she felt her body to be a thing most mottled and melted, an Easter bonnet blown off by a storm. She didn't want to join a gym where others might look upon her physical disgrace; instead, she'd petitioned her husband, a urologist with family money, for the funds to set up a fitness chamber of her own, the Gold Valley Ranch, which of course was not going to be any kind of a ranch at all, there being no plans for cattle or horses.

Donovan could tell from the scanty and clumsily gilded biographies on the brochure that the three-member staff had virtually no scientific or business acumen among them. "Ms." Colterblake, as she called herself, appeared to be abetted by old dolls who were interested in the declining fortunes of their own carcasses and no one else's. The director of diet services was a "former actress" who, he believed, would be most open to things experimental, unproven, and theatrical.

So Louise Craythorn skipped lunch to meet him and felt, as she later confessed to her daughter, immediately self-conscious about doing so. The facility had looked fabulous upon completion, but one year in you could see that the wiring had been hastily pasted in—to wit, the many dead lights around the joint—and that the grouting, especially in the whirlpool and shower areas, was significantly cracked. A crafty young masseur had made off with the sound system and all the ambient soundscape cassettes. So she was apologetic, the more so as the meeting went on, because she was impressed and wanted him to like her. His diet she guessed to be worthless, as most diets were. But there was a gentleness about him, a hurt boy's pain that softened his every sentence; and coming off an ex-husband like Louise's, a rather loud character of the genus Abrasivus Annoyingus, she was ready for some gentle.

"You have such a lovely accent," he told her. "Like Grace Kelly. Are you from these parts?"

"Well," she said, reddening but pleased that a man had finally taken note of her intricately carved consonants, "I went to school in Switzerland."

"Switzerland?" he inquired. "My."

She told him she'd seriously think about his diet, but in the meantime, would he like to have lunch? There was no written proscription against dining socially with a snake oil merchant. Before long he was coming over to the house for tense and uncertain dinners. Louise liked Donovan, liked him more and more all the time, but "Ms." Colterblake had no intention of forsaking Pritikin for some untested plan that quite hideously suggested you force Black Forest cake to share a plate with puréed turnip. Donovan couldn't accept that it was out of Louise's hands and kept badgering her in bed, where she was at her most vulnerable.

Another problem was that Louise's daughter hated him. In one sense, having Donovan sub for her own dad was a good deal for Martine. He yelled a lot less. He convinced Louise to install a hot tub in the basement. And after

Donovan moved in, they went on family trips, an idea the Professor had condemned as extravagant.

But the girl found something truly repellent about Mack Donovan. Perhaps it was his dress, the blouson sleeves and velvet pants that had him looking at any given time like the flautist in an English progressive rock band. Or his hair, which he grew out until it hung in slovenly houndish flaps about his face. Or the way he kept grabbing Louise right in front of Martine. It was all these things, but most of all it was the way he was slowly inhaling the family fortune.

Martine took particular offence at the way he would sit hawing in front of *Happy Days* with a giant box of diet caramels at his side, as if the energy crisis, the ecology, and world famine weren't happening. She couldn't believe her mother was that stupid. She'd been an actress, she was still so beautiful—this was the best she could do? And when business dwindled to virtually nothing, when Mack Donovan's good luck finally ran out and he started to spend all his time in front of the television, with caramels now that weren't even dietetic in nature, and beers, and licorice, and Quarter Pounders, too—when this happened, Mack Donovan couldn't stand it any more and had to throw himself out, fleeing back to California. Louise was too nice to do it.

Mr. Mack Donovan
197 Garland Avenue
Toronto, Ontario
Canada
M4T 2E3

Cynthia Macdonald

Dear Mr. Donovan:

re: CounterACTION!

*We have received numerous customer complaints on
the subject of the above-named diet. A recent analysis
conducted by our resident nutritional advisors has
determined that the program makes a number of false
claims, several of which may result in injury to adher-
ents of the program. Among its potentially harmful
assertions:*

1. Soft cheese is preferable to hard because the latter
   is harder to digest.
   As yet, this idea has not been scientifically proven.

2. Vegetable oils have fat-burning properties.
   *Vegetable oils are fats themselves. This statement is
   therefore absurd.*

3. Pectin is a major digestive enzyme.
   *Pectin is not an enzyme at all but a thickening
   agent, often used in the making of jam.*

4. Romaine lettuce is a healthful source of Vitamin R.
   There is no such thing as Vitamin R.

*In addition, the CounterACTION! program urges upon
its followers the ingestion of less than twenty per cent
of the Recommended Daily Allowance of thiamine,*

calcium, iron, zinc, copper, niacin, riboflavin, and
thirty-seven other essential nutrients and minerals. As
any continued propagation of the program may result
in harm to its followers, we request that you refrain
immediately from publishing and distributing
CounterACTION! materials, and that you stop selling
any supplements or additional materials associated
with the plan. Failure to do so could result in criminal
charges against you and your employees.

Several years ago Martine might have penned this letter herself, had she only been able to get hold of the government stationery. But rather than wallowing in joy, she felt, of all things, the alien urge to say something comforting to her mother. "Mack probably didn't know about all that stuff."

"I'm sure he didn't," Louise plunged. "And what's more, the recipes tasted perfectly good, which should count for something — and they worked, which is what people want."

You idiot, Martine thought, her compassion fully eclipsed. The guy's sole purpose in life has been to bilk you white and still you leap to his defence, even as he's probably buying some fourteen-year-old starlet a wheatgrass shake in a Pasadena shopping mall. This is what I could never stand about you, Mother: you give so much, others have no option but to take.

The Professor had spent nearly every night of their marriage away in Africa, or at political meetings, or at the office setting up committees that would ultimately eject him for "personal reasons"; the few hours he did pass at home were all devoted to putting Louise and her rich parents down.

When Martine once dared to wax bitterly about this dimly remembered scenario, Louise corrected her. "Well, your father is just like that. He's a socialist."

"Yeah, a *National* Socialist."

"Please."

It was this sort of bovine loyalty that had catapulted Martine ever back to the Professor's side, the side that welcomed and understood anger. Not that Louise's loyalty couldn't be taxed to its very limits. From birth, Martine saw it as her mission to do just that. There was the time they found themselves together on a beach, the Christmas Pépère Berthiaume had decided to take them all to the Caribbean. Martine was only about four. She was determined to fashion a castle out of dry sand, no matter that Louise kept telling her it would never hold. "Just try adding some water, sweetie, it will work much better," she said, her soothing voice rising a little with each refrain. "How do you know?" barked the little girl, and even then she could see the hot words behind Louise's huge eyes, awaiting but never achieving expulsion: "Because I'm twenty-nine years old and I've built a fuck of a lot of sandcastles in my day, that's how I know!" But of course she would never say that.

Martine folded the letter and put it back in the envelope. She touched her mother's hand and watched the powdery plum-coloured eyelids flutter shut. Strange that she always had makeup on. "So what will you do now?" Louise asked.

Martine shrugged and ran a finger along the chenille bedspread, which was now indistinguishable from the pale nightgown and skin of the woman who lay beneath it. "I

don't know. There's this place I heard about." She mentioned
the hotel downtown, the one with the red velvet wallpaper.

Louise gave a sort of palsied half-smile. "Oh, that's the
most beautiful place—didn't I ever take you there, for your
birthday or anything? No? It was always the place to go,
years ago, you know. Sharon told me it's gone to seed,
though. She and Mott went there on their anniversary and
they had to watch one of those terrible acts, where a horrible
man talks and you think it's his puppet—what's it called?"

"Ventriloquist."

"Mmm. But it was always the best, though. They had the
most extraordinary chandelier in the lobby, I wonder if it's
still there. Do you want to work there?" she asked hopefully.

"I was thinking about it."

Louise's eyes opened and she started into a kind of syrupy
whine, grabbing her daughter's hand and stroking it. "It
would be such a step up, *chouette*. You could be a concierge,
or a hostess. Not like that awful place you were at. Go, go.
See if they have anything for you."

$\mathscr{M}$ARTINE REPORTED TO THE CONCIERGE, a fussy young man in a threadbare gold Nehru jacket. "Good morning, mademoiselle. Can I help youuuu?" he asked, cocking his head like a terrier in a bank calendar.

"I'm here about a chambermaid job."

The young man's caramelized unction vanished instantly, along with his bizarre Toulouse-by-way-of-Iowa accent. "Employees entrance," he said. "Around the side."

To get to the housekeeping offices she had to walk through the kitchen, through the stench of meat, fruit, onions, and chocolate being cooked very badly at the same time. The hotel's restaurants were known to offer the worst expensive food in the city but were still able to survive on a pre-war reputation for fanciness and elegance, though you'd have to be over eighty to recall a dollop of whipped cream free of powdery lumps, or a filet of sole unbathed in rancid cooking oil.

Alms

The woman who interviewed Martine seemed to be the unhappiest person alive, someone who'd voyaged past tears and anger into a sunless patch of soul scattered with garbage and burnt trees; a once-beautiful girl who might have been a model had destiny not decreed her Supervisor of Housekeeping Personnel and shut her up in this horrible basement, sandwiched between the monstrously redolent kitchen and the laundry room, which was full of tank-topped clods much given to swearing and sexual harassment. The woman hired Martine on the spot and took her on a tour of the hotel's cobwebby bowels, showing her the locker room, the boiler room, the dusty time clock cracked and invaded by flies. Martine was then handed a blue cotton shift and told to report for training the next morning at 6:15.

"Remember," said the woman. "Use the employees' entrance. It's against hotel rules to enter through the lobby."

But Martine did enter through the lobby, the next morning and every morning thereafter. The concierge never noticed, since he was usually replacing the cartridge of his fountain pen or filling a rack with brochures for the zoo. Just off the lobby lay Martine's one daily pleasure, unbuttered brown toast and coffee in the Princess Café: a treat that put punching the time clock and buttoning herself into the sad little cotton dress on the verge of worth it.

Of course, the Princess Café couldn't even get unbuttered toast right—it was invariably burnt or soggened by drips of milk—but hotel restaurants were exciting places to eat, like airports. To be in them was to be an adventurer stocking up for the next exploit. There were, however, rarely any fellow travellers here at six in the morning.

One started showing up, however, and almost every morning. He was small and apparently weathered by life, with receding brown hair and an exaggeratedly correct bearing. Agreeably natty, Martine supposed, if cheerful in a way that suggested mental imbalance. His face was off, too. With its autumn sunburn and bad teeth, it hinted at failure, but he could obviously afford to take his meals in the bosom of the British Empire. Strange. Usually, the shaggy little man ate in such a hurry as to not remove his beautifully tailored topcoat, but one day he did and Martine was shocked by the outfit underneath.

He was a Catholic priest. Not a typical one, but then maybe this was the "new breed." The Church did need to get with the times, everybody had been saying it for years, but still—Martine had known a priest or two in her time and this guy wasn't them. Even the youngest among them suffered from a severe funkiness deficit; how she had secretly mocked poor Father Pendergast, her catechism teacher, when he returned from a trip to Broadway and insisted on humming the overture from *Jesus Christ Superstar* while going about his sacerdotal duties.

The priest always ordered a huge breakfast of French toast, bacon, home fries, and eggs, and Martine noted that he wolfed everything down, even the homely little parsley sprigs. One day he took out a cigarette and lit it, an affectation less *outré* than the purple sunglasses he sometimes wore but just as notable. He smoked half the cigarette, then got up, donning his topcoat with ceremonial care. He gave a last, loving brush to his cuffs and headed for the exit with a considerable spring in his step, apparently juiced by Christ the Lord—as if he were born, when Martine really thought about it, to such eye-catching garb; but while she was thinking this he noticed her doing it and stopped before her table.

"Hello!" he said, in an embarrassingly familiar way. Martine returned the greeting, then recoiled. With coffee this bad, did she also have to endure missionary zeal? He sensed her discomfort and stepped back immediately. "Well, good day, then," he said, and left. The next few times he saw her, he would only grin shyly and from a distance, which she didn't mind. Though somehow his interest in her only made her think of hell—and of how she, a designated felon, was quite likely going there.

She turned out to be a perfectly lousy chambermaid. The worst, perhaps, in the history of the British Empire. Martine was shocked by her own lousiness—she was so fastidious, after all, and had grown up in Moore Park's cleanest house. Then there was her stint picking up after the Pines. But the aesthetic perfection of her surroundings had mostly been Emelda's doing, and Martine found it impossible to replicate it in her new workplace. She could never get the bedspreads flat enough, or vacuum every last speck out of the carpeting. The intricacy of the hospital corner eluded her. She kept forgetting to turn light bulbs off before dusting them and, as a result, a few of them exploded in her face. Black hairs lay stuck in bathroom tiles like mocking vipers; she sponged them up and they stuck to her wrists and dress. She dreaded being sent to the eighth floor, everyone did. That was the private domain of Lumira, a stern giantess of unspecified ethnicity who literally dragged Martine around by the ear from bed to bathtub to closet, yelling, "Dis is no clean rooms! Dis is no clean rooms!" Martine was so terrified of not finishing her work on time for Lumira's inspection that she started taking shortcuts, like cleaning the drinking glasses with the same cloth she'd just used to scrub the inside of the toilet. Naturally she vowed not to do this when Prince Philip came for his annual visit, should she land the honour of cleaning his biffy. Which of course she would not.

The other floor supervisors had their own problems. Once Martine came upon a room that was most intractably unclean; if there was ever a room that cried to be released from the bonds of its building and thrown out onto the street, this was it. The suite was liberally daubed in blood—sheets, carpets, room-service menu, even the ceiling. The tiles in the bathtub were dotted with pretty starlike spatters and the doorknobs stained with the dried maroon whorls of a big man's desperate fingertips. But there was no body anywhere, and the windows were all locked shut. Martine called the fifth-floor boss in for a look. She was a quiet Jamaican woman named Edris whose black eyes were filmed so thickly with boredom she seemed bound to consciousness by the thinnest of filaments; sometimes she'd dab at those eyes with the worn pink Kleenex she kept underneath her stretch watchband. Edris waddled into the suite on swollen calves and started filleting its drawers and bedclothes as if looking past the bloodstains for a better reason to be there. "Probably somebody had a fight in here, I think," she shrugged, then turned out the lamp on the night table. "Just go on to the next one."

Alms

And what reason was there to clean these rooms anyway? Nothing matched anything else, the art was atrocious, the furniture creaky and water-stained. Paper peeled from the walls and loosed crumbling plasterwork on worn carpets. The new hotels, by contrast, were chic and fresh with panoramic lakeviews and orchid petals floating in the toilet water. But this hotel was mired in the ideals of empire: subjugation and sobriety. Everything was dank and old, including the employees.

Martine had one friend among the other maids, a drained little Portuguese widow named Maria—or called Maria at any rate; her real name was Eufemia but her co-workers could never manage that so she'd just given up and let them have their way. The other maids stuck together and were always going out after their shifts to drink fuzzy navels and have a few laughs, but Maria was forever alone, imprisoned in a language that few of them spoke.

Every day she took off her turquoise dress and put on a black one with a matching head scarf. She and Martine trained together, an experience which left Martine in knowledge of the Portuguese words for *canker sore* and *pillow*. Like Martine, Maria couldn't work hard enough for the trainers' tastes, something Martine thought they might laugh about together, but Maria wouldn't play. She was over forty and well past laughing at her own incompetence.

Still she was kind; not a quality she could express in words, but in furtive grins, in the flans she sometimes baked and brought to the locker room, in the way she would touch the tassels of Martine's old muffler and say, "Nice. You pretty scarf." But one day an American guest accused Maria

of stealing an emerald bracelet and that, of course, was that.
It reminded Martine of how the Professor used to accuse
Louise of leaving cash around to test Emelda; anyway, from
then on the hotel's worst chambermaid had to content herself
with the society of women like the lemon-faced Geraldine,
inheritor of Maria's locker, who'd worked at every hotel in
the city and was on her third stint at this one. "You do shit
rooms," she told Martine, "but you're a summer maid, so I
don't know what you're still doing here." Martine protested
that she'd only started in the fall.

"Right," sneered Geraldine. "Little rich gals like you come
in here on school break and think they can clean rooms. It
takes years to clean one right." About which she was correct.
She was far less correct on the subject of black people,
abusing the Jamaican supervisors when she was forced to
submit to them and, being something of an éminence grise in
the world of chambermaidery, never paying for it. One
weekend a convention of black teachers came to stay at the
hotel and this was more than Geraldine could take. "Look at
this room," she'd say, inviting Martine into an averagely
lived-in suite. "If they wanna be that dirty, I shouldn't have
to pay for it. Why should we clean their rooms? Eh?"

I should really let her have it, Martine thought. If she were
Jeremy Pine, I would. But I'm just too tired now, and I don't
have many friends. "I don't know," she replied absently.
"But then, I don't know why I'm cleaning anyone's room."

In spite of all this human and architectural ruin, however,
Martine sometimes felt a bit soft about the hotel, like when
she left for the afternoon and the sun hit the limestone just so.
This thousand-room hulk had survived wars and depressions

and millions of private tragedies and celebrations—most of them taking place well outside its walls, but what of it? They were all over and this building wasn't; it saw history and sneered in its face. It wasn't impressively bullet-pocked like, say, the Dublin post office, but that was just the point: the great hotel wouldn't tolerate bullets or any other such nonsense. It had imposed itself on the city and was not going anywhere, and for that she befriended it.

Martine felt, in fact, unworthy of the place, since she was only up to one of its challenges—toothpaste splashes on the mirror. A spritz of Windex and a pass with a dry towel and these were gone in seconds, though not so the sad picture that remained carved in the glass: the wraithlike young loner at her labours.

Guests rarely saw her, so guests rarely tipped, except the Japanese, and there weren't many of them at this time of year. In fact, Martine saw more call girls than guests, since the former tended to roll out of bed just as the maids started work, and could sometimes be seen padding to the elevators in stockinged feet, swinging high-heeled sandals beside them. Martine would stand at her trolley folding towels, wondering the usual things you wonder about such women. Were they spiritually *there* for the sex or did they astrally project themselves onto a beach in Antigua while, say, Mr. Ogilvy in from Winnipeg was bucking away? Whichever, theirs had to be a painful, dangerous, and unenviable lot. Still, they gave every appearance of not caring, dangling unlit smokes between their lips while they buckled those impossible shoes; their insouciance made them compelling to Martine, Martine who was, now, always worried—worried about not preparing Mr. Ogilvy's room on time, worried about hair in the drains, worried about a broken arm from Lumira, worried, worried.

Once, when she was in the Princess Café, she saw a woman she swore was one of the call girls sitting with the ratty priest. It was hard to tell out of context, but who else would wear six-inch heels at that hour? Martine watched them from afar. She thought the call girl might be confessing, but the two of them were laughing awfully hard for that. The call girl finished her cigarette, then got up, smoothed her sparkly red tube dress over bow and stern, and put on her coat. Then, to Martine's horror, she actually leaned over and *kissed* the grinning priest. Only on the cheek, but still . . . Martine looked around. The few other people in the café didn't seem to care or notice. But the priest saw Martine looking at him and grinned (as was his embarrassing wont). She returned to her toast and avoided his glance until it was time to go.

Maybe it was a Mary Magdalene thing, she thought. Maybe the priest was trying to lead this scarlet harlot unto goodness, and cigarettes, laughter, and kisses were nothing more than the tools of the New Breed. Martine accepted that. She had always been a pious child, but she considered herself flexible. In fact, there were times, when she threw open the curtains to Room 1203 or Room 847 and saw the hard bright sun falling on the busy world below her, that her piety returned, along with her faith in the easy fix. Catholic school had invested her with the idea that bad problems could only be addressed instantly; with a touch of Christ's fingertips loaves and fishes would abound, lepers could be made whole.

"Be not afraid," went the hymn, "I go before you always."
Believing herself to be nothing more than God's pull-toy had
given her strength. Strength to run away from Jeremy Pine
when she stole some of his Hallowe'en candy and took it
downtown for the porepeople. Strength to stand up to teachers, parents, anybody who tried to tell her not to give meat,
milk, fruits, *and* vegetables up for Lent.

But she would only submit to her own version of God, and
she'd long ago discarded the fierce, caftanned codger of
childhood imaginings. She no longer cared too much for that
Kid of his, either—he was far too human, the biblical equivalent of Frank Sinatra Jr., and a chicken-hearted dude given
to whining about why he should die (Awww, Dad! Do I
hafta?). Between the ferocity of God and the frailty of Jesus
lay the perfect, invisible saviour, and Martine always
preferred a saviour she couldn't see.

She had actually saved money from this job, and before long
had enough for one month's rent, if not two. The next
morning she sat at a table near the door and scanned the
apartment rentals section of the *Toronto Star*. A little while
later the priest came in and sat down. Not at his usual table,
but right next to her.

Martine grimaced and kept reading. It was like Flavio
back in the high school cafeteria, though Flavio, at least, was
way better looking. There were, as usual, few other
customers: the priest obviously *meant* to sit here beside her.
"Good morning," he said with customary merriment. She
gave him a pained smile and went back to the paper, but he
wouldn't stop looking at her.

"Beautiful day," he said.

"Isn't it?" he said.

"Well, anyway," he said, and began whistling.

Now, nothing sent blood rushing behind Martine's eyes faster than whistling. And tuneful, practised whistling, such as the priest engaged in right now, was the worst. Pépère Berthiaume even had in his collection a double album of a man whistling Christmas carols: a slow abrasion to the soul and to the senses. Fortunately, at the height of Martine's fury—on the point of her addressing the matter—the priest stopped.

"I was just wondering, miss," he said. "Are you by any chance looking for a place to live?"

The question was far too intimate for him to be asking. Insulting, too. What was he proposing—that she be stashed away in some group home with his other friends, fallen wenches in tube dresses whom he aimed to make whole with prayers and porridge? Did he think she was one of them? But then you couldn't lie to a priest.

"Uh . . . kind of," she told him.

"Really," he said, spider-cool now. He grinned again, revealing a jumble of crooked, discoloured teeth. If I had teeth like that, I wouldn't ever smile, Martine thought. Even if I felt like it.

"Well, it just happens that I've got a place in my house, in the basement actually. It's not far from here, and it's only"—here he motioned to the waitress with his hand—"two-fifty a month. You'd never see me because I'm never there. I didn't want to rent it out before, but the thing is, my ministry could really use the cash. So if you're interested . . ."

Weird, Martine thought. Not interested. At least, don't think so. On the one hand, she admired his obvious independence and probable commitment to the Lord's work, if the collar counted for anything. On the other, there was the time she saw him reading the sports section and heard him mutter under his breath: "Goddamn Leafs." At least, it sure sounded like that.

"Here—Wanda, give Martine your pen." The waitress placed a pen primly down on the For Rent section, over ads for apartments which were, admittedly, twice as expensive as the one the priest was proposing.

"Take this number down." Martine wrote the number hesitantly on a little corner of newspaper, which she tore off, folded, and stuck in her wallet in order to satisfy the guy, who watched her, intense as a starved vole.

"I'm Father Kearney," he said, offering a scarred hand that was surprisingly big, given his general smallness and wiriness. "You're Martine."

"How did you know?" she asked.

He looked at a spot just above her right breast. He looked—did he?—one half-second longer than he should have. "Name tag," he said.

She gave Wanda her pen back and asked for the bill.

But how, she wondered on the subway home, would a priest have a room to rent? Louise would know—she had a cousin who'd gone out to minister to the flock in Shapdoe, Saskatchewan. But it was hardly conceivable that Cousin Père Pierre roomed with anyone else, let alone a young woman.

When she got home the house was dead. For a second Martine thought she had lost her hearing. She mounted the stairs with a higher degree of dread than usual and tapped open her mother's bedroom door. In bed *comme toujours,* motionless *comme toujours,* all nightgown and splayed hair.

"Mama," Martine said, roughing Louise's slack shoulder. "Mama, I want to ask you something."

There was no response and Martine shook harder. Nothing and nothing. Martine grew frightened and finally resorted to yanking her mother's hair in order to rouse her.

"Einhhhh?" Louise said suddenly, casting about like a ghost.

Martine wanted to slap the laziness right out of her, strangle her until she was forced to stand up, brush herself off, and do something.

"You sleep so much, Mama," she said tightly, but with terror in it.

Louise pushed her hair back and groped through the wads of tissue for her glasses. There were new wrinkles about her lips, which bore the stains of old lipstick. "I don't," she said, affecting a false brightness.

"Why don't you do anything any more? You never go to the opera committee, you never see Sharon . . ."

"That's not true, I saw Sharon today! We had lunch at Holt's. You think I always sleep, because you're only here when I sleep. During the day I'm very busy."

Martine snorted. When Louise was sweet and apologetic it was easy to feel for her, but when she showed the least sign of armature her daughter always felt like punishing her for it.

"I had a question to ask you," Martine said, "but I'll come back when you're more alert."

"*Mais non* — Martine, *p'tite étournette!*" Louise took the girl's hand and gave it an industrious rub. She was suddenly so vibrant with life, not at all like someone only several minutes out of Nod. "Don't be silly. You ask me whatever you want, you know you always can."

Martine sighed. The question was no longer important and it dropped from her like shale off a cliff. "Okay. I just wanted to know. Do priests live with other people or by themselves?"

Louise flopped back on the pillow and rubbed her eyes. "Why do you ask me that?"

"I'm just wondering."

"Well, if they're Franciscans — yes, Franciscans live with friends, just in regular houses. Usually in poor neighbourhoods though."

Two-fifty a month. That's why.

"All right, Mama. Sorry to wake you."

OVER THE NEXT FEW DAYS, she went and checked out other apartments, but none of them were right. It was always one little tragic feature or other that got her. A horribly outdated light fixture. Pink-and-peach linoleum. Coffee grounds on the floor by the sink. She realized much later that the coffee grounds must have been mouse excreta, but she had never had access to such a thing in Moore Park and didn't see it immediately for what it was.

Nor did she like the way the landlords would show her blank-eyedly around, flipping light switches while they picked their teeth and checked their watches. They didn't look at her or ask her anything about herself. Which would have been all right—she was a loner, too—but their demeanour actually suggested hatred, instead of a mere lack of interest.

It didn't matter anyway, since most of the apartments were too expensive. But one cold afternoon after that, on a day so windy she could hear the weather blowing murderous oaths at her as she tucked in one imperfect hospital corner after another, she found the ring.

She was wandering alone on the sixth and entered a darkened suite. Its occupant had checked out the day before but had barely disturbed the room while he'd been there, so it hardly needed cleaning. On the bed was a tiny velvet box. There was a note on top of the box, scrawled by a shaking hand.

To the Chambermaid:

Like you, my late wife worked as a chambermaid at this fine hotel, although this was long ago now in 1928. Elsie made many friends and always remembered her time here with great fondness. In fact, I believe it was the greatest joy of her life apart from the years we were fortunate to share together. We were not blessed with children and I know, if Elsie could say it, she would want a girl like you to have this ring. If you don't think it is pretty, I'm sure you could sell it and use the money as I realize a chambermaid's pay is not high.

All the best to you in your life.

Sincerely,
George Woodley

She opened the velvet box to see a dimmed and puny diamond sitting atop a thick gold band. It slid with some difficulty over her thin but broken finger, which had been left unset after a skiing accident ten years before. There was no question of keeping it. It was the ticket out of Moore Park.

Martine lay down on the bed, closed her eyes, and listened to what was now the lash of the rain. She thought of all the future six and eight and ten o'clocks that would see her mother waking up and reaching in vain for her *"étournette,"* her angry brown starling, for a trace of the baby softness she hoped might yet be buried in the felt of her child's cape. Could Louise survive the removal? It was not Martine's question to answer, and she cursed her mother for making her think it was.

After tucking the ring back in its box and sequestering it among the bath oils on her trolley, she finished out her day, went downstairs to empty her locker, and tendered her resignation to the supervisor, who accepted it as a matter of course.

After a sneering farewell to her little turquoise maid's uniform, she acknowledged her hunger and was gripped by a curious need to slake it. With only two of her servings so far accounted for, she could eat well tonight.

The Princess Café was not the best place to have supper, but it was close at hand. She settled herself at a small table in the back and placed the suitcase in front of her. It was her first opportunity to really look at the menu. She could choose among "Medaillons de veau *Duc d'Edimbourg*"; "Potage *Diana*"; and "Ragout de lapin *à la Reine*." Everything was named after one member of the English royal family or another, except for the limp and oversauced vegetables—

which weren't worth naming after anybody, except maybe Princess Margaret. It was also fairly curious that all the dishes had French names; it was as if, after sampling the disgraceful rabbit stew named in her honour, the Queen had ordered that it not be spoken of in English.

Martine ordered the "Paillard de poulet *Prince de Galles*" and a strawberry milkshake. Then she heard a whap of familiar laughter from the kitchen. The door swung shut but, looking into the little round glass portal from afar, she could just behold the priest—Father Kearney, he'd said his name was. He seemed especially animated and, if her vision served, was wearing his purple sunglasses in spite of the grey autumn rain outside. While she was wondering at the meaning of this, Wanda came to take her order. She spoke in the same tone of tearless despondency that marked all the hotel's employees.

"Don't even think of ordering the soup. Cook gave it all to the Refuge."

Looking out the columnar leaded windows of the café, Martine could see the strange little cleric loading numerous trays of sandwiches into the back of a white truck, as well as a virtually uncarryable white plastic bucket of what Martine presumed was "Vichysoisse *Andrew.*" There was a man with him, who appeared to be his driver. Sort of a man, anyway. He wore filthy jeans, a wool cap, and blue basketball shoes with shredded toecaps. His hair was long and greasy, and Martine could almost smell him from where she sat.

"The Refuge?" she asked.

The waitress shrugged. "You know, that restaurant that Father Kearney runs. For the poor folks. And let 'em have the damn soup, I say."

Martine looked out the window with a cynical wrinkle of the nose and watched the priest get into the passenger side while the dirty man started the truck. "I mean," said the waitress, "you'd really have to be on the skids to eat that stuff."

Martine didn't want soup, though. It was the one thing she truly never ate, not after the botulism thing at Pépère's company.

The accident happened a long time ago; a little boy in Montreal had died, although Pépère's lawyers were able to successfully argue that his congenital intestinal problems would have done him in anyway. One other person had also died, but she was old and so nobody really cared. Then the scandal itself died, as scandals will; the lost money was all remade and Pépère's torn prosperity so skilfully mended that eventually he was even able to reminisce tearfully about the affair at Easter dinner one year. *"Ce p'tit monsieur là,"* he said in reference to little intestinally compromised Bruno Poirier of Montreal, P.Q. "Well, let's hope he went to a better place than this one."

Martine extracted her notebook. She felt sick with the great weight of glutinous, well-besauced chicken inside her. The rice, spiced and salted and choked with butter. The mangled asparagus corpses, which had crushed themselves in her mouth and slithered to mute rest at the pit of her gut. She had not eaten so much at one sitting for months, not since Christmas in fact, when she always starved all day so she could eat an authentic four-course feast as a special gift to Louise—who always watched her eat, one tear welling at the corner of an eye, hoping it heralded some new normality.

Alms

She wrote it all down, but the milkshake tripped her up. Did the whipped cream and maraschino cherry count as part of the drink, or did they represent two separate servings in themselves? She flipped back through the notebook to see if this had ever come up. Pages and pages of fine psychography, the "felon's claws" hanging off the lines like icicles. A typical entry:

March 12

1 potato chip
1 glass orange juice
1 medium pepperoni pizza
3 cantaloupes
2 raisins
1 licorice cigar
1 can condensed milk

Aha! The pepperoni on the pizza had been included. But then, Martine agonized, it was *embedded* in the cheese, while the whipped cream and the cherry floated on top, so where did that put her?

This was madness, that she knew. She wished she could stop. A couple of months back she had, but it only lasted a day. Without the notebook, her very life felt flabby and shapeless. That day she ate what she wanted, when she wanted — which left her wanting nothing, like the dead. Each ritual food list was a sign that she had lived through yet another neatly moulded day, that she had not let herself fall from the invisible ledge on which she stood. Each bit of food

121

withheld gave her something to yearn for. But the routine was getting hard on her, taking too much time. She must simplify matters.

Eight servings from now on.

She tucked the notebook back in her bag, left the restaurant, and walked down to a pawnshop, where she exchanged the Mrs. Woodley ring for a few hundred dollars. It was surely worth more, but what the hell. She was free to go now.

On the streetcar she started thinking about Father Kearney, how he'd struggled with the bucket of awful soup, handed it off to that horrible man, climbed in the battered truck in the darkening cold to go who knows where, and still seemed so happy. The whole picture endeared him to her. She decided that the patchy hair and the cursing must only be bait for the heathen, similar to the artfully constructed five o'clock shadows worn by undercover cops. But why the happiness? Was life, perhaps, not so bad down here?

The more she thought about it, the more detached she became from Moore Park: home, when she finally got there, felt newly foreign to her. She sidled into the den like a burglar and turned on a movie, with the volume low so as not to wake Louise. The movie was called *The Sorrow of Solitude;* it was several years old and Martine recalled that it had bombed terribly in the theatres. It was the true story of a young French girl who, while bravely ferrying secrets to the Resistance, was caught, raped, and shot by the Nazis. Watching it, Martine felt a blade of compassion knife through her—not for the real French girl, whose tale was probably overembellished—but for the star of the film, a young actress named Juliet Whitewell. She'd won the part after a well-publicized casting call and much had been expected from her, but after the film's leaden failure the returns only diminished for poor Juliet; bit parts in sitcoms, paper towel commercials, and lately, the worst fate of all: "spending time with her family." Martine had followed the girl's descent avidly. She had seen *The Sorrow of Solitude* before, attracted by the title, and was enchanted by Juliet's performance, which was, in the critics' eyes, marred by a near-total lack of charisma. She was a beautiful girl, but it was a beauty unlit by humour or warmth or talent of any kind. Pure beauty, Martine thought. She crawled to the television screen and spread out her hand and pushed it through the thin gate of static onto the stern, pale face of Juliet Whitewell, a face which, when she looked very closely at it, was broken into a hundred thousand infinitesimal dots.

To leave right now would be best, before Louise had a chance to wake up. Martine felt that she would not be able to bear the canine puzzlement on her mother's face when she found out. It would be more comfortable to deal with her on the telephone from downtown, when Louise was as faceless and absent from her as the African poster children.

But where could she go? The pink-and-peach-linoleum landlord would never receive her at this hour, and all other landlords would be asleep. Save perhaps one. Yes, she had a strong feeling that that landlord would be awake.

She went into the mauve room and rooted around in her closet for the black duffel bag she'd always taken to summer camp. It still had a training bra stuffed in the corner, from the summer she was twelve, stretchy and white with a dainty pink rose in the centre. There was also a letter the Professor had written her from Africa.

May 15, 1975

Dear Martine,

Good to get your letter and, if memory serves me correctly, a very happy birthday to you. I'd like to tell you things are fine here but, as usual, they are not. I've made the acquaintance of a little boy about your age. Life is very different for him. His name is Kwao and he lives with his mother and five brothers . . .

Blah blah blah, Martine thought, crumpling the thing and pitching it into her porcelain wastebasket, on which a painted lord and lady danced a merry gigue. She folded her jeans and packed them, along with seven pairs of underwear and an equivalent number of sock pairs. The weather was turning and sweaters would be needed. She put in a notebook for financial calculations, and her toilet kit, which contained nothing but toothpaste, toothbrush, mascara, tweezers, and a jar of something called Nightime Miracle Emulsifier. This last she never used, but its blue bubble-filled jelly was often comforting just to look at.

Books. She looked at her shelves, still home to the preferred stories of her childhood: *A Tree Grows in Brooklyn*, whose waif heroine dreamed of eating charlotte russes at the Sherry Netherland Hotel, and poured her beloved coffee down the drain just to feel the eroticism of wastefulness; *A*

Little Princess, who went from riches to rags, tortured in her garret by fantasies of steaming curries and gold-threaded quilts. *The Little Match Girl, Jack and the Beanstalk, The Little Drummer Boy, Oliver Twist, Huckleberry Finn, Cinderella, Little House on the Prairie:* poor kids the lot of them, glamorous exotics. She thought of taking them all with her, as tour guides.

She went down to the kitchen and randomly chucked an ill-considered bunch of housewares in her bag: some cutlery, a potato masher, dishtowels. What would she not be able to do without? The food processor, to be sure, but it was impossible to fit in the duffel. If she ever ate, she'd eat out.

She dragged the packed duffel into the front hall, hoping but knowing that its comical jangle wouldn't wake her mother. She looked up the stairs to where the cream carpeting seeped over the top step and into the untroubled perfect nothing of all the rooms upstairs.

Au revoir.

"*T*WELVE MERSEYFIELD AVENUE, please."

"Where's that?" asked the driver.

"Uh—I don't know. It's not that far from . . ." She gave the name of the hotel.

The driver unclipped a dog-eared city guide from his sunshade and began flipping through it. "L-eight. Oh. You sure you want to go there this time of night?"

"I'm sure."

The driver shook his head and replaced the book. He started the cab up and drove her down Mount Pleasant, eerily empty and soothing. The great road rolled beneath them, bordered by moon-splashed thickets of green. A large purposeful building greeted them on exit; life insurance, Martine surmised, was its chief reason for being, but though she had seen this building thousands of times she had never really thought about it. She thought about it now, as she did

all the buildings they passed. There was much art and industry in the first few among them: the steak restaurant, the
bohemian hotels, the head office of the pizza company. But
then a certain blandness set in and she couldn't quite tell
what the buildings were for, though their stained yellow
brick betokened something one wouldn't advertise. Then a
men's hostel. Then a women's hostel.

The driver turned east and they passed a long black fence
covered in angry paper signs, most of which were hanging in
the wind. There was a woman in a sequined miniskirt, notice-
ably pregnant. There were figures she dared not look at,
marked by open black coats and wavering gaits. At length
they came to another broadly lit street and a derelict hotel,
lately famous because a long-time inhabitant had been
discovered in one of the uppermost rooms having sex with
the corpse of his wife. She'd been dead for long enough that
her face was largely eroded, the newspaper said, and the man
wept bitterly when they handcuffed him and removed her.
Much more romantic, Martine thought, than the one marriage
I ever saw.

They went down a series of rather jaunty residential
streets, with stained glass on the doors and plump cats sitting
sentinel in the windows. Martine was just about to relax into
the back seat when the buildings hardened again, became
boxy and flat and surrounded by dust. Not a soul on the sidewalks. One squat brick horror gave way to another and she
was on the point of ordering the driver to go back, it was all
a mistake, when he made a left turn. Not far enough left,
mind you, for her taste, but at least 12 Merseyfield was a
house, and a thankfully big one at that.

The porch was lit, as if someone expected her, and there was light coming from the hallway. She imagined the priest to be in his kitchen, reading Teilhard de Chardin by candle-light. She rang the bell tentatively.

Lace curtains covered a small pane embedded in the door, and through this she watched him come barrelling down the stairs. She instantly regretted the fear she must naturally have sparked. But as he made for the handle he seemed neither fearful nor bothered, but happy—*still!*—a happiness that kicked insistently through his smile, the broad grey cradles under his eyes. He wore a lushly coloured housecoat and matching corduroy slippers, as if he were off to some upscale slumber party. The door flew open.

"I gave at the office," he said mockingly.

Martine had expected the priest to be sleepy enough that she might control things, but he was, sadly, even more alert than she had ever seen him. "I'm sorry to disturb you at this hour . . ."

Yes? He looked to be thinking, with his quizzical little eyes: *Do* go on, my girl. There is nothing more entertaining than the spectacle of the wrong trying vainly to be right.

". . . but I was wondering if you've rented the room yet. Father."

Father Kearney stretched and invited her in, barely suppressing laughter as he watched her lug the clanking duffel bag inside. "As it happens, I haven't," he yawned, looking at his watch. "But there's a lovely couple coming back for a second viewing at one-thirty—so you may be out of luck."

Martine stood, hand still on the bag's handle, waiting. On her lunch break she'd noticed a run in her nylons and gone across the street to buy more. The transaction was completed within seconds and involved no eye contact at all between her and the clerk; and now, under the wildly interested stare of this strange landlord, she wished anything that all goods and services could be exchanged with that kind of speedy impersonality. He led her through the rather vast foyer to the living room, which was also large and carpeted in an impressive rose-coloured Persian. Louise had a rug like this rolled up in the back of Martine's closet. There was a lot of room for it, since Martine had never had very many clothes. The auctioneer had sung its praises thus: "Ladies and gentlemen, this carpet is so stunning that even if you didn't have a place to put it—even if you just stuck it in a back closet somewhere—it would still be worth it!"

Father Kearney pointed at an elegant club chair.

"Sit a minute, my dear," he said. "I'm just going upstairs a second to take care of something."

Odd, she thought. It was as though he were going to tell his wife . . . but that would be impossible, of course. Probably just going to turn off a tap. She placed the duffel bag on the carpet and looked around her. There was a dainty gold crucifix over the fireplace, fresh flowers on the mantel. The coffee and side tables were too futuristic, though, and didn't sit well on the Persian; Martine wondered if he'd bought them himself, or if they'd been given him by the diocese. There was a haphazard war of modern and antique being waged all over this room, actually—ruched curtains in a blue-and-white triangle pattern, Royal Doulton figurines, and a huge welter of stereo equipment, black and streamlined with flashing coloured displays and neat Blaupunkt speakers. A tacky setup, all in all, but an expensive one, too.

The decorating missteps were a shame, because in many ways it was the perfect room for an elegant tea party, and it was impossible to believe that not two blocks away all manner of indignities were being suffered. But then churches always had to look the part, didn't they?—and church is exactly where Martine felt she was. The building was sealed against anything truly ugly, she was sure of it. Pain and poverty were close at hand, but so was luxury; if she lived here, she could travel the alpha-omega of human experience in a single walk home.

The proprietor was a bit off, though, but at least he decorated himself well. After a minute he ran downstairs again, this time with a lit cigarette and an insouciantly held ashtray, a flat tin plate that asked you to visit Niagara Falls. "Come on down to the basement," he said.

They went back through the foyer again and he opened a large wooden door. She worried that they would constantly be running into each other at this door or just inside it; and, as if he knew exactly what she was thinking, he laughed and reminded her that he was "hardly ever there." She couldn't imagine why this would be so, but didn't ask. The priest took Martine down a staircase that was small, but big enough to wind slightly. It let onto a vast expanse of freshly installed flooring, grey with funky mint-and-pink accents. The walls were white and he told her he'd just had them painted.

"I went with eggshell," he told her. "But I could have had bisscue. What would you have done?"

" 'Bisscue'?"

"Yeah, you know. Is that how you say it? B-I-S-Q-U-E?"

"Oh, bisque."

"Yeah . . . uh, so do you like it? What do you think?"

Martine shrugged. "Walls are walls. I don't really care what colour they are."

"Huh," he said, then proceeded to show her the stove, the fridge, the bathroom and light fixtures. A lot of effort had gone into this basement. The bathroom was a symphony of gold and marble, with zebra-patterned wallpaper and a pink plush bathmat. He's angling for a woman to move in here, Martine thought. But it was really all too much. It was a mobster's bathroom. Father Kearney seemed proud of it, though. He stroked the oversized faucets as if they were cherished pets, and started in on the Homeric tale of their purchase; but, seeing Martine didn't care, he stopped, extinguished his cigarette, and said simply, "Tell me about yourself." He squinted at her through the cigarette smoke, as if preparing to cast doubt on whatever it was she had to tell him. She felt like a lump of clay about to endure the sculptor's enthusiastic squeeze.

They stood facing each other in the hallway, each leaning on opposite sides of its fresh white walls. "Well," she said, "you know where I work."

"Sure, but where do you come from?"

To tell him the truth would be to mark herself as soft, pampered, and idiotic. But the thought needled her again: lie to a priest and you risked eternal damnation. "North," she said.

"Northern Ontario?"

"No, just . . . north."

He disposed of his cigarette in a tidily lined wastebasket and looked at her with a kind of reproving hurt. "Oh. You'll tell me more when you want to, I guess." He looked at the sunken duffel, from which a pot handle protruded. "So you're takin' the room then?"

She nodded.

"Great." He wheeled toward the staircase with a vigor that seemed only to increase the longer their conversation went on, and began climbing. "First and last, starting from, let's say, the fifteenth, which is coming up, give you a few days free, and—aren't you coming?"

Martine stood against the wall. "No. I'll pay you now, if that's okay. I'd actually like to sleep here tonight."

The priest choked out a laugh. "But you don't have anything to sleep on! Let me go upstairs, I'll get you some blankets at least—"

"It's all right."

"A pillow! You need *something*."

"I'm fine."

He pouted in resignation and looked at his watch again. "Okay. It's only a few hours till Brown Toast Hour anyway, eh?" He laughed and she smiled politely in return. He cleared his throat. "Well, pay me when you can." He stamped up toward the door on thin fuzzy legs.

"Oh, by the way." He turned from the door, knob in hand. "I may be a man of the cloth, but I do allow overnight guests. If you were wondering."

This surprised her. But then maybe he thought of fornication as a sort of methadone: a transitional pleasure that eased you into a cure. And a nice offer, but Jeremy Pine was gone and the Flavio file was closed for good. "That's kind of you, Father, but I won't be having any guests."

He looked bewildered, as if he'd been slapped, and Martine instantly regretted the certainty of her tone. The guy was only trying to be nice. But there was something of the Labrador retriever in him, and she worried that any friendliness on her part would be met with twice the amount on his side, and *that,* she feared, would be too much for her to handle. True to his way, though, he quickly became jaunty again."Suit yourself," he said. Then he smiled and was gone.

She realized, before curling up on the cold if stylish floor, that she'd have to maintain the fiction of her employment at the hotel in order to fool the priest into thinking she had some income. Rising and exiting that early wouldn't be a problem though. Six-thirty, striding empty streets with the day all to herself, was when she had always been happiest.

She managed a strained nap with the duffel as her pillow, though she kept waking up and wailing silently at the sight of the tragic little window above her, which she now noticed was covered in a thick prison-style grate. She was not aware until now how accustomed she had grown to waking up under the mauve bedclothes and looking at Mémère's silver brush and comb set on the vanity; and the remembrance that she had not even packed it struck her as unspeakably sad. But that silver-and-mauve life had only been good in sleep. By day it was erosive and stupid, like floating on seafoam so thick you couldn't feel the water underneath, and what made the sea if not water? Thank God, Martine thought, waking to the eggshell walls of her new existence, I'm swimming in it now.

It couldn't have been much past six and the sky was still an uncooperative deep grey. She got up, batted at the tangled thatch of her hair with her hands, and decided to take a walk outside. But there was nobody around. She looked down the length of Merseyfield and was reassured by its quiet, neutron-bombed feel.

There was a marked contrast between the priest's house and everyone else's. The others were thin and porchless, in one case even doorless. She passed a school, which looked like any other save for the extra quantity of garbage floating around its empty playground. From the garbage a single used needle rolled past her, through the fence but too close. The virus, looking at her again. She was terrified of it and saw it everywhere in people; a tiny red mark on the hand or neck of a Helping Hands client and she would scoot her chair back a discreet inch or two, though she was more frightened of someone noticing her cowardice than she was of the disease itself.

She came out onto Queen Street. Not nightclub and bank-tower Queen Street, but one of its more desolate intervals. This was the real city now, the one jammed with striving folk who were white, black, and gold, but mostly colourless, its streets a festival of asphalt, metal, and wire—never wood, never leaf. Big downtowns like this one wedged three storefronts in a space plainly meant for one and two families into apartments the size of pillboxes.

She was hungry now. It was going to be nice, not having to shake off Emelda in the mornings or her mother in the evenings: voluptuous encroaching women waving drum-sticks and loaves. She could eat at her own pace, and more importantly, she could not eat at her own pace. But it would be all right to eat now. Maybe a doughnut to celebrate her daring descent from uptown.

She walked into a place called the Koffee Kave. There was only one other customer, a wrinkled old man wreathed in oddly girlish grey curls. He sat at the table with nothing before him, wrists and hands poking delicately from the sleeves of a thin baseball jacket. He watched Martine buy a cherry Danish and take it to a table across the room from him.

But as soon as she sat down, she didn't want it any more, and why that was she couldn't say exactly; there were always so many reasons to give up on food. The place reeked of smoke, that could be one thing, and the cherry filling was fluorescent, and Martine knew the old man's eyes were boring into her back. He had nothing in front of him, no cup nor plate.

She could leave. But she would still feel his eyes on her back. She looked at the Danish and it looked back at her, its pastry flesh chapping, its pink-red centre as terrible to behold as the bleeding eye of a Cyclops. She picked it up in her napkin, walked to the old man's table, and dropped it before him without word or glance. Then she left, and whether he thanked her she didn't know.

Daylight the colour of dirty sheets now: not a sky under which you'd picnic. She preferred to watch the sidewalk as she strolled, with its palette of dogshit, potato chip packages, and dust.

She passed a hardware store (closed), a second-hand bookstore (closed), and an open store above which hung a sign that said S and S Convenience. This she entered, to buy food in case of some speculative future hungriness.

The place looked like it was either starting or finishing its life as a store; there was hardly anything in it. Only a fair bit of cheap metal shelving, holding not very much at all. Like shopping in Tashkent. It stank of pet urine and indeed three mangy cats could be seen prowling the rows. The stock was sparse and weird: extension cords, some packages of nails, squashed bread, a great heap of soap with severely outdated packaging—the model had a beehive hairdo. There were also some cans of Berthiaume soup, but only Cream of Celery. A dimly lit refrigerator in the back housed milk and some processed cheese. "Are you . . . in business?" Martine asked.

"Of course," said the owner, whose eyes were hugely magnified behind thick lenses.

A quick walk around revealed some antediluvian carrots, which Martine decided to buy, thinking she could revive them under cold running water. She picked up milk and bread, too.

"The truck didn't come yet," the owner apologized as she approached the cash register. "When he does, there'll be more."

It better be a pretty big truck, thought Martine.

When she got home, she found an inflated air mattress with a thick down sleeping bag on top of it lying before the entrance to her apartment.

The priest.

She ran up the stairs and into the foyer; she called for him to thank him but he didn't answer. Then she remembered: he was hardly ever there.

Grateful for both the bedding and his absence, she descended to her apartment and hauled the gift inside.

ITHIN A COUPLE OF DAYS she managed to have a phone hooked up. She called Louise.

"Martini!" her mother exclaimed, but the exclamation was false and stale.

"Hello, Mama."

"But—oh." Sheets rustled, something heavy fell to the floor; the latest Shirley MacLaine autobiography, probably. "Martini, where are you? At work? But you're *bad*. You haven't come to see me."

She sounded worse than ever. Martine swallowed. "I called to give you my new phone number, Mama."

"Ohhhhh," the older woman breathed. "That's—what?— but you come to see me, now. I need a hug, *minou*. Where are you? Are you at work?"

The coquettish mewl terrified Martine. She supposed the "trick hip" was at it again, a hip tricky enough to call bursting plastic vial after bursting plastic vial into its service. They were all lined up in the medicine cabinet like obedient little soldiers in thrall to the doctor's command. Rpts: 4. Rpts: 3. Rpts: 6. What a marvellous hip, that it should have the power to make pills jump and frolic so! A hip like that could play Vegas!

But Martine was far away now and there was nothing she could do about it. Louise would just have to take care of herself, even if doing so meant lying all day in perfumed sweat, oblivious to hell's nearby blaze. The Professor had left her and she'd carried on; so had Mack Donovan; maybe Martine could leave her, too.

"I'll come soon, Mama."

She hung up fast, before her mother could say anything else.

Martine didn't try to get a job over the next weeks. She had enough money to survive, and learning to take care of herself took up most of her time. A certain routine developed. She'd go to S and S Convenience, buy increasingly large bags of groceries—the guy was right, there was more food after the truck came—keep a fraction of them for herself, and give the rest to a beggar outside. There was always a beggar outside.

The routine became insidious habit. She winnowed her expenses severely and enjoyed seeing how little she could spend in the course of a day. In rationing she found strength she had lost, mooning over that Chilean goody two-shoes back at Helping Hands. She felt she could live forever on the contents of one bizarrely stuffed duffel bag, never stopping to work or socialize; she could spend her whole life walking the length of homely, tired Queen Street. Once she started hacking away, she couldn't stop. It was fun, almost. She wore and rewore her black woolen V-neck beyond when the elbows began to fray. She rarely sprang for bus fare, preferring to walk everywhere. Where was there to go, anyway? And didn't it just tingle to look at how much she'd saved at the end of the day.

She cut, and she cut some more, and when she walked past the panhandlers and the stray dogs and the little kids playing with sticks, it became almost easy to think: but you've got nothing on me, folks.

At night she watched the odd scuttle of a cockroach beside her pillow. As a child she'd heard of these bugs and imagined them as huge and greasy, with giant poisoned antennae. But they were actually so little! So cute! And if their number transcended the bounds of adorableness, well . . . at least they were company. And they were quiet.

Naturally, she ate less, too. She had always been a "finicky" eater, but that wasn't quite the word for it any more. Eight servings were quickly reduced to six, and the portions were getting smaller. When her eyes crossed involuntarily, when black spots multiplied before them, when she felt herself going under, she would rush to the kitchen for a medicinal speck of food. For a few days she went on a diet of mint gum and Fresca, cold ingestibles that might, she reasoned, have powers to frost her digestive tract into submission. She remembered the patch of Orwell she was reading when she first saw Flavio in the cafeteria that day: *You have talked so often of going to the dogs, and well, here are the dogs, and you have reached them, and you can stand it. It takes off a lot of anxiety.* She marvelled at the way her empty belly grew in the way of one regularly filled with food—not in the physical sense, but in importance; it demanded to be heard, it easily bested the brain in the race for chief organ. Water could mute its rantings somewhat, but of course it never shut them down completely.

One night Martine swore she could see her midriff swelling toward the cracked bathroom mirror, a kwashiorkor pout forming. If she kept on like this she'd be one of the poster children. But it was probably her imagination, the mirror showing her what she willed it to.

She lifted up her shirt. Was that a distinct throb she saw, just below the shrinking breast? *My heart and proof I have one,* she thought. And wasn't it true that if you buried your life pulse under too much béchamel sauce, you lost sight of its very existence? Until one day it lumbered to a halt, freighted down with grease in place of sensation. She sat watching herself, evening shadows playing on her pale ribs, the whole picture framed by arms that seemed infinite but for the bony fingerclasp that ended them.

This diet was her new job, and in many ways it was a job like any other. The world requires industry and initiative, and this was the brand Martine had to offer. It was the kind of hard work that made a mockery of all other hard work. Most importantly, it was work that she knew would produce results. You couldn't say the same about other projects that required such consistent and life-threatening application. Love, for example.

One night she had a dream.

Alms

She was standing in front of the family refrigerator, although she'd already eaten her daily rations and wasn't permitted any more. Still she opened it. Only one thing there: Louise had just baked a Sacher torte for her art gallery committee meeting. Martine squinted at the cake through the slitted eyes of a trained fighter.

En garde!

She felt in fact like Bruce Lee, prepared to chop the cake in half if it made a move on her. It flirted with her, like some beautiful heavy-lidded Viennese lesbian. Just try it, lady, Martine raged. You think you're so tough? You're nothing but eggs and sugar and cocoa while I—I am bone! Flesh! Blood! I could flatten you in one swat, turn you into screaming jammy crumbs, leave you begging to be put back together. At which the Sacher torte pouted and seethed. It ignored Martine's fury. It pulsed with just-baked sex. It said: *Komm, kleine.* A torture of apricot jam spilled from its dark cleft—dripping, sun-coloured viscera, magnetic to the eye. The chocolate frosting shiny and tuxedo-black. Underneath was the cake itself, its moist ebonous walls studded with small caverns, and inside each cavern a small circle of air: innocent air, to eat it was to not eat at all. Maybe, she thought, I could just eat the air inside the caverns and not the sugary black sides— but would that be possible?

Martine pressed her lips to the cake. They flattened into the icing while the jam strained toward her teeth, but still she resisted. *O liebchen, komm, komm . . . just one millimetre closer, komm.* Martine's lips went deeper and deeper into the icing until they finally hit the rich dark cake. She sucked air greedily out of the holes for about five minutes before Emelda wandered into the dream and asked, horrified, "Martina, what you doing there?"

Food started to fascinate her, where before it had just seemed an irritant. Sometimes she would stop into a supermarket just to pick up an orange and count all the dimples. Once she bought a pint of strawberries, took them home, and tried counting all the seeds. Could a strawberry seed count as a serving?

She thought of little Bruno Poirier dining on a fatal bowl of Berthiaume soup; it helped to do so and her appetite waned but did not quite die. In any case, hunger reminded her body that it could need something even more than physical touching. She had never been comfortable with the role her body played in sex, anyway: bodies were nothing more than barricades against the celestial interchange she thought it should be. She saw herself as neither man nor woman now, just a wheelless car of bone and thought, fuelled by calories left over from her opulent past. A minute on the lips, a lifetime on the hips: that's what Louise used to say, each time she caught sight of a brownie or slice of cheesecake.

In many ways her transformation to poreperson had been complete. So why was it, when she walked by the same loners and losers and kids with sticks, that she still felt pampered and soft?

Because: she had the Elsie Woodley money and they didn't. At this point three hundred and eighteen dollars stood between her and the world's savagery. There were also the handful of designer garments with which Louise had vainly tried to improve her, and the loose change rattling around in her jeans; surely a purgation of all these would finally unshackle her, enable her to cross over. She would be "cleaned out," as they say in poker—a pejorative term, but why should it be so? Cleaning out an attic or a desk was a worthy and necessary thing to do—how was cleaning out your pockets any different? It would be the sort of thing that brought order, that allowed you to start again in a new and better way.

She contemplated destitution for a few days, the perversity and the freedom of it, the (perhaps undeserved) rotten rap it had been given. Then one day, early on a sumptuously bright and blue morning—weather that laughed in the face of comparative delights like food and money— she decided to do something about it. She walked back to her apartment with a hard, soldierly stride, trying hard not to think about the conclusion she'd come to, or about anything, for that matter. She stowed much of what she'd brought to the apartment in a garbage bag, leaving some clothing, toiletries, books, and a towel, then dashed with great purpose to the Don River Bridge before rational thought could intrude. The comforts dropped, one by one, over the bridge, and Martine felt light and silly and giddy as they did.

She saved the Woodley cash for last. She thought of scattering the bills like twittering birds into the pretty blue day, but that just seemed wasteful.

She looked at her watch. Still early enough for the Koffee Kave. She zipped up her purse and started walking, trying not to think of anything as she watched the sun hover over morning commuters, blessing them with the free luxuries of light and warmth. Indiscriminate in its choice of whose path it cared to light: the great white communion host, held aloft by unseen fingers.

When she got there the man with girlish grey curls was still there, sitting alone at his usual table. He had a coffee cup in front of him and his eyes were fixed on something going on in the corner; a mouse ferrying home of piece of pastry, maybe. Martine sucked in her breath and walked right up to the table. Within seconds she had whipped out the thick mattress of Woodley bills and plunked them down before him, barely glancing at him before she wheeled back around to run out the door.

"Wait," the man called. "Hey!"

She stopped, shamed as a thief though she was quite a thief's opposite. She turned to see the cashier's blank look, to hear the vaguely interested murmuring of other customers. The man held the money up, as if she had dropped it by accident. She walked back to him.

"I don't need that," she said quietly. "You can have it."

"Well, there's quite a bit here, isn't there?" said the man, counting it slowly. "Are you sure about this? It's an awful lot of money, miss."

Martine felt foolish, as though she had mistaken one dollar for three hundred of them and had been unveiled as an arithmetical ignoramus. It was becoming apparent to her that giving did not make her feel any better — in fact, it made her feel worse. She instantly wrote off that hoary old Kelly Centre high as some youthful pleasure now outgrown, like the merry-go-round at the park.

But the man had . . . tears in his eyes? Either that, or an infection. Whatever it was, Martine couldn't very well walk away from it.

"You're a very kind young lady," the man said. "A very kind young lady. But why do you run away like you done something wrong?"

"I—I just," Martine said. Everyone was staring now. "It's awkward, sort of."

He looked at the money skeptically. "Did ya rob a bank?"

"No!"

"Simmer down, I was just wondering. I mean, there must be coming on two hundred dollars here."

"Three hundred," Martine corrected. People were staring.

"Three—hm. That's a lot. And it might get stolen, too." Martine was horrified. It was as if he didn't want it. It was as if she'd complicated his life, made it less livable. Maybe this guy wasn't even a poreperson! She was a reporter, she should have researched him. She set to thinking about all the people she could have helped—men, women, children, a dollar for each one: three hundred and eighteen people, and here she'd shot the wad on *one*. Who didn't even want it that much. She had an urge to ask for it back.

Before she could, though, the man wiped his eyes and tucked the bills away in the inside pocket of his jacket. He kept a hand on them, which gave him a sort of Napoleon effect. "Well, it's nice anyways," he said, "and you shouldn't never be ashamed of being nice." Then he offered her his free hand. "Name's Albert Swanson. From Kenora, Ontario." She took it; it was warm from the coffee cup.

"Martine. Craythorn."

"But don't you go giving me any more doughnuts, now. That was nice, too, but I don't need you to do that."

"I won't," she promised.

She walked back to Merseyfield Avenue with nothing but her keys, unsettled by the encounter, unsure of what it taught her. But free, at any rate, of the demon money.

There is a moment between when a catastrophe is ordered and when it arrives that can only be described as funny. The car is hurtling toward the tree and you still have your teeth, your face, your brain, just like anyone else does, but the great joke is that yours are soon to be shown for the cheap gimcracks they really are. Thus it was that Martine sat on the bare tiled floor of her basement apartment that afternoon, laughing and marvelling at her own ability to go on in the face of authentic poverty.

But late that night it hit her. She was swaddled in the priest's sleeping bag—not hers to throw away—when terror wrapped its slimy arms around her midsection. Her rent was due in a week and she was too shy to ask for an extension; not for her the brave assertiveness of the people she'd met at Helping Hands. What had she been thinking, that she could just photosynthesize like a plant? Was she made of marble? She needed food and a roof like the rest of these scrabbling saps, and though she'd all but conquered the food, the loss of a roof . . . oh, anything but that. Yes, she'd heard of folks living in cardboard boxes in Los Angeles—but that was Los Angeles, where you could curl up in a cozy blanket of hot smog at any time of year. Homeless in wintry Toronto and you'd die. Wouldn't you?

The priest was a good man, though. If ever there was a landlord who'd understand, it was he. Martine had the feeling that he might even be entertained by her problems. She slipped out of the sleeping bag and threw the cape round her T-shirted shoulders. She had no watch but knew it must be very late, the same point in the night, perhaps, as when she'd first arrived at 12 Merseyfield. Indeed, there was some pretty audible scuffling in the kitchen as she mounted the stairs.

*S*HE STOOD DUMBLY in the main foyer, waiting for Father Kearney to emerge from the kitchen. In a minute he did; it was dark there, and the streetlights outside illumined a little square of clerical collar. He was munching on something from a brown paper bag.

He looked surprised and even frightened to see her. Several weeks had passed since they'd last spoken. Her sunken face was only the frontispiece of what most people would find an alarming work, she knew. Even the cape could not hide a suggestion of knobbed red elbows, visible ribs.

He asked her to sit on the steps beside him. "You all right?" he asked.

She told him yes and looked at her hands.

"You just want to sit a while?"

She nodded, and sat, and felt a bit lost. The subject appeared to be unbroachable, and meanwhile he just kept crunching. Candy, from the smell of it. Finally she looked up at him. He'd tried to tame his sparse hairs with an apparent mixture of turpentine and airplane glue, and his undersized head looked like an eightball. This ridiculous picture gave her the confidence to start talking.

"I've been having," she began sheepishly, "a bit of a rough time."

"I'll say. You look like crap. I mean—hell—I mean, you look bad."

The almost-swearing stunned her into further silence; she tried to bat the ball back but couldn't think what to say. So they sat in continued silence, with him crunching on whatever was in the bag. Martine liked its sweet, familiar smell. After a while she said, "I never heard a priest say 'crap' before."

"Well—" he put the bag down and thought for a second— "I took a Berlitz course in Presbyterian a while back but I didn't do too good. So I decided to stick to Low English. But I never take the Lord's name in vain—no, ma'am, that's the one thing I don't. As long as I stick to that one they oughta let me keep the membership card and decoder ring, don't you think? You're Catholic, right?"

She was surprised by this. "Uh, yeah."

He plucked her left hand delicately from her knee and set to appraising its fingernails and knuckles. "I could tell. These are Holy Rosary hands."

She tried a curt laugh, curiously unruffled by his theft of one of her preferred extremities. "No. They're not."

He turned the hand over and subjected it to a series of strangely pleasant palpations. "Too pale for Blessed Trinity

. . . but the nails, the nails give it away. There's a French manicure in the not too distant past of these here nails, yes sir. The Great Kearnino says: Our Lady of Perpetual Help."

"You're right!" she exclaimed, forgetting that she'd done, all too soon, the one thing she meant never ever to do. She'd given her provenance away.

He opened his eyes, wide. "*Chawmed,* I'm sure."

Two seconds in and exposure was turning out worse than she'd imagined it would be. But he said nothing further about it and merely lit up a smoke, after which he thrust the cellophane bag in her face. "Want a Ding Dot?"

He told her to take as many as she liked. Ding Dots were candies made of hardened malted milk that were covered in chocolate or coloured sugar, depending on which struck your fancy, and Martine had held a great affection for them in childhood. Somehow the priest's offer was so much more concrete and helpful than a set of Hail Marys, so she took a few. She cradled them in her hands a while, rolled them around, knocked them together. She picked one up and sniffed it.

Father Kearney took out a Swiss Army knife and took the candy from her. He cut it in half and presented it gingerly; it was only a half-inch wide. "Okay like this?" he asked her. She nodded. "I'll save the other half for later," he said. He held it high enough to indicate that he meant for her to take it directly into her mouth, like a communion wafer. But she had always found that form of acceptance especially degrading; she took the candy in her fingers, rolled it between them, and stared at it. Then he cut the others in like fashion and told her he'd save those, too. She popped the one little bit she held in her mouth. It tasted untellably good. "I've got more if you want 'em," the priest said eagerly. He watched her eat. The watching hurt.

"You're going to have to write that down," he said.

She was shocked; but of course he'd seen her notebook, back at the Princess Café, the notebook she even now felt pressing against her rump, flattened in her back pocket.

"No, I won't."

"Sure you will. I'll get a pencil for you." He handed her the candy bag, then nipped into the kitchen and was back before she could say anything. "Here," he said. "I *know* you have it on you."

At that Martine felt obligated to take the notebook out, even though he hadn't exactly asked for it. She reached behind her, looking at the floor the whole time.

"Can I have a look?" he asked.

She gave it to him. He flipped through it slowly, page after page, not saying anything. Finally he closed it.

"You're weird," he said.

She grabbed the notebook back from him and stared at her knees. "You don't have to tell me that."

"Hey—hey, I *like* weird! Only normal guy I know is the one who comes to read the gas meter. Weird's good."

"I . . . don't think you're right about that. Not in this case." Still, what he said was a relief. Most people she knew could not even bring themselves to acknowledge the note-book. Whenever Martine produced it, Louise would turn away. Jeremy went in more for the harsh reprimand, while the *Attitude!* people seemed to think that ill-disguised gossip was the best way of dealing with the problem. But nobody had ever come close to approving of the notebook, until this guy.

He jumped up to dump the Visit Niagara Falls ashtray in his kitchen. "Everybody has a thing they're dealing with," he called out. "So that's yours."

"What do you mean?" she asked. Then she thought of the people he usually surrounded himself with: call girls, porepeople, the man with the shredded basketball shoes. They all had things—did they ever—but he couldn't very well be equating . . .

"This is not a thing," she said.

"Oh, I'd say it's a *hell* of a thing," he laughed.

She put the notebook back in her pocket. "Call it what you want."

He popped back out of the kitchen and sat beside her again. "Hey, how come I haven't seen you at the Princess Café lately?" he asked.

"I . . . eat breakfast somewhere else now."

Father Kearney looked doubtful. "Uh-huh. You got fired, right?"

"No!"

"Don't sweat it, I've been fired way more than you."

Before we start, Joe, Martine recalled herself saying, *you might be surprised to know that I failed some courses, too.*

"Right," she smiled uncertainly.

"Listen. One of my waitresses at the Refuge has been out a week with some kind of jaw problem. Anyways, it's been hell on the other girl that works there, she can't handle it by herself. If you need something to tide you over, you know, just until you get something else—it's not far from here."

She straightened and rose. "That's very kind of you, Father, and I'm a great believer in volunteer work, and I probably could use a new job, when I think of it. But I have to think of the rent, right?" Or maybe I don't. Please say I don't.

"Eight dollars an hour," he shot back proudly. "Nine. Hell, make it nine."

She looked through the lace curtains on the front door and imagined all the establishments not two blocks away, the ones she walked by each day through hardening fall winds. The deli that wouldn't need any counter help, if she asked. The dry cleaner who'd pretend not to understand her. The notary public who'd laugh at her typing.

Father Kearney saw tiny cells of agreement at play in her weakened mouth and dawdling feet. He decided to multiply them. "You probably never waitressed before."

"I have so!" she shot back, although he was right, and she was going to have to do some fancy fabricating if he called her on it.

"Relax," he laughed. "Nobody's going to tip you anyway."

He told her he always walked there, though less hardy mortals would have called it a streetcar ride. That afternoon, wind rattled the trash cans and whipped debris onto the widening holes in Martine's black jeans, the only pants she had left. The September issue of *Vogue* had come and gone and she plainly had not read it. Huddled into her cape, she thought the weather might prove fatal to her before she got there, but Father Kearney obviously thought she could handle it. He kept trying to light a smoke while walking and the picture was comical, especially as the hair he had so assiduously plastered down yesterday had broken free of his scalp and was standing straight up to the wind in little glue-slicked posts. He wore an expensive-looking down ski jacket over his uniform.

"I go to the galleries all the time when I have a chance," he said. "Do you go?"

She swore he'd become a different person since she'd let the Perpetual Help thing slip; sort of mock-butlerish, with exaggeratedly courtly gestures. She thought he might be making fun of her, but there really was something of the aesthete in him.

"No. Art, paintings, that's really my mother's thing. I don't—"

"Well, there's a painting I saw at the Selden Gallery that looks just like you. Old-fashioned, kind of like, except painted in the modern day. A girl brushing her beautiful dark hair. With one hand over her head . . . kind of like—hey, you ever take ballet?"

Now he was getting personal in a sort of creepy way, like a louse crawling along her scalp. "Of course," she said sourly, "and tap dancing and riding and skiing." The people she hated most were those who forced her to be cruel to them, even though they hadn't done anything cruel to deserve it. "Any other questions?"

"Hey, relax," he said. "It's just you have a nice long neck, you know. I just thought."

It was a compliment she couldn't thank him for. The misplaced flirtatiousness of it cancelled out any civility it might have borne. Which reminded her. She, who had become too accustomed in youth to having needed things drop mysteriously from the sky, hadn't thanked him for the bedding.

But he hadn't brought it up either, so.

"You brushed your hair," he tried again. "It looks good, that's all."

She stopped, wrenched by anger. "Please stop talking about the way I look, all right? I really don't think I owe you that. Attractiveness."

"Hey, you don't owe anybody anything," he said, excited. "But try telling them that."

"I'd just rather we kept my appearance out of it."

He held up his hands as if under arrest. "Okay, okay. It's cool."

His small, unshaven face was alight with mirth; maybe any woman's anger would be amusing to him, she saw, like pink steam issuing from the little china nostrils of a ceramic bull. A woman's anger lacked potency, and so could not inspire fear. There was nothing for it but to ignore him.

He kept chatting though. "I have to warn you that some of the people you're gonna meet tonight are . . . a little different from what you're used to."

"I used to work at Helping Hands," she said quickly, looking straight ahead. When she looked straight enough ahead she could see through to the bank buildings, which reassured her.

"You did?" exclaimed the priest. "You worked for the Frito Bandito, down there in Parkdale?"

Martine was shocked at the nickname and wondered if it might be a real one; if the two knew each other; or was it— as it immediately seemed—a nasty racist epithet, conceived and employed behind poor Flavio's back? Would a priest do that, even this one?

"Flavio Vargas," she replied. Saying his name was so intensely pleasurable she had to say it again. "I worked for Flavio Vargas."

"That's who I mean. I know about him. Big success. Very young, to be running an organization like that." Martine smiled proudly, as if she'd been his mother instead of his word processor. "He's a nice guy," the priest continued, "but—well, he runs a different kind of ship. You don't have to wipe your feet at *my* door, for example. You don't have to disinfect your fingers before you take a cookie. But you worked for Flavio, eh? Who would have thought?"

She offered him a look so even and cold in composition that its message could not possibly elude him. It was a look she reserved for the excessive, the mendacious, the slangy, the gluttonous, the invasive; a look that saw years of meritorious service in her school hallways, and in valiant nights spent chipping away at the Louise/Mack Donovan axis. It was a look that let others know they were as dung to her.

It could not possibly elude him, but it did.

"Although, I've got this theory of Flavio. Here's what I think—"

"Father, can we—is it okay if we just be quiet for a while? I'm not used to all this talking, this early in the morning. I'm sorry. I'm just not very good at it."

"Oh. Okay."

They turned onto a little dead-end street off Queen and stopped in front of what looked, from the outside, to be a lamp store. It was a small establishment with a large sign in front of it that said LUX in authoritative if dirty neon. How sad neon looks in the day, thought Martine, though she had the feeling that this particular sample didn't come to blazing white life at night either.

"Welcome to the Fiat Lux Refuge," said Father Kearney, opening the creaky little door and striding with great purpose across the store's distinctively lampless interior.

Indeed, it was not a store, but a kind of restaurant with eight card tables, four against each wall. Each was covered with a vinyl tablecloth in a red-and-white check pattern, and had as a centrepiece a juice tumbler filled with a single plastic daisy. The place needed a coat of paint and a major sweep; Martine discerned bacon bits, dust, and assorted other moltings and sheddings in the corners, as well as an obvious mouse hole. The chairs stacked on top of the tables were of the same turquoise plastic school-gym variety as at Helping Hands, and a couple had angry shards ripped out of them. There was a crucifix hanging crookedly over the food counter and a votive candle burning incongruously in the corner: errant scraps of Jesus.

Next to the crucifix was a huge hunk of cardboard, ripped from a box. On it were the words LOVE THY NEIGHBOUR AS THYSELF, with the red paint dripping off each letter like blood. Next to that was a large headshot of Princess Diana, pasted onto cardboard and decorated with a moustache.

At the end of the restaurant a woman stood at a counter, fiddling with a recalcitrant coffee maker. She was fairly young, though everything about her seemed acceleratedly old, from her cheap white blouse and homemade skirt to her mop of sandy permed hair; her poor head looked like a tumbleweed, though she'd tried to subdue the fact with bobby pins. Under the blouse was a complicated neck brace, which prevented her from moving with any grace whatsoever. Her eyes were red, shrunken, like broken tail lights on a toy car. There were coffee grounds all over her prissily manicured fingers.

"Coffee maker's on the fritz again, Father." She trained her red eyes on Martine, an act that only seemed to redden them further.

Father Kearney tapped the machine, as if such benediction might fix it; when it did not, he muttered something about going to see Frost's cousin, whoever Frost and his cousin might be. Then he disappeared into a back room, leaving Martine with the tumbleweed woman, who was arranging sushi on an aluminum platter. "I don't know so much the folks will like this, Father," she whined. Then she inspected Martine again. "Is this the girl come to take Dianne's shift?" Her boss ignored her. He was talking to someone else.

The man he was talking to was the driver from the hotel, the one with the basketball shoes. He'd come out of nowhere, though his smell preceded him. It was the smell of booze, yes, but it portended worse—separated gums, crumbling glands; a soul long dead but locked in a body by waxy skin. His hair was dirty, his big eyes goggled. He carried a battered red box.

Father Kearney looked deep into the man's eyes. "Frost, can you drive today? Martine, take a look for me. Is he too drunk? You know about drunks, you worked at Helping Hands. You might've run into a guy or two that got his hands on Flavio's Lysol, eh? What do you think?"

The other woman leaned over the small tap behind the counter and washed hands that were coated in sticky rice. "Why don't you ask Mr. Frost himself?" she interjected. "He's the one who studied to be a doctor."

Martine despised this person (and her instant certainty that Martine had *not* studied to be a doctor), but was glad to be saved from giving an opinion. The man could barely stand.

Father Kearney stood back and regarded his chauffeur. "You're right. What's you're, uh, *scholarly* feeling on the matter, Doctor?"

Mr. Frost opened his mouth; Martine expected dead leaves and the corpses of insects to tumble from his tongue. "I am the master of all I survey," he slurred.

But the priest still looked unsure. He undid his own belt, pulled it from the loops, and straightened it out across the floor. His pants sagged pathetically over boxer shorts and Martine closed her eyes. "If you can walk this," he said, "you can drive today."

The man stomped on the belt obediently, but tripped before he could take a second step.

"Close enough," said the priest.

He reinserted his belt and slapped Frost on the back, almost hard enough to tip him over. "We're not going far anyway. And you'd be a lousy driver no matter how much Lonesome Charlie you didn't drink." Adjudging him nonetheless fit to go out in the world and do whatever it was they did, the priest motioned for his friend to follow him. Then he grabbed a couple of California rolls and stuffed them in his mouth. A horrible look overtook him.

He choked the food down, then wiped his mouth with a handkerchief from his pocket. "We get some pretty bizarre stuff in here," he told Martine.

"Sushi," Martine explained quietly. "It's Japanese."

"Oh. Well, they're better at cars and radios," he laughed, then daintily handed Martine a dirty apron and pointed at the tumbleweed woman.

"This here is Glenys—we'll be back in a few hours. You need anything, you ask her or anybody else who comes in." Then he was gone.

Gone. She mistrusted Father Kearney, sure, but she hardly wanted him *gone*. "It's not far from here," he'd said—about his house, but just maybe about this place, about all the places in and out of which he darted like a maddening elf—"and you'd never see me. I'm hardly ever there."

She stared into the space where the men had been. Surely the man wasn't really drunk? "Drunk" was probably some joke code-word between them for "weird." And there was nothing on the law books about driving while being a little weird.

"Well, he didn't look right to me, but then it's none of our affair, is it?" Glenys said.

"No, I suppose it isn't."

"Here." Glenys thrust a mittful of drop-spattered cutlery at Martine. "Follow me and set these around after I wipe down the tables."

The two women walked about the room silently, setting all the tables in this way: wipe knife fork wipe knife fork. It was the middle of October but, curiously, little touches of Christmas clung to the restaurant's decor: a broken

crèche in the window, a forlorn card tacked on the wall.
MAY THE SPIRIT OF THE SEASON LIVE IN YOUR HEART LONG
AFTER THE SEASON IS ENDED said the card.

"You're a student, I'd expect."

"No. I'm . . . an actress."

Why she lied she couldn't have said. Maybe it was only
that, in this moment, she so desperately wanted to be her
mother: airy with disdain, sexily plump, and padded against
pain with Berthiaume soup money.

"Have I seen you in some of the shows?"

"No."

"Oh. Well, I'm working here right now, but I have other
plans. I'm going to study occupational therapy one day
because there's a greater need for it than even most people
know. And believe you me it's not pretty when you're going
to work hurt. I've been dealing with this neck for going on
two years now and there just doesn't seem to be anything to
do about it. Mr. Frost, who comes in, suggested a bag of
frozen peas to me, but that didn't work for long. Mr. Frost
studied to be a doctor, you know . . ."

Martine let poor Glenys drone *ad sominem* about the
various grotesqueries that signposted her life—her neck, her
shoulder, her sister Bonnie, her other shoulder. It turned out
that she was something of a career volunteer. It was, Martine
figured, the only kind of job that would have her, though it
sounded like even non-paying employers found it hard to
tolerate her constant illnesses and cloying personality: they'd
all fired her, too.

Glenys was quite up front about her dismissals, which, it
appeared, were as routine as coffee breaks for her. She'd

started out with the suicide hotline but was let go when, despite her best efforts, it became known that she was actually killing more people than she was helping; callers who'd started out very tentative about suicide committed it wholeheartedly after a few minutes on the line with her. "I'd tell them about my troubles, too, of course," Glenys said proudly. "Oh, I'd let them know they weren't the only person suffering in this awful world." She then decided to bestow her favours upon the local senior citizenry, helping them run errands or steering them through the aisles of the IGA. "But I don't know what happened there," she said sadly.

Martine did. She guessed that Glenys's clients simply weren't able to stand her—the way she likely bellowed in their ears about yams at three for a dollar, dear! High in vitamin C, sweetie! The worst part of chronological aging being, of course, the way it threw you in constant league with these sorts of youths, the ones who were just plain *born* ninety. Glenys admitted that one old bird had actually run away from her on a scheduled outing and called the police, who managed to handcuff the bewildered volunteer before everything was straightened out: incredibly, Glenys's whining, throat-clearing noises, grinding banter, and antiseptic smell all turned out to be perfectly legal. So was her face, one of those faces you hated yourself for disliking, large and specked with untrustworthy little features. Her big indulgence was lipstick, Maybelline's wildest, stuff that set her mouth to shimmering in expectation of some improbable kiss.

This unremunerative life had only been made possible through the good offices of Glenys's roommate and sister Bonnie, a dental hygienist and woman who believed her older sister to be an ailing, brilliant, saintly genius, exempt from the ordinary rules. Reading between the lines of Glenys's story, Martine divined that the older girl had spent a concentrated thirty years running Bonnie's self-image into the ground, which would have taken some doing: Bonnie was a gorgeous teenager and frequently reminded of this by assorted swains, modelling agents, teachers, and relatives, including their late parents. But with the onset of adulthood and the disappearance of such people Glenys set to work draining her sister's rosy cheeks with a nightly selection of mildly lacerating comments, the cumulative effect of which was not meant to be felt until twelve, thirteen years into the project, by which time Bonnie would be (and, to hear it told, was) almost as faded and unappetizing as her older sister and protector.

Bonnie would be the only one to buy Glenys's number, the only one who wouldn't believe that she had begged some orthopedist to let her keep the neck brace. The folks at the Wheelchair Basketball Association hadn't trusted her, nor the directors of Camp Watchanabee, nor the unwed teen mom who'd grabbed poor Glenys by that stupid brace and whirled her into the radiator one afternoon, apparently driven mad by the alternating sounds of a wailing baby and the charmless throat-clearing of its "attendant." *Hch-hch-hchmmm* went her throat, filling each silent minute, epiglottis sticking and unsticking ever on forward and always. Thank God for that brace though. Without it she might have been throttled to death years ago.

They finished setting the tables. Until the customers came there were no especially ugly jobs for this girl to do, a state

Cynthia Macdonald

of affairs that obviously frustrated Glenys, who squinted foxily at Martine. "Father Kearney often has . . . friends come to help him here, you know," she said with transparent revulsion. "But then, of course, none of them last."

Glenys explained that they—she and Father Kearney—had been operating the Fiat Lux Refuge for about a year. It was a sort of café for the poor, where fifty cents bought you a meal. The Refuge was something less substantial than a food bank or soup kitchen, but much warmer, more informal. So informal, in fact, that it was often hard to tell the employees from the patrons; a couple of regulars, the absent Dianne and the almost-doctor Frost, had become full-time employees. If your fork was dirty, you went round the counter and looked for a clean one. If your coffee was bitter, you made a new pot. She also said that your fork was frequently dirty, and that your coffee was always bitter.

The hotel and several others like it supplied the Refuge with daily leftovers from their business meetings and wedding receptions. These made up its ever-changing menu, a carousel of stuffed porcini mushrooms, gravlax and capers on croissants, aïoli and crab on pumpernickel rounds. Much of the stuff was darned strange, Glenys admitted, "although if folks are hungry enough they'll eat anything." Desserts were always popular, she said. "Chocolate-covered strawberries is everybody's favourite. We sometimes have fights over those."

"What about candy?" Martine asked, remembering the Ding Dots from last night. They had tasted so good she could think of little but them, and had skipped breakfast in anticipation of fuelling herself on more. "Don't you serve people candy, too?"

"Oh, that's another business of Father Kearney's and I don't know anything about it," Glenys muttered, wiping a tumbler with a dirty cloth. "Anyways, we're not supposed to go in the back room."

The door opened and two customers entered, a woman and a teenage boy. The woman, heavy-set and bleached blonde, picked a table close to the kitchen and set about berating the boy into doffing his ripped jacket. Once she'd succeeded, she sat in a grim stew of expectation, clutching a copy of the New Testament to her considerable self.

"Hello, Muriel," Glenys said. Then she parked herself behind the counter, picked up a magazine, and opened it to an article on colon health. "Why don't you go take Muriel's order, dear," she wheedled Martine without looking at her.

Martine picked up a tray and held it like a barmaid, horizontally against her hip. How earthy this feels, she thought, how very . . . down-home. But the second she started addressing the customers, things imploded. Her words were tentative and lousy with ersatz gaiety. She had never before served strangers in so distastefully direct a way. Or maybe she'd never served them in any way. *She* was the one who got served.

"Whaddaya have today?" the woman asked.

Martine tried to explain about the sushi but Muriel wasn't interested, so Martine offered her instant coffee instead. "Disgusting stuff," was the reply. "And I don't ever take it. No strawberries today?" The boy, slow and hunched, wore a torn Lionel Richie T-shirt. He reached for his jacket and took out a bulging orange-and-yellow change purse appliquéd with the letter *M* from which, once opened, sprang a knot of bills—a couple of ones and twos, twisted together into a kind of lumpy monetary scone, and in the middle of them a hot green twenty. Twenty whole dollars. Martine stared at the bill with a strange hunger: what she would do for twenty dollars right now.

"He's savin' up for Lionel Richie," his mother explained. "Manny, put that away now." Martine didn't understand— was Lionel Richie destitute these days? She guessed that "Hello" had not been as successful for him as "Three Times a Lady," but still. The boy set the money aside and fished out a dollar from the bottom of his *M* purse, which he then gave to Martine.

"I'll go see about the strawberries," she said, but before she could disappear she heard his mother grumble: "I bet she thinks the Lord's looking at her."

Martine took the remark quietly, but it festered within her all night as she slogged from table to table pouring Sanka and sympathy, for which she got nothing but this grim, smirky position, this look that made her want to throw down her tea towel and order pad and scream: Jesus, throw me some sugar, would you, people? Would a smile really be too much? Three hundred and eighteen dollars—is that how much it takes?

But there were few smiles as the night went on, no thank you's; well, maybe one or two, but the gratitude was far from unanimous. She needed gratitude to assure herself that the Refuge's patrons were benefiting from her services, that they were all right. And that she, Martine Craythorn, was a bloody significant improvement on all right.

Now at Helping Hands, she had to admit, most people had thanked her and she hadn't even noticed. But the kindness of others was not nearly so interesting to her as her own, and how little, she thought bitterly, hers counted for on this cold blue globe.

These new porepeople all smoked cigarettes, which drove her crazy. Two of them discussed a wrestling program they had watched the previous night, and another moaned about an experiment with hair dye that hadn't quite turned out. Cable television, hair dye, cigarettes: it got so that every time a client came in admitting to some activity not strictly necessary for life's bitter continuance, she scowled at him. But she could not afford to look as sad as she felt. Open wounds invite infection.

She had to do most of the work, too, while Glenys made an intensive study of the colon health article and tended to her aches behind the counter.

The regulars all came, apparently. There was a rumpled old character named Suleiman who spouted senseless parables at her as she set a succession of Styrofoam cups full of tea before him. He wore a set of keys around his neck, keys that (he told her) once opened a house before it burned to the ground, and started a car before it was stolen from him.

"Who holds the real power, the tree or the seed?" She smiled waterily when he said these things to her, and then other things like it. She wondered if someone so extraterrestrial in outlook was capable of leaving a tip. Near the end of the night, though, he said something that made a little sense; a line from some poem Martine vaguely remembered, offered as they watched Muriel's great backside waddling out the door with her poor son trotting behind.

"Some are born to sweet delight, my dear," he smiled, "while some are born to endless night."

It was a line that angered her, too, since it implied that Suleiman could still perceive traces of sweet delight in his waitress. Everybody was on to her, it seemed.

There'd been a table full of Spanish-speaking refugees, some wearing suit jackets, all wearing buttons that proclaimed some message of Salvadoran solidarity. They gabbled away importantly, *taca-taca-taca,* submitting to the homeliness of English only when the salt shaker needed filling or a napkin was required. Such requests Martine tended to with great speed and joy, since it was almost as if he were there again, the boy with the bookbag, giving her the third chance she needed. But when she hovered too closely, one of the suit-jacketed men stared her away with a frown that broke the last of her heart.

And oh, the cigarettes. Most restaurants had two sections, smoking and non-smoking, but the Fiat Lux Refuge was divided along different lines: smoking and Vimy Ridge. Martine coughed, sweated, endured. As it turned out there *were* strawberries and she'd had a few to keep going, but truly, she wasn't well nourished enough to stay on her feet this long, nor to tolerate anything but benign behaviour from the clientele. An unspeakably grubby man called her over at one point and brandished a drooping lettuce leaf before her. "Would you eat this at home?" he growled.

"No," she replied with quiet haughtiness. "But then I don't eat much at home anyway."

"I suppose you don't think beggars can be choosers, eh, girl?" he lectured, climbing to his feet. He was well over six feet and he frightened her. His snarled black hair and beard hinted at nests of paper and gunk that would shame an animal; his fingernails reposed on thick crescents of silt. "I know how to eat good. And I know how to eat well. And what I had here tonight was neither." He shuffled out on dreadful feet, having left her the poignant gratuity of a burning cigarette.

Martine almost wept in the wake of such ferocity, but Suleiman pulled her over and comforted her. "Never mind, Miss Lady. He was asking for money from the people leaving the movie film *Princess Bride* and business was very good. Now the theatre has changed it to *Fatal Attraction* and he is making completely nothing."

Eight-thirty came; Father Kearney and Mr. Frost had not returned. Nobody seemed in a hurry to leave, either. Martine grabbed a second to ask Glenys when she might be able to go, but Glenys was in the middle of a phone call.

"All right, dear. You take care. I know how it is. This neck is giving me the devil. The arthritis, too. You take care now." She hung up and sighed. "You're going to have to come in tomorrow, dear. Dianne's got an awful trouble with her jaw and she can't make it until next week."

Martine protested that she had things to do, but Glenys's ears were plainly too delicately placed on her head to accept even a word of such violent objection. "You tell Father Kearney, dear. Now I don't know where he and that rascal Mr. Frost are tonight, but I think it's about time we closed up—*hch-hch-hchmmm*. Finish up, folks!"

The remaining patrons pushed plates and cups away, struggled into second-hand jackets. Slowly they rose and formed a sad cordon that limped toward the door, heavy with life, bidding the women good night.

Glenys cleared the table—no doubt to appear active in case the priest should walk in—while Martine carted the cutlery and tumblers downstairs to wash them in the bathroom. The place was still set up to sell lamps, and in the year since the Refuge had been open, nobody had thought to make it more restaurant-like. There was no refrigeration, nor any visible place to cook anything. The only thing it had in common with other restaurants was mice.

While she was downstairs she heard the door burst open, the slam of purposeful feet. She marched upstairs with an armful of clean cutlery and saw the returning few: Father Kearney, gobbling leftover bread and picking fish off the sushi to clear his way for the rice; and, at the table closest to the door, an even more decrepit Frost with someone new.

She was a teenager from the look of it, quiet and serious in a tight denim skirt and leg warmers, with another bad perm and about twelve studs snaking up the cordillera of her left ear. Smoking, of course. She helped Frost open the red box and unfold a sort of game board within. Then she shuffled cards and they set to playing whatever game it was.

Father Kearney finished off the rice greedily, then buttonholed Martine. "So. How did it go? Make any new friends?"

"I'm not here to make friends," she said quietly. She passed the cutlery to Glenys, but Glenys was in no position to receive it. She had already put on her coat and shut her handbag, out of which stuck the colon health magazine. "No, ma'am," she sniped, frowning at the forks. "Union rules. Oh, by the way, Father," she said on her way out. "Dianne's not back tomorrow and your friend doesn't seem to care for the work so I'm not sure what you're going to do, but of course you'll think of something." She bade everyone goodbye and marched out of the restaurant on worn heels, casting an acid look at the teenage gameswoman.

The priest took the cutlery himself and started sorting it. "Well, of course. I mean, who would want to make friends . . . *here*? I mean, it ain't like Groping Hands or anything, where you've got the cast of the Waltons coming in and singing hymns to get a can of creamed corn, right?"

The remark was so strangely vitriolic that Martine thought he might be drunk. There was a new laxity about his mouth, a certain gloss to the eyes, and then the new stage patter, courtesy Mr. Hyde. Cousin Père Pierre was also said to have had too great an affection for the evening sherry, she remembered. But not while he was out working, and not while he was taking direct care of a man who was also drunk—professionally and constantly so, it would seem.

Drunkenness wouldn't excuse what he said, anyway. Martine was actually nostalgic for Helping Hands tonight; it was so much better run than this place. Clean, obviously. With administrators who were calm and efficient, and clients who mostly spoke politely and tried their best to make better lives for themselves. And the more Father Kearney made fun of Helping Hands, the more she missed it. "A crumb for the children," he continued, fashioning a head scarf for himself out of a dishtowel. "A crumb for the children, please, Mr. Che Guevara. Then I'll be off to my shoebox for some more suffering under the one naked light bulb left me. It was my uncle Theophilus left it to me, yes sir, and a prrrrrince he was!"

She bowed her head in anger, though to the priest it might have looked like prayer. "Aw, I'm sorry," he said, folding the dishtowel. "I just like to make fun of those guys, but it doesn't mean anything. They're kind of holy rollers, you know." There was no irony in the remark. "Anyways you gotta admit, it's different over there."

"Yes, it's different."

"And it's more . . . to your taste?"

"Flavio has some pretty good ideas," she said calmly. "He hired a cat, for example, to get rid of the mice. And it worked."

Father Kearney exploded in clownish laughter. "He hired . . . a *cat*? Only Flavio,"—he bashed the dishtowel against the counter in hilarity—"only Flavio Vargas would put an ever-loving cat on the payroll. Dental plan and stock options, too, I bet."

Martine blushed. "Got. He got a cat, that's what I meant. And he has these little fridges, which I'm sure you could get—"

Here the priest launched his arms in the air, describing a wild circle as if he were trying to lead her in aerobics. "No, no, my dear. You don't know how much these fridges cost. Now it's fine for Flavio, right? He gets the charity bingo money and buys himself the word processor and the fridge— now don't look at me like that, I've done my research, I know what he's got going on there. But you answer me this, Martine, Our Martine of the Perpetual Help. Where do you think the charity bingo money comes from?"

She really had no idea where any money came from. "Charity bingoes, I suppose."

"Here, I'll tell you." He leaned in close and she could smell that in fact he had been drinking. "It comes from Muriel, doesn't it? Muriel and her welfare cheque and the cheques of all the Muriels in his neighbourhood, and Mr. Clean-As-You-Like doesn't think a thing about taking their rent money and buying himself a handy little fridgeroo for his non-dairy creamer. And while he's at the store, maybe he thinks: Wouldn't it be nice to have one of these for my apartment, too? Well, you won't catch me." He leaned back again and crossed his arms.

"He wouldn't do that," Martine said.

"Oh, yes, silly me, of course he wouldn't. No, he'd use his *government* money for that."

Martine made no reply, hoping he'd get the message that this was not a fight worth having.

"I suppose you'd rather not come back tomorrow," he said, defiant. His tone implied that she wasn't man enough for it.

She wasn't; she didn't like it here, not one bit. Maybe tomorrow she'd try her luck at a temp agency . . .

"Of course I'd *like* to," she said, "but I can't. I have a dentist's appointment."

"Aha," rejoined the priest with more of a flourish than the battered little room deserved. "The problem with Perpetual Help teeth, you know, folks, being all the perming and setting they require."

Martine was overcome with rue for the way in which she'd revealed her family parish, which wasn't really her parish at all, and if the priest could only have seen the Professor walking by it and spitting his gum on the pathway, he'd know that. From now on he would only see her through the sparkling golden scrim of privilege, unless she clawed the damn thing down. Which she immediately resolved to do.

"Shelley!" Father Kearney yelled at the teenage girl. "What are *you* doing tomorrow night?"

But neither Frost nor Shelley were listening to him, absorbed as they were in the strange game, which seemed to require a lot of arm-waving and calling out of dates from Frost, a lot of sitting still and smoking from the girl. "January 26, 1965!" he grumbled at her. "You'll never get this one."

The priest scrutinized Martine. "Of course, you have to go to the dentist, my dear darling. Hell, I should go to the dentist. Do us a favour and take all mine and Frost's teeth with you. Shelley!" he called again, though Shelley seemed to have slipped into a kind of catatonia. Then Frost proceeded to slump and fall asleep on the gameboard, his lips blubbering open, his dreadful head surrounded by myriad tiny cards crammed with tiny black writing. "Forget it, Father," came the girl's dead voice. "Can't do it. Gotta study for my math mid-term."

"Huh. Hey, let me tell you everything you need to know about trigonometry," replied the priest. "Past Grade Thirteen, *it doesn't come up*."

"I'm in Grade Ten."

Father Kearney cast a worried look at Martine. "Yes, well, no need to get technical. But look at our Dr. Frost here—he was the cat's own ass at algebra, calculus, all that nonsense, and now see where he is."

"He's, like, ten feet away from *you,*" said the girl, crunching on a lollipop.

"Fine, fine," the priest sputtered, waving a dishtowel at her. "Go do your math test. Who am I to stand in the way of human effort? Glenys hates you anyways. But you, Perpetual Help—maybe I could sweeten the pot for you. Every woman has her price, isn't that what they say?" Every woman *you* know, thought Martine. "What would you think of this?" he announced. "Rent's due soon. Work for me one more night and I'll waive it for a month."

What?

"You heard me. One night's work. One month free."

"Hey, man," the girl interjected. "If I'd have known you were so hard up—"

"Ah, no!" Father Kearney commanded, showing her the flat of his hand. "This is a one-time offer for our friend Martine. I know she did a great job tonight. It's a signing bonus."

If Mack Donovan as Don Bates had taught her anything, it was to jump on ridiculous generosity before its nature became clear to everyone concerned. She could either spend one night here or endless years in a cream-coloured blouse, suffering the regular inhalation of some Pine replica's eau de cologne, listening to the thrum of the photocopier, the fart of the watercooler—the sheer expectedness of it all had once comforted her, but she realized now that it had also protected her from the things she feared most. Or she could go back-packing in Europe, get a master's degree; there were many clean untroubled tributaries down which a trained oboist and highland dancer could swim, but she knew where they all led: to a careful shot-by-shot remake of *The Louise Berthiaume Story*.

"Sure," she told him reluctantly. "My teeth can wait."

Then she grabbed her cape and prepared to leave before the priest could realize the monumental stupidity of what he'd done, he who couldn't even afford a miniature refrigerator. But he hadn't clued in yet. "Great," he said, clearly seeing himself on the fat end of this deal, "and now we'll just have prayers and close up for the night."

Martine didn't want to spend a second longer in this ragged room than was absolutely necessary. "I'm a little tired, Father. My first night and everything."

"Yes," he said, "well, you're hardly walking home by yourself, though."

"Oh, I'll be fine. I'll see you all tomorrow."

"Wait!"

She turned to see him extract a crumpled hillock of bills from his pants pocket, from which he peeled off three twenties. "Keep the change," he said. "This is for tonight, plus cab fare."

She took the bills and folded them primly, then placed them in her back pocket with the notebook. He carries a lot of money with him, she thought. And he can't afford a fridge?

"Look, stay a bit," urged the priest. "Really. It's dark and cold—you shouldn't even be walking out to the corner by yourself. The service is only a minute . . . actually . . ." He beheld Frost and the girl, both comatose in their own way and hardly primed for prayer. "But then, why don't we skip it tonight. This lot's hardly up for it."

Martine winced. He was too small and thin to protect her, hardly bigger than she; well formed but marked by a littleness that mitigated against manly work, like Eohippus, the tiny prehistoric horse who walked among dinosaurs. He was just drowning in his habit, for example. Maybe he thought his collar was enough to ward off any evil they might encounter. "No, I'd really rather be alone," she said.

"Martine—"

"She wants to go by herself, let her go. Jesus, are you deaf, Father?"

The priest whipped around in a gesture that advertised anger but delivered far less. "Look, Shelley—if I'm going to start the damned argument, the least you could let me do is win it." He turned back. "Fine, darling, go have yourself killed. You can't do nothing about people wanting to off themselves and why should you try."

"Five o'clock tomorrow?"

"That's what it is."

The night was cold and even the high street was more than usually empty. It was garishly lit, as if to set her in perfect relief for the bogeyman: a slow-moving target, a morsel that begged to be swallowed. Nocturnal strolls had never bothered her too much, but the priest had succeeded in transmitting a bit of his own terror. He obviously knew things she did not. A car rolled by her, the approach of its engine deafening, and only when it passed did she realize the extent of her fright. There were no streetcars. Even S and S Convenience was a tomb, its shelves shrouded in mournful blue light.

Martine reached into her skirt pocket and closed fingers around keys, making a weapon of the largest and sharpest. She passed a gap between buildings and heard a rustle—of raccoon? Rat? Or something bigger—and it was something bigger, too, that much her nerves told her. She walked faster, faster. She told herself she didn't hear it, but one block later it could hardly be denied. The bloodied bumps of him behind her, him, the matted horror.

The beggar who could be a chooser.

She was a woman, and thus acquainted with a certain fear of nighttime walking. In Moore Park, whenever she'd sensed such bumping behind her, she'd travel up the bright green of a nearby lawn, pretending that the yellow light of whatever faux-Georgian or mock-Tudor manse that lay at the end of it burned just for her. And when the putatively criminal dog-walker or cyclist passed, she'd travel down the lawn again and continue her scurry toward home, finally arriving there, bracingly awake.

Fine. But here there were no lawns up which to travel, no lights toward which to walk. Murder and rape rolled calmly behind her because, here, they could afford to take their time, nestled comfortably in the brain of a real monster: a were-wolf, with the long nails and coarse hair, the encroaching stink and mass of his kind.

She turned down Merseyfield, still trying to convince herself that it wasn't happening. God, what a lavish table murder and rape had set for themselves! The great empty schoolyard, with its cornucopia of black corners—why, the werewolf would be rubbing his red hands together, smacking the cracks in his hard black lips. *Last time you serve me wilted lettuce, girly.*

She was almost running now, running being the thing she didn't want to do, the acknowledgement of her status as prey, and now she really was running, and he behind her, grunting, "Uh! Uh!" and she coaxing what breath she could from the cold masonry of her chest, legs afire with pain . . . and down, and down, and then the worst: the realization that she had dropped her keys.

She yearned to cry out but the street was a morgue. She dared not turn to see how close he was. If she ran back to get the keys, she would meet him halfway; but if she didn't, she would run up against the flat unyielding thick of her door, no one there, no lights on. She ran next door, home of what Father Kearney had in passing called "the winners of the World's Grumpiest Family contest" and she pounded, she keened: someone please answer, someone please hear past your television, your baby's cry. But the World's Grumpiest Family wasn't home.

Martine looked tremulously up but could not see him anywhere, although not seeing him was far worse than its opposite. He could be in the bush behind her, he could dart out from a corner of the playground. She sunk to the stone path in a dog's resignation to its fate. She was a piece of clutter now, inhuman. She had never felt so sapped of will in her life; the ugliness was upon her and she awaited the curl of a red tentacle around her thin useless neck.

But as she hugged her thighs to her chest, coiling into the shell of her cape, she felt a sudden stab of metal at her thigh.

Her keys. She had shoved them in her pocket after all. This gave her the courage to uncoil and run up the porch, just as she heard someone yelling down the block.

Whether it was her private monster or someone else's, she didn't know. Maybe she hadn't been followed at all . . . but it could have happened, she told herself. This is where it happens all the time, and nobody pays any attention.

Her mind would rape and murder her, if nobody else got there first.

She opened the doors and staggered down the steps to her darkened apartment, then went straight to the sink and took out a large bucket the priest had left there. Dirty, dirty: there was nothing left in her apartment and still she felt dirty.

She filled the bucket with boiling water, took it to her room, and pushed both bedding and clothes into the hall. She dunked her towel in the water and scrubbed baseboards. Walls. Floor. She scraped sticky dust out of the silly gilt and frosted-glass light fixture, then scalded herself in the shower. She dusted the light bulbs and watched some pillbugs writhe to death under steaming streams from the bucket.

At some point the birds took up their perch on the wires outside and things seemed clean enough. Finally, she went to bed.

*S*HE WENT BACK to the Koffee Kave one morning, several weeks later, and bought herself a cherry Danish and a coffee. Albert Swanson wasn't there, so she kept them for herself.

There were two other customers here, though, both of them men sitting at the other end of the room. The one facing her had long but tidy hair, and wore a new denim jacket. He looked like a folksinger who was trying hard to be cool, without realizing that folk music itself was twenty years out of fashion. The broad back of the folksinger's friend was hunched over a doughnut, his bright yellow head bobbing into it and away from it and back. What conversation took place between them looked minimal.

Martine had only ever known one person with hair so yellow—like a pile of straw, flattened in places, from which some indolent barnyard animal looked to have just risen.

That sweater, too, expensive but run to ruin, with one hole under the arm: it was him, she decided. It was Elliott Pine.

Elliott—the lowliest of Pines, the one who'd been thrown down stairs so many times by his relatively golden brother Jeremy that one day his straw-covered brain just submitted, as all brains so treated will, to a life of meanness and stupidity; Elliott of whom parents Jane and Jim never spoke at dinner parties, with his dopey three-eared friends and criminal record; Elliott who had kicked her beloved Flavio in the head, that awful day in the schoolyard. Martine hated Elliott, but if in fact that big back across the room belonged to him, she was glad. A man who took breakfast in this part of town was necessarily unhappy.

But then, when had Elliott Pine ever been anything else?

Martine grew up thinking of Elliott as a great pink mattress you heaved down the stairs or over a cliff for kicks, which is mainly why, when she saw him sitting in the emergency ward of the Toronto General Hospital one evening back in junior high school, she didn't say a word to him.

He'd escorted Jeremy there when the older Pine had, after two large pre-cinema cocktails of tangerine liqueur mixed with twelve-year-old Scotch, sliced off the very tip of a pinky in the theatre's door jamb. While he was in being bandaged up, Elliott was left alone in the lobby, and, seeing Martine in her candystriper outfit, stared at her. She caught his eye, too, and was forced to acknowledge him. She went over, sat on one of the orange plastic seats, and waited for him to talk.

"Hi," he grunted.

"Hi."

She noticed he was reading a yellowed pamphlet. "What's that?" she asked, just to scratch some silence off the moment.

"It's a thing my dad gave me," Elliott muttered from underneath the curtain of straw. "It's about a king in Messatamia."

"Mesopotamia?"

"Yeah, that. It's about a king who had a great fortune and lost it because he didn't keep enough for himself. It's priddy good."

Martine knew the pamphlet for an eternal constant (in French translation) on Pépère's desk in Montreal. It was called *Reward Thyself Unto Thyself,* and it was written by someone with the fragrantly Mesopotamian name of Edwin Q. Candlesworth. The pamphlet detailed the story of a king named Omar and his flock of sheep. Omar's sheep-management techniques increased his wealth over time, and by ignoring his fellow shepherds, who begged him to share, he became the richest man in the kingdom. Wise shepherding brought him the Mesopotamian equivalents of swimming pools and colour TVs with remote control, as well as a long and fruitful marriage to the caliph's daughter, a bedizened voluptuary in a solid gold brassiere. "Many laws must you follow, but this and this first," said the pamphlet, "reward firstly thyself unto thyself."

Jeremy swaggered into the waiting room, his finger entombed in gauze.

"This is such a cool look," he said proudly.

Jeremy was newly impressed with his younger brother, too, though Elliott seemed to Martine just as silent and lumpen as ever.

Cynthia Macdonald

"Elliott," Jeremy said vividly. "Tell Martine what you did yesterday. Tell her."

Elliott muttered and scuffed a licorice wrapper around the linoleum with his left foot.

"He's too shy. Well, get this—Elliott stole a city bus!"

Martine wondered aloud where you would put a city bus.

"What do you mean, where did he put it? I'm saying he gets on the 32B at St. Clair West while the driver's gone in for a coffee and drives it away with like fifty people in it."

"More like eight," corrected Elliott.

"So anyway, Elliott's driving and the people are all in a flap because they're getting hijacked, and Alison Jackson's mom is in there and she's going, 'Elliott Pine! Elliott! What are you doing?' Then the best part is he crashes into the gate outside the old folks' home. Oh, Elliott, you gotta do it again. Martine, you come with us and we'll be in the bus next time."

Martine was impressed that someone would kidnap Mrs. Jackson, a veiny-nostrilled crosspatch whose terrification would, admittedly, make for good fun. It certainly made Elliott seem more worth anyone's time . . . but why did he have to hang his head like that? Why didn't he put on a good show the way Jeremy did, with his peacock walk and pretty face? Jeremy gave the impression of someone who was going somewhere, and not in any old broken-down Toronto Transit bus either.

In fact, she had lately become more interested in Jeremy, who was growing taller and better looking with each passing month. So a few weeks later, when she came upon the two of them setting fire to larval caterpillars on the merry-go-round at Rosedale Park, she stopped to say hello. Jeremy didn't

184

mind. Martine had always put up with his misdemeanours and had never told on him. It was hard to find girls who were cool about caterpillar murder, and about leafing through Jim Pine's snatch rags, which is what they did the following week, and about klepting a bunch of freezies from the 7-Eleven, which happened a few days after that: on a Sunday, when Martine would ordinarily have been at mass.

The brothers had intercepted her on her ten-speed. "Mass!" Jeremy derided. "Who goes to mass if they don't have to?" *They* had to, a fact that Martine had always envied, but they always went *en famille* at nine o'clock, leaving the rest of the day open for mischief. It was such a beautiful day though, beautified all the more by lanky Jeremy in his Darryl Sittler jersey. "Come on," he urged. "Five Mr. Frosties is my record. One of every colour. We're going for ten today but I need extra manpower." Martine told herself that it would only take an hour, after which she could make the noon service; but twelve-thirty found her sitting on the merry-go-round under a glorious spring sun, laughing with her new old friend and his silent brother, sucking on illicit freezies and *being a kid,* and she felt no guilt about any of it. The following week she skipped mass again.

This adjustment in her Sunday schedule coincided with a certain change in her reading habits. She chucked *A Tree Grows in Brooklyn* and became an avid consumer of Louise's more lurid paperbacks, like *Fear of Flying* and *Kinflicks* and *Looking for Mr. Goodbar* and *My Secret Garden* (or at least certain parts thereof). The clitoris was invented in 1973 and these were its user manuals. Martine found the books to be inspirational and edifying, and toyed with the idea of getting

Jeremy over for a literary salon of sorts in order to analyze the ideas advanced within; Twinkies and Southern Comfort would be served. Which book to choose was the question. Every mother on the block had an impressively stocked library, and not just in paperback either. Sharon Colterblake had what appeared to be a thousand-page tome in her living room called, provocatively, *The Female Orgasm,* and why the book was so big and why it was sitting in a Moore Park living room, between the candy dish and the April tulips, were questions that colonized a good part of Martine's newly teenaged brain.

But how to get rid of Elliott? He seemed to be a necessary part of everything Jeremy did. As sidekicks went though, he wasn't too bad, being stone silent and interested in only one thing—driving, a skill he'd honed on Jim Pine's many and various golf carts. Even though he was years away from being able to get his licence, he was really good at it. It was a useful skill, the teens discovered, since it meant they didn't have to live out their adolescence on a splintery old merry-go-round. And getting the old Mercedes for a spin wasn't much of a problem, since the Pines had too many cars and too many children to notice the kind of blank spots around their garage and dinner table that would have given other parents pause. Thus did Elliott become the wheelman for his brother's first, and most questionable, business ventures. He was thirteen when he started.

If they wanted to pull a runner at Olympic Pizza because they couldn't afford the tab—not with the extra Cokes they couldn't—he'd buzz them out of there so fast the stung waitress could only gape in admiration. If Jeremy had to pick up a nickel bag from some dealer up in what he called "Browntown," Elliott would power the Mercedes there without complaint and sit reading a Richie Rich comic while his passenger completed the score. If Jeremy had the post-spliff munchies at 1 a.m. and *totally* needed some stolen taco chips, they could roust him out of bed and he'd pull up to the curb with the instantaneity of a pushed button. He'd heist the chips, too, with dip if they wanted. Elliott was the dray horse, so he did it all, big dumb Elliott did it all.

Sex, drugs, theft. Each sin was giving onto another in Martine's life and they were all incredibly fun, and that shouldn't have been so, but what could you do? One night she lay between the Pine brothers in Rosedale Park, completely wasted and looking at the stars. The three of them had smoked a joint, shared a wineskin full of purple Freshie mixed with vodka, split two of Louise's Seconals three ways, snorted nutmeg, and rubbed cayenne pepper on their gums (Elliott had somehow heard that prisoners got high by raiding the jail kitchen's spice cabinet). Martine felt dreamy and perfect, listening to the brothers fight—"No *that's* Orion, you dipshit!"—and before her eyes a picture swam and took shape in the fluid firmament above: it was a picture of her, just a little while ago, shaking hands with the lady from the Kelly Centre. Did lying here like this feel better than that?

But—what if you could put them both together, wouldn't that be the best? Good and bad, side by side, one no more important than the other. What if you could?

Naturally, Louise was horrified at her daughter's deepening association with Jeremy. She had always disapproved of what few friends Martine had almost had, probably because they were so resolutely *not* Carolyn Colterblake. A Pine she could have tolerated—one of the older ones, the ones who held solid career-track summer jobs working for their respectable daddy. But Jeremy? And, worse than that, Elliott?

At a certain point Jane Pine discovered that her sons had been joyriding in the Mercedes and she grounded them for two weeks; but since she had four other children, a husband and three housekeepers to govern, she quickly forgot the length of the sentence or if she'd even been the one to pass it.

Which left the brothers free to commit their first truly criminal act—robbing their own house, which wasn't going to be hard since they had an obvious inside line on where the rest of the family was going to be: in Aruba doing something called "windsurfing." Daisy, the overnight maid, was nominally in residence, but she saw Pine vacations as a chance to enjoy a succession of all-night potluck suppers at the homes of her friends. So the path was clear, but when the time came, Jeremy told Elliott he had to stay in the car. He wouldn't even let him rob his own *room*.

"You're like Michael Collins, Elly," he said.

"Who?"

"The astronaut. Michael Collins stayed in the space capsule the whole time, but he still got a parade and stuff when he got home. You're our Michael Collins."

Which left Martine to wonder who she was, since they didn't exactly have stewardesses on board *Apollo 11*. Jeremy expected nothing from her except her presence; as he once said gallantly, while fashioning a spliff: "A lady never rolls, and a lady never pays." He accomplished all the larceny while she just sat and watched, an impotent Bonnie to his wildly inventive Clyde.

She felt sort of bad about the Pine break-in, but couldn't consider it to be a crime, really. It was their own house, after all, they were teenagers, and it was all insured. It wasn't too much trouble for her to square this new sub-Martine with the one who initiated a bottle drive for the children at the Kelly Centre. Especially if she just stayed in the Mercedes with Elliott.

She convinced herself, too, that things were just as light and merry when Jeremy decided to break into St. Joachim's the following night. The plan was that Elliott would idle outside in the car with Martine while Jeremy broke into the principal's office and robbed the petty-cash box. He'd emerge only minorly enriched for their trouble—maybe a couple of hundred bucks or so—but the incidentals would make it worth it: their private dossiers, a snapshot or two of the bathing-suit-clad principal on a cut-rate Florida holiday. A giggle, clown stuff.

Elliott eased the car up to the side of the school. Metal grates covered the basement windows, as at an asylum, but these had been in place for fifty years and crumbled even under the tentative hacks of Jeremy's hammer.

Jeremy actually looked quite the scofflaw this evening. His mom had ordered a real punk leather jacket for his birthday from England, which, to her horror, he had ripped up quite jauntily with a letter opener.

"Tell that goof to turn the lights off," he yelled to Martine in the car, rust spattering his dandyish burglar clothes.

Elliott doused the headlights and hunched over to squint at his comic book. Sometimes he reminded Martine of Cadbury, Richie Rich's thin and bloodless butler—but a Cadbury given to blushing, a butler with a trust fund and an impossible thatch of straw-blond hair. Elliott didn't seem to know he was dumb; it was one of the many things a dumb person wouldn't know.

Jeremy wrenched the grate away and tried to jimmy the window lock, but jimmying not being his strong suit he ended up taking hammer to glass, which showed him for the amateur he was.

"That was bad, that glass," Martine said to Elliott.

"Yeah," he agreed.

She'd tried to "cultivate" Elliott for the past couple of months—that was the phrase her mother might use; she was sure there were depths there worth plumbing. She'd asked him questions about himself and he'd lob her a series of dead-end monosyllables: "yuh," "s'pose," "right." Did he ever think about anything, this giant underbaked loaf of a boy, besides comic books and cars? It wasn't as if he'd sprung from idiot loins—his father was impressively wealthy, head of a company toward which Elliott was comfortably destined. If he ever graduated.

"Good comic, Elliott?"

"S'okay."

And now here Martine sat again, trying to talk to him. She always started such conversations certain she could excavate an actual person from the layers of grunting gristle. But it was a project, like all her other attempts at goodness, that tended to weary her after fifteen minutes of earnest digging.

She always gave up, disliking him a little bit more. She knew his mother wanted to ship him off to Switzerland at some point, to a lycée for wayward teens. But repeated blasts from an alpenhorn and curative hypodermics full of goat's milk would probably not change him. He would still be Elliott, whatever Elliott was.

Jeremy came tearing out of the school with a sheaf of wanton pages. He tumbled into the back with Martine, knocking his lit joint into the car's upholstery. Neither brother paid any mind.

"Let's see," said Jeremy. "Let's see—by the way, Pine Junior, put your ass on the pedal, please, as if I should have to tell you—let's see." Elliott tore out of the parking lot. "Craythorn Martine, Craythorn Martine . . . 'quiet student,' 'well-mannered student,' 'tendency to daydream'—fuck me, what a *dullard*! Let's take a look at Elliott's IQ. I wonder if it registered." Jeremy shuffled the papers around. "Pine, Pine . . . what? There are a bunch of different numbers here. I don't know which one to pick."

"You know what you do?" said Martine. "It's like the grocery store. If there are different prices on something, you take the lowest one." She said this monotonously, in the way of one who was only here for the makeout session after. She'd conjured up a rather rococo oro-digital manoeuvre while exercising her tendency to daydream in class the day before. She thought she might as well try it on Jeremy as on anyone else.

"So, eighty-three," mused Jeremy. "Yeah, sounds like Elliott. What do you think, bro? Do you remember that test?"

Elliott was silent for a minute more.

"Is that the one where you need the pencil?" he said finally.

"Most tests you need a pencil, doof."

"Yeah, but I meant . . . you know."

"He means an HB pencil," Martine translated.

Jeremy laughed his special failure-deflecting laugh, one he trotted out whenever he was in trouble or losing an argument. Then he blanched and he slammed his fist in the door. "Fuck. I think I left the cash box in the parking lot." They took a vote on it, but nobody wanted to go back. It wasn't as if they were in it for the money.

Ten minutes later they found themselves in the Pines' den. Louise and Mack were away that weekend, too, and Martine told Emelda she was sleeping at a friend's house. But she was only a few doors away at the Pines', lolling on their overstuffed leather furniture, taking inventory of all the expensive pieces her friends had been too stupid to steal: Inuit soapstone, Lladró figurines, pewter ashtrays, and scads of Italianate knickknacks. They'd left all these behind and stolen two huge macramé wall hangings instead; maybe, like their sister's flamenco-dancing clothes, these were just something the Pine brothers had grown tired of seeing and that made their theft worth it. Elliott manned the remote control, cool as the undead, snapping past the faces of Elizabeth Ashley, Hogan and several of his Heroes, and assorted other actors who in Draculan fashion only made themselves known late on Saturday night. Then he slowly vibed to his own redundancy. Drugs procured, made presentable and presented, he was no longer needed; his brother and his girlfriend had clearly forgotten him, with Martine rolling hornily on the couch pawing at Jeremy and Jeremy shouting theatrically while reading from his own dossier: "Disturbs class frequently!" "Will not listen!" "Suggest psychiatric help!"

When he'd read his fill he grabbed Martine and rammed his face into hers. She undid his belt and led him by it to his parents' antique four-poster, giggling and giddy, leaving Elliott with the remote control and a pile of potato chip bags.

Martine woke to the sight of a tentative shaft of light stabbing the broadloom before her. She gathered her things and stole out of the room before Jeremy woke up. It had all been something of a botch, really. Mutual misunderstanding had resulted in a number of misplaced teeth and Jeremy had suffered an uppercut from one of Martine's vagrant elbows, after which he'd cursed her, turned over, and gone to sleep. It was weird: back when they were kids Jeremy had taught Martine everything she knew about sex, all of it spoken into her back during math class and all of it hard to believe. She found the idea of fellatio to be particularly incredible. "It's true," Jeremy hissed. "You do it on your knees."

"Like praying?" she asked, disgusted, rejecting the implied similarity of the two acts.

"Yeah, but with this you get an answer."

Martine wondered if sex was ever going to get good; these early days of her love life were not going well. On her fourteenth Hallowe'en she had gone to a party and retired to a closet with a thoroughly costumed stranger. She made him take off the red nose but still ended up with red and white face paint smeared all over her face, throat, and shoulders. At the end of the evening it looked as though a clown had been dropped on her from a speeding F-16.

It had only been practice for Jeremy, and now the big collision had come and gone, and it was so much less than she'd expected. As she struggled into her black T-shirt and staggered to the bathroom to splash water on her face, she wondered if they were "going around" now, or even "going out." She wasn't keen on either and thought fleetingly of joining the Inter-School Catholic Fellowship crowd, whose many good works would leave her no time for bad teenaged sex. But, she thought sadly, she probably wasn't worth good works any more.

Elliott was still in the den. Not watching or reading anything, just being Elliott in the den.

"Elliott?"

"Oh, hi. I thought you might like me to walk you home."

She realized her fly was open and tried lying on the floor and zipping up her jeans, but that was a production she didn't have time for. Elliott wouldn't understand; Mrs. Pine frowned on jeans.

So they loped out the door together. Martine's eyes were all but welded shut by reclumped mascara.

They walked uncomfortably down the street. "Did you hurt yourself?" he asked.

"No. Why?"

"I just heard someone . . . never mind."

It was dawning on her that Elliott might be some kind of voyeur, that he wasn't dumb at all, that he had some secret hotline to the real floridity of her mind because it matched his own. People who say nothing, she held, cannot possibly be thinking nothing at the same time: nothingness cannot spread itself that thin. She sensed that each was cracking the code of the other, but it brought her no feeling of fellowship. It gave her the creeps, actually.

"Do you want to get breakfast?" he asked.

Ugh. Now he was going to hit on her? Over breakfast no less, a big boy lapping up a big plate of bacon in some glaring pink-and-yellow breakfastorium, hardly candlelight and roses, my friend, and just who the hell do you think you are, anyways?

"No, I think I'll just go home if it's all the same."

"Okay."

So he dropped her off. And she didn't thank him.

It was one of those Sunday afternoons that began with knocks on the door and stupid questions, both of which came to Martine's ears in a manner dulled by the heavy down of her ruffled bedspread. She had crawled into her bed and slept way into the afternoon, by which point Louise had returned.

"Martini?"

"Ungh."

"Jeremy's on the phone. Don't be too long," said Louise. "I'm expecting a call from Sharon." Martine shambled down the hall, still in too much of a fug to properly attend this call from her "boyfriend."

But pillow talk was not Jeremy Pine's purpose. "We've got trouble," he said weakly. "The night janitor got our licence plate. The cops took Elliott away while I was out walking the dog and they called my parents in Aruba.

They're on their way home. He's going to rat on us for sure. Expect your next call to be from one very pissed cop."

"A cop? *I* didn't do anything."

"Right on, and I guess you spent last night at the roller-drome with your pal Carolyn Colterblake. We're all sharing the heat from this, Craythorn, and if you tell on me—the point is, just cool it." He hung up and Martine shivered; they stood to go in for a major fall. If the school authorities knew about the IQ papers, they'd probably find out about the lockers—how Martine and Jeremy kept small things they'd shoplifted in theirs, and Elliott kept the pot. She spent the rest of the day wondering how many people would come to visit her in jail. Her friends wouldn't, because they'd all be in jail, too. Her mother would go in for a few tearful visits, but the routine would ultimately prove too painful; their connection would sputter and die, though it was possible that later she'd come to think of the whole relationship as a kind of ongoing charity benefit for which you didn't have to buy a dress, and hence worthy of "cultivation."

Word of her incarceration would somehow wend its way to her father, and he'd tear himself away from whatever he was doing—teaching in Toronto or agrarian reform in Upper Volta—growl at her, jet right back, and that would be the last of that. The growl would be Professorese for: Crime is the province of the poor, and what in God's hell do you think you're playing at?

Martine tried to eat her supper but couldn't. Still, the evening wore on and there were no more phone calls, not from the police, the principal, nor any representatives of the Pine family. Thankful confirmation, maybe, that girls weren't thought capable of such acts? Especially "well-mannered" girls whose fathers laboured on behalf of the world's starving and whose slight physiques precluded the smashing of locks and windows.

Now her thoughts turned to whether *she* would visit Elliott in prison, and she decided she would. It would be the least she could do.

It crossed her mind to skip school the next day, but justice wasn't so blind it couldn't find her cowering over coffee in Olympic Pizza. Canonization was off the table now, and perhaps graduation. She decided to face the bear and felt very *croix de guerre* for doing so.

Jeremy was sitting at a table in the cafeteria, his warm complexion bleached white. "Elly took the whole rap himself," he said astoundedly. "They set a trial date and shit. But he won't even talk to me about it. It's fucked, man. I mean, it's not like I asked him to play it that way, right?"

Martine was frightened as to what Elliott's strategy might mean; she knew better than anyone that self-interest always lurked behind self-sacrifice. "But then," she said, "he never talks to us anyways."

"Yeah. How about that? He never talks to anyone."

Quietly penitent, they attended most of their classes, then returned to the cafeteria for lunch and picked with wordless fear at a communal carton of fries. Casting about for spiders in their midst.

"Good thing Elliott's not here," Jeremy opined finally. "More for us."

Martine quailed at the possibility that their poor driver would be tried, convicted, and jailed like a man instead of bunked up in a cushy training school like a child, but Jeremy dismissed that possibility. "My dad'll get him the best lawyers."

"Not if he figures out you took his macramé."

"Look, nobody even noticed the macramé. Can you believe that? Anyway, that stuff looks really hideous when you're not stoned. Getting it off the wall was, like, a public service."

She wasn't impressed by the way he grabbed at his knuckles, blushed, stuttered, and worried. He had gone overnight from insouciant cowboy to spoiled and spineless brat. A weakling, she thought. Weaklings all around me.

Elliott did return to school the next day, but, little by little, he stopped hanging around with them. He had no choice in the matter, since he was given detention every day after school on penalty of failing; and one afternoon, Martine was leaving school and tried to scurry by him, so awful did the sight of him scrawling out math problems seem to her. But he caught her. "Martine?"

She forced herself back three steps to the open doorway.

"Hi, Elliott. How—how are you doing in there?"

"Oh, fine."

"Well . . . thanks. For not saying anything."

"It's all right. You didn't do anything—it's not like you ever did."

She smiled falsely and turned to go but he wouldn't quite let her; there was one more thing he had to ask of her, that one last fateful thing. He looked up at the lights and worried his pencil between pink fingers. "I'll be finished here in five minutes," he said, "if you—if you want to go to Olympic."

Martine combed frantically for an excuse. Homework wouldn't cut it, because he knew she never did any. "It's Tuesday, isn't it? I have . . . er . . . ballet."

"Maybe next week then."

"Sure," she replied, and, guilt shooting like a geyser up her fool spine, added, "Thursday?"

Her appetite disappeared, which was the usual response to any blip in her life's rhythm; she couldn't imagine choking back pepperoni and unwashed mushrooms with Elliott, she'd order water. And the talk . . . she was no longer curious about him, she figured she'd served in those trenches already and didn't know why this gruesome finale should be tacked onto the tour. The days ticked toward her ghastly date and she dreaded its advance. What if he moved to kiss her at the end? He was bigger than she was! She knew of a camping store where you could get bear repellent, which was ten times more powerful than Mace . . . she'd wear something foreboding, black and tentish . . . burlap would do . . .

Thursday morning was bright, cool, charged with sun and promise for everyone but Martine, who stayed home from school with a "cold."

So she skipped out on their date: but Elliott didn't call about it. Maybe he didn't mind. Every single minute of that day, she wondered what he was doing, then resolved not to think about it any more.

The criminal troika fell apart after that. Martine saw Elliott plenty as the rest of high school passed, but they never spoke. Jeremy lost touch with him, too, even though they lived in the same house. The older boy immediately swore off drugs and crime, at least the kind that might pull you down to the lower orders. Elliott, on the other hand, went deeper into it. He started attracting boys far worse than Jeremy to himself, boys who not only robbed their own living rooms but those of strangers. Luckless, dirty boys. Boys who kicked immigrants in the head. Elliott grew larger, coarser, uglier as time went on, a pathetic stain in the margins of Moore Park life. Parents came to shudder at the sight of him, for he represented every dark alley their children might go down.

Several years later, Martine got another call from Jeremy, who told her to check inside the morning paper for a small headline several pages in.

TWO ARRESTED IN SEXUAL ASSAULT CASE

Police held two men in custody last night in connection with the attempted sexual assault of a 21-year-old woman. Charged with kidnapping, forcible confinement, and attempted sexual assault is Edward Conrad Witschel, 25, of Pickering. A 16-year-old juvenile is also charged with kidnapping and forcible confinement. The two will appear in court today.

"They can't say his name" said Jeremy sadly. "But I can. Elliott Thomas Kerrigan Pine. That's his name."

It must be another Elliott Thomas Kerrigan Pine, said Martine. But Jeremy assured her it wasn't.

The folksinger caught her eye and held it. It was only for half a second but it was fatal. It prodded Elliott—and it *was* Elliott—to turn slightly, curious about what his friend might be seeing.

The big face had been planed and edged by reversals and he stared now, unflinching. Martine resolved not to look away first. The folksinger patted his hand and left the two of them to square off against each other. Martine hoped Elliott might follow the folksinger out but his look seemed to imply some mission. Eventually he got up and sat across from her.

"Hi," he said.

He started speaking, but with effort, as if each heavy word had to be heaved onto a wagon and trundled outside his body. He told her he'd run into some bad luck back there in high school, "and it *was* bad luck, too," he assured her. "The guy just told me to drive, so I drove. I didn't know he was going to do . . . *that*."

Martine was quiet.

"You don't believe me," he said.

"No." She didn't want to cultivate him any more. She wished he would go.

He hunched farther into his sweater and hung his great yellow head. "That's okay. Nobody believes me. But at least I paid for it, eh? I paid and I'm paying. Can't find a damn job."

He was eager to talk, which was odd, even though the talk took the form of irregular blurts. As he enumerated the losses of his young life, Martine found herself buying him a coffee. He was so pathetic she couldn't do any less. Goodwill had nothing to do with it. The Flavio beating, the kidnapped woman: these sat like shadows in the corner, and chilled her eventual parting words to him.

He came again the next day, though. This time he was alone. He bought the coffee before she could object, and launched into more tales of family estrangement and friendlessness. His brothers, sisters, and parents were all conducting their lives very happily without him, he said; it was as if he'd never been born.

He kept talking, and talking. It was the damnedest thing. In the middle of one of his stories, Martine put a hand over his and stopped him. "Elliott—why are you telling me all this? You never said anything before."

Startled by the question, he couldn't answer right away. "Because," he said at last, "I guess I don't have anyone else to talk to."

So Martine listened. Was it only that she wanted to be in the presence of one whose foot had touched Flavio's head? Or did she actually pity this creep? She had always been a sucker for this kind of sticky threnody—watch it, she told herself. On the other hand, it would be just like those Pine idiots to cut him off, to dump him like some low-performing junk bond.

Whatever it was, she felt anxious when he didn't show up the next day, anxious and not a little homesick. She was about to go when he lumbered in, alone again. She called him over with a feeling of inexpressible relief. What, she asked herself, is wrong with me?

He asked her what she'd been up to.

"Do you remember Flavio Vargas?" she asked, her voice hard. "I was recently working for him. He's done very well for himself."

"Is that that Spanish guy from St. Joachim's?" Elliott asked.

She nodded slowly.

"That guy—" Elliott gasped, shaking his head. "I tried to save that guy once, you know. Pat Murphy and them were wailing on him." Martine said nothing in response. "But I guess you don't believe that either," he sighed.

She didn't really, but the possibility of its being true needled her all that day and into the night. The next morning she opened the conversation herself.

"Did you really do that, Elly? Try to save Flavio?"

His eyes bugged. "Of course! What—you don't think *I* was beating him up, do you?"

She shook her head hastily. They drank their coffee for a while. The folksinger passed by the window and Elliott waved to him.

"You know," said Martine, "I might know someone who could use a driver."

She wrote down the Refuge's address and gave it to Elliott, not a little hesitantly. She'd been working there for almost a month now and it sure wasn't getting any easier. Father Kearney had only wanted one extra night from her, but she found herself going back and back again; the sick waitress had not returned, Glenys was as lazy as ever, and Martine had the growing sense that it would all fall apart if she didn't hold it together.

And yet she was seeing less of Father Kearney. He was leaving earlier each day to go on his "runs" with the ramshackle Frost, who really (she was certain of it now) had no business driving. Where did they go? What did they do when they got there? It took less than half an hour to pick up supper from the hotel; what went on the rest of the time? Like the priest, she had no driver's licence, so she couldn't offer herself as a substitute chauffeur. But she could offer Elliott. Maybe he could find out.

He looked at the paper. "What is this place?"

"It's a—soup kitchen, I guess you'd call it."

Elliott made a face and looked out the window. "I was thinking, more like, I don't know. Something in an office."

"An office? Elliott. Come on."

He said he'd think about it and that's the way she left him. Thinking about it.

$\mathscr{M}$ARTINE WAS SURPRISED to see Father Kearney and Frost at the Refuge when she arrived late that afternoon. They were surrounded by white boxes and their eyes were gleaming. Glenys was opening the boxes and clucking over their contents. A woman Martine had never seen sat in the corner watching them, a sallow-faced person in her late thirties with a sheaf of brightly coloured flyers in her lap and the obligatory cigarette between her fingers.

"We're gonna have a party tonight, yes sir," said the priest.

Martine walked over to the boxes and saw they were full of food. Which she expected—but there were so many of them. The number was truly unusual. "What's this about?" Martine asked.

Frost belched. "The secretary for Mr. Earl Passmiller committed a grave error. She booked his retirement party for

the evening, and his fatal myocardial infarction for the afternoon. When it really should have been the other way around."

"Poor bastard," said Father Kearney, opening a box, and
Martine was about to be shocked by this but he cut her off
with a gasp. "Oh, my Lord in heaven. Oh, but would you all
have a look at this," he exclaimed, pointing inside.

It was a huge, perfect cake, lavishly and intricately frosted
to create the image of a beach scene at sunset. Deep purple
icing was overlaid with orange and yellow, for the sky; down
toward the middle warm colours met up with the bright blue
of waves. Here the icing was whipped up in a choppy, white-
capped impasto. It smoothed out where the waves met
cookie-crumble sand. There were even girls on the beach,
hula dancers with leis made of tiny candies and black-licorice
hair. Underneath the scene flowed one carefully scripted
word: *Farewell*.

"And look here, Father," said Glenys, who'd opened three
more boxes of strangely perfect food. Generally the stuff
they got was fairly well mashed up by the time it got there,
and it was hard to make it presentable. But there wasn't a
crumb out of place in this shipment: there were mini-quiches,
chicken wings, spring rolls, mushroom puffs, cheese cubes,
melon balls, and several large trays of fresh vegetables.

"Crew-dites," said Father Kearney.

"Cru-dee-*tays*," Martine corrected.

"But look at this grub," he cried. "So beautiful, every bit
of it. We'll have to have a special grace for this, won't we?
Come around everybody, let's join hands."

"Oh, for Christ's sake, Father," said the sallow-faced
woman.

"Exactly," he said.

The group formed a circle reluctantly; Father Kearney sometimes called for prayers at the end of the evening but nobody was ever into it except for him. They all watched tolerantly as he closed his eyes and bowed his head. Then he said, "Martine, would you recite the blessing, please?"

"Me?"

"Yes, you. You're the only Martine here."

She took a breath and hoped it would come back to her.

"Uh . . . bless us, O Lord," she started. "In these thy gifts . . . which we are about to receive . . . from thy bounty, through Christ our Lord." She held Father Kearney's warm hand on one side, Glenys's cool one on the other. The moment took on its own soft character: there was no strain in her muscles now, no pain behind her eyes.

"Amen," she said.

In the stillness that followed Martine opened her eyes and looked at all the food. It did seem curiously beautiful to her, a series of rare and glistening artifacts awaiting classification. And Father Kearney was right—the cake was miraculous.

He broke from the circle and crossed himself. Desperately, it seemed to Martine, as if quadrisecting his chest with a razor. Then he snapped his fingers and smiled.

"Let's eat!"

There was more than enough for everyone who came that night, and everyone did come. The crudités went first, well before anything else, which surprised Martine. What could be duller than cucumbers?

"When you eat from a food bank, you never get beautiful tomatoes like this," Father Kearney said, holding one up to the light and turning it right and left. He hated food banks and always spoke as if the people who worked there were bent on destroying the health of their clients, instead of keeping them alive. He was sure they'd all be closed in a couple of years. "Canned stuff, peanut butter, that's all these guys get to eat. That's why a lot of them are so fat, see?"

Martine looked sadly at Muriel, who was slowly savouring a plate of sliced mushrooms and red pepper slivers; and then at her own thin fingers, in which she held her notebook. She knew that the road between her and Muriel was long, very long—but what strange turns in it, too, turns she'd never counted on.

"Isn't it a great night?" Father Kearney asked, still holding the tomato aloft.

"Sure it is," Martine agreed.

He placed the tomato on a plate, looking at her all the while. Then he added some carrots, and cauliflower. A mini-quiche, two mushroom tarts, and he was done. He held it out to her shyly.

"Do you—I mean, would you like this?"

She smiled and took it from him, and before long the plate was empty.

It was nice to have him there all night, for a change. Night after night Martine and Glenys oversaw the restaurant themselves, serving and cleaning like docile dogs. Things only ever picked up on the priest's return, which was always so energetic as to make one think he'd just come back from a month of mountain climbing. Even battered Frost usually took on a celebratory air somewhere between leaving and re-entry. Father Kearney truly seemed to believe that he was running a nightly party, one of the best in town—that Suleiman was a titled marquis and the Salvadorans had pages devoted to them in Debrett's Peerage. But tonight, in everyone's eyes, was an especially special party.

As the night wore on Martine found herself looking out the front window, hoping Elliott would come. If he came upon this scene, he'd surely want to work here, Martine thought, because he'd assume it was this much fun every night. But he didn't show.

Later, as Martine was wiping the counter, she noted the presence of several brown bags full of bottles in the corner.

"Father?" she asked. "What are those?"

The priest put a finger to his lips and whispered, "*Champagne*. Sssshhh."

One of the bottles was open, though, and Martine looked from it to Frost, who was gadding from table to table with a Styrofoam cup, more talkative and happy than usual. She picked the offending bottle up and started pouring it down the drain.

"What—what are you doing?" Father Kearney shrieked under his breath. "Martine, it's a party! C'mon, let him have fun, just for one night!"

She watched the champagne fizz and dribble down the drain. "There's too much here for one person anyway," she told him. "You can't let him have all of it. You *can't*, Father."

He crossed his arms and leaned against the door, the door to the back room that no one ever went through but the men. "I guess you're right," he said. He thought for a second. "Maybe *we* should take it home. Would that be all right?"

Martine smiled. She adored champagne. "Yes, I think that would be all right."

"And we'll drink some together?"

She laughed. "Yes, fine. We'll drink it together."

Father Kearney punched a fist in the air. "Yesssss!"

The new, sallow-faced woman didn't take part in the festivity. All around her people were eating and horsing around, but she was here to work and let everyone know it. She went from table to table, slowly tacking her coloured flyers to the wall. "Take a load off, Dianne," someone counselled. "Sit and I'll fix you a drink," Frost begged. But she wasn't listening. There was something frightening about her way with the pushpins; she wielded them as if she were puncturing skin. Her thin flowered blouse was hardly the thing for such angry shoulders. If Kearney had any thought of "converting" this one, Martine thought, he'd have some time of it.

When Dianne passed by Martine, she thrust a pile of flyers in her direction.

"Help me," she commanded.

The pages advertised a benefit for the Refuge, to be held in two weeks at, of all places, a swank Forest Hill address. It was the first Martine had heard of it. "What is this?" she asked. "Who's holding it?"

But the woman wasn't listening. She was trying to force a pin into one of the metal brackets at the back of the room, which had once displayed a variety of sconces back when the place was a lamp shop. The bracket was painted purple, so she mistook it for plaster; the pin snapped and boomeranged into her cheek. "Shit!" she yelled, holding her already bruised

Alms

jaw and rounding the counter for a bandage or an aspirin.
Martine trembled and, noticing the jaw, realized that this
was *that* Dianne. The Dianne she was filling in for. Which
meant—she thought, with a sadness that surprised her—that
they probably wouldn't be needing her any more.

"Cold water, dear," droned Glenys. "Run some cold water
on it. Is it cold enough? I said cold water, dear. Warm won't
heal the cut. Cold—"

"Piss on it, I'm finished anyways," Dianne snapped, then
wriggled into her jacket and pulled a wool cap over her head.
She turned to Martine before leaving and said, "You do the
other wall. Whoever you are. Please."

Which Martine did, if a tad resentfully. But she slipped
away early, when she realized once and for all that Elliott
wasn't interested in the job. Just as well. He didn't belong in
an office, but he probably didn't belong here either.

On her way out the door she tried to hide herself in a forest
of Salvadorans so the priest wouldn't see her. He was too
eager about the champagne date, and she knew he wanted to
have it as soon as possible. In the warmth and whirl of the
party it had seemed like a good idea, but now she wasn't so
sure.

So Martine scuttled home and, as was her custom, turned
regularly to make sure she wasn't being followed.
Fortunately, he hadn't seen her leave.

The problem was this: Father Kearney loved the company
of women—a little too much, considering what he did for
a living. Glenys told Martine that the last time they'd had a
party of such magnitude at the Refuge was when a jilted

bride came in to donate her entire uneaten (and undrunk) wedding feast. The priest thought it beastly that she should be deprived of her wedding night and immediately took her out for a little consolation.

Women sometimes, in fact, accompanied him on his "runs," but they were usually seen once and never again. There was the teenaged Shelley from the first night, for example. Glenys was obviously scornful of these ringers and hissed about them.

"But who are they?" Martine asked.

"Oh, they're his *friends,*" Glenys snorted. "He's trying to convert them all, you know. But good luck. You'll never see one come back and help the way we do." Glenys was rapidly accepting Martine as a colleague and kindred spirit, which depressed her more than anything.

There was one repeat among the women, or so Martine could swear: one Saturday night she came home to find a familiar character in the foyer of 12 Merseyfield. She was tall and electrically blonde and no Catholic from the looks of things; she recognized Martine, too, and greeted her warmly with an English accent. On the way downstairs Martine placed her as the call girl from the Princess Café. "Hallo, dahling," she trilled. "Just been out for a bit of shopping, we have."

Indeed. If this was conversion, it was conversion of a most appealing kind: there were bags from Holt Renfrew and the stereo store, plus a new framed lithograph for an upstairs room. This, from the man who couldn't afford a tiny fridge for the Refuge.

But the call girl was probably doing pretty well, so maybe the stuff was hers.

"Look at these!" she said, rummaging in another bag only to come up with a full set of purple satin sheets.

"Are they yours?" Martine asked.

"Oh God, no, they're Father Cliff's. He's got quite the lair up there."

Purple satin sheets: what would a priest be doing with those? On the other hand, on the other hand . . . maybe this woman was just a housekeeper, or something. Didn't Bing Crosby have one in *Going My Way*? Yes—although not one with breast implants. This woman was more likely a Mary Magdalene figure, risen from the swamp of self-gratification, still good for the odd back rub but nothing more. But then who were Jeri, and Kelly, and Shelley and Lynn—relievers? No, no, no, Martine said to herself, grab hold of yourself here. The guy's a priest, a sinner every bit as much as any of us, but the sinning doesn't go that way. This Kearney lacked the sinister edge required for womanizing, the forked tongue and fake green eyes of a Clayton Pine. He was too like a leprechaun, a little leaping pesky elf-man; he reminded Martine of a constant birthday party fixture from back in her childhood, a man who dressed in a green felt hat and buckled shoes and called himself Finnegan Dunnegan, who strummed songs of his own devising on a guitar he never bothered to tune, songs with lyrics like *dum-diddle-diddle-dingle-dangle-doo*. This priest was like that, and surely a confrere too of the unfunky curate from St. Joachim's with his Broadway records, of Cousin Père Pierre with his Hummel figurines—of course he was, with his sheets and his paint chips and his brass bathroom fixtures. He was gay, had to be. Heterosexual men did not revel in the shininess of their doorknobs. They did not fuss and dust and tweak the way this Kearney did whenever he walked in the Refuge door. His affection was for the feminine, not the female; he clearly preferred shopping to anything else he might do with a woman, and shoppers, Martine had heard, tended to pair off.

But even if he was gay, he'd still have to be celibate, and in the end she still questioned whether a man this insistently alive could really bury all his need for human connection under a pile of bags from Holt's. She wondered this about all priests, but this one particularly. All the more so, now that he'd expressed a desire to drink champagne with her.

And there was much else about him that resisted interpretation. At first she had considered Father Kearney to be the new breed, but he now appeared to be his own breed. He retained enough tradition in him—clothing, prayer, undoubted kindness—to make him seem a man who'd started out right but had fallen away. Could be this world had made him fall away. This third world within the first.

As she got ready to crawl into her sleeping bag, Martine noticed that the green light on her answering machine was flashing on and off. Louise again. I really do have to call her, she thought.

W HEN SHE WENT TO WORK the next day, she realized sadly that her job was probably over, and just when she was getting used to it. Dianne was there again, drinking dreg-laden coffee with Muriel, Manny, and Glenys. It was too early for customers. When Martine joined them, however, they didn't ask her to leave or wonder why she was there again; Muriel, in fact, told Manny to "move over there, so's Martine can sit."

They were discussing the upcoming benefit.

"I'm wearing a nice red skirt I picked up at the Smart Mart," Glenys said, "and also a pleasant blouse I made myself from a Butterick pattern."

"A peasant blouse?" Martine asked.

"That's what I said."

"I'm showing up in what I got on," Dianne put in, "and if that's not good enough for Frost's mom, then she can kick me out."

Cynthia Macdonald

Martine leaned forward. "Frost's mom?"

"You heard it," said Dianne, picking a bit of tobacco off her lower lip. "Frost's parents live up where the sun always shines. They give Father K. lots of dough to run their kid's life for him, make sure he pays his rent on time." She yawned. "Usually they just send a cheque, though. They don't come in person, we never met 'em before. I bet they sterilize the china after we leave."

"Jews," said Muriel, clutching her New Testament to her chest.

Dianne ground her cigarette out violently. "Muriel, shut up about that shit for a second, would you?" she barked. "Besides, they're not."

"Well, they're some rich," Muriel snorted. "And Frost's dad was in that camp in the war, too."

"Yeah, well."

They all sat in silence for a second, smoking and chewing their coffee.

"But I'll tell you one thing," Muriel continued. "I haven't worn a dress since I was carrying with Manny and I'm not getting another for this. Take me as I am—I'm with you, Dianne. What are you wearing to this thing, missy?"

Martine had no idea; she'd hardly been counting on a Forest Hill party when she threw most of her clothes off the Don River Bridge. But Muriel answered for her.

"Probably that cape, I guess. You don't seem to own anything else. What's under there? I wonder."

"I'm sure it's one of these Academy Awards outfits," Glenys snickered, "with the diamonds and emeralds and such."

"Naw. Skin 'n' bones," mused Dianne.

The three women looked at each other conspiratorially and Martine felt herself shrink. Mere hours after her return, and Dianne had already consolidated a feminine junta whose purpose was to make her life intolerable. This—this whispering, sniggering, excluding—she judged to be established practice, the usual way they dispensed of Father Kearney's "girls."

Then Manny spoke. "Leave Martine alone," he said. Then he went back to leafing through some magazine with his beloved Lionel Richie on the cover.

The women did leave her alone, but in so cold a way that Martine felt that she had no choice but to go and start setting the place up by herself. There was old, old knowledge in the looks they traded. And when the priest came in ten minutes later—when he saw that the tables had been wiped, the floor swept, the vases refilled; when he said, "Hey girls! Come on, Martine can't do this alone!"—well *that,* she knew, was the end of her. As far as some people were concerned.

"Come on, ladies!" he repeated.

The three of them straggled slowly up and out of their chairs. Like thick-stemmed weeds.

Father Kearney stood close behind Martine as she spooned non-dairy creamer into the little tin bowls. "I mean," he said, "we're a team, aren't we?" He said it not quite loud enough for the other women to hear. She tried not to pay him any attention, and quickly placed the bowls on a tray, scooting out from around the counter to distribute them: table one, table two, table three. Some magnet had her walking robotically from one to the next, and she was determined not to look up at the priest.

But my job is over, she thought. I'm not even supposed to be here.

She realized that life at the Refuge was taking on something of the comfortingly dull automaticity of *Attitude!*, another place where the employees had had no time for her. But at least here she had a patron, someone looking out for her. A little too much, really. In his own way, Clayton Pine had been preferable.

She couldn't work the thought out, though, because when she got to table seven she was arrested by the sight of somebody standing outside the front window.

He was wearing that fancy sweater with the holes in it, a sweater that hardly protected its wearer against the cold in which he stood. She beckoned him inside.

"Sit down, Elly," she said. He parked himself at table seven and looked around. It was hard to tell what he was thinking, as usual, although he might have smiled a bit when he saw the Lady Di moustache picture.

"We're not open yet," Dianne said, and so coldly that Martine felt she must see everything in Elliott's past: every piano lesson, every plane ride he ever took.

"Now, Dianne, that's no way to treat a guest," Father Kearney admonished, and rushed over to him, hand poised as always for a shake. "Father Kearney's my name and what can we do for you today?"

"I asked him to come, Father," Martine said. "He's an old . . . friend. I thought you might be able to use him sometimes. For driving? He's a very good driver."

The priest looked him over warily. "But we already have a driver." Frost was present, but in no position to listen in. He was slumped at table one, apparently asleep.

"Just in case Frost needs a rest every now and then," Martine replied swiftly.

Of course, Frost looked in no shape to drive today, or even to get up. His face was so flattened to the table that he was likely breathing through his ears, if at all. And Father Kearney would need a driver today, as he did every day; like Martine, he seemed not to have a licence himself, or perhaps it had been taken away.

He frisked the young man with his eyes. "You look like a serious fellow. What's your name?"

"Elliott Pine, sir."

He pointed at Martine. "And are you two . . . *special* friends? Martine had to run out early last night. Was it—to see you?"

They both blushed and Elliott told him no.

"But you've known each other a while, I gather."

"Since we were kids," Elliott said nobly.

"Well, Martine's a good Christian. Too good, some might say, but heaven even makes a place for folks like her. Are you like that?"

"I don't know," Elliott stammered. "I guess you'd have to decide that on your own."

"Can you drive a truck?"

"I can drive anything."

The priest crossed his arms in the way he obviously thought made him look important. "Still. Frost won't like it when he wakes up and finds himself rolling around in the back, will he?"

Elliott turned to go, but Martine took him by the elbow and bade him wait. Then she asked Father Kearney for a private word. This he granted her, but instead of leading her into the back room, as she'd expected, he stalked passed Elliott to the frigid street.

"This guy could help you," she told him when they got there. "He's had a bad break. He just finished—uh . . . well, you know, *doing a little time*."

"Oh yeah?" asked the priest, deeply interested now. "Why, what for?"

This was the sort of job experience that seemed to get Father Kearney's ear like nothing else. When he spotted a fallen bird, you could instantly hear him rustling eagerly in his pockets for a splint.

"It doesn't matter," Martine said. "I'm sure—you have my word on this—I'm positive he didn't do what they said he did. He's a good guy, Father. He'll help you out. And Frost will understand. It's just for when he's, you know, tired."

The priest regarded her a moment and she couldn't tell if he was staring at her, or whether her face was an object that just happened to be in the way while he thought it over.

"I mean, Frost really shouldn't be driving," Martine said. "Ever."

Father Kearney looked down at the sidewalk. "I know," he said mildly. After a bit he jerked his head in exasperation and muttered, "Bah, I'll try him out. Why not, we hardly have anything to do today. Especially since . . ." Here he looked through the window at sleeping Frost, whose red box lay beside him on the table, like an obedient pet.

"We'll try him out," the priest repeated. "If you like him, he's okay by me."

And so, unbeknownst to him, Frost was demoted. In the weeks that Martine had been at the Refuge he had in fact changed for the worse. Every night she watched him distribute the strange, scrawled cards across the board for another round of the game he loved to play, which she knew now was called "Calendar." His fingers had grown more shaky with time and last night he couldn't even pick the cards up; Martine did it for him. On the cards, she noticed, were inscribed a series of minor dates and events: FIRST USE OF INSTANT REPLAY ON TELEVISION. INDUS RIVER TREATY SIGNED BY INDIA AND PAKISTAN. AUGUST STRINDBERG IS BORN. The handwriting was uncertain, the pen faulty.

She played Calendar with him once. To do it she had to flick a complicated tripartite spinner which landed on a random year, date, and month combination. Then she had to name not one but two events that happened on that day — so if she'd landed on November 22, 1963, it would not have done to say the obvious; she'd also have had to know that Hud was number three at the box office that day, C. S. Lewis had also died, and that a congressman from Iowa had filed objections to the Equal Pay Act. At a certain point, when the score was 24–0, she tried to make up an event, but Frost only bared his teeth and demanded that she prove it. Frost was not only the sole possible victor at Calendar, but the only player who ever earned a single point.

"This is stupid," Martine said toward the end of their game, as she threw the spinner onto the board. "How do you expect me to win a game against the person who invented it?"

"Uh-huh," Frost slurred belligerently. "Well, then I'd ask you this: how many World Series rings do you think Abner Doubleday ownnnnns?"

"I don't know," Martine pouted. "I don't even know who he plays for."

Frost reared up and shouted down at her, his breath a rain of sour gas: "He doesn't play for anyone, Ms. Einstein! He invented fucken baseball, didn't he?" He started repacking the box angrily, with a childish lack of care. "In April, 1839. Not sure of the day, but no one is."

"Well, we can't all be as smart as you," Martine snapped, reeling from his breath.

"Nope. Yea verily but we can't," Frost growled.

But she would not be vanquished by a loser, no matter the terms of the game. She would just have to argue herself unto victory. She followed him to the door. "There's no real practical reason to know all these dates, is there? There's nothing you can do with that kind of talent, am I right?" He grunted with such disgust that she immediately feared he might spit on her, black tarry slime from the devil's very throat. But he just continued on for the door. And that was the last time she'd see any vivacity at all from Frost.

I've killed him, she thought.

Her guilt about their fight swelled by the day. She hit on the idea that if she showed some respect for Calendar he'd come off this funk, or binge, or whatever it was that had him staring slack-jawed out the door or slumped on the table every day. To that end she'd stopped by a library to look Abner Doubleday up in the encyclopedia. She photocopied articles about him and committed them to memory. But when she brought this knowledge to Frost, when she shook his arm gently and said, "Hey . . . I found out more about that Doubleday guy. He was a Civil War hero, you know, born in 1819—here, I have the date somewhere," he brushed her off, made her feel like a buzzing hornet.

She decided not to tell him that there was some doubt about Abner Doubleday's having invented baseball in the first place.

Even Father Kearney's usual good spirits were tested by Frost's decline. He counted on the uptown elegance hidden within the man's rotted packaging. Without that sparkling inner life, Frost was no better than any of the other winos shambling about on the sidewalks outside, whose faces told not of things lost but things never had.

But they couldn't just leave him at the Refuge today—leave him there, and have him wake up to find that he'd been replaced by yet another high-born lowlife.

Kearney strode back inside and turned to Elliott. "Let's take you on a little run and see how it goes," he said. Then he went over to Frost and shook him gently. "Time for tennis, old bean. Jeeves has come to warm the limo for us."

The men left, simple as that. Martine had entertained the fleeting thought that she might get taken along, too, as a sort of finder's fee, but of course she was left behind here, in the fields, with dreadful women who hated her. Meanwhile—she reflected with her mother's traditional distaste toward the boy—*Elliott* was allowed to go. Back in the day she'd always felt bad about his being Michael Collins, staying in the space capsule, but geez—at least

Michael Collins got to go into space! Martine was no better than an astronaut's wife!

Kearney did warn her at the outset that he'd never be there. He even paid her anonymously: popped an envelope full of bills under the door while she was sleeping. Why couldn't she "never be there" for a change? She always planned to collar him in the foyer to ask about it, but where was he for her to do that? She thought of the purple satin sheets, and decided that she couldn't very well go upstairs.

Dianne grabbed a handful of knives and forks. "Let's set the tables," she ordered.

Some people lead such apparently undesirable lives that it is tempting for the better-favoured to believe that misfortune must come naturally to them, that they must want it that way. When Martine saw old Suleiman caning his painful way down the street into the Refuge each night, his worn nylon windbreaker ridiculous in October, lethal come November, she thought, Well, at least he has his poetry . . . at least he has . . . he has . . . but poverty must have its compensations! I can't see them, but they must be there! A mere lack of money needn't slit the soul! Look, he's even smiling!

But Dianne offered her no such out, because Dianne was miserable, bitter, and hard.

Martine put the knives down blade out, as she'd been taught to do, but then Dianne angrily went around behind her, changing them to blade in. "It's blade out," Martine protested quietly. "No," Dianne replied, "blade's supposed to face you, otherwise it's rude to your dining companion." Martine continued to set the knives down her way, though her hand shook as she did so. "Yes," she said at length, "but if it's blade in, it's rude to *you*."

Dianne stopped and looked at Martine, her eyes the colour of dried blood. "So who's more important — you or someone else?" Martine was too scared to continue the argument, but inwardly she seethed. "I think" — crunching the words, hoping Dianne would not hear her — "*I* know which way the blade goes."

"If you know that, then that's all you probably know." So ended their conversation.

It was a slow night, ferociously rainy, and Glenys knocked off early with a headache. Dianne and Martine decided to wait out the weather a bit after they'd finished cleaning up and the customers had all left. Dianne took a smoke break at one table, while Martine sat reading the paper across the room.

"Community service?"

Martine looked up from the fashion section, startled. She thinks — she thinks I'm here because I'm a criminal? "Of course not," she laughed nervously.

"No shame in it. That's how I started."

It was terrifying to contemplate what sort of criminal this woman might be, though Martine was certainly curious. But to ask might be to call a knife into her throat, blade right-side up.

"So you know Father, then," Dianne said, a little sarcastically. That was the choice: in this realm bad sluts got taken shopping and good maidens polished cutlery, and there was really no third type of woman unless you cared to create one, which Martine did. "I don't know anybody," she said proudly, not realizing that a third type—flaming lunatic—also existed, and in great numbers, and it was under this column heading that Dianne was now mentally marking Martine's name in indelible ink.

"I see. He try and feel you up yet?"

Martine sat back in her chair and stared. She wasn't sure if she heard right. "Of course not."

"Sure he must have. He does everybody," Dianne replied, her words carried on an impossibly large cloud of smoke. "Anyways, Glenys says you're staying with him."

"Well, but, uh—it's—it's not like that."

Dianne shrugged and stared into the red-painted sign, the one that encouraged you to love your neighbour as yourself, relishing (Martine was certain) the panic she'd just set off. But Martine calmed, after an admittedly frenzied couple of seconds. She didn't trust anything anyone said here, and if she were asked to pick a side, it sure wouldn't be Dianne's.

"You from Toronto?" Dianne asked.

"Yes."

"Where?"

Oh, but Martine wasn't about to fall into the Perpetual Help trap again. She looked back down at her newspaper, at the pretty models with their ice-cream-coloured sweaters and teased, fountainous manes, their little rolled socks and jelly sandals. It occurred to her that the newspaper was at least three months old. "North," she said.

"Jane-Finch?"

"Around there."

"Hmm," Dianne said. "You don't look Jamaican." She stubbed out her cigarette.

The two women waited for the rain to stop, but it didn't stop and it didn't stop, and it kept not stopping until someone was forced to say something else.

"I got a skirt you could wear to that party," Dianne said.

Martine looked up.

"You could keep it if you want. Doesn't fit me any more." She put on her jacket and cap, flipped her long hair back. "Has a top that goes with it. I'll bring 'em tomorrow." Then she got up and left.

When Martine got home she felt the perverse instinct to check her messages. Just get it over with and call home, was her thinking. She had convinced herself that feeling bad about ignoring her mother's messages was equal to the decency of returning them. But the first message wasn't from Louise at all. It was from her grandfather. Pépère was in town; he said that Louise had been taken to the hospital, but he didn't say why.

Martine splurged on a taxi to the General, site of some reasonably heroic candystriping back in the day. She was not worried, not worried at all. If she just kept breathing in short, light puffs, she could stem the dread, at least until she got there. There was every chance it was just liposuction, which Sharon Colterblake had recently undergone. Or maybe her mother had finally had the trick hip replaced—which would be a good thing, even if the hip had formed, of late, her personality's very nucleus.

The hospital felt clean and safe and the sight of so many worker bees in white and pink was delightful to her. She decided there could never be any real illness in a place like this. She thought, at least more gets fixed here than doesn't.

Cynthia Macdonald

The sight of sick people in their wrinkled blue johnny shirts was also strangely cheering. You couldn't tell where such people came from or what they looked like before they got sick. Some of their flesh was light, some of it dark, but apart from that they all appeared to have hatched from the very same egg and for that she envied them. They had fellows, millions of fellows, all across the world wearing the very same uniform. Their boneless hands and downward mouths would be pathetic in the outside world. Here, they were just ethnic folk dress.

On her way to the elevator she passed by a sign with a black arrow under it: HIV Primary Care Clinic.

Louise was in a private room on the tenth floor, surrounded by flowers. Pépère was sitting on the bed at her feet. *"Ohé!"* he called, springing from the bed and enveloping Martine in a suffocating embrace. *"Tapasgrossi d'puis-ladernière foisk'j' taivu,"* he said, or something like that. He insisted on speaking French around Martine, even though his English was perfect and he knew she couldn't understand him. She just nodded at everything he said in his own language, and took his speaking of it as a welcome break, since she violently disagreed with everything he said in English.

Louise had, apparently, fractured her tibia. Skating, she said—if you could believe that, which Martine couldn't. Louise had in fact been an accomplished skater in her youth—"almost in the Ice Capades" was the motto traditionally attached to that youth—but her daughter could only dimly remember her actually taking to the ice; though it was a nice memory, too, the sudden confidence in this ordinarily

fragile woman as she propelled herself backwards in powerful, simple waves, tilting impossibly to the side as if she
might fall over, but she never did; and for her to resurrect that
memory in Martine, for her to try and pretend she was still
athletic like that, graceful like that, was somehow wrong.
Unacceptable.

On the other hand, Martine was astonished to see that her
mother was smiling and alert. Rosy. Groomed. Uppers?

"She was doing a jump," remarked Pépère sourly. "I don't
know why! I taught her to skate myself. Obviously not too
well, *hein?*"

Louise looked apologetic. She crossed pale hands and
looked down to the untouched dinner tray that sat before
her. "He won't let me eat the soup," she laughed. "It's
Campbell's."

"Pig slop," spat Pépère. "But give it to Martine anyway.
She could use it."

"*Je ne veux—je n'en veux*—I don't want any," Martine
said.

"Sure, if you say," he shrugged. He was chewing gum, as
usual. For all his millions, Pépère was really quite the hick.
He had always been rather awful to Louise whenever he
came to visit, criticizing her for this or that every time she
approached the table with his toast, his butter and jam, his
coffee, his paper. When they visited him in the great house in
Outremont, he usually rose early and went out golfing or to a
meeting, leaving them with the lavender-scented Mémère,
a kind but distant woman who was always in bed with one
complication or another from the lupus that eventually killed
her. Pépère was, comparatively speaking, quite lively and

entertaining, with his great plume of cottony white hair and bowed, jangly limbs. Martine found it hard to take him as seriously as Louise did.

"Well, do I stay longer?" he now spluttered. "Have we covered everything?"

"Oui, Papa," Louise whispered. "I think that's everything."

"Good!" He jumped up and patted her on the affected leg, which made her wince. *"Ecoutetuvasmappelertantôt,okay?"* he grunted. Then he kissed Martine and left.

Whenever Pépère was around, Martine became instantly defensive of her mother. She could not bear his insistence that everyone be as successful and hard-working as he—risen from nothing, recipient of the Italy Star, hero of the Royal 22nd Regiment—had been. "A winner, Martine!" he'd yelled at her one day after unearthing one of her more notably gory report cards. "Don't you want to be a winner in life?"

"For every winner there has to be a loser," she'd told him. She was cleaning up after a lunch that only he'd eaten, watching him hold court at the great harvest table in their kitchen. "It's much better to *make* one than to *be* one, Pépère. I mean—look—because of me, someone else doesn't have to suffer having the lowest marks in the class." He hadn't found this funny.

"You're like your mother," he said, swatting the air with her report card. "You know she could have been in a play with Christopher Plummer? But she turned it down. Why? To marry that *cris' de* Farmer Trotsky!"

Farmer Trotsky was the Professor, whom he despised—even before the man left his daughter high and dry in a big old house. They'd done nothing but argue from the day they met—or at least from the day the Professor discovered the story of Rodrigue Brault's leg.

"It was a lawful protest, On-Ree. I can't believe you called in the police to beat up your own workers."

"They were there to keep peace and I'm not gonna apologize to you if someone got out of hand! I didn't mean for that to happen and you know it!"

"He never walked properly again. He had eight goddamn children."

"How do you know all that, *hein*? How do you know how he walks? Maybe right now he's out playing for the Expos, stealing the third base—how would you know he's not? Are you his buddy or something? *Defender of the people*. Have you ever even talked to any other French Canadian, outside of this family?"

"Oh, don't give me that crap, On-Ree. You play mister big nationalist now—but where were you in the conscription crisis?"

"I fought for my country!"

"Yeah, well it's hardly *your*—"

Here the Professor looked over at his terrified wife, who was standing with a tray of cocktail sausages at the entrance to the kitchen, the girl he married because she was so talented, so beautiful, so kind, but above all so *oppressed,* and it came to him now that—on at least the last of these counts—he just might have been wrong.

"Such arrogance," Pépère said to him, in a controlled voice that was full of hate. "Look up from your little pile of manure, *mon fermier*. Telling a Québécois what it means to be Québécois—if you could listen to yourself!"

The Professor pushed his chair away from the table and stood, the better to loom over his father-in-law. But he was shaking, anyone could see, uncertain now of his own certainty.

"Some of you *need* telling," he burst, at last. "Not most of you, but some."

Later, after the death of poor Bruno Poirier, the two men never spoke at all, but by then the die was cast. Pépère had even flirted with the idea of disowning Louise after the wedding, but he didn't. Secretly he loved her too much. This was the thing about Louise: everyone loved her, and everyone kept it a secret.

"Your mother was almost in the Ice Capades one year. I'm damn sure she never told you *that*," he told Martine, that day he found her report card.

Louise hadn't, actually. But Pépère had, over and over. Sometimes Martine would catch him looking at his daughter with the most extraordinary admiration; he would marvel at her for minutes at a time, until he recalled her most fundamental life choices, which made him snap out of it and start grumbling at her. Over time the grumbling had its effect on Louise.

"Oh, that's just a silly old thing," she would say whenever Martine dug up an old picture of her, radiant in a bathing suit, pouting beneath the brim of a wide-brimmed hat; she'd modelled, too, and no wonder. Her eyes alone stopped Martine's heart, the fresh blue honesty of them perceptible even in black and white. "I was just play-acting, really. What did I know?" In these pictures she was the most stunning thing Martine had ever seen, and it was sad to see her soft-pedalling the power of them in order to make Martine feel just as beautiful, because it never worked.

On the back of the picture in green ink: August 1961. "A month before I met your father," she said, and it was surpassingly odd, Martine thought, to think that her parents had ever met, married, and set up house. Another in a series of fantastical tales told at bedtime by a mother to her child: the wolf who dressed up as a grandmother; the princess who slept for a hundred years; the bears who ate porridge and slept in real beds; and, least believable of all, the Saskatchewan farmer who fell for the pretty French girl.

"I see they have that HIV thing up and running," Martine said. "The one that you had the Fandango in the park for."

"Yes," replied Louise, zealously spooning soup now that her father had gone. "It's only been open for a week. Sharon did such a great job organizing that party, she always does." Martine flinched. She looked nervously at the giant vial of white pills that now stood beside her mother's hospital bed. It was twice the size of the ones she kept in her medicine cabinet at home.

"What are those, Mama?"

"Oh—just some pills they gave me for the pain. Very intensive aspirin, I suppose."

"Do you think . . . do you really need them? You have aspirin at home, I mean."

Louise put her spoon down and looked at Martine with mild surprise. "Yes, but the pain is very bad, *chouette*. I had a pin put in my leg. If I only took regular painkillers—well, they wouldn't do enough."

True. Who was this girl to advocate a deepening of her mother's pain? "Rpts: 3," said the pill bottle. At least it wasn't six. Yet. Martine turned to look at the bile-green hallway and said, "I suppose you'll be needing a lot of help. At home."

Here Louise took her hand and affected her old brightness. "Ah, Martini, don't worry about me. Sharon's picking me up on Thursday and she'll be all the help I need. I have Emelda, too, of course. You just continue on with—with whatever it is that you're doing."

Martine gasped. "I'm sorry I haven't called, Mama. I . . . I wanted to."

Louise gazed at her with a calm neutrality Martine had never seen; her hair was pulled back, her eyebrows expertly plucked; and the younger woman felt newly conscious of her own chapped lips and uncombed hair, accessories Louise had recently favoured but strangely did not now.

"Are you all right?" her mother asked.

"Me? I'm fine." Martine patted herself, a little wildly. "No broken bones here. I'm fine. I'm fine."

Louise smiled. "Great," she said, then started on her green Jell-O.

What was wrong with her? Here was a woman who, when alert, would practically threaten self-immolation if Martine so much as left half her cereal in the bowl. But now she sat, still and lacquered as a painting, even though her daughter had obviously never been in such trouble. Where was the flailer, the cajoler of yesteryear? Where was the woman who ran for the Yellow Pages, the white pages—*Oh, is there a doctor I can call?* The woman who went to the Mount Pleasant Library and came back with a pile of books with titles like *Understanding Your Teen: Problems Defined, Problems Fixed*—"defined" printed in angry Martine red, "fixed" below it in serene Louise green. "The book says she has to gain weight before she can gain weight," Martine once heard her weeping into the phone. "But how can I get the weight on her? Maybe I could slip it under her pillow, like tooth fairy money . . . or sneak it into her Christmas stocking, I don't know. Oh God, Sharon, I just don't know." And this was back when Martine was eating ten servings a day!

But fate had finally returned this child to her, scarred and battered after uncrewed months on the high seas, and now that it had happened she just didn't seem to care any more.

"Mama," Martine said, "that story about skating—it isn't true, is it? What were you really doing?"

"I was skating."

"Come on. If you fell down the stairs, you can tell me. I won't judge you. Who was with you? Was it a man? Did Mack come back?"

"No, no, I was alone. I just felt like skating. That's all."

It didn't make any sense. It was like a reel of film with hundreds of frames blacked out in the middle, a film there was consequently no point in watching. Women are reliable, creatures of pattern. If a woman drinks one bottle of rosé on Wednesday, she can generally be counted on to drink two on Thursday and three on Friday. She doesn't go fucking *skating* in the middle of it all.

And the worst part of this senseless recovery was that Sharon lay behind it. Sharon Colterblake, not Martine Craythorn, was the big star of this maddening and gap-ridden film; Martine didn't even get a walk-on. "You'll be better off without me," write the suicides, and sometimes they are right. But Martine had no taste for suicide. That was for others. For her mother, maybe. She'd thought!

"Mama," she said, "you're acting sort of . . . I don't know. You're acting sort of different."

Louise put down her spoon. "This food is terrible," she laughed. "Oh, I was a little gloomy after Mack left, wasn't I?"

"A little! *After* Mack left!"

"All right, all right. But it's over now, so." She smiled to signal that there would be no more talk of it, that there would perhaps be no more talk of anything at all. Martine was free to go and Louise would not ask where.

I'd believe in redemption, Martine thought. If I could just see its gears and pulleys, if I could just learn how it worked.

"Your father's been calling for you," Louise said. "He really wants you to take Obike to the Science Centre."

"What did you tell him?"

"I said I didn't know where you were," Louise said, then started laughing. "And you know what he said? He told me I was an *uncaring parent*." She laughed a little harder at this, and Martine couldn't help but join her; soon their giggling bordered on the helpless. But then Martine sobered, got a grip on herself.

"Mama, do you . . . do you really not need me? At home, to do anything?"

Louise picked up her daughter's cold reddened hand and rubbed it. "I don't *need* you. I love you, and that's much more important."

Martine sat back in the chair and looked around the blocky white room, enlivened by the sort of autumn flowers she hadn't even thought to bring. There was a little ridge of cards by the windowsill, too. At least someone had brought them, there was comfort in that. She stared at her mother's half-eaten tray.

"Do you want some of this?" Louise asked, surprised. Martine picked up the spoon and the little Jell-O container and finished off the dessert within seconds. Then she plunked them back on the tray and scowled, like a grumpy toddler.

Louise smiled. "You're okay," she said. "You don't know it yet, but you are."

Sure, I'd believe in redemption, Martine thought. If it ever happened to me.

*T*HE BENEFIT AT FROST'S old house was nigh. What
little clothing Martine had stored on Merseyfield could not be
worn there: the bright discomfort its designers had cleverly
snuck into it had all been soaked out in a dingy laundromat.
And the skirt and top that Dianne brought for her—or rather,
pitched at her upon entering the Refuge the following
evening—only sort of fit, but it would have to do. Too many
sequins, too much sparkling lurex thread for Martine's taste;
excesses of black Orlon hung in mournful hammocks from
her vanished breasts. She put the outfit on anyway, worked at
her hair until it sprang at the brush's touch, then applied
some rust-coloured blusher she'd found hanging incongruously off a nail at S and S Convenience.

But I'm . . . devastating! she thought sourly, inspecting
herself in the bathroom mirror. She really couldn't tell—
either she looked passable or even more horrible, like some

anthropomorphic mop. Others would know. They always did. "Martine, you're so pretty. If you just gained ten pounds, you'd be even better." This she had often heard, but was never able to understand. It was like telling a blind painter to slap more red on the canvas. Where is the canvas? she wanted to ask. And what is red? The odd time she would catch sight, say, of her left knee, and it would appear to her so un-left knee-like that she could only agree with them. But the image never stayed with her. She had been pretty, and now she was ugly, and her experience in the world was no different one way or another.

Now it happened, later that night, that the silk and the powder were not lost on Father Kearney, but given their recent friction on the subject of Martine's looks, he could hardly comment on them with impunity. "You ready, my dear?" he barked, rapping on her door. And when she answered it: "Oh!"

He looked surprisingly presentable himself, having been treated to a shave and haircut by Dianne that afternoon. Even two floors above, Martine had been able to hear her barking at him: "Stay still, for Christ's sake! I can't work a miracle, but I don't want you scarin' little kids either." Yet she had worked a small miracle.

"You look . . ." Martine blurted.

"Like what?"

"Like—a priest!"

He coloured deeply in response. "Thanks," he said. "I guess."

In the taxi on the way to the party, they started talking about Frost. Martine refused to believe that he came from where they were bound. The street was one of the city's most opulent. If he had fallen from that lofty a perch, how could his parents ever bear it?

"So where does he live now?" she asked.

"Not too far from us. He's got a little room down the road a piece." Father Kearney gathered his fingers in front of him and frowned into the bony latticework. "He's doing good. I know he's been a little off lately, but he's getting better. He'll be great tonight, you'll see."

The taxi passed two giggling girls with giant, moussed hair and fingerless gloves: not a care in the world, Martine told herself. Wish I were one of them.

"He drinks all the time," she said. "Doesn't he?"

"Well, he *is* a drunk, Martine. He's only doing his job." She didn't laugh, so he ignored her and kept looking out the window. "Would you look at these new townhouses," he said. "I'll bet they're not so nice inside, though."

She pressed on. "What's this about Frost being a doctor?"

Father Kearney continued to stare into the townhouses, craning for a view of the dining-room tables, the happy families around them. "Oh, that. Well, we all have things we were *going* to do, don't we? How about you, Perpetual Help— maybe you wanted to lead safaris in Africa, or be a great artist, or . . . ah, don't we all have those dreams, and don't they hardly ever work out. There's only one thing you can do about them, if you want to stop yourself from going mad. And that's pretend they all came true."

Father Kearney asked the driver to let them out before they reached their destination. "Let's walk a bit," he suggested. The taxi stopped on a quiet street festooned with great, slumbering maples. Martine strolled the sidewalk with an exquisite sense of relief, which she tried not to show: she felt home again. But Kearney refused to play cool. He gaped at each splendid gingerbread estate as if it were on fire. "The house you grew up in," he asked, "was it like these?"

"I suppose. They're really all the same, these places."

He wrapped a protective arm around her. He was her chum now. He was gearing up for another great time. "Aha, no, no, my dear, no. Maybe the people in them are all the same, but the houses themselves, they've all got their own character. Aren't they something! Look at this yellow fella with the shutters—a gorgeous big wreath on that door in a week or two and he'll be a living Christmas card." He shook his head in awe.

Martine did not like or understand this arm around her, this talk of houses. The priest wore Jeremy's brand of cologne and pressed his fingers into the still-soft way station between her back and her front, though she was sure the pressing was only due to his enthusiasm for the shutters. What might she say that would shake him off? "Frost's parents," she tried, a little too loudly. "Do they support him?"

It worked. He released her and resumed walking. When he spoke again, he sounded almost angry. "An odd question from you, Martine. I didn't think you were the type to care where the beans were coming from."

She was surprised and not a little angry herself; but she had asked for it, this new assault on her origins. "I was just wondering," she said.

"You pick some strange things to wonder about. Why don't you take your eyes off the sidewalk and look at the scenery for a change. You'll see sights a hell of a lot prettier 'n cement."

They passed another house, a beautiful, still thing. On the porch, two delicate hanging lanterns bathed a pot of oriental cabbage in soft white light. There were a jumble of pumpkins in different sizes, to celebrate Hallowe'en just past: one for each family member, Martine presumed. It was prettier than cement, yes.

"You know, I've been wondering about something, too," said the priest. "I know you worked at Helping Hands before. Did you ever do any other kind of work . . . of that type?"

"What do you mean?"

"Oh, soup kitchens, food banks, that sort of thing."

Martine laughed regretfully, recalling her failures chez Flavio and the Reading Action Committee. "Actually, I'm not so sure any of those places would have me any more."

"Of course they wouldn't!" the priest exclaimed. Which alarmed her.

"What do you mean?"

"Because they're all such perfect little people working at those places, Martine, all of them rackin' up anecdotes for their eulogies while helping the downtrodden. The men don't wear suspenders like they do on Bay Street, but I see 'em. When really they're just doing—in a far less efficient way— the government's job. The government should feed its poor. People can't do it themselves, and they're plain arrogant to think they can."

Now he was getting into politics and what could bore her more. The word "government" induced conversational polio in all who uttered it, as far as she was concerned. So she was quiet for a while, but then the obvious occurred to her. "But you . . . you feed them, too, Father."

He was ready for this. "Oh, I give 'em coffee and maybe a little snack. A place to sit. But no one's gonna get three squares from me. I'm not God—I don't pretend I can keep anyone alive."

"Yes, but . . ." Yes, but one night she'd stayed late at Helping Hands to prune the files, chuck the records of clients who'd stopped showing up. There was banging on the door and she was the only one there. She'd walked up to the door—thick, well locked, unwindowed—and said, "Yes?"

"You have anything to eat in there?" came a man's voice, muffled by the door. "I'm hungry. You got something to eat?"

She shuddered. "Sorry, we're closed."

No reply, but then: "I'm hungry."

"You can go downtown, to the Good Shepherd or something . . . I don't know . . ."

"I need a token for that, though."

Martine looked up at the sign on the wall. *Rule Four: Do not ask staff for money, credit, subway tokens, etc.* Then she thought of Maureen, Methadone Maureen, who was always asking for extra cookies, tokens, and spare change for "my friend's little autistic girl." Don't believe a word of it, Claudia had warned.

"I'm sorry," Martine said. "You can come back tomorrow." She stood by the door for three tense minutes, until she was satisfied that the man had given up and walked away.

Yes, Father, but there's the matter of the meantime: the meantime between now and when the government, or God, or whoever, gets its act together and fills all the bellies properly. In that meantime, who's going to do it, if not you or me? She wanted to say all this and was just about to—but here was the priest, already striding up the Frosts' long stone walkway and there was no time. A big smile he had on, too, as if he'd heard the "yes," and deafened himself to the "but."

Frost's gracious mother seemed happy to receive them. "Clifford!" she exclaimed, but with a slight European accent: Cleeford. "Don't you look nice tonight." She kissed him on both cheeks; they seemed awfully familiar with one another.

Martine took to the living room with an ease that embarrassed her, and tried to remind herself how much she'd always hated Louise's dinner parties, funerals where the corpses outnumbered the mourners. But it didn't work. She closed her eyes and inhaled the canapés and artificially freshened air; she hummed imperceptibly along with Bach's French Suites, plinking from a hidden stereo console. She looked over toward a large Chinese planter and saw an authoritative, handsome man in a Hugo Boss suit standing next to it, conversing with grace and ease; he was uncannily endowed with Frost's pale, bulging eyes and sandy sweep of hair, and though the white teeth and easy laugh seemed grafted on, loaners, she had no doubt it *was* Frost, made suddenly clean and brilliant. But as she strode toward him with congratulatory zeal her eye hooked on another, more familiar presence in the opposite corner. Holding a red cardboard box and a glass—of water? Sure. Well, at least he was standing up. Bathed, shaven, and with laces in his basketball shoes. But still a far cry from the suit-clad doppelgänger.

Alms

All the Fiat Lux Refugees were there, except Elliott. The Salvadorans, Suleiman, the whole roster, including Muriel, who still clutched her New Testament and kept her eye on Manny as he perused the massive record collection. "He lost his purse, you know," said his mother. "And with all his Lionel Richie money in it. Idiot."

Martine watched the boy's wretched hands riffling through the albums. Mozart, Beethoven, Miles Davis, an assortment of Broadway soundtracks, some Polish folk songs. No Lionel Richie. She remembered that twenty-dollar bill, all folded up like some crippled origami swan. She had one of her own to give him now, she could make it right. Rule Four, though. Rule Four. If she made the giving extracurricular, where would it end?

Father Kearney swilled his sparkling wine and suppressed a burp. "Why are all these toffs looking so glum?" he wondered. "This is a party."

"It is that crash with the stock market, Father," Suleiman told him. "Terrible thing. You might not get very many donations after all."

"Ah! Is that it? Buy high, sell low," the priest exclaimed. "I keep telling these guys, and telling these guys—but do they ever listen to me? No, and look what happens."

"The stock market," said Muriel through vicious little teeth. "Well, let me tell you about *that*." She set to thumbing ferociously through her good book to find a passage probative of her general views on the Devil, the Zionist Conspiracy, and the NASDAQ, but Father Kearney grabbed her hand.

"Never mind. What we don't get, we'll just steal," he said with a wink at Martine. At once his attention was taken by a guest across the room. A young woman. He motioned violently to Frost, who shambled over obediently.

"Frost, who's that young lady in the corner? The one dressed like Stokely Carmichael."

"Oh," said Frost, "that's my cousin Christina. Who hates me. I mean all my relatives hate me, but she's the president of hating me. I'm sure my mom's sister forced her to come. She just came back from Thailand or some place like that. She writes travel poetry."

Frost explained that Christina was very "international." She had a degree in Latin American literature and always dressed like a gift-shop souvenir. She had lovers in all ports, men of the earth, intensely tanned goatherds and artisans. Usually these were married guys with about seven children who would be left screaming and hungry when Dad went traipsing off for moonlit swims with his freckled Canadian trollop. One time Christina had been bold enough to move in with her lover's family in Indonesia, forcing his benighted wife to feed and shelter her. Two of the children tried to poison her, though, and she almost died—an experience that led to an entire book of poems called *The Curare Cycle,* which had been reviewed in the local paper. The headline read: BLAME THIS ONE ON BLUE CROSS.

"That's quite the dashooky thing she's wearing." Father Kearney sipped his drink and stared at the girl intently. She was pale, a little plump, and very pretty; one imagined the hair underneath the turban she wore to be glossy and fair, like that of Mrs. Frost.

"Yeah, well, I don't think real African tribeswomen wear shoulder pads under *their* outfits," Martine sniffed.

Curious, though. Martine felt jealous, and her jealousy was reflexive, the sort of thing she always felt in the presence of confident, physically plush girls. But she also thought Father Kearney might be staring at the girl, and not just her outfit, and that bothered her. Why should it, though?

"A pretentious getup, to be sure, but it does inspire a certain . . . curiosity in a man. Frost, how come you never mentioned her before?"

Frost laughed and stubbed his cigarette out in a delicate porcelain vessel clearly unmeant for such defilement. "Well, Father, she was always a little *young* before."

"She's a little young now," laughed Father Kearney, a touch too loudly; several chiffoned matrons looked over at him with pursed lips and Martine stepped warningly on his foot, with more energy than was absolutely needed. He cried out in pain and scowled at her, but his interest in the girl was undiminished. He pulled Frost toward him. "Now then, Doctor. Introduce me to cousin Christina, an intrepid woman of . . . of . . ."

"Great intrepidness," said Frost.

"Yes, an intrepid woman of extreme intrepidness, never at home anywhere and looking for spiritual sustenance. I know the type." Father Kearney always knew the type. "She's been voyaging the seven seas in search of a guy like me. Do you think she likes priests? Frost, what're my chances?"

Martine was confused and sickened by this conversation, this attempt to parody a man screwing up his courage to pick up a girl at a party. Either he was being cruel to such hopeful, lovesick, gentle men, or it wasn't a parody at all.

Frost, however, was practically retching with glee. The subversion he somehow thought was inherent in their attendance here had him laughing almost continuously. "Maybe— maybe if you told her you were a missionary!"

"You know, I *was* once," Father Kearney giggled into Frost's neck, "but later I felt—I felt it was time to move on to more exotic . . . positions!"

Martine silently wished them both dead. Sexual innuendo did not suit either of them and they had no right to it. In her mind they were not and would never be Real Guys, football-watching, backslapping, beer-drinking guys, and if that's how they saw themselves tonight—well, how pathetic.

She looked around and noticed Dianne sitting on a couch by herself, looking extremely uncomfortable and sipping at a can of ginger ale. She was wearing a stretch-denim pantsuit and the flowered blouse; she *had* put on something nice, after all.

But the poetess was advancing, and you could see from Father Kearney's face that he could barely believe his good fortune. He stood up straight and cleared his throat.

"Father Clifford Kearney," he said, offering his hand, "and may I say what a delight it is to finally meet you."

"Enchantée," replied Christina, with only the slightest trace of revulsion. A waitress came along and offered them some bruschetta, which she pronounced "brooshetta."

"No *broosketta* for me," Christina corrected briskly. *"Mille grazie, signorina, ma non ho fame."* The waitress retired with a baffled expression.

"I hear you're a poet," said Father Kearney jauntily. "I'd love to experience some of your work."

"Well, then you're most welcome to read it," she snapped. "Papers Bookstore. Eight dollars." Her English was flecked with unsetttling notes of Urdu and Catalan.

"I already read it anyway," blurted Frost.

"Is that true, Alexander? Tell me, which poem did you like the best?" She was too smart, this Christina, smart enough to know that nobody had bought her work and nobody ever would.

"I . . . can't pronounce the name of it," Frost replied, surmising that one or another of the poems would sport some puzzling foreign title.

" *'Kalispera'*? Or *'Nemo Me Impune Lacessit,'* perhaps?"

"That's the one, that last one."

"But that poem's in Latin, Alexander. Surely you've learned a little of that, keeping the company you do? But then you're probably the modern sort, aren't you, Father, breaking out the guitar at mass and all that? Probably don't go in much for Latin."

Father Kearney's face fell. Within seconds anyone could see that he detested pretty much everything about this woman except for her creditable figure, over which his eyes seemed to be blinking recklessly. "Oh," he said off-handedly, "we're about as modern as you can be."

Christina took in the questioning looks of her aunt, her aunt's friends, her curious uncle in the corner. She paused so that this "priest" character might notice them, too.

"Modern, you say. And here I was thinking you were the reincarnation of Saint Francis of Assisi. But the fawns and the fishies wouldn't swarm around you, would they, Father?"

"I beg your pardon?"

"Have you ever been to India, Father?"

"No . . ."

"If you love poverty so much, why don't you buy a ticket? Haven't you had it with spoiled nutcases who drink themselves silly every night and make their mommies throw parties for them? You should see the real stuff. Children who've had their eyes gouged out by their mothers so they'll be able to beg a better price. Men in diapers with no limbs, wheeling themselves around on boards while their sores drip into the dust you walk on."

Frost snickered. There was too much drama in her point for her to properly make it. She was not the best representative horror ever had.

"At least," said Kearney quietly, "our beggars have the good grace to cover up most of their sores."

"Listen, Father. You need my aunt's money so you can prop these losers up and help them keep ripping people off. Well, you're not getting any from me." She pointed her wineglass at a desk with a cash box on it, where Glenys was sitting and taking donations. "I bet you think you're unhappy. I bet Alexander thinks he's unhappy." Here she gestured at Frost. "But you really don't know unhappiness, do you? You *know* you don't know it."

Kearney gripped his glass tightly, but Martine could see he would not be squaring off against this girl in her own constituency; and in the sad submission of his eyes there was even a touch of agreement. "It's an argument that could never end," he said.

"That's all right," she said, eyes infernal, "because I'm not in any hurry for it to end."

Alms

They were all three silent for a minute. Then Frost belched
loudly, inducing disgust in the poetess and the tweedy
lawyers who surrounded her. "Excuse me," he said, covering
his mouth. But Christina just shook her turbaned head and
walked away.

Kearney stared after her, touching his fingers lightly to his
lips. Then he shrugged and took a sip of his wine. Ah, well,
he seemed to be saying, I've struck out before.

Martine watched him, standing there alone. She wanted
to wrap a friendly arm around him, take him into a corner,
and tell him that you can't act too interested with rich girls.
Nothing drives them away faster, you have to play it cool.
But this poor clown could never be cool. He looked especially small now in his oversized habit. Was it a one-size-fits-
all proposition? All, she supposed, except for him. He
reminded Martine of a Save the Children ad right now. She
wished she loved him, so someone would love him.

But she didn't love him, and to avoid him she walked into a
nearby library and contemplated the Book-of-the-Month Club
titles that furnished the bookshelves of Gregory Frost, Q.C.
(she had seen his name on a notepad by the phone). On the
outer shelves were a series of books with long Polish words
snaking up the side; these must have belonged to Frost's
mother, the blonde lady with the smoky accent. There were
pictures there, too, of two little boys in dungarees and welling-
tons, proudly holding up freshly caught fish. Then the same
little boys, smiling down from the branches of a tree, blond
crewcuts swallowed by sunlight. One of these was Frost.

The travel poetess had a point. Perhaps she had read the
article in the paper the other day, which proclaimed that

twenty-three per cent of all porepeople had video cassette recorders. Christina wouldn't like this. She'd probably grown up with an image of the poor as uniformly "deserving"—old, sick, children; not one of them ever snapping or lying or spewing hatred; people who, in spite of their terrible lot, always seemed to be trying, and never getting, because getting wasn't part of the deal. The rules were clearly written in storybooks. You'd never catch the Little Match Girl wasted in a back alley.

And Christina's words weren't lost on Martine, because when she watched Muriel cuff her son across the head with her Bible, or when she was summoned to table two by a pervert who rubbed her leg as she set his coffee down, she, too, felt sick with disappointment. She had wanted them to save her, and they weren't doing their bit: their patient, mute, smiling, forbearing *bit*.

Like Father Kearney, Martine had spent a long time preferring to see things as they were not. But once in a while she'd be confronted with a snapshot of human pain so vivid she knew a plane ride couldn't take her to much worse: a black word, a scar, a bruise, and she just knew. Knew, too, that it was one thing to free yourself of money, quite another to free yourself of all the times you were never hit, molested, utterly abandoned. It would be impossible. The only thing to do was to enjoy what you had.

Which was, of course, also impossible.

A buffet was set up in yet another adjacent room—a pointless sort of room, neither living room nor den—and at the end of it, a handsome young man in a chef's hat lay two tiny slivers of beef onto massive white plates, which were then dribbled with a teaspoon of burgundy sauce and garnished with mint and a couple of gooseberries. Suleiman held his plate before him and inspected it, apparently hunting for food. What little there was looked humped, huddled, marooned in whiteness, as if it were a research station in the Antarctic. Father Kearney came and joined him, followed by Dianne. They all stared at their plates in shocked silence. "This may be Martine's speed," the priest said quietly, "but I don't know about the rest of us."

"Nouvelle cuisine. For my old man," Frost explained. "My mom's always trying to get him to reduce."

"Well, it's very pretty, at any rate," said Father Kearney.

"I'll go try to scare up some potato chips for you ingrates in the kitchen," Frost grumbled.

It was a buffet that took the mickey out of buffets and for that Martine considered joining it. There was something assembly-line about buffets that had always done in her huge but highly cancellable appetite; she flashed back to her eleven-year-old self, standing in line at the yacht club, the slow anaconda glide of people ahead of her, insatiable grown-ups spooning and picking from huge bowls of salad, cheese platters, trays of cherry-topped cakes. The sight of anything in large amounts had always disgusted her. So when another waiter passed by in the hallway proffering a small platter of "beggar's purses," she took one of those instead: the tiny perfection of an hors d'oeuvre was more to her liking. This particular treat was unfortunately named under the circumstances but delicious all the same: chèvre and porcini-mushroom purée wrapped in a tiny crepe, the parcel held together with a slender chive thread. Martine took one into her pink napkin and stared at it for a while, then squired the treat into the darkened lee of a winding staircase, where she swallowed it whole, feeling the creamy chèvre pervade her like a lover. She closed her eyes and sank to the floor, a wanderer home again.

She caressed the varnished wood of a stair just above her. If she did go home to Moore Park, she'd certainly be taken back. Her mother was not a cruel woman; she only lived to protect. Take the time the Professor brought a hobo home for supper. An authentic, full-service hobo, right down to his ruddy face and shopping bag full of broken effects. The Professor had seemed rather proud of his find. "Louise," he proclaimed, "this is Bill. Bill, meet my wife and daughter."

"Hello, girl," Bill said. "I've got one about her age, too." Louise frowned and crossed her arms. Her look said: You had one about her age in 1923, you old drunk. Drunk he did not appear to be; he was, however, the single dirtiest person Martine had ever seen. He frightened her terribly.

"Well, what's for dinner, Louise?" asked the Professor, with too much eagerness. "Bill and I are starving."

But Louise just stood there with her arms crossed.

"Bill's not staying," she said.

Husband and wife stared at each other as the kitchen air fogged with hatred. "Bill is starving," the Professor insisted. "He hasn't eaten in days."

"Then you can give him some money and send him to McDonald's."

"He needs a family. He needs someone to talk to."

"Then he can take a bath, put on something nice, and come back when he's ready to look human."

"He *is* human, whether you think so or not."

"He's scaring Martine. Anyone who scares my child does not eat in my house."

"Bullshit, Louise. That's just bullshit. You can hide your baby under your skirts all you want, but when she grows up she's going to find it isn't all beer and skittles out there."

Martine started to cry. Louise gathered her to her hips defiantly.

"Look, folks," said Bill, throwing up his hands. "I didn't mean to cause a commotion here. You were just going to have a nice supper together and I don't want to interrupt. I'll just go back downtown and get myself some soup."

"Thank you, Bill, that's a very good idea," barked Louise. She stalked to the oven, ripped a drumstick off the chicken she was roasting, wrapped it in a bit of paper towel, and thrust it at the hobo. "My husband will give you a ride. Take this with you in the car."

At which the Professor intercepted the drumstick, threw the paper towel on the ground, and slowly, ostentatiously, rewrapped the chicken in a fifty-dollar bill he'd just extracted from Louise's nearby purse. Then he took Bill by the arm and led him out the front door.

"Lovely to have met you," Bill managed before the door slammed behind him.

Still shrouded under the staircase, Martine saw Frost sitting in another pointless room with his phone book beside him; across the coffee table was Elliott, who'd shown up after all and had hidden out in this little roomlet the whole time. Elliott was wearing a rather nice suit, come to that, though, of course, his clothing always looked like it would rather have been on somebody else. The two men were eating greedily and playing Calendar in utter silence.

Soft and utter silence. Probably the best way to handle affliction of any sort. When Martine almost failed Grade Five, she'd had sopping hugs from her mother and icy words of reproof from her father. Pépère flipped his thick white wig. Everybody had an opinion, that was the problem.

They put her in summer school with seven other dolts and reprobates, including Jeremy. She was the only girl. The teacher was a quiet man named, oddly, Mr. Champagne, and as it happened he came from her own school; Grade Six was his normal house specialty. He was an ex-priest—hadn't been man enough for the job, or was forced to leave, who could say. Martine pitied him. He was too diseasedly tall and mournful looking not to be mocked by children, even Catholic children, and constantly, too.

"Long division," were his first words to the class, and he'd hardly turned to the blackboard before the spitballs started, then a hunk of paper, then a sandwich. But he didn't mind. He just went quietly through the work, stopping once to wipe egg salad from his glasses. He didn't smile, he didn't not smile. He got it done, speaking in numbers instead of words, and in time they all caught up and were more or less ready to start a new year. He did no more nor less than was asked of him.

Why hadn't she remembered that guy all this time, all this time she'd spent ladling on the gloppy gravy of goodness?

Tutting, shushing, complimenting, stroking, backing away, inching forward, worrying about whether she liked them, whether they liked her, about whether they were "good" or "bad." Who cared? They were people; she had a job; the important thing was just to do it. Like Mr. Champagne. Like Elliott.

Who currently was, it goes without saying, having the tailored gabardine pants beaten off him by Frost in what must have been an especially one-sided game. Martine couldn't hear them, though. She was prevented from doing so by the susurrations of a kaffeeklatsch emanating from the kitchen.

"Too good, Shirley, she's too good. My God, what that woman has been through. I wouldn't have the strength for it. We don't know how lucky we are, with our children healthy."

"And, you know, I don't think he even appreciates how much they do for him."

"I think Renata's just relieved this minister has taken over. I think she's about had it."

"No, I'm sure he's a priest, Rita. Catholic."

"Of course, I forgot. But, my God, how sad. Do you remember we used to drive Alexander to his chess tournaments, so polite —"

"Oh, I know —"

"—always the top of the class—"

"A shame."

"A life wasted—"

"—is what it is."

"There's nothing they can do about it either."

"I don't know about that—he won't see a doctor, he won't go to the meetings—I mean, Renata has done everything, and to be perfectly frank, I stopped feeling sorry for him a long time ago. Do you remember the clinic in Vermont?"

"Oh, sure. He was fine after that."

"For a while, but then he went back like he always does . . . You know, I always thought it was Renata's fault, the way she used to be so obsessed about keeping his nails clean—do you remember?"

"Oh, she was so fussy about that!"

"Well, I know her therapist told her to do this, but I'm not sure it's the right thing. Really, she's lived her life for that boy. That man, I suppose he is. A sort of man, anyway."

You got that right, thought Martine. Hail Renata! And Louise, and all the other parents who only lived to protect. How could you blame them? You could not. It was their friends you hated, the Sharon Colterblakes and their heavily scented ilk, flapping their glossy yaps in kitchens across the nation about whose life was worth living and whose was not. "Louise, I tell you, my Carolyn is going to ruin her eyesight with all this studying. I know she has to do it if she wants the scholarship, but I do worry." "Well, it's better than Martine, isn't it, destroying it in front of the television like she does." "Oh, isn't it true, Louise. I suppose I should count my blessings." There couldn't be much good in these mothers if these were their pals. And did they ever stop to defend their children? Might another conversation in another kitchen feature Carolyn as a sorry egghead, and Martine and Frost as the bright, unusual pearls who were truly "going places"? As if.

That's when Martine knew for sure what side she was on.

She saw Father Kearney skulk into the hall alone. Curious that he'd let that bitch travel poet win so handily, she

258

thought. A Christly turning of the other cheek, maybe? Or economic necessity—her aunt, after all, was holding the wallet tonight. None of those seemed to hit it for Martine, though there was one last possibility: sheer kindness, of the sort displayed by Louise when she used to let her daughter win at Crazy Eights, over and over again. Kindness, yes, but with a serrated edge; Martine had never forgiven her mother for dousing her in these delusions of false victory. Clever, cutthroat kindness. She had to hand it to him.

He saw her hiding underneath the stairs and his eyes gleamed. "Hey, Perpetual Help—what're you doing under there?"

She tried to arrange her legs demurely in front of her but couldn't. In any case, there was no time to before Father Kearney started pulling at the hem of her skirt. "Come! Let me show you around upstairs."

She stole up guiltily behind him, but as they rounded the first spiral she instantly regretted doing so. Glenys and Dianne were standing beside each other at the entrance to the kitchen, watching the pair ascend with smirking faces. The beverages they gripped threatened to bubble and smoke. Martine turned away.

Once having ascended the stairs, Father Kearney hopped through the hall like a man at home, knocking open all the doors with his fist. "Bathroom," he said. "Andy's old room, that's Frost's brother. Sewing room or something now. Gosh, that cousin of his sure wanted nothing to do with me, eh? I mean, who am I, the Swamp Thing? Come here."

He tiptoed reverently to the end of the hallway and opened the door slowly to reveal a large and elaborate master bedroom, in the centre of which was a giant bed covered in a red brocade spread. The walls were papered in red, too, and there was a large wooden crucifix over the bed. It was an opulent but ghastly place. It looked all set for an exorcism.

Father Kearney lured Martine into the ensuite bathroom, which was silvery white and comparatively cheerful. "Look," he said. "I wanna show you something." He opened the medicine cabinet and there, nestled among the unguents and lotions and bottles, were two overripe bananas. "See?" he said, pointing them out. Martine didn't understand. Then he pointed to the back of the toilet, where a bag of gingersnaps sat next to a pile of magazines. He opened a cabinet under the sink and pulled out a bag of red licorice, then helped himself to a stick.

He pulled her by the hand back into the bedroom, and toward the bed. She pulled the other way, frightened.

But all he wanted to do was turn over a giant pillow, underneath which lay a large cache of Ding Dot candies in little single-serving bags. "Aha!" he exclaimed. "I knew we'd find something good."

Martine asked him what the point of all this was. Chomping on the licorice, Father Kearney explained that Frost's father was in the habit of keeping food in unexpected crannies all over the house—everywhere he went, in fact, in his briefcase and glove compartment, too.

"How do you know this?"

"Because Frost and me go way back. We were in high school together fifteen years ago, you probably didn't know. 'Course, I come from the other side of the tracks myself. I used to hang around here all the time. Mrs. Frost couldn't stand me. Until I became a priest, that is. Then she figured I'd probably be the one to save old Alex."

It was inconceivable to Martine that the two men had gone to high school together, and that they were only in their early thirties. Father Kearney looked forty at least. Frost looked fifty.

They'd been partners in Grade Eleven chemistry, apparently. Frost was the smartest kid in the class. "He won all the prizes then," said the priest. "He was really smart, this gangly Polack kid, best in the class. I guess the teacher thought he'd be a good influence on me, but the reverse happened. He fell in with a bad crowd, and the bad crowd was me.

"His brother was a big thing, too, in medical school then, so his mom had high hopes for Frost, but I kind of wrecked *those* all to Pittsburgh. Aw, she hated me back then, wouldn't let me in the house. Then one day in chem class I asked him if he might be able to cook up some—oh, forget about that, you don't need to know that story. Anyway, we got up to all kinds of mischief. You know when they have those contests on the radio and the forty-third caller gets a prize? Frost fixed the phones so that we'd always be the caller. He was amazing. We won all kinds of stuff, concert tickets, a couple of trips. We even ran off to Paris for a week and his dad sicced Interpol on us . . . I thought of all kinds of ways to make money—like, we'd go door to door and ask people if they'd ever been ripped off by guys selling stuff door to door. If they said yes, we'd tell them we were collecting money for a special fund to stop these horrible kinds of guys, and of course they'd give it to us. Morons."

"Rotten little pranksters," said Martine. To confirm for herself that that kind of rottenness had had its day and was now over.

"Yeah," he agreed. "We were bad. 'Course, that was a long time ago."

"Sure. I wasn't the best kid either."

He seemed surprised by this. "You weren't?"

"Well, no. Elliott's never said anything?" Father Kearney shook his head, but looked hungry for more information. She didn't want to go into it. "Uh, I—let's talk about it later. Now tell me, why does his father do that—hide the food everywhere?"

The priest sat down heavily on the great bed. "He was in Dachau for five years. He'd be dead if he were Jewish. But he was in the Polish resistance, so all he got was the starvation part." He ran his fingers over the red brocade. Its sheen seemed to mesmerize him. "He was just a teenager when he went in. Name was Filipowski then."

"So he—he eats a lot now, to make up for it?"

"Are you kidding? You saw him."

"No, actually, I didn't."

"How could you miss him? Guy weighs about three hundred pounds. He's had two heart operations already. He's made quite a life for himself here, but I don't know how. All he freaking does is eat. He's gonna die of eating." At this Father Kearney grabbed a bag of Ding Dots and offered one to Martine. "Here, even you eat these."

She took it and held it a second, then returned it to the pile. "No, he needs it," she said. "He needs it as much"— she turned the bag over so that its brand name would greet

Mr. Frost instantly the second he next turned over his pillow—"as I don't need it. And that's a lot."

The priest looked at the opened bag in his hand and made a face. "All right, Martine," he said. "Few enough like you around, I'd suppose." Then he put a soft hand on her shoulder and directed her back toward the stairs. "Bet you always picked the four-eyed kid first for basketball, too."

*F*ROM THE OTHER SIDE of the tracks, he'd said. Father
Kearney had grown up accustomed to less than what Frost
had, but how much less? He *was* sort of rough-hewn, with a
turn of phrase that was sometimes too forced. But he was
a gentleman, of the kind they didn't make much any more.

"If you didn't grow up around here," she asked in the taxi
back home, "why did you go to school with Frost?"

He looked out the window and placed a finger on the
glass. "Had to take the bus uptown, 'cause they booted me
out of the Catholic schools in my neighbourhood."

He was a bad little kid, he said. The smallest boy in
Grade Five. Outlaw swaths of hair running past each other
on his skull. A crudely pasted nose and mouth, both of them
daubed with woe: a dunked rodent. He wore his sisters'
hand-me-downs. Exhibit A was a pink blouse from his
sister Katie by way of his sister Rosemarie that he knew

would seal his fate as far as the crueller boys were concerned; a blouse that would sentence his face to a semester-long series of mashings against the crumbling brick wall just outside the gym.

"I'm not wearing no girl's shirt," he told his mother.

"Oh, Clifford, your friends won't hardly notice what side the buttons are on."

"But it's pink."

"And there's no ruffles on it either."

"But it's *pink*."

"'Tisn't pink, my kitten, it's cerise, and it's perfectly lovely."

He soaked it himself in bleach until his hands burned and the pink swam in peninsular tongues down a white front. The shirt was ghastly now, a stiff, stinking thing. But his other two had great holes in them and it was winter.

He behaved unusually badly the first day he wore it, hoping his actions might detract from his wardrobe. He yanked braids. He turned his eyelids inside out. Then he trapped a daddy-long-legs near the fence and pulled a tiny limb off during arithmetic. His classmates watched in awe as the bodiless thing bent and straightened for fifteen whole seconds before Sister noticed, and Sister was not normally a teacher you wanted to notice you. But she did nothing. Maybe she was sorry about the shirt.

At the end of the day he figured he'd made a clean breast of it. But as he tried to hop over a chain that separated the school from a ravine that led to his house he was intercepted by three big boys: Fergus Day from his class, with a couple of subalterns he'd called in from somewhere.

"Hey, Pinky. Are you hungry?"

Clifford tried to dodge them but it was impossible. They smashed his mouth into the frozen chain and he gagged. It was so cold he feared his tongue might stick to it, but the runnings of tears and blood kept it slippery between his jaws.

"Hungry little guttersnipe," said Fergus, pinning his prey by the neck with a big mittened hand. "Eat your Christmas dinner, gutter kid. Mmmmm." He squeezed the little boy's neck harder. "Yummy cold metal." He let him go and Clifford slid, minus three teeth, to the gravel. "Now he needs dessert," said the boy. "Let's get him it."

One of Fergus's henchmen produced the perfectly intact corpse of a squirrel—a strange sight to Clifford, since all the dead squirrels he'd ever seen had come to obviously violent ends. This one looked stuffed. But Clifford could see it wasn't when Fergus took out his jacknife and made an incision down the animal's belly. The hide proved hard to cut, and Fergus gritted his teeth as he tugged the knife down toward the pubis. Viscera stained his mittens. He took one of them off and cut more savagely; blood browned quickly on his fingers and thumb. The squirrel's face, meanwhile, remained serene, with wistful black eyes and a mouth slightly open as if in song: *laaaaa*. Before long, it became a furry bowl for its own true black-and-red self. Wind punished the grey fluff while the boys stared hard into the guts. "Eat it," Fergus commanded.

Clifford stuck a shaky finger in and licked. The squirrel didn't mind, *laaaaa*. Clifford's mouth was already swimming with blood and this didn't taste much different; what seemed truly grisly to him was Fergus's face, the hatred between his eyes. One buck incisor sat on his lower lip, like a gun on a pillow. Such viciousness—and all because of a shirt. Clifford almost forgave him. Not because it was in his nature to do so as a Catholic, but because he hated the shirt even more than Fergus did.

Some rustle in the distance alarmed the criminals, and Fergus whipped round to check it. Probably just another squirrel, looking for her missing mate, but they couldn't be sure. "We gotta get," Fergus yelled, with a final whap to Clifford's head.

Clifford went back to his apartment building, ran straight to the bathroom, and pounded on the door. The Russian was in there taking a crap. The Russian, who probably wasn't Russian but sounded it, was a boarder who lived off the kitchen with his old wife; they ate with the Kearneys and shared their toilet. The Russian had a great passion for the toilet, sad to say, and on more than one near-accidental occasion Clifford vowed that when he grew up he'd get a nice big shiny old shitter that was all his own and nobody could ever use, ever, ever, ever. Finally, the Russian emerged with a smile and the boy cleaned up as best he could. The shirt was set anew in bleach.

Then Clifford ran out the door in his undershirt and jacket, the bloodstains on his dark pants barely visible. He couldn't think of anything to do so he pushed a rock down the road for two hours with a stick. "Clifford?" he heard his mother calling at intervals. "Clifford, are you there?" Yes, I'm here, he thought bitterly, remembering her syrupy advocacy of the lovely "cerise" blouse. But *you* aren't here. You never are. Most times he defended his weird mother against the verbal assaults of fearsome Rosemarie, but tonight he wouldn't. She'd have to bloody well fend for herself.

When he finally came back in, Teresa Kearney was crocheting in the kitchen. She had been crocheting the same object for several months now, a vaguely bag-shaped thing of no possible use to anyone.

Rosemarie walked by and noticed her. "What the hell are you going to do with that?" she derided.

"It's just something to do while I hum," her mother replied, mid-hum. Humming was one of Teresa's principal occupations. Coughing was the other: she was a birdlike woman, apparently on the way out, both in the mental and physical senses. Her great dream was to visit Hawaii, and accordingly her humming taste ran to hoary luau tunes like "Down Mauna Kea Way" and "Hawaiian Wedding Song," with the coughs for percussion.

She hummed that night while heating the soup and serving it to Clifford, who was still in his undershirt, which she didn't notice. She did see he wasn't eating, however, and called him on it. He told her he wasn't hungry.

"Well, that's fine," she said merrily. "You look like the Prince of Wales and that's the only thing that matters."

There was no point in telling her he had three fewer teeth than he'd used to eat last night's bread and soup. Katie wouldn't see it either, she not being quite right in the head, slurping her soup loudly between tired Rosemarie and Mrs. Russian.

But you couldn't get anything by Rosemarie. "Jeez, what happened to your face? Your lip's all fat on the bottom."

"Is not."

"Fergus Day again. You better tell your principal."
Clifford said nothing.

"Well," his sister said, frowning, "I will, then."

"Now, Rosemarie, if he says his lip isn't fat, then it isn't,"
Teresa piped. "It's *his* lip, so he should know."

Rosemarie dropped her spoon heavily in the bowl, causing
the soup to splash up onto Katie's neck. "Oh, for Christ's
sake, Mother. Face the real world for goddamn once. Just
look at that window. Take a good look at it."

There was a small window in the kitchen with a sizeable
hole in it, made by Teresa with a broom handle when the
landlord threatened to kick them out the last time. "There are
bad fairies in this house," she'd theorized, "bad fairies
making things hard for us, with no door to fly out. So we'll
have to make one." Now it was getting to be winter, and the
fairy-hole wasn't half so cute any more.

"Yes?" said Teresa. "I see it. What about it?"

"You don't see it! That's the thing!" Rosemarie slumped,
incredulous, looking around at the various beaten, stupid,
old, and crazy people who surrounded her. How she got in
this situation she'd never know. She was fifteen, normal, and
counting the billion minutes until nursing school. "Open your
eyes, for the love of Christ! Open your *stupid* eyes."

But Teresa's expression did not change; she still looked
gay and girlish, even with all the wrinkles and the mouth that
looked poised to quiver.

"And if I opened my eyes, darling Rosemarie," she said,
"what then do you think I'd see?"

With that she rose, humming, and cleared the bowls.

The taxi stopped in front of 12 Merseyfield, but Father Kearney didn't acknowledge its having done so. He was still in that drafty kitchen, five blocks and twenty-three years down the road. Martine paid the driver and pulled her companion out onto the sidewalk.

"Father—you don't have to tell me these things," she told him as he somnambulated toward the front door. "If it makes you uncomfortable."

He opened the door, let them both in, and proceeded to relock it behind them. "You're right," he said. "Always running my mouth off. Gonna get me in trouble one day. Not like you, eh? Only saying what needs to be said. I should shut up sometimes." He smiled sadly. "Well, good night, my dear." Then he turned toward the stairs that led to his purple-sheeted bedroom.

Martine couldn't bear to see his shoulders that way. "I meant—"

The priest turned around. "What?"

"I meant, I *enjoy* listening . . . I thought it might be hard for you, to talk about that stuff. That's all."

He grinned and went back to his old self. "Talk! Hard! Me? Darling, my larynx is like the laundromat round the corner—open all night, and everything that comes out of it is nice and dry. Though I can't promise you it'll all be clean."

Within minutes Martine found herself settled in his kitchen. The room had an exaggerated "farm" feel: bright yellow walls and a big pantry, a flouncy calico valance over the window, with matching potholders hanging by the stove. A little too much; Louise would sniff if she saw it. At odds with the farm stuff were the countertops, which groaned with

270

shiny appliances lined up in a row, a presentation that made the place look like a laboratory, or a store. Martine noted the presence of a food processor like the one back home.

Father Kearney set about introducing her to the machines.

"This is my juicer, I call her Anastasia. And here's my toaster, Paulette by name—not as compliant as I'd like, but she gets the job done."

"You gave your kitchen appliances names?" Martine asked.

"Why not? They're my best girls. They'll never yell at me or break my heart." He curled an arm around the cappuccino maker. "This is Simonetta—a glamorous Italian. Would you like a cup of her? She won't mind."

"Yes," Martine said, warming slightly to the idea of these strange housemates. "Hello, Simonetta."

"And . . . a cookie? To go with it? Maybe?"

"Sure."

Father Kearney clapped his hands together and set about fixing the snack. "I was going to open our champagne but I guess we've both had a bit to drink, so we'll have it later. Hey, but—what about your notebook? I didn't see you with it tonight."

"Oh, I filled that one." Martine accepted a gingersnap and bit into it. "I suppose I should go get another."

"I've got paper and a pen. If you want."

She shook her head and finished the cookie. "No, thanks."

He broke into a wide grin. "Martine! You don't use it any more?"

She put down her gingersnap. "Yeah, yeah, yeah," she said. "So what."

271

"But that's wonderful!"

It was embarrassing and she didn't want to say any more about it. "Tell me more about Rosemarie," she said, "and all that, and everybody."

Nobody ever did tell the principal; two more fights with Fergus Day and Clifford was out of that school. Needless to say, there was no severance package. By that time it was close enough to summer for young Clifford to knock off the rest of the year and hang out by the Don River, rafting down it on giant hunks of cardboard that came from the soda pop factory. Sometimes he'd climb up the fire escape to the roof of the smallest factory building so he could watch the sunset from there. And every now and again he'd "borrow" a bike from outside the Old York Coffee Shoppe and go down to take a ferry to the marina, the place he loved best. The following summer he spent most of his time there, and the next one after that.

Freshly adolescent, he had pursued but one career: altar boy at St. Anthony's. There he filled cruets with wine and water, lit candles, bore the cross, and excelled at all of it. He had no other talents. The lusciousness of the priestly vestments appealed to him: they were the only beauty in his life. He loved his snowy-white surplice, longed to complement it with a chasuble, cincture, maniple, stole. How he wished he could put them all on, run home, boot the Russian out of the john, and stare at himself in the cracked mirror of the medicine cabinet. He thought, in fact, he might like to be a priest someday, even if it were just for the clothes. How happy it would make Teresa, too.

One day, down at the marina, he met a man named Lloyd
L. Llewellyn who asked him what he wanted to be. But the
man looked disappointed with him.

"No money in that, kid. No money and definitely no
pussy."

"Oh."

"I mean, sure you'll go to heaven, but say there ain't no
heaven? Get paradise to come to you."

Through a little door they watched the man's girlfriend
slowly rubbing suntan lotion on her bronzed belly. It was a
film so erotic Clifford thought he might have to be hospital-
ized, but the man didn't seem as interested and kept talking.

"Now, if it's charity you're after, well, that's not a bad
racket at all. Full of women and they're all very big on
giving, if you get my message. Let me tell you a little story.
A few years back I come into a pretty good nut and I decide
to put a swimming pool round back of my place.
Everything's fine but the old ball and chain feels guilty about
it. She tells me one day how sick she is about wearing chin-
chilla and going to the golf club and now here's the swimming pool—every time she looks out the window she's
reminded how terrible it is that her life's so great. So she says
one day, 'Now you look here, Lloyd, I'm going to go down
to the Kelly Centre and see if they don't need me.' Right—
like working with kids who put their brains on backwards
is going to help her feel any better! But she goes. They put
her on the fundraising committee 'cause she's so rich, but
it turns out, big surprise, these people know nothing about
making money. So she says, 'Lloyd, *you* started your own
business'—I'm in precast concrete—'*you* got the know-how,

you go tell them.' Hey, it's a roomful of women, no need to convince me. So I go down and make a big speech to the board. And the director—well, Chip, she's got a face like a can of crushed toes, but I can live with it. I'm a good boy, I eat what you put in front of me. There are starving bachelors in Africa, you know what I'm saying? I take her out for coffee after and she says, 'What about direct mail?' I tell her it's fine for some, but the personal encounter is always better. I tell her not to be too strict about the non-profit angle either. A little on the side never hurt a girl. 'A little on the side?' she asks me.

"Next thing you know we're in the bridal suite at the Lakebreeze and she's telling me, 'Oh, Lloyd, you're so compassionate for a businessman, I never thought I'd see the day.' I think: You got that right, sister—nothing turns me on like little crippled kids or whatever the product is you're turning out down there. Anyway, off goes the Cross Your Heart, and let me tell you, Chip—Andrew Carnegie didn't know shit about endowment! Ha ha ha! Then she gets on her knees and gives me one *hell* of a generous donation. Holy Christ, kid, I should have issued her a tax receipt for that one. The least I could have done. Charity, yes sir! Old charity's fine by me. Sure it begins at home—but it can end up someplace a hell of a lot more interesting."

They went back to watching the sunbather outside. "Is that . . . one of them, sir? Clifford asked after a bit. "One of the charity ladies?" He was young, but smart enough to know he probably wasn't looking at good, guilty Thelma.

The man twirled his cigar ruminatively. "Naw, kid, that one's a taker. Gimme gimme gimme, that's the name of *her.*" Twin images of the glistening woman danced in his sunglasses. "Of course, that type has its bright side, too. Eh, Chip?"

Father Kearney placed a cup before Martine and she stared at it. For a second she thought about the coffee maker back at the Refuge, how it was always half broken and never replaced, how Suleiman and the Salvadorans et al. suffered through their turbid coffee without complaint night after night. While back at the priest's house, actual cappuccino was frothing forth regularly—with cinnamon on top, no less. A contradiction. But it sounded like he deserved it, after what he'd been through.

"You had an interesting time of it," Martine said. "Didn't you."

The priest leaned forward on his elbows. "Interesting? That's an interesting word for it."

She took a sip. "I wish I knew you back then."

His eyes widened. "What? Aw, you woulda run so far. You would've got lice by looking at me. Ha." He saw she wasn't laughing and blushed. "Hmp. Who knows, though. Maybe you would've been friends with me after all. God knows, you're weird enough." He scratched his knuckles and looked around. "We did well tonight, eh? The Frosts really came through."

"But then what happened?" Martine asked. "After the boat?"

Clifford went home that day and thought about charity: its pros and cons, its curves and contours. When the weather got too crisp for him to continue hanging around the marina, he took the man's advice and founded an organization called the Children's Tumour Foundation. He went canvassing door to door for funds. He really did plan to give the money away, though to whom he was not sure, but when the first snapping green dollar was placed in his hand he saddened at the thought of parting with it . . . *Maybe just a wee bit off the top for my troubles,* he thought. Anyway, he only got five apartments in before the plan fell apart, since the "tumorous" child whose snapshot he flashed in his doorway speech was actually Rosemarie's best friend, who lived in the neighbourhood and whose adolescent form was unquestionably ridden with the very best of health. Still, what might have been a disgrace for the altar boy turned out to be anything but: thinking fast, he decided to turn over the ten dollars he'd collected to the church, an action he convinced everyone had been his intention all along. As a result he became something of a minor hero in his community—his stock even went up in his new school, to and from which he was allowed free and temporarily bruiseless passage. Sulking in the bedroom she shared with her siblings, Rosemarie suspected some poisonous ulterior truth.

Her brother ignored her. Victory made him cocky. Lloyd L. Llewellyn held distinction in one hand and riches in the other. And why shouldn't I, Clifford argued in his prayers, have both, too? And God answered back: Why shouldn't you, indeed.

The boy started to nick more and more little things from stores he'd wander into—candy, magazines, pencils. At mass on Sundays, he developed an unhealthy obsession with the collection basket, with its bills cresting up like meringue peaks on a fancy dessert. He looked longingly on the St. Vincent de Paul box, regularly stuffed as it was with plump envelopes full of cash and coins. He couldn't muster the necessary legerdemain to swipe from the basket, but the box . . . he could get into the box, no problem. Since he was charged with sweeping up after mass, he had easy access to it and helped himself, at first timidly, at length boldly. He kept the money uneasily, reminding himself it was destined for the poor. But at night, when he looked at the cracked blue ceiling of the tiny room he shared with Katie and Rosemarie, it was easy to convince himself it would only go to boys like him anyway.

At school, he watched the cans mount in the Christmas hamper outside the hallway. There were a lot of things his mother liked there: wax beans, canned peaches, soup. She's frail and getting frailer, thought Clifford. If I steal things for her, he reasoned, the villainy of my other thefts will be annulled.

So steal things he did, leaving school each day in a worn duffel coat heavy with cans. Two or three weeks later he was caught in flagrante by one of his classmates and set on the road to another expulsion. But his resolve remained unaffected. He swore then and there that he'd much rather walk among the red-handed than the brown-nosed.

Martine was touched by his story, by how much it recalled her own days of petty thievery. He'd had reasons for it, too, which she had not. How much harder it must have been for him to climb back out.

"When did you change?" she asked.

"Change? Oh, I've not changed. I'm same as I ever was."

"No, but when did you stop stealing."

He smiled hugely, then laughed. He clasped his hands together and blushed again, staring at the hand she'd just brushed with her own as if it had been autographed by a movie star. "Aw, I'm not really attached to dates like that, you know. The alcoholics love that routine: I had my last drink at three seconds before midnight on March 27, or what have you. But you know what they say about the Catholic church—it's a hospital for sinners, not a country club for saints. I'd be arrogant if I told you I'd changed too much. I'd be lying to myself."

Martine had never warmed to this idea of sin being something you couldn't avoid. You could avoid everything if you wanted to. It had proven rather easy where she was concerned. Anyway, absolution was an idea always used in defence of the most appalling behaviour: a few Hail Marys and the sin was gone. But where did the sin go?

"You want another coffee? Cookie?" he asked.

"No, thank you."

"Just say no, eh? What a person you are, Perpetual Help. Myself, I've never refused second helpings—of anything."

"But you're just as skinny as I am."

He laughed. "Yeah, well, that's because nobody ever *gives* me second helpings!"

His laugh dwindled away until he was doing nothing but looking at her. She looked down in shame. The Professor had once warned her against this kind of guy, the kind who punctuates his remarks with long stretches of silence. He had told her that kind of guy is mentally choreographing the rest of the evening, and the bunny hop won't be among the steps. But before too long Father Kearney spoke.

"You're okay being alone all the time, aren't you?" he said. "You don't always have to have people dancing around you. I wish I was like that."

Martine was shocked. Few aspects of her character had ever been envied. In fact, not since the Kelly Centre fundraiser had she been singled out for salutation in that way. If others looked favourably on her, it was for her birthday booty, vacation destinations, lack of curfew and siblings, ability to wear most shades of orange—yes, all these had set others to cooing appreciatively. But her essence, her very Martinosity, was routinely ignored. She felt sure it would die along with her.

But he was right about her relation to solitude. She loved being alone more than anything. A trip to the circus or date with a boy was fine, but to sit alone and ponder circus and boy was far better. Trips and parties and meetings with others were nothing but preludes to the great gorgeousness of being on her own and retreading such things in her mind.

"I mean," he continued, "if I'm by myself for even an hour, I can't stand it. I always have to call someone up and go somewhere, do something. Doesn't matter who it is, I'll take anybody."

"Maybe you're in the wrong profession."

He laughed. "Hey, you're right about that. Maybe it's you who should have been the priest. For example, you don't need . . . well, forgive me for saying it, but it doesn't exactly look like there's a boyfriend in the picture. Forgive me for saying it."

"No, there isn't. But—"

"But what?"

He was a little too interested in what she had to say, but that was all right. She trusted him now. She saw how he drew others in and yet she trusted him. He was not a handsome man, no; in fact, now that she really looked at him, he was downright ugly, patched together from leftover scraps down at the face factory. But the nose might have been patrician had it not been knocked in so much. Proper dental attention would surely have righted the sad crash of teeth. Even the eyes were different colours, and she wondered if they'd started out that way. Pity softened her before him, made her feel something very like friendship.

"Well, there was someone, as a matter of fact. But you know how it goes. He's got someone else."

"Oh." The priest rubbed at a spot on the table, then picked up the cups and took them to the sink. As he rinsed them, he began speaking again. "Okay, but I wouldn't waste my time pining. It never works, I oughta know. Been through so many broken hearts I'm a freak of medical science. But tell me— this guy, what's he like?"

"He's . . . good."

"Good?"

"Yeah, he's a good person. Just a truly fine, brave, honourable human being. That's the main thing to say about him."

Father Kearney looked puzzled. "What in God's name would you want with a guy like that?"

She waited for the ironic laugh but it didn't come. He really seemed to think these qualities undesirable in a man.

"Is he one of the parishioners then?" he asked. "At Perpetual Help?"

"I'm not a churchgoer, Father. And you're really asking me if he's rich like me. Well, he's not. He wasn't even born in this country."

She was afraid to tell him who it was; she thought he'd keel over. Father Kearney despised Flavio and never missed a chance to tell her that he did. Though it was probably a big act, Martine figured, since it was impossible to hate Flavio. She should know, she'd tried it. In any case, she felt flooded with the sudden desire to talk about the guy, as she had never done, to dissolve in girlish gab. She pouted, she grinned. She brought her slender arms out before her and stretched sensuously. Whose arms are these? she thought. They can't belong to me—romantic me, the loveliest maid in the village, waving from a throne on a parade float, Queen of the May—

"All right, Miss Guessing Game. Stop squirming around and tell me all about Dudley Do-Right, as it seems you're so eager to do."

(Martine noticed that whenever Father Kearney was nervous he started frantically nicknaming the hated people under discussion. The Refuge landlord was "Mr. Hand-Over-the-Cake"; Muriel was "Frau Schnickengoebbels"; Glenys was "Our Lady of the Blessed Spinal Curvature.")

She drew her arms in and sat up, businesslike. "Promise you won't get mad?"

"At worst, I'll sentence you to a few prayers."

"Very funny. Well, it's Flavio." She looked up to check his reaction. "Flavio Vargas."

Cynthia Macdonald

The priest stood very still. He thought a minute, then straightened out the dishtowel and hung it slowly on a rack. Martine started to worry. It didn't look like he approved of her choice, but come on. No sensible man would be jealous of Flavio, would he? Because no sensible man would see the point. There was simply no contest to be had.

Father Kearney put his hands in his pockets and looked at the light switch, as if to sugggest that within seconds it would be flicked off and the evening would be ended.

"You know him well?" he asked calmly.

Good Christ, why did I tell him? "No, I—barely. I just think he's good-looking, it's stupid. Plus, there's the girl-friend, so . . ."

"Oh, I see. But that's your type, eh?"

"If you're only interested in one person, you don't have a type," she corrected.

"One person, that's no fun."

"Oh really? And what would your type be, Father?"

He took his hands out of his pockets and crossed his arms. He smiled and shuffled. He crossed one foot over another and looked at it. Then he said, "I don't know. All of them, I guess."

"What do you mean, 'all of them'?"

"I mean, fat and skinny. Tall. Short. Black, white, brown, yellow, purple. Long hair and short. Blonde black brown redhead. Grey. White. At a certain point I thought of, you know, declaring a major, but I never got round to it. My God, ha, it's funny . . . but I even find *you* attractive sometimes." He hastened to bury this. "And Glenys. And Dianne. And even bloody Muriel, for crying out loud. Hell, I'd take youse

282

all, God help me." He hugged his arms tighter across his small chest, as if to stanch a wound. "I'm not what you'd call a stout-hearted man."

There was a gay little clock above the stove, with a yellow plaid face that picked up the colour in the walls. Martine and Father Kearney listened to this clock tick for what felt like minutes.

"You're not really a priest, are you?" she said.

He looked up in surprise. "Why, yes! Of course I am."

"A Catholic priest."

"Sure."

"Roman Catholic."

He frowned, clenched his chin between thumb and forefinger. "Now that," he said, "that might be pushing it somewhat."

She didn't understand. There were other flavours? He told her not to worry and produced a business card, but it didn't clarify matters much: "Father Clifford Kearney, S.Sax." S.Sax, Martine thought. Soprano Saxophone? Some weird all-musical order—a Singing Nun kind of thing?

"Society of Saxons," he said proudly. "I'm a Saxon Catholic."

Martine knew the Pope wouldn't like this, not one bit, and her first instinct was to thank "Father" Kearney for the cappuccino and bolt the room. But then—was the Pope's opinion that important?

"Look," he said, then pulled a chair theatrically away from the table and gently grabbed her hands so she couldn't go anywhere. "I know you have certain attachments to the Church. What Catholic doesn't? The incense, the prayers, the hymns. That's all so great, isn't it? Or the peace that comes over you when you cross yourself, when you feel that communion wafer melting in your mouth. Believe me, nobody finds it more beautiful than me. But the Church has problems these days, you have to admit, and maybe you're not as comfortable with it as you used to be. Now, let's say you kept all the good stuff and threw away the bad—and you know what I'm talking about when I say bad, Martine. The boys, the poor little boys. The nun who bashed you over the head with a bell because you didn't line up straight after recess. Sure, I'm not perfect. I may have known a woman or two in my time, but I never led any inquisitions. What's worse? Say you could throw all the crap out and keep what you liked, would you do it? Of course you would. Well, that's what I've done. That's what being a Saxon Catholic is all about."

The notion struck Martine as overly sensual. Suffering through the Church's missteps was part of the deal; Catholicism without sin was hardly entitled to the name. But the sinning had been overplayed, too. "How about Mother Teresa over in India?" she asked. "She's Roman, and she's part of the good stuff."

"Yes, well, she's just too busy patching up babies to change over. She'd like me a whole lot better than the Pope, you know. Women tend to."

Martine could not believe the guy was trying to assert stud rights over the *Pope*. Anyhow, in spite of everything, there was more "good stuff" about the real Church she might mention—Cousin Père Pierre, the Sistine Chapel, Christian Assistance scholarships, the courageous and funny saint she'd heard about who, half-roasted on a spit, commanded his torturers: "Turn me over, for I am not done." She could go on, but Father Kearney was too good a salesman. He went too fast to let you think.

"We Saxons broke away from Rome in 1724, or 1742—I can't remember which. Frost would know, he's good with dates. Aw, look, I wouldn't blame you for having doubts. But when you really wake up to what I'm saying," he insisted, wagging his finger at her, "you'll realize you don't belong anyplace else. Helping Hands, Perpetual Help, what nonsense. All that fancy help to go around and none for you. You think some of that star power will rub off on you? It won't. That little old lamp store down the block, that's your Vatican. What it lacks in glamour it makes up for in all the ways that count." He knocked at his heart with a fist and even she, tired and weak and not overlong in the world, flinched at this hokey finale.

But he was right. She thought of those awful women in Mrs. Frost's kitchen and their denunciation of Frost. How their clucking would turn to trills if Flavio, and not Frost, were the subject. For Flavio was one of them now. Probably not even Chilean any more; maybe even planning a name change, like Grzegorz Filipowski did when he came to Canada. You joined them if you could. But Martine had never been able to.

"Oh, another thing," said Father Kearney. "I'm sorry about what I said. About the people in those big houses being all the same. They're not, are they?"

"No," Martine smiled, "they're not."

She said good night to him and he shook her hand, as if she had just passed a job interview. And she did feel curiously tranquil in this world right now, as she had not before; surely a world in which she could do good, while still surrounded by all of her natal comforts, was a perfect one.

She went downstairs, opened the door, and shut it behind her. She looked at the bare walls, sink, sleeping bag, books, phone, table. Not much to look at, but it hardly mattered when there was a cappuccino maker so close at hand.

She was home.

*M*ARTINE WOKE LATE and called Louise, to check on her. Since the hospital visit, something alarming had happened: Louise hadn't called. Her daughter had just gotten used to cringing every time she saw the green answering-machine light flashing every time she entered her apartment, and now she cringed for the opposite reason. It had only been a week, sure, but what was with this woman? So Martine panicked and decided that from now on she would call every day, so that if Louise didn't call, Martine wouldn't even notice that she hadn't called—because *she* had called.

Louise answered on the first ring sounding alert and sunny, in spite (or because?) of the extra painkillers. Even her "hello" was weird: focused, with it, to the point. It was like they'd thrown in a free brain transplant while patching up her leg.

"Mama. You sound *okay* today."

"I know I'm okay. I'm always okay, aren't I?"

"Uh . . . yeah."

"But listen—Jane Pine just came by for a visit and you'll never believe," she said. "Elliott. He's become a born-again Christian!"

"Oh," said Martine. "Oh, but that's good, isn't it? Compared to what he was before?"

"Ah, no! His mother's in a real flap about it. You know, she'd rather he was still importing the drugs or whatever it was he was doing. He's joined some cult downtown, she says. He keeps calling her and talking about Jesus and kindness to others. My God, poor Jane—she thinks he's going to turn into one of those guys on late-night television. 'At least I have five others,' she said. But it *is* bad, Martini. I think it would be about the worst."

"A Christian? A Christian is the worst thing you could be? Come on, Mama. Think about what you're saying." Louise was talking so fast. Was this how she used to talk? Before Mack Donovan, before the Professor, before Martine?

"Well, they try to shut out others, you know. Who aren't like them. If you don't join them, they think of ways to get you to do it." She was so sure of herself, businesslike, opinionated; how could this have happened?

"Like when my cousin Pierre went into the seminary," she was saying. "Everything was suddenly Catholic or it wasn't. The spoons, the trees, the floor. Everything was either for the Church or against it. So black and white."

"Hey, you always talked about how great that guy was!" Martine cried. Cousin Père Pierre was the only person in her family Louise even admitted to liking. "I can't believe I'm hearing this from you. *You're* the one who sent me to Catholic school."

"Oh, that was just to make your father mad. In those days, anything I ever did was only to bother him. Anyway, Jane's going to send out the, the—what do you call them—the deprogrammers on the little guy, there. He lives downtown, she says—not far from you, I don't think."

If I tell her I've seen him, Martine thought, she'll have me deprogrammed too. She pictured herself and Elliott locked in a hotel room, while men in black suits denied them protein and waved business school applications in their faces.

"Are you all right there, Mama? How's your leg?"

"I'm fine, *chouette*. Now I'm sure you have things to do. I'll call you soon."

It dawned on Martine once again that there were some critical things her mother didn't care about. Like where her child was and what she was doing. She sounded happy to hear from her, and just as happy to hang up. Some horrible experiment had taken place in Martine's absence, a rewiring so radical it could never hold. There were drugs that made you confident, and successful, and strong—but Martine still preferred the ones that had made Louise groggy, for groggy was the mother she knew.

Before leaving for work, Martine stood dumbly in the vestibule in a half-conscious wait for Father Kearney. They didn't, as a rule, ever go there together, but she wondered now if things had changed. Now that they were friends, sort of. He didn't come down though.

There was a sound from upstairs, however, an awful sound, like the lament of a ghost in a dark wood. Then vomiting, then silence. She heard the priest whispering; it sounded like there was another man there with him. "All right now," Father Kearney was saying. "Just calm down."

Martine did not know what any of this meant and stood redundantly before the staircase, its rose-pink runner lit by rainy daylight. "Everything okay?" she yelled. "Do you need any help up there?"

There was a long pause and then another moan, in the dark folds of which she was sure she heard the word "no."

Nobody needed her today. She backed slowly away from the stairs and out into the cold rain, having offered what she could.

Upon entering the Refuge Martine noted the presence of only one customer: the beggar who could be a chooser.

She hadn't seen him since the night she'd imagined him following her home. Tonight he was wearing a denim jacket cut off at the elbows and filthy white cotton pants, greyed to the colour of a sea squall. He was a huge man and it was all too small on him. Suleiman had told her he was quite a successful panhandler and Martine assumed it had been an inordinately good day, that he'd made his quota and knocked off early. So he'll be in a good mood today, she thought with relief. He won't yell.

And he wasn't in yelling form. In fact, he didn't even notice her. His watery eyes seemed blinded by some fantastic carousel rotating behind them. "Pretty balloons, pretty balloons," he droned. "All the girls love the pretty balloons." The drawstring around the waist of his pants was open; he wore no underwear and his pubic hair was horribly visible.

Martine edged away from him toward the counter and hissed at Glenys, who was as usual buried in a magazine. She was the only other person there.

Glenys's boiled stare took hold of the man. "Sir!" she managed ridiculously. "Sir! Sir! Oh, gosh, if I could call Father—but then he and Mr. Frost are gone to pick up the coffee maker . . . Sir!"

Martine stopped for a minute and considered the moans at the top of the staircase, what they might have meant. But there was little time for such thought.

The man leaned forward and raised his voice about the balloons. The voice's very sonorousness scared both women and they froze behind the counter. His hand moved down to his near-bare genitals and he grasped at them, perhaps not to masturbate but in fact to cover them, protect them from some perceived assault. "Pretty balloons," he went on. "Oh, they love them, the pretty-in-the-sky balloons, *they* love *them,* they do . . ."

And the two ladies bountiful stood behind the counter in their little skirts, one barking impotently, one wiping forks and polishing the petty cash box and generally doing things that required her to look down and away from the sight. This went on for a while, during which time the beggar who would be a chooser would ardently hitch up his pants for minutes and just sit there in near silence; but Martine refused to take his order, and Glenys would not approach him. Not that he demanded any service.

Eventually Muriel entered with Manny and tried lancing him with a series of evangelical bons mots, but the beggar didn't pay her any attention, in thrall as he was to the balloons and the pretty girls. Muriel gave up, grabbed Manny by the shoulder, and left for the Koffee Kave around the corner, and so did the Salvadorans, who were so immediately repelled by his open pants that they were not three steps into the Refuge before leaving it. The man was clearly bad for business, and meanwhile there were two round aluminum platters of pinwheel sandwiches to be eaten. "Well, we might as well give them to him," said Glenys, who over the half-hour he'd been there had become rather used to his droning and babbling. "No other takers tonight."

But Martine pretended not to have heard and she continued to play at wiping and cleaning. She hated and feared this beggar, this beggar who once dared to choose. She hated the size of him and the space he consumed. She hated his senseless little chant about girls and balloons. She hated the way he was so very not in a jail or hospital.

At last there was a clattering at the back and Martine exhaled lavishly—Father Kearney, with Frost and Elliott. Father Kearney who would know what to do. *The dead ariseth, and appeareth to many.*

The priest burst through the door and ripped off his old muffler. Elliott was in his way and he pushed him against a wall, then loped to the table, grabbed the offender by both shoulders, and yanked. But the yank didn't work. The great man was much bigger than Father Kearney. "Get up, Raymond!" he yelled, but it was more of a chirp than a roar, he was not good at anger. "Get . . . get up, will you?" he grunted, and began pulling inefficiently at his victim's oil-soaked windbreaker, once, twice, until finally the beggar who would be a chooser flopped on the floor on his hands and knees.

Alms

His pants slipped farther down and he grabbed at them. He tried hitching them up, but his fingers were poor instruments with which to do it. "Ah!" he yelled, terrified and shaking. "Ah! Ah!"

The priest wrung his hands. He seemed at a loss about what to do while Raymond knelt before them all: Elliott standing against the back wall, Glenys with her magazine, and Martine and Father Kearney directly over him. At least Father Kearney finally had him where he could handle him. He instructed Martine to open the door so he could roll him out of it. Like a barrel, or a log.

Raymond lay on the sidewalk for a time, shaking and rolling. He was yelling but they couldn't hear him. They all watched in nervous silence, until he stirred, rolled, placed the flat of his palm on the sidewalk, and began to pull himself up. He tried and fell; his big knuckles scraped concrete.

The sight sickened Martine. Earlier she hadn't cared whether biology or free will had brought the man to this behaviour: if he couldn't help his repellence, she couldn't help her disgust. She wanted him up, she wanted him gone. But now—at the sight of him trying to get himself away, to satisfy all those who wanted him away—she felt those big hands straining against her conscience, a thing she had always hoped was made of harder stuff than the sidewalk. She was only partly relieved when, after several attempts, he succeeded in dragging himself up the street.

Father Kearney rushed to Martine and made a grand gesture out of throwing his coat around her shoulders. "You're okay?"

"She's fine, Father. Raymond didn't do anything," Glenys spat, angrily flipping the pages of her magazine. "And so long as you're asking, he didn't do anything to me either."

The priest ignored her. He led Martine to a table close by and sat her down. "Here, I'll get you a cup of coffee. I brought you a new machine for it."

A new machine: not for the Refuge, not for the clients, not for Glenys; the machine was for Martine, all for Martine. Something not quite right about that.

"Where will he go?" she asked. "Raymond, I mean."

"I don't know," he said, walking behind the counter where a new coffee maker sat. "Not my problem. Maybe the hall monitors will pick him up, with his pants hanging like that."

"Hall monitors?"

"That's what he calls the police," volunteered Glenys, banging with dissatisfaction at the little steel coffee maker, which was a far cry from sleek Simonetta. "Oh, dear," she said. "No, this wasn't the kind I was talking about. It's too small."

Father Kearney glared at her. "Well, I brought it from my own collection, and if people don't like what it gives off, they can damn well go outside and slurp from the puddles. Me and Frost didn't have time to get another one. We were busy."

Martine recalled the moans at the top of the staircase. "Where is Frost?" she asked.

Father Kearney ignored the question while plugging in the kettle. Then he turned around and bashed into Elliott by mistake.

"What are you still doing out here?" he yelled. "Why aren't you in the back room like you're supposed to be?"

Elliott stood still, perhaps so shocked by the priest's uncharacteristically cruel tone that he didn't seem able to move. He held an envelope in one hand, exactly like the ones in which Father Kearney enclosed Martine's pay. But it was much, much fatter.

"And put that away," the priest yelled. Elliot stuffed the envelope hurriedly into his jacket. Then he opened the door to the back and rushed in, slamming it behind him.

Father Kearney shook his head in fury. "Moron," he muttered.

Glenys was now frantically paging through her magazine, in a desperate flight from eye contact with anyone, and Martine knew that if anybody was going to say something, it would have to be her.

"He's not . . . what you said, Father."

The priest strode angrily over to table one and threw himself down into the chair. "Ah, come on, Martine. That guy's two Mormons short of a choir and everybody knows it."

"That's a terrible thing to say."

"All right," he said, agitated. "You want me to apologize, is that it? Be a good, polite little boy, like your bandito there across town? Never say or do or think a bad thing? Well, that ain't me, my precious, and if you look hard at yourself, you'll realize it ain't you either."

She took his coat off and hung it across a chair. "I think I'd better go," she said.

"Nah—wait," the priest snapped. He closed his eyes, calmed down. "I'm sorry. I *am* sorry." He took a deep breath, walked over to the back-room door, and turned the knob. "I am . . . sorry." He closed the door behind him.

At that moment Dianne walked in, apparently wracked by something. Every part of her looked like it hurt. She installed herself in Raymond's vacated seat with ostentatious slowness. Martine turned away from these new overtures of hypochondria, which she knew meant she'd have to do all the work yet again, for whatever part of the night still remained.

Glenys, who always had a lot of time for the phantom aches of others, put her magazine down and busied herself arranging pinwheel sandwiches on a plate for the ailing woman. "If he doesn't get us a new coffee maker," she nattered, "I don't know so much as we'll be able to keep serving it. And you can hardly have a café without coffee, now."

The chatter was ragged but light. Martine wondered whether Glenys had seen the overstuffed envelope. Even if she had, she gave the strong impression of not wanting to acknowledge it; to keep in perpetual motion, walking, wiping, clearing her throat so she didn't have to. This is what she did while Dianne and Martine sat immobile at different tables trying not to look at each other. Islands in a lonely archipelago.

Dianne sniffled, refused Glenys's offer of more coffee. Either she had a cold or was crying; the truth was probably both. The others listened for interminable minutes to her discomfort. "Where's Frost?" she said at last, wiping at her nose.

Glenys unplugged the kettle and spooned instant coffee into a Styrofoam cup. "Guess he wasn't feeling up to it tonight," she replied.

"Well, that's too bad," Dianne sobbed, "because I really felt like playing Calendar tonight. I'll play with you guys, though."

She was repellently, hugely sad, and it made Martine uncomfortable, since she was starting to see the Refuge in the way that Father Kearney did. Sadness was for the social worker, the doctor, the probation officer. Sadness had no place here.

When nobody replied, Dianne redoubled her keening. "November 12, 1983, folks. I said November 12, 1983. Does anyone want to take me on? Glenys? Martine? You try."

"I don't know," Martine said. She wanted to go, but Dianne's intensity was such Martine feared she would spring from her chair and try to block the door.

"November 12," she sniffed, "1983."

Father Kearney emerged from the back room. He walked over to Dianne, carrying the coffee Glenys had prepared. He put his arm around her and took out a pack of smokes, offering her one. They huddled together like that, smoking, not speaking, for what seemed like a long time, and when nine o'clock came around she got up to leave. The priest escorted her gently out by the elbow like a gentleman on a skating date.

He returned with a determined look and walked over to the little shrine in the corner, where Princess Diana's picture shared space with the votive candle and the sign LOVE THY NEIGHBOUR AS THYSELF. Then he crossed himself and said a short prayer. When he finished, he spoke quietly.

"Listen," he said to Glenys. "I'm going around back to help Elliott for a minute. But Dianne says she wants to come back tomorrow, so I'm going to take Martine with me—"

"What?" Glenys spluttered.

"Frost is pretty out of it and I don't think he'll be better by tomorrow. We've got a couple of errands so we'll have to leave early—and of course, we have to get the coffee maker."

"But you saw Dianne tonight, Father, she can't hardly work!"

"Says she can. It's just the anniversary, you know, she's feeling a little off."

"But—but—well, how about Raymond, what if Raymond comes back?"

"He won't."

Glenys fumed impotently in a desperate search for something to say. "But it's Friday, Father. Who knows who'll come in and—oh, why're you taking *her*? She's only worked here hardly any time at all—and you never take your waitresses out on a run! Never! And we haven't had a proper coffee maker for weeks and maybe you don't know but I've been having to run to the Chinaman's to buy instant with my *own* money."

Father Kearney grabbed his coat and said, "So get your sister to come help."

"You know very well my sister wants nothing to do with you, *Father*."

Her sarcasm came at him like spittle; he seemed suddenly to realize that his clericalism was a big joke to everyone but him, just another eccentricity, like Frost's cardboard box or Suleiman's poems. He slumped against the counter like a man who'd once had control of his people but had now lost them, to drink and madness and petty mutiny. He looked to the back, where Elliott worked in silence, the only one who never gave him any guff. He fingered the plastic stem of a flower. You could tell from the freshets of blood at his temples that he was considering another cast of characters, another refuge: good, credulous, meek, stupid people, the kind who could make it work. "You'll do it," he said quietly. "I know you will."

But Glenys wasn't finished. "And I never seen you act like that with Raymond before, did I? You always said to let him be when he's like that. Let him be and the others can either listen to him or go to Koffee Kave, that's their choice. 'Concerts of the spoken word'—that's what you always call them. But tonight you throw him out. In the street, like an animal."

Father Kearney wrapped his arms around himself and hugged, like a little boy. It was true, Martine saw it in his eyes; he'd broken his own rules and couldn't quite bring himself to believe it. When he finally spoke he was hardly audible, since a large part of him agreed with what she'd said.

"But you always wanted Raymond thrown out, Glenys. You've been nagging at me for not ever doing it. What about the time I stopped you—when you went after him with the broom, don't you remember that?"

Glenys opened her mouth to release a rebuttal but none emerged, at least not immediately. "The thing is . . ." she said. "Okay . . . all right, maybe I did . . . but for good reasons! You put up with him when he's going on, and you even agree with him, and you always take him seriously and say things like, 'Oh, is that so, Raymond? I never looked at it that way before.' Then one day you waltz on in here and kick him by the seat of those rotten old pants—and what is it for? What is it for? It's all to impress your little country-club friend, that's what. Well, you can try all the tricks you want, Father, but you're never gonna see limousines pulling up outside of *here*."

Cynthia Macdonald

The priest just looked at her, with that open, blank look Martine was slowly coming to know. She now understood where the broken nose and the crooked jaw had come from: he never fought back.

She gathered her cape around her and said good night to them. Father Kearney snapped to attention and reached for his scarf. "Yes," he said with an embarrassed little chortle. "Leaving—that sounds like a good idea, right about now."

"Oh, isn't that just so nice," Glenys snorted, watching the pair get ready to go.

Martine realized how it looked and hated it, too. She told them both that she'd be leaving alone, but he, of course, wouldn't hear of it. He reached out awkwardly and placed a gentle hand on what he guessed to be her shoulder. It was thickly protected by the cape but the touch still frightened Martine, especially when he said, with pleading eyes, "Aw, don't listen to her. I never do." She removed the hand as politely as she could, and told them both she'd see them tomorrow.

On the way home she heard steps behind her. The steps were so loud she knew they had to be real, and when she turned around she was chilled to see the advancing silhouette of Glenys, her tumbleweed perm backlit by street lamps.

The women walked single file for a time, with Glenys about ten steps behind. Finally, she tired of that arrangement and slithered up next to Martine, opening her umbrella close enough to scrape with its spokes.

"I guess you're pretty proud of yourself, eh? It's all just coming together sweet as you planned it, isn't it?"

300

Naturally Martine said nothing, which gave Glenys the courage to continue. "Well, you should know it won't last too long. I've seen 'em come and I've seen 'em go, and let me tell you, go is what they always do in the end." Martine made an acute left turn onto a side street and tried to outwalk the harridan, but Glenys kept the pace up. "You don't even know anything about him. I've been with him for two years, so I'm the one to ask. If you want to hear stories I could tell you, yes, I could."

"If you think he's so awful," Martine said, "why do you stay with him?"

"I'm not staying," Glenys shot back. "Oh, no. I'm leaving, soon as I can get into occupational therapy I'm leaving. I've had it with his nonsense. He's no priest like I've ever seen, but what can you do. He forced me into all this—but I'm leaving, yes, I am."

Martine stopped. "He forced you into this? What do you mean?"

Under an umbrella on which nothing landed but cold fall air, Glenys beheld Martine with a sour grince of the lips. She looked suddenly consoled that the girl would soon discover what life with this man was really like; that she had one rosy toe in the Lake of Despond and the rest would soon follow, foot, leg, the whole package of transitorily girlish parts. That she would never get over this, this, whatever you'd care to call it, *affair*—yes, that would be it, *affair;* that it would tug at her later in a life marked by stronger and better comforts, and it would destroy all those comforts for her. Because how could you get over a priest who'd left you high and dry? It'd be as though God himself had come in for a wee look, sneered, laughed, and left.

"Make me a cup of tea, dear, and I'll tell you," she smiled.

They stopped in front of the house. Martine was loath to invite Glenys in, but there was no way of finding out what she meant without it. So she let the woman follow her through the lace-curtained door.

They settled themselves in Martine's spare little kitchen. Glenys looked around disapprovingly.

"I've read that book," she said, staring at a paperback by Martine's sleeping bag.

Martine couldn't believe it. *Anna Karenina*? Glenys? What do you know.

"I'm really enjoying it," Martine said as she took tea bags out of the cupboard. This information was a sound for the sore ears of an academic's child. Perhaps she hadn't given Glenys enough credit. Why, it seemed like forty, fifty years ago that she had been at the university herself, yet here was someone with whom she could discuss Tolstoy: here again would be the scent of tweed, the taste of sherry, the roar of the hearth fire in the faculty club. Well, maybe not quite. But Martine decided to ask her opinion anyway.

"Tolstoy is so sensitive," Martine said, "the way he deals with adultery—don't you think?"

"Adultery?" Glenys exclaimed. "*Hchm*. Well, *I* certainly didn't get that from it."

Deflated, Martine set a teacup before her. Then Glenys launched into her story.

"*Y*OU KNOW, OF COURSE, that I'd had some trouble with the volunteer jobs I'd held," she said delicately. "So I decided to start a project of my own."

Nobody, Glenys reasoned, could dismiss her from something she herself had started. After mulling over a few options she settled on the idea of a young Catholic singles group, run out of the basement of her local parish. Not that she personally wanted a husband. The thought horrified her, and even worse was the prospect of her sister Bonnie's being snapped up by some sweating streetcar driver. But it was the only idea the pastor at St. Anthony's would consent to; he reasoned that a knitting circle "wasn't in line with parish objectives," and the Sunday school was already well staffed. Add to which, Martine figured, he couldn't bear her bothering him all the time: give her a project, close the discussion, get her off his back.

So she had no choice. But all would be well, if she only ran the thing properly.

It was at this time that Clifford Kearney started attending mass at St. Anthony's every Sunday, front pew always, resplendent in a flashy three-piece suit and tie. He'd lately returned from a stint "building housing for the poor in Costa Rica," as he told old Father Fodor, and was looking for another opportunity in social service. He was keen, well groomed, and confident—a real gentleman—and the pastor had noticed him immediately from the altar. After a few such Sundays, Kearney struck up a friendly acquaintance with "Father F." He reminisced with him about his own days on the altar at St. Anthony's and complimented the priest on his trenchant homilies. The older man was glad of Kearney's company and found him a welcome addition to his grubby benumbed flock, though he didn't half believe his tales of European travel and advanced philosophical study. Intelligent he was, but there was still a strong whiff of the sewer on him. Still, he had always been drawn to men with big ideas and inflexible spines; he was not that kind of man himself.

One Thursday, Kearney took Father F. across the street for tea and made a proposal. What if he started a drop-in centre for the poor, a sort of café—not just a grimy soup kitchen, with watery macaroni soup and such, but a classy sort of alcohol-free bistro with breadsticks and fruit punch served in fake crystal. A touch of the Left Bank on the wrong side of the tracks. What did the old priest think?

Father F. was skeptical. Did it ever occur to the young man that crystal, fake or otherwise, might just be *lost* on some people? All very well for us, but . . . he cradled his Styrofoam teacup and gazed disconsolately at a fly hopping across the sugar lumps. It would never get by the pastoral council. And anyway, the night Kearney wanted was taken because of the Catholic singles group. Not that Father F. saw much of a future for that particular venture. The gal who ran it hadn't attracted many people to her group and what few she had were still most definitely single. But he told Kearney to take it up with her, if he was interested in "something social."

And why not, thought Clifford Kearney. I'm a Catholic boy and plenty single, too.

Catholic singles night was held on Wednesday. On Kearney's first visit it had attracted exactly three other participants, two girls and a guy. Perfect, thought Kearney. A double date. And the choice is easy—the one in the neck contraption isn't to my taste, but her friend isn't bad at all. Nice smile—maybe she's got legs, too, though it's hard to tell with that tarpaulin she's wearing. As for the guy—no problem moving him over, weedy little fella, well, I guess I am, too, but this one's got that lobotomized look you get when you been punching a cash register in some hospital cafeteria all day, *kaching, kaching*—oh, gosh, this'll be fun. He rose to address the singles.

"Hello, everybody! My name's Clifford and I love to dance! How about you, there, you in the corner? What do you think about dancing?"

Bonnie gave him a demure look and glanced nervously at her sister, who was standing over her with crossed arms. "She doesn't care to dance," said Glenys evenly. "And anyhow, there's no record player here."

"What?" Kearney clutched his breast in mock surprise. "Why, how can we have a party with no dancing? How 'bout you, sport, you like to shake a foot, eh? Am I right? You look like a swinger."

The man looked past him and sipped catatonically from a cup of Tang.

"Well, this is your lucky day, young Catholics! Because I just happened to bring the party with me!" It was true: under one arm Kearney hefted a portable eight-track player; under the other, a collection of outmoded "hits" with which to feed it. It was a Kearney sort of thing to do. His mother had always brought her own food when invited to other people's apartments, and his sister Rosemarie only read her own books in libraries. It was a Kearney thing not to trust what was offered in strange places. "You know, when I think that the best minds of our generation are hopping it up at Studio 54, a scant plane ride away . . ." He sauntered over to a card table set up in the corner, pushing aside the tray of date squares, the punch bowl full of Tang. He set up the player and popped in an old *Sergio Mendes and Brasil 66* tape that both looked and sounded as if it had spent a great deal of time underwater. "I know it's a den of iniquity, but such fun they're having! We should be having it, too!"

The neck-brace girl crossed her arms tighter and pursed her greasy purple lips together. Kearney realized he was probably courting suicide; it was she who kept the basement keys, it was she he was meant to woo. But he couldn't help himself—these were the kind of stiffs who tipped over if you so much as blinked at them. Plus he'd get Mrs. Neck Brace onside in the end, on that you could count. She wanted him, he could tell. She was hurting. She'd be lucky to get a feel from her gynecologist.

Bonnie rose and padded toward the bathroom. Kearney smiled broadly at her, grabbed a date square, and planted himself in the centre of the large room. Getting a little affection out of these religious ones was always an act of back-alley curettage.

"Okay, here's what let's do. I'm going to finish consuming this delicious baked good—say, did you make this?" Glenys said that no, her sister did. Her sister who was now in the bathroom. "That's your sister? And very pretty she is, too. What's her name?"

"Bonnie."

"Ah, patron saint of breads and pastries!"

"I don't believe so."

"Oh. Well, anyway, what's *your* name?"

Glenys thought, No man alone behaves with such sure-ness, such ironic contempt for a strange crowd, unless he is deranged. And why's he dressed so fancy? Cufflinks, even, and are those see-through socks?

"Okay, here's the thing, guys," he went on, rubbing his hands. "Last year I completed a fantastically great tour of Central America and I was lucky to learn a thing or two about the dancing they do there. Oh—but here's the lovely Bonnie." He gave her a courtly nod as she scurried back to her chair. "It's very . . . well, why don't I show you." He marched over and thrust the crook of his elbow at the dental hygienist. "May I?"

Bonnie glanced up at her molten sister and knew it was not all right, but she got up anyway and let him lead her to the centre of the room. He pulled her toward him in a way that was both intimate and chivalrous.

"It's very sensual, as you can see," he said softly. "Glenys and what's your name . . . Tang-drinking guy . . . why don't you watch us for a second or two and then you guys can give it your own go."

But neither of them made a move. Bonnie tried but couldn't take her eyes off the hurried knot of this strange man's necktie. He was small but so was she, and glad of it, too: if he were any more imposing, she might buckle with shame, though why she couldn't exactly know. This proximity to his flesh was bad enough, the knobbed throat rising arrogantly out of its crisp collar. "Just let yourself go," he whispered, "I'll lead you through it."

So she did; she let him do it all, and it was a system that worked. Before long, they were like a perfect machine, gliding with liquid ease across the dance floor and looking shyly into one another's eyes. "You're good at this!" he said.

But right at that point the music slipped into a state of suboceanic bubbling so loud that neither of them could ignore it. They stopped dancing, jolted out of the reverie.

Glenys snapped, "Well, now, naturally we'll be taking that off."

"Cost me a quarter at a garage sale," Kearney laughed.

Then the other man—single, Catholic, but by no means young—finished his drink and began groping around for his coat.

"That about does it for me, ladies," he said with a frown at Kearney, and then he walked out.

They all listened for a spell to the clatter of the man's feet on the stairs leading to the street. "I think you can go now, Mr. Clifford," said Glenys. "I think we were handling this just fine by ourselves."

"I can fix the tape."

"Nobody wants to dance."

He helped himself to a brimming cup of Tang, then took a silver flask from his jacket pocket, and sprinkled a few clear drops from it into the cup. "Well, Bonnie seems to—"

"Bonnie is not interested in your attentions." Glenys said, at which Bonnie excused herself and repaired once again to the bathroom.

"Look," said Kearney, as he helped himself to another date square. "If you think I'm after your sister, I wouldn't worry. See, I'm not exactly available. I'm in the seminary."

Glenys's eyes narrowed to the point of disappearance. "The *seminary*?"

"Oh, yes. I'm on summer break, I'll be ordained next year. I just like to dance is the thing."

"Well, goodness, Father—"

"Not *Father* yet!"

"Well, my goodness, Mr. Clifford. I didn't really know and I'm sorry. I'm honoured to have you here, and if there's anything we can do to make your visit comfortable." She brushed imaginary date-square crumbs off her skirt and plumped her perm with her fingers. "I hope you're enjoying the Tang?"

"It's excellent Tang, really. Very well stirred. Actually, while we're on the subject of snacks, I'd like to propose a little idea to you."

Cynthia Macdonald

Glenys coloured and turned away—the very idea of it was too delectable for her hearing, someone proposing an idea to her instead of the other way around. Someone fixing to hire her, and a clergyman, too, or close to it. Kearney saw his chance and pounced. "I've been thinking that we could turn this singles night into a kind of café, you know, a sort of . . . bistro for singles. I know where to get better snacks than those date squares," he stage-whispered, lest Bonnie hear over the flush of the toilet.

Glenys stiffened. "But singles night is Wednesday," she said. "Wednesday is a good night for singles, because if you met somebody, that would give you time to organize a date for Friday or Saturday or some such."

"Hey, relax. I'm not asking you to change the day. I'm just asking you to change the orientation a little."

"But it's—singles night, it's—"

"Yours?" Kearney grinned and stared at the lap of the freshly returned Bonnie, hoping to make out the roundness of a thigh as she arranged her defenceless calves beneath her. "My dear, it would still be yours. I just want to help you out a little. I could bring a lot of singles into this place, believe me."

Of course, he didn't mention that there were, by the terms of polite society, very good reasons for the singleness of the people he had in mind.

Glenys agreed reluctantly—how could she not? He was going to be a priest in a few months while she would stay the same, come from nothing and bound for nothing. She handed over the reins.

As the weeks went on, though, the worst happened: she lost what control she'd had over the enterprise. The basement filled up, to be sure—but my Lord in Heaven, what did it fill up *with*. Dead-eyed women. Shaking, babbling men, one of whom insisted he had a piano up his rectum ("Well, for God's sake, play it!" Kearney commanded. "It couldn't sound worse than my eight-track!"). There were derelicts who'd try to curl up in the corner for a nap, prior to a poke with a broom handle and a gallant bum's rush from Kearney. One night there was one who wouldn't budge, perpendicularly plopped against the radiator, and poke poke poke went the broom until he finally stirred a bit.

"Frost?" Kearney tried, tentatively. The bum grunted and stirred, then covered his head with his arms.

"Alex? Is—is that you under there?"

"No," was the bum's muffled response. "It's the Sultan of Brunei. My Concorde took a wrong turn and I crashed into a tree."

Kearney threw his broom down and jumped in the air. "Filipowski! Doctor! *Kuzyn!*" He lay down with the filthy man, started pawing him, hugging him. It turned out that they'd known each other a long time, and Kearney was so thrilled by the reunion that he barely appeared to notice what state his old friend was in.

"Get the fuck off me, Clifford," the bum snarled.

Kearney ignored his rebuke. "Now, of course, you'll have to come back home with me. You look like shit, Frost—excuse my French and don't tell the cardinal. You haven't been sleeping rough, have you?"

Frost rolled over on his back and stared at the ceiling fan. Everyone had gone and they were the last two in the place, along with Bonnie and Glenys, of course.

"Good thing my parents sent me to summer camp," Frost growled. "The survival skills have served me well."

"Oh, but we can't have that," said Kearney. "A man of learning and breeding such as yourself—no, that'll never do."

So Frost became a kind of VIP around the place; he always had to be served first and best, and Bonnie had to take it when he criticized her baking. Yet in time that baking wasn't even needed any more, as the basement began receiving the nutritious overflow from office parties, daycare centres, and fancy restaurants, courtesy, usually, "some woman I know's husband." Kearney seemed to know many women who in turn had many husbands. But if he'd lost the need for Bonnie's date squares, he hadn't lost the need for Bonnie, though she felt disgusted by the unpredictability of what singles night had become, and visited only at her sister's periodic insistence.

One night, though, Glenys took to her bed with an unspecified orthopedic ache and sent Bonnie out instead. Bonnie whined, wrung hands, puffed forth with tiny excuses not to go, but nothing worked. To stay home would be unsisterly, not to say unchristian.

She was grateful when it all went relatively quietly. No florid psychotics or real fights of any sort. Several people tried to converse with Bonnie, but she just nodded and went back to rinsing the plastic cups and throwing out the scraps. Two regulars got in a polite argument over whether she was deaf or some kind of immigrant. She found this sort of funny; really, she thought, it wasn't so bad here.

But later she found herself alone with the would-be priest, after all the "young singles" had departed. He sat on the

counter and watched her dry the last of the cups in silence.
She tried not to look at him looking at her. He wore a proud
look, though whether he was proud of her or proud of himself
for having her there—or proud of what might happen later—
she couldn't tell. By her reckoning he had no cause for pride.
He wasn't meant for the priesthood, she could see that, and if
her sister didn't see what was right in front of her, it was
because she was too kind for her own good.

"Bonnie . . ." he opened tentatively. "Bonnie, I have something to ask you."

She dropped a cup, which bounced vigorously on the
carpet as she knelt to pick it up.

"I don't," he said, "exactly know how to ask this, but . . ."

"Don't," she said, shaking.

And before he got the chance to explain himself, she'd
risen, grabbed her purse, and hightailed it out of there. She
never came back, either.

For the next ten singles nights Glenys was left, strange to say,
on her own, running the place and kicking out customers
when their language or behaviour offended her.

"We've got to have some rules in here, Mr. Kearney," she
said.

"Oh? Then you go ahead and make them, my dear," he
replied. "I've never really been one for rules."

Glenys liked kicking people out: it proved to her, at
least, that she was more than just the person who made the
coffee and washed up. After a while, though, the glister of
co-running the bistro began to tarnish. She noticed that,
when he was there, the seminarian was not substantially

different from the flock to whom he ministered. He laughed at their filthy jokes, played cards for money, bummed smokes, and even pinched the buttocks of young women he didn't know. For a few months she told herself she wasn't really seeing such things; she didn't want to. The priest was too nice to her, too smiling, too gracious. "What would I do without you, Glenys?" he said one evening. "What would I do?" And if at home poor Bonnie darkened at the mention of his name, what of it. She'd always been too dim for her own good, Glenys thought.

During those months Glenys reclaimed some of her old identity, sanding down calloused souls whenever she could get hold of them. She developed a sort of mentoring relationship with a schoolboy who started showing up at singles night for lack of anything else to do—under her tutelage, he even placed third in a schoolwide math contest. But when she assumed it her right to attend the Christmas concert at his school, he threw a fit. "You're not my mom, volunteer lady," he shrieked, right in the gym, right in front of all the teachers. She wasn't his mom, he was right. She'd temporarily forgotten the rules.

Some time later, the basement flooded after a heavy rainstorm. Kearney had directed Glenys to open the café by herself and she went in the back room to assess the extent of the damage. There she found about twenty large cardboard boxes full of potato chips stacked against the wall, the bottom ones soaked and ruined. Must be for the Sunday school, she thought. Enticements for the kids. She ran up to check with Father Fodor.

The old priest tried to look busy with paperwork, the better to be rid of her. "There aren't any potato chips in the basement. Now, if you'll excuse me, Glenys—"

"Oh, sure there are, Father," she replied, surreally bright. "Big cases of them. Anyways, the bottom cases are ruined and they must be for the Sunday school. *Hch-hch-hchmmm.* The kids definitely won't like to have their chips all wet and I thought you should know."

"Well, I'm sure Agnes would have told me if . . . no, we didn't buy any potato chips, I'm sure of it." He filled his briefcase, snapped it shut, and stared at her evenly. "Anything else?"

"Nothing." She waited while he put on his hat and coat. She had counted on his concern and felt deflated. "So, well, I'll ask Father Kearney, in case he knows anything about it."

The briefcase's handle slid in old Father F.'s grip. "*Father* Kearney? But . . . you mean *Mr.* Kearney. My goodness, Glenys, he's not a priest."

"Yes, I know, but—soon."

"Soon? I don't think so. First I've ever heard of it."

The next day she watched Kearney stalk over the sodden broadloom. He looked desperate and powerless, and the longer she watched him, the angrier she got.

"Damnit!" he yelled. "Damn, damn, damn."

How, she wondered, could I ever have trusted him? A priest, indeed!

"Ruined. Ruined six ways from Thursday," he said.

Glenys saw that there was much more in the boxes than potato chips. There were jujubes and candy corn and marshmallows; canned goods, too, tomatoes and peas and Bing cherries. All nonsense the café would never use, yet it all seemed to belong to him. As he beheld dripping bag after dripping bag, she took in the ostentatious pleating of his pants, the cufflinks he wore even on hot days: how false all this seemed now. She cleared her throat and spoke.

"Mister Kearney."

"What," he muttered, kicking in the cardboard mush wall of a box.

"May I ask what all this is for, sir? We don't seem to have a call for any of it at the café."

"I'll explain it later. Right now I don't have time. I lost about seven hundred bucks 'worth of food here. Man!"

Glenys let him root around a bit in this way and, at length, managed to call forth what little she owned in the way of his favourite quality: balls. "I hate to say it, but how on earth did you pay for it anyways, *Mister* Kearney?"

He stopped inspecting the bags for a second and examined her in silence. He drew himself up and straightened his tie, as if he were suddenly reminded of his true station in life. "Do you have a problem, my dear?"

She took in a breath. "I do. Yes. In fact, I would like, if it wouldn't be too much trouble—*hchm*—to hand in my resignation."

"Ah," he said, slapping bags vigorously back into the box. "Well, one of these days I'll get a desk and a secretary and you can get her to type it up."

"Mister Kearney, you know what I mean."

"That I don't, Glenys, that I don't. Is this how it works with you? A little rough weather and you bail?" He was hefting and throwing the bags with something too like violence for her comfort. "I need more help than I ever did with this place and you just stand there like a . . . like a . . ." He met and tugged on a bag so heavy it finally defeated him, then approached Glenys and placed both hands on her shoulders. She started back and stumbled. "Glenys," he beseeched, "just let's stop all this silly talk now. Please go find me a mop."

"Yes, and I understand all that, but—" trembling now— "but . . . I really want to quit."

"Look, Glenys," he said, taking her hands in his. "Please. I *need* you here, you know that. You've seen the other girls, they can't handle it like you can." The other girls were friends of Kearney's brought in from time to time, young and well-groomed and stupid girls at that: this here's my friend Renée, he would say by way of introduction, my friend Sharon who's at the university, my good friend Julie I've told you so much about. Glenys always took care to ride them especially hard. She made them empty the mousetraps, for example, and made them wait on table one, by the door where the glue sniffers sat. The "friends" would invariably vanish after a single shift: not one had come back yet, praise God. "Nobody's good with the customers the way you are," he continued, and she thought: You got that right, brother.

He frowned and took a little stroll around the room, calmly inspecting its stains and failures. "What if . . . say, Glenys, what if I were to put you on salary?"

"Salary? But, Father—you don't have any money for a salary."

"Oh, but I'll find it. I'll have to. You make the best coffee in the city. I can't afford to lose that, can I?"

An acid grin settled on the bottom of her face, like sediment in an old bottle of vinegar.

"I guess I do, don't I? I guess there's none who can make it as well, though the good Lord knows I've tried to train them."

"And so have I," he smiled. Then he returned to the boxes, presumably to stave off any further talk of money. "Now, Glenys. Shall we see about that mop?"

The next week though, disaster struck. Father Fodor invited Glenys up to his office and informed her he was cancelling her group. Glenys protested that they'd cleaned up the carpet and there was no need to worry, and what could you do about an act of God anyway, but it was useless. Father F. said the spot had already been granted to a bereavement support group. *Death,* Kearney muttered to himself when told of it. Personally, he found *life* far preferable, but in the end it didn't matter.

The husband of his dear, close, good friend Janet owned a lamp store not far from there that had fallen on hard times. The husband hadn't been able to sell it so was forced to rent. Kearney would have preferred donated space, but put up more than cheerfully with the new expenses he was bringing upon himself.

Then another curious thing happened. Kearney and Frost scared up a big white cube van and started driving it around. At first they'd stay away from the Refuge for an hour at a time, then two; after a couple of weeks they were barely stopping in, leaving Glenys to muse sadly about how, once again, she was running things on her own. At least she was getting paid.

Alms

One afternoon, Kearney showed up with a pile of boxes from the Princess Café. "Tally ho, my dear," he called to Glenys. "We'll be late tonight." He put the boxes down and, and as he did his coat flew open. Glenys stared.

Instead of the three-piece suit he usually wore, he was now dressed in a black shirt, pants, and clerical collar. They were far too big for him and Glenys's stomach cramped at the sight.

"I see you've taken your orders, then," she said. *"Father."*

"I sure have," he said, buttoning up his coat. "Isn't it a wonderful day?"

After hearing this story Martine was taken by what she had always considered the world's most horrible feeling: that she wanted to leave, but that to do so would only be to proceed onto a street that was equally leavable, and no train, plane, or space shuttle could deliver her anyplace better. One hell would only give onto another.

"He *stole* the clothes?" she said.

"It's what I'm telling you. I don't know how, but I'm sure of it. He'd tell me if I asked, though. When he thinks he can trust you, he tells you everything, even if you don't want to know it."

But this story was naggingly incomplete. Martine wanted to know: why *not* ask? Why not find out what was in the boxes?

"Oh, that's his business," said Glenys, as if it were obvious. "It's not really important."

"So you stayed with him—even though you thought he was a fraud, even though he stole your job, even though he seems to be running some seedy operation you don't half understand—you stayed with him because he complimented you on your coffee?"

Glenys clutched her handbag closer. "Like I said, I'm leaving." She looked fearfully about the small, white, unadorned apartment, as if its walls were kept standing by the hidden bones of countless runaway girls. "And so, I would imagine, after listening to me, are you."

Martine rose from her chair and took the cups over to the sink. "Yes, I suppose I will." She turned on the hot water and let it scald her hands, thanking God there was still some pain in the world that was simple, elemental. "Some time."

"So you won't go tomorrow, then? On the run with Father?"

"I . . . I don't know." She had to see these things for herself, after all. To take Glenys at her word would be unthinkable.

"You don't know!" Glenys cleared her throat and slapped her handbag on the table, loud as a bomb. "After all I've been telling you and you don't know! *I* have to work there, of course. I've got no place else. But you—you could go to Holt Renfrew now, couldn't you? Be a saleslady or some such, fold the cashmere scarves . . . Well, this is really just the prettiest picture, isn't it? Dianne's baby died and you're making her come in to work for you so you can go gallivanting about the city with your boyfriend!" She struggled into her coat and stole up next to Martine.

"In 1983," Martine said. "Was that what she—" She clutched the sink and looked determinedly into it.

"Well, that's hardly a long time ago, is it? For a little boy to die!"

Martine coloured. "How did he die?" she asked.

"Oh," said Glenys, shaking her head. "He had a bad heart, and the doctors left him waiting too long in the emergency."

"That's awful. Did Dianne sue?"

Glenys sniffed. "Sue? Right. Look, don't ask me any more about it. I don't butt into private matters."

Neither do I, Martine thought. That's the thing.

"That's awful," she said. "My God. That's a horrible, horrible shame."

"Well, then—why would you go? With a man like that?"

A man like that, indeed. Martine recoiled in shame that she'd ever believed, liked, or trusted him. She thought of that envelope full of money and felt sick; she wanted to run back to Moore Park immediately, but how could she leave Glenys and Dianne, Frost and Elliott?

"It's better for all of us," she said, "if I go."

Glenys buttoned her coat rapidly, straining its fabric over her neck brace. "I already know all I need to and so do you."

"Yeah, well, something's going on here."

"Doesn't matter what it is. I told you these things for your own protection and you can leave or stay with me. It's your choice." She moved in close, smelling of canned beets and library fines, of everything small and nagging in the world.

"Keep your nose out of it," she said. "That's the best thing. Look at Miss Hall down in Washington. She just typed some letters and shredded some others and didn't know one from the other, and now there's pictures of her dancing in the party pages—no jail for her. Well, none for us either, *if* you stay in your place."

Martine froze. *Jail?*

"But doesn't it bother you," she asked in a thin voice, "that he's doing something wrong? And that you—you work for him, so you're in on it, too, whether you like it or not."

Glenys clasped her handbag, cleared her throat, and sighed in an offhand way, as if she'd just accomplished some tiresome but necessary task. "Yes, well, some of us can't afford to lie around in bubble baths all day thinking about those things."

When Martine said nothing, Glenys picked up her gloves and tried furiously to pull them on over stiff fingers. "I see," she said, her tone strained. "*Hchm*. Go with him, then." She gave up on the gloves and closed her eyes. "Just, please, don't tell anyone what you see. Have some kindness in your heart. All I can do is beg, and I suppose . . . well, I suppose that's what I'm doing. Thank you for the tea." With that, she left.

Martine had always envied Glenys, in a way. That neck brace made for a collar bigger and whiter than the priest's. It was never the woman's spinsterhood, physical malaise, friendlessness that she envied, no, but her mind: clear, cold, and unpolluted as an ancient river. The words "sort of" or "maybe" never fell from those incongruously painted lips and Glenys had, until now, always seemed stronger for it. No time for rumination in a world full of lazy people and unfinished work. She always zeroed in on what she wanted to see, and sheared off what she didn't without a second's regret. It was the kind of decisiveness she felt rising in herself, right about now.

*F*ATHER KEARNEY WAS SITTING on the stairs of the foyer, smoking, with the Niagara Falls ashtray balanced on one knee. "I told Elliott to pick us up here," he told her. "If it's all right."

He was uncharacteristically quiet as they waited. Every so often there was a groan from upstairs, against which he appeared to grit his teeth. "Frost," he said. "I'm taking care of him upstairs for a while."

"Is he . . . very bad?" Martine asked.

"Ha," the priest replied, as though she had made some ironic or wry observation. But that was all he had to say about it or anything else. She thought he might want to talk about where they were going today, what they were doing, but he remained silent and kept smoking. "Father," she asked a minute later, "what will I be doing today?"

He ground out his cigarette and thought about it. "We're going to be making a few stops, holding a couple of meetings.

Just come with me when I tell you to. You don't have to say anything—just be your usual classy self." He smiled, then went quiet again. They sat and waited. Every so often he started to express a thought, but then it fell apart and he stopped himself: "Did you ever—aw, forget it," he said.

She did forget it. She wasn't the type to press. But he was acting very strange and she wondered about everything he was hiding.

"Oh," he said suddenly, and began to rustle around in one of his pockets. "Here. I found this a while ago and I thought you might like it. See? It's got your initial on it." He handed her a small orange-and-yellow change purse with a large red *M* on it.

Martine beheld the tiny purse, which felt empty. "This is Manny's purse," she said.

"Oh. Manny? Like, Muriel's Manny?"

"Yeah. There was a lot of money in it." She stared hard at Father Kearney but his expression did not change. "He was saving for Lionel Richie, whatever that means."

"Huh," said the priest. "It was empty when I found it. Poor kid. Around here nobody holds on to a lot of money for very long." He smiled. "But it's not empty now. Open it."

Martine unzipped it and looked inside. Two tiny jewels glinted in the darkness. Earrings.

"Do you like them?" he asked.

"I . . ." Very small, but were they actually diamonds? They terrified her. As she was formulating her answer the horn honked outside.

"Well, do you?" Father Kearney pressed as they climbed into the cab beside Elliott. No one said hello to him; he started to drive anyway. "What do you think?" the priest continued. "They're pretty, aren't they?"

Martine zipped the purse back up and handed it back to him. "I can't take these," she said.

Father Kearney was dumbfounded. "Oh, I see," he said.

Then, to Martine's surprise, he started laughing, hard. "I'm sorry, my dear," he said. "I'm sorry for laughing, I don't want to embarrass you. But you see, these aren't for you."

"They aren't?" Martine said, shocked.

"No. It's my mother's birthday. I just wanted to see what you thought, you being a lady of taste and good sense. But then Elliott here told me that you don't even like jewellery. So I guess you're not the best person to ask," he finished, his laughter dying. "I guess I should have listened to him."

Martine felt her cheeks burn. She folded her hands on her lap and tried to think of something to say. "They're beautiful earrings, Father," she managed, and though ashamed she was also relieved beyond measure that they were for somebody else. "I'm sure your mother will be very happy with them. Are they diamonds?"

The priest curled his fingers over the little purse, which disappeared in his grip. "Yes," he said. "They were."

They were driving to Scarborough and the traffic was bad. As Elliott guided the big white truck creamily through all the cars and lights, Martine thought how strange it was to be sitting up front with him, instead of in the back the way she used to. He was less like a chauffeur this way, more like an equal. He still didn't say much, even though the three of them were crammed pretty close together. There was no room in the back, since it was loaded with boxes.

"Father," Martine asked, "what's in them? The boxes?"

His reply was as casual as her question; he'd been morose for several kilometres and was probably happy for the distraction. "Well, you see," he told her, "what we're carrying here is food of various types—candy, soft drinks, a fair number of canned goods. We keep some of it in the back of the Refuge but most is in the warehouse up north. What's it for? Well, I suppose you might call me a . . . food broker, kind of. See, companies give me food they can't sell: smooshed bags, boxes with dents in them and that. Then I sell it at a reduced price to vendors who can't afford the top-priced stuff, and the money I make goes to keeping up the Refuge and paying salaries. It's a win-win situation. Got it?" he asked, bright as a penny. "Up to date? Good. Now, the first thing we have to do is get a proper coffee maker, or Glenys'll roll up one of her health magazines and beat me to death with it."

Well, that all sounded simple, Martine thought. A win-win situation. No spiders under this rock.

They were actually going to get the coffee maker from Frost's cousin, a man more newly arrived from Poland than the rest. He operated a store called Tommy's Appliance Repair on a forgotten street that was free of character, a street that, like the others around it, was thick with the dust of failed mercantilism. On the way there Father Kearney related the long, sad tale of Tommy, who had been bothering Frost to come into his shop for many years. "Don't you have something's broken, Alek?" he imitated in a whiny singsong. "I can fix anything, you know. Anything." Weddings and

Alms

Filipowski family reunions were always, for Tommy, nothing more than good occasions to hustle business; even the funeral of his own mother found him pressing embossed cards — TADEUSZ (TOMMY) K. FILIPOWSKI YOU NAME IT WE CAN FIX IT — into the hands of startled mourners. Because of this annoying habit, he hadn't been invited to his aunt's benefit night. He was the second least-popular person in the family.

Elliott cruised the streets slowly, silent as usual. Finally he settled on a parking space that was comically inappropriate given the truck's size, though he somehow wedged it in. Good old Elliott, Martine thought. He stayed in the car while the others entered the store; this, she surmised, was how it always went. He was still Michael Collins, and so used to it by now that he didn't complain about it any more.

Inside, Tommy was so excited to see them he tottered about the room with the inefficiency of a blind penguin, banging into disabled microwaves and typewriters. "It is a shame not to see Alek," he sweated. "But you are his friends, he has told me — please, you are welcome here."

Martine winced at the awfulness of how glad he was to see them. It shouldn't have been so pleasing. Tommy ordered his teenaged assistant to the back where the coffee maker was, and in the meantime Father Kearney busied himself looking at the pictures on the bulletin board beside the cash register.

"Lovely." Kearney stretched the word out like taffy, which suggested he was talking about something he oughtn't, namely, a picture of a girl. Tommy allowed with embarrassment that it was his daughter. "That's your daughter?" the priest replied in disbelief. The girl in the photo was lying on a beach in a red bikini, and it suddenly struck Tommy that public display of such a thing must have been shocking to a priest's eyes. In an effort to prove himself a decent father, Tommy quickly extracted snapshots of his other daughters from a filing cabinet, pictures of younger girls in satin dresses and hair ribbons.

"There's Basia—but she's bigger than that now! Taller, I mean." He blushed and adjusted a pen in his breast pocket. "Well, you must tell Alek to come. When he's feeling better."

While he was talking Kearney kept examining the bikini girl, an art lover to the last. Then he seemed to remember that Martine was with him. He tore his eyes from the photo as if it were sunlight in his eyes and stood up, correct, smiling away at the one he'd brought to the dance.

She avoided his gaze, twiddling the knob of an old radio. Please stop looking at me, she felt like saying. But Father Kearney kept smiling, stupidly, in the evident belief that he was on the threshold of some very exciting project.

Tommy's assistant brought the coffee maker out and plunked it on the counter. "There," said Tommy. "I know it doesn't look very good, but it will make you some coffee, sure thing." He punched the cash register triumphantly. "Forty-two ninety-nine today, please."

The priest turned to him, pursed his lips together, and became very serious. "I'm sorry, Mr. Filipowski, but there seems to be a little misunderstanding here. You see—well, this is rather delicate . . ." He laughed and rubbed his hands together nervously. "Actually, sir, we were under the impression that this was a donation."

Alms

Tommy looked stricken, but recovered quickly. "Oh. Excuse me. I didn't know."

Father Kearney continued, in the same mellifluous salesman's drawl he'd used the other night in the kitchen. "You see, we're a charity, Mr. Filipowski. We don't have much money. And our clients dearly love coffee—it's one of the few pleasures many of them have."

Tommy had to concede that this was true, and felt so guilty for even thinking to charge them that he immediately offered filters and warranty protection and periodic visits to tighten the screws.

"Ah, thank you so much, but that won't be necessary," the priest demurred generously.

"No, please," said Tommy. "Here. Sanjay—give them that television, too, that little Panasonic. Your poor people will enjoy watching that."

Father Kearney thanked and thanked again, though he seemed to take the man's sacrifice as his due. People are eager to show priests how good they are, Martine saw, but priests— especially fake ones—always know theatre when they see it.

"Say hi to Basia for me," he said, then ushered Martine and the new appliances back to the truck.

Out on the street he reverted to his old good humour, whistling as he tucked the coffee maker behind some boxes in the back. Then he pulled the door down to lock it and said, "Our Dr. Frost would have liked that. Little family reunion."

Adjusting her seat belt, Martine felt strangely as if she had just witnessed a beating. The priest could easily have paid for the coffee maker, and his doing so would have meant a lot to that guy. Why didn't he?

329

Diamond earrings, she reflected, were paid for with this kind of thing.

"We going by the Ding Dot place now?" Elliott asked, trundling along. Sitting beside him, Martine jumped. It was shocking to hear him say anything, even the least little thing. Father Kearney was whistling, slouched against the window and oblivious to anyone but himself.

"The Ding Dot place, ho!" he barked. "But first S and S."

Elliott flinched a little at the order, but otherwise stared grimly ahead. He made no attempt to converse with Martine, of course, even though they were only separated by a half-inch of space. It was revelatory to be beside him. This way she could see his profile—with the same expression he must have worn back when they were kids. Tight-lipped, unhappy, troubled by an occasional sigh. Hands firm on the wheel. Suddenly the truth came to her: it wasn't Father Kearney who hated Elliott. It was the other way around.

Martine wondered how this had come about. Had Elliott respected the priest, then grown away from him after too much mistreatment? He was a born-again Christian, supposedly. But Martine had never believed that story. The truth was probably that Elliott hated everyone, herself included— and you couldn't entirely blame him.

Father Kearney couldn't have known it. No man could behave in so carefree a fashion if he knew that there was even one person on earth who hated him that much. And hating him so much wasn't such a bad idea right now, Martine thought. The priest insisted on reminiscing about the teenager in the red bikini, and she feared he might do this all afternoon.

330

"Pretty girl. I always wanted a summer place, you know," he gushed. "A nice big place opening onto my own stretch of beach, and then every morning I'd take my coffee out and see what sort of ladies had washed up on it. Elliott—you must have had a place like that somewheres."

Martine wondered if he was planning to invade it for some lakeside chicanery that, though temporary, would drive property values down well into the next century. "My family's is in Quebec, and Elliott's is in the Kawarthas," she intercepted.

Father Kearney asked, "Why, there's more than one Kawartha? Goodness, I didn't know. You see, I come from the kind of people that don't think summer is a verb."

His words were light but still testy. And when he spoke them, he looked at Elliott. And these kinds of "conversations" probably happened every day. Martine decided to take up the cudgel on poor Elliott's behalf. He would never do it for himself, after all.

"What did you do all summer, *Father,* if you weren't water-skiing with us?"

The priest cleared his throat and sat up straight, the picture of clerical rectitude. "Why, I was honourably self-employed in a variety of interesting occupations." There was music in his voice. It was still all a joke.

"Self-employed, Father? Why? Because A-1 Burger wouldn't hire you?"

He stopped looking at Elliott and hung his head. Finally he spoke. "No," he said. "No, there's no way they would have, would they."

Martine sank in her seat, a bit sick. No joke any more and he was trying to make her feel guilty, but it wouldn't work. Father Kearney's way was to skip the war and go straight to the medal, the honourable martyr who would rather submit than fight back, but she wouldn't let him do that this time; the medal would be pinned on someone else. "Well, Elliott didn't ask to be born where he was," she said, "so lay off him."

The truck was thus plunged into complete silence, which shamed Martine in spite of herself. In the movies, when a major argument was won—when the *coup de grâce* had been delivered by the repositor of all that was good—music swelled, backs were patted, the presence of a just God was felt. But in real life there was nothing but quiet, and a series of nagging questions for the victor: did I actually win? Am I, in fact, right?

They stopped in an alley behind S and S Convenience. There were leaking black garbage bags by the back door, and a cashier from the nearby Koffee Kave was shivering on a smoke break and flicking flies off his apron. The priest got out and rapped on the door. It was quickly answered by the man in the thick black glasses. He looked unsurprised to see Martine, who believed herself to be his only customer.

Elliott got out to help Father Kearney unload boxes. The boxes were all labelled Mr. Goodsweet Bananas and each of them featured a blue cartoon banana with the raised eyebrows and big smile of a bright child. The men didn't ask for Martine's help and she wondered at the necessity of her presence. If the priest only wanted a decoration, why didn't he just string her from the rear-view mirror?

When they were finished they set off again, this time for the Ding-a-Ling Nut Company. They weren't far from the

Refuge now and the darkened sky imparted an even more sinister cast to the neighbourhood, which was rich with decrepit office buildings whose every grimy window featured piles of paperwork framed by dirty drapes. The company manufactured, among other things, Ding Dots. Father Kearney had a meeting scheduled with some publicity person there; all in a day's work, Martine guessed, but there was a bad smell to it. She couldn't shake the sense that they were not on their way to the Ding-a-Ling Nut Company at all, but to some deserted cabin in a wooded grove where horrible acts could be carried out without impediment. She listened to the hum of the van's heater, to the empty rattle coming from the back; boxes which might well contain not bananas but ropes, lead weights, and wire cutters. She had a premonition of herself sinking in a murky lake, her torn cape floating free of her condemned body. But then, it wasn't as if she had other plans.

As they neared the Ding-a-Ling factory, they were hit by the scent emanating from within. "Check that," said the priest. "Peppermint." Martine permitted herself the luxury of deep breath, and with it a lung-bath of sugary gas. They stopped in front. Father Kearney wanted Martine to come with him to the meeting, but he had other plans for Elliott.

"Elliott," he said, still smiling, trying hard to be serious about the matter. "Could you go and check on Frost for me? Here, I'll give you the key. When I left him he was a little restless. I'm worried he might not have got to sleep properly. Just give him something to drink if he asks for it." Martine knew he didn't mean hot milk.

Elliott nodded, took the key, and was gone within seconds.

The remaining pair walked into the lobby, a sobering sight in their respective collar and cape. The receptionist sat up a little straighter on their approach. Beside her desk was a life-size statue of the Ding-a-Ling Man. He was a jaunty fellow whose limbs and torso were constructed of giant fibreglass candy canes. They had little chips in them as candy canes will, but he had been in the lobby a long time and retained his shiny painted smile. He wore a natty boater, which he tipped cordially between candy-cane thumb and candy-cane forefinger.

They were ushered into the offices of Ms. Debra Garlick, Associate Marketing Representative, a correct and pretty young woman with pearlized nails and eyelids. Father Kearney brightened at the injection of this sort of company into his day and he shook her hand with undisguised brio.

Ms. Garlick had not counted on two visitors, and she excused herself to seek another chair. The priest smiled gaily at her, after which he leaned in close to Martine.

"Now, you just sit quiet. Not that I need to tell you. But a few smiles might help—show off that beautiful Moore Park dental work." He winked and patted her hand. "She'll just ask a few questions and we'll be on our way."

Ms. Garlick returned with a chair for Martine. She took her seat briskly and knitted her sparkle-tipped fingers in front of her. "I must say that we admire very much what you're doing, Reverend. The objectives of your organization are really in line with where we're at in terms of community outreach and we do see the potential for some synergy here."

Father Kearney nodded vigorously about the synergy and shot a look at Martine to get her nodding, too.

"Our CEO wants to continue his involvement in the sort of thing represented by your organization and, at any rate, it's only a question of whether you wish to access any additional product lines. Your organization has quite a few children in its client base, I take it. They do enjoy the candy, don't they?"

Martine had a vision of Manny with his ancient eyes and raw red mouth that wouldn't smile, and mused that he hardly counted as one child, let alone many. But she said nothing.

"Generally, we provide fresh fruit and granola for the little ones," said the priest gently, "but the occasional treat is well appreciated, I can assure you."

Fresh fruit and granola? thought Martine. Little ones?

Ms. Garlick told him that while *her* organization obviously didn't deal in fresh fruit, there was a candied-fruit line that *his* organization might find very enticing indeed. Oh, it was all good and everyone would walk away happy, today and evermore. In fact, what they were looking at here, as Ms. Debra Garlick pointed out, was not so much a win-win situation as a win-win-*WIN* situation. "Goodness, we've never had one of those before," she said. "Now, about the tax receipt for today's shipment—"

"Ah yes," Father Kearney jumped in, "I'll take care of that now if you like." He extracted a receipt book from the inside pocket of his coat. "Here's our non-profit registration number—I'll write it at the top here. That's what you fill in on your tax form."

Ms. Garlick looked a little worried. "I was going to ask that you send us a confirmation letter when you get your shipment, Reverend. I'm new here and I'm not sure what the procedure . . ."

"It's okay, my dear, I spoke to Don about it last week—"

"Well, Don's out of town now . . ."

"I know, but that's fine, I'd better take care of it now since I'm leaving town next week, too." Father Kearney kept chattering in a hypnotically soothing way. "Don and I discussed the exact amount, so there won't be a problem there—glory to heaven, are those real topaz?"

Ms. Garlick touched her left earlobe. "No, no," she said, blushing. "They're just paste."

"I could have sworn," he continued. "Such a beautiful colour, with your eyes—a perfect match! Here, then." He finished writing out the receipt and blithely went over it with her. She tucked it uncertainly in the file, then took a pair of hairnets out of her desk.

A brief factory tour was the plan. There was a long hallway with a viewing area where Martine and the priest could see the Ding Dot "kreme" being squirted, iced, and packaged. In the hallway there was actually a giant portrait of the company's chief executive officer done entirely in Ding Dots, but it was dangerously unprotected by glass, and while Ms. Garlick had her head turned Father Kearney impishly picked one of these off the subject's chin and ate it, leaving the poor CEO with what appeared to be a shaving nick.

"Now, Reverend," Ms. Garlick said smartly when the tour was completed. "Before you leave I'm just going to get our photographer in here to take a little snapshot for our newsletter. If you don't mind."

"A photograph? Good idea," said Father Kearney. "And where would you like us to pose?"

Alms

But Martine couldn't do it, couldn't do it at all. Even in a hairnet, she would still be recognizable to whoever came across the newsletter in the future. "Father, I think it's better if you do it alone," she said. "It's your organization, after all."

"But you're a very big part of it, Sister."

Sister?

"No, I—I'll wait outside for you. Thank you. Very nice to have met you, Ms. Garlick. Thank you. Meet you outside." She walked confidently to the elevator and, once inside, backed against the wall and slid. Down.

*S*HE WAITED FOR HIM OUTSIDE on the sidewalk across the street, and when he came down twenty minutes later he looked very happy. He knew he'd pulled off a good one. He'd placed but one finger on the old building's side and still it crumbled before him. "That portrait of 'Our Founder'— done in Ding Dots! Could you beat that?" He sat down on the curb with Martine and rocked back and forth with pleasure. "Do you think they wheel out a lard sculpture of him for the Christmas party? Ice, more likely. So Little Miss Perfect in there—Ms. Garlick, what a name—can watch her boss's face melt while she sucks on the Ding-a-Ling man's candy-cane legs . . . oh, hey, Martine? What's wrong? Didn't you have a good time?"

The creep of disillusionment is slow and thick as lava down a mountainside; in the end it always engulfs the idea that there ever was an illusion at all.

"She really thought you were a priest, Father."

He gasped. "But I am one. I *am* a priest." His gaze was strabismic, his hands unquiet; his hair seemed to thin even as they spoke. Only his clothes were still and perfect. Without them, he seemed of little value.

"You don't know how much I wanted to believe that," Martine said.

He stopped twitching. They sat about two feet apart and he let his hands fall dumbly between his legs. For lack of anything better to do he leaned forward and looked down the hopelessly empty street. "Where—where's Elliott anyway, huh?"

He ached to fix it, Martine could tell. He threw his hands up and tried. "I'm sorry, love. It's just that . . . I mean, every time a person like that says *synergy*, doesn't it drive you crazy? Or *win-win* or *interface* or *impactful* or *liaise*? And her bloody tax receipt, Martine—when the candy's all going to waste anyway! A company can't just give it to you out of the goodness of its own heart because—and here's the thing you have to understand—a company doesn't have a heart. We've got blood in our veins, and they've got—I don't know, copy-machine fluid, or something. So goddamn their money and goddamn their charity, too, is what I say . . ."

He thought for another minute, then went on. "And what about *her*, that little machine cog in her high heels: *Oh, but I'll have to check that with Don . . . well, that's not what Don says* . . . She can't even make up her own mind, Martine, because she doesn't *have* a mind. You know what her skull's filled with? Kreme, that's what. Sugary, white, Ding-Dot kreme. And I just thought"—he tried to touch her but she flinched away—"I just thought you felt the same way I do about all this. I'm sorry."

She was sitting up straight in the way she always had, though she felt slack and beaten. "Clifford," she said. But she couldn't use his Christian name, it didn't feel right. "Father. I know you think Ms. Garlick's a hypocrite—and believe me, I'm one, too, and so is everyone I know. But you, Father. A fake priest." She shook her head. "You have to be the worst hypocrite of them all."

As soon as she said it she felt him smile. No edict carved in granite was ever going to make much of an impression on Clifford Kearney. She knew that women always lobbed noble moralisms at him, before hitching up their undies and going home to their boyfriends. Why start listening to them now? The smile turned into a laugh.

"Well, at least a hypocrite," he said, "is always doing something *half* right!"

She couldn't smile with him and he knew it. They sat like that for a few minutes more and still Elliott did not come. Father Kearney checked his watch and took out a smoke. "Your little . . . what's his name there, Flavio. I guess you'll go back to him, eh?"

"I don't know."

"No, no, you should. He's a good guy, isn't he? I've read about him in the papers. Only—what is he, twenty-three, twenty-four? Big, strong guy. Lots of awards. Bet he could be prime minister if he wanted. Of course, the good Lord's going to slap the bill on him some time, we know that. God always makes time to burn down our house or put us in a coma when he thinks we could use it. But here's what I don't get: why is this Flavio slopping around in the world of bad luck before he absolutely has to?"

Martine had no answer to this, and so he pressed on.

"I mean, do his clients really need that kind of yuppie crap waved in their faces every day? Wouldn't they rather be with people who understand them—*vulnerable* people, Martine, *sensitive* people? People like us."

Martine shivered. The sky was darkening; the Great Barkeep telling these last two stragglers to go home. She sighed. "Losers, you mean?"

"Ah, another word from the good folks who brought you *synergy* and *liaise*. I see you've memorized their dictionary."

He managed to light his cigarette, even though it was windy and cold. They sat apart but together, watching lights extinguish here and there in the building before them. Mr. Grey in accounts receivable; Mrs. Wilson in sales. Both had homes and both were going to them.

"I know it doesn't mean much to you," Father Kearney said, "but I'd do anything for you. I really would."

No man had ever told her that before. She used to dream about Flavio saying that sort of thing to her. The priest watched her; she knew that what he saw was a girl wishing someone else had complimented her.

"I can't help you with this," she said tightly, "this problem you have. With me."

He smoked in silence a moment. "That's all right." His voice was high and thin. "I'm sure I'll be able to work it out."

"And," she said, twisting the knife, "you should really save your kindness for others. It's wasted on me."

"I know." He threw the butt on the ground and stamped on it.

The big white truck now rumbled down the street before them. They had been sitting there a long time. Elliott pulled to a stop and waited patiently for them to climb in beside him, then explained why he was late.

Frost was vomiting blood when he got there. Elliott first called an ambulance and then Renata.

"Did they take him to St. Mike's?" the priest asked quietly. Elliott nodded. "Well, hurry up, for God's sake!"

Elliott kept driving, staring at the road, utterly impassive. "I'm not sure you're exactly the guy his parents want to see right now," he said simply.

Father Kearney looked as if might reply to this, but in the end he couldn't. "Yes," he said, "I suppose you're right." They seemed to be rambling toward home, though only Elliott knew for sure.

"Will he survive?" Martine asked.

Elliott shrugged. "I don't know," he said. "If he does, it would be good."

She shivered. But then so much went untreated in men like Frost and still they stayed alive. Sinus infections lasted for years and minor cuts yawned into chasms. Frost could lie dead, look dead for days, and not be dead; and now that he was finally nudging up against his own extinction, it came as both the most and least surprising thing she'd ever heard.

Elliott made a right onto Queen Street, and Martine guessed he was headed for the Refuge.

"I guess I always think of him like he used to be," Father Kearney said suddenly. "Like he could just take care of himself. I always think that, you know, today's the day he's just going to wake up and be the star again. The doctor." He tapped the window with his fingers. "If it wasn't for me, he'd be teaching at Oxford, I swear."

It was partly to console, but mostly to take the priest down a peg that Martine told him: "You may not have as much control over other people as you think. He's sick—anyone can see that."

Father Kearney kept staring out the window. "Sure. 'Mentally ill' is how Flavio and your pals would put it. But I think Frost himself put it best once. We were eighteen or so at that point. He told me that he was a kind of single-electron molecule, fine on its own but in trouble if it met up with a—what did he call it—a reagent, like heat or light." He looked out at the billboards and the sandwich shops, the absence of dogs or trees. "And I was the heat, or maybe the light. Maybe both. Without me, the whole experiment would never have happened."

Elliott was about to turn onto the little side street that was home to the Refuge when the priest suddenly leaned over and grabbed his wrist. "Don't," he warned.

"What?" Elliott said dumbly.

"That car." Father Kearney pointed to a burgundy sedan, not the sort of vehicle you'd notice if it weren't parked outside your restaurant, and with a man sitting in it, too. The man looked familiar to Martine. Had he come around before, disguised as a customer?

"Flip off that turn signal and drive," he said. "Drive straight toward my house, anything, but just keep going

343

while I think." He gnawed on a thumbnail and turned to Martine. "I'm sorry, my dear. I just don't like the look of that guy out front."

"Who is he?" Martine asked.

"He's probably nobody," Elliott put in. "He's probably just picking up his dry cleaning—I think it's still open . . ."

"And what the hell would you know about it?" the priest snapped. "That guy's bad news, Elliott, I should know. I grew up on these streets, you people didn't, and I've got a good feel for when someone's trouble."

Martine had to ask: "Trouble?"

"Just take me home," Father Kearney cut her off. "Then you and Elliott can do the hotel and the warehouse. I just have to think about some things, that's all."

Elliott pressed his foot on the gas and motored obediently toward Merseyfield: the wheelman, Martine thought sadly, for yet another criminal.

And once again, she knew, he'd get dragged under. Like the Frosts, his parents had surely given up by now. Martine had never intervened all those years ago when Jeremy used to hurl him down the stairs; she told herself then that Elliott liked it. But who could like pain? Over and over again. She'd got him into this, and now she had to get him out—but how?

When they got home the priest leapt out of the truck, distracted. Then he stopped, rubbed his mouth, and looked around him. "Uh . . . okay, Elliott. So after the warehouse you'll bring everything back here, including Martine. Then you and I will have a meeting and consider our next move."

Elliott leaned forward and started the engine. "Whatever you say, Father."

"Elliott," Martine said after they pulled away, "there's something you should know." No response. "Elliott, can we—can we pull over somewhere?"

"Can't. We're in a hurry, you heard Father."

There was no other way. She would just have to say it. Reach the warehouse, and they'd surely meet up with another burgundy sedan. "Father Kearney isn't what you think, Elliott. He's not a real priest."

No response.

"You could be in trouble here and I know you don't need any more of that."

Nothing. Like talking to a tree.

"This business of his," she continued stupidly, "I'm not sure it's exactly on the level. I mean, I don't know what it is. But that man outside the Refuge . . . I think he may be a policeman."

She saw the colour drain from his face. "Can't be," he croaked.

"Yes, Elliott. He is."

"No, you're wrong. The car's not right, for one thing."

"Look," Martine said, "I know your dad will come through for you, with the lawyers and everything. And I'll back you up, you have my word on it. I got you into this. I think of that every day, you know. I think of that all the time."

He took her advice, pulled over into a near-empty parking lot and stopped the truck. It was as if the idea had robbed him of breath. He clutched his stomach and she wondered if he was going to be sick.

"Elliott?" she asked, alarmed. "Are you all right?"

He turned to her and gave her one of those patented looks he had, one of those non-expressions that betrayed no emotion whatever. Then he pulled his sweater up slightly and she saw something black taped to his broad, pale abdomen. A truss or something. A bandage?

But it had wires snaking out of it, ugly black ones.

"I know your dad will come through for you," Elliott mimicked. *"With the lawyers and everything!"*

He broke out laughing. Then he got out of the truck, made a phone call, and returned to his stunned companion. Now it was his turn to talk.

"That stuff he told you," he explained after starting the truck up and making his way south, "is kind of true. He does get extra food from these companies, stuff they can't sell. Thing is, they don't expect *him* to go sell it. They think it's all going to, you know . . ."

"Porepeople," Martine said robotically.

Elliott took his eye off the road to look at her, and stayed looking at her for so long that he looked set to career into a mother pushing a stroller; but somehow he divined the woman's presence and got to the brake in time, gently, in complete control. He headed for the expressway and kept explaining.

"But he doesn't give it away, he sells it. And some of what he makes goes to, like, salaries and rent and running the Refuge, that's true. But there's still a lot left over after that."

"And he keeps it?"

"Yeah, he keeps it."

But how much does he keep? Martine wondered. The dollar figure probably wouldn't mean much to her. He was prosperous, comfortable, perhaps inordinately so, but given the neighbourhood any kind of prosperity seemed out of place. At any rate, others skimmed more off the top for their troubles—Elliott's father, for example, or Pépère. Granted, they did it all in the open, but was it really so different?

"How do you know all this?" she asked.

Elliott parked the truck in front of a giant garage, set in the back of an old building near the Exhibition grounds. "I'm paid to know it," he said. "Well, not in *money* I'm not. But the cops had me cooked on something else I did and now I'll walk free. Who cares about money, anyway? Freedom's better. I'll take freedom any day."

He opened the heavy door by himself and invited her inside. Her mouth suddenly filled with a terrible taste, though she hadn't eaten anything. The folksinger guy . . .

"That man. In the car, out front."

"Yep," Elliott said. "A hall monitor."

There were cardboard boxes everywhere, piled to the ceiling in places. Blue and black ink proclaimed their contents—soda pop, candy, bananas, soup. Anything you could eat or drink, actually. Clearly some of it had rotted; the air carried the sour, sugar-breakdown smell of food garbage, and rats skittered in the corners, stopping to gnaw on scavenged hunks.

"Will he go to jail?" Martine asked.

"Unless he can figure some way out of it. He's a charming guy, though. He'll find a way."

He hefted a large box handily and made for the truck.

"Will I?" she asked. "Will I go to jail?"

"No. The rest of you guys are fine. Though some people I know might want to talk to you."

"Well," Martine said, "they won't get much out of me. I don't know anything, do I? I knew nothing."

Elliott started for the truck. "Right," he said.

She tried to lift one of the boxes but it was too heavy. She struggled, struggled, but had in the end to give up. Elliott, having loaded three boxes already, hoisted hers without any trouble. "This is the last time I do this," he said. "Gonna have to get another job." Showing off, he piled another box atop that one and staggered away. "Hey, if you hear about something—let me know!"

They finished loading the truck and climbed back in. Elliott wiped his hands on his sweater and sniffled; he had a bit of a cold. "Street smarts, ha! If there were any such thing as street smarts, you think so many of these guys would be in jail? Let's take the long way back," he said. "It's nice talking to you. We never really talked before."

They drove along the lake, but Martine couldn't think of anything to say. That was fine. It was Elliott's turn to talk now.

"He liked you, you know. Kearney. He thought you were a real *lady*. He used to say, 'What do you think my chances would be with someone like Martine?' And I'd say, 'Father, are you kidding? What are you after *her* for?'" He snorted.

"What do you mean?" she asked, offended.

"Come on."

"Well," she said haughtily, "your brother sure liked me. He was always asking me to marry him."

Elliott laughed. "Yeah, well, let me tell you something you might not know. My dad had this rule: he used to tell us you should never marry for love. Because if you're in love, you're exposed. You could get hurt. You could give away the store. He said a family is a business—and would you go into business with a lover? Of course you wouldn't. That's why I think Jeremy liked you: he was afraid he'd never meet anyone he loved less than you." He smiled. "You were perfect for him."

He turned onto a residential street full of tall thin houses. "You know what he used to call you? The Stick. 'I've got a date with the Stick,' he used to sing. 'I think I'm going to be sick . . .'"

Martine screwed her eyes shut. "Stop," she begged him.

"Sorry," Elliott said. "That was mean, I shouldn't have told you that."

They passed a gaudy plaster fountain crowned by a urinating cherub. When Martine saw it she felt a flash of grief: it meant they were close to Helping Hands.

There was a lot of commotion even two blocks from its front door. Television vans and cameras, and many more cars than usual, including a limousine. There were also a number of teenagers with gelled hair and expensive leather jackets. "Aw, how the hell am I going to get through this?" Elliott muttered, honking his horn. He tried backing up but another van was coming up behind him. They were stuck. Martine rolled down a window and asked a harried police officer what was going on.

"Lionel Richie," the policeman said, "the singer. He's in there doing some charity thing before his concert. Let me get this guy to back up, I'll get you out of here."

While Elliott was backing up, Martine remembered the little purse, with the *M* on it. She wondered if it really was empty when Kearney found it.

This time Martine stayed in the truck while Elliott did all the work. They had made their way across town to the hotel; they had to finish up, after all. Kearney had asked them to.

When they got back to the Refuge, bearing trays of tartlets and smoked salmon on pumpernickel, they saw that it had been abandoned. The folksinger had left and the door was ajar, but Glenys and Dianne weren't there, and neither were any customers; a Closed sign hung askew on the front door. Some of the stacking chairs were turned over and broken plates were scattered on the floor.

"They must have searched the place, then gone to his place to pick him up there," Elliott said. "Let's see if his petty cash is still there." He led Martine to the back room, which was dank and poorly lit, considering it had once been the storeroom of a lighting shop. Empty shelves lined the walls and the floor was littered with boxes, some empty and overturned. Elliott rucked up the carpet in one corner and jimmied a couple of floorboards. He took out a small cash box and counted the contents. "Fifteen hundred . . . sixteen . . . yep, it's all still there. One thousand eight hundred and twenty-seven dollars and sixty-four cents. Don't ask me why, but it's always that amount."

"He doesn't use it?"

"Naw. He just likes to have it around. 'For a rainy day,' he says. Well, it's a rainy day. I'll ask them to let him keep this." He stuffed the cash box back under the floorboards. "He'll need it, it'll be the only thing he has left."

"It's not that much money," Martine said.

"I know. What a loser, eh?"

"Yeah," Martine replied quietly. "What a loser."

They shared the food. Martine insisted on reserving all the chocolate-covered strawberries for herself. It was odd; this was no time to feel hungry, much less to do anything about it, but she was and she did.

While they were cleaning up, Elliott said, "By the way, those earrings *were* for you."

"How do you know that?"

"Because," he smiled, "he doesn't have a mother. His mother's dead."

*T*ERESA KEARNEY WENT from frail to sick to dying within months. Rosemarie grudgingly made her meals and applied the plasters, but Clifford was his mother's preferred caregiver at the end. He would take a warm, wet sponge to her feet and talk to her for hours about God and Hawaii, her two favourite subjects. He would reapply her lipstick for her, a hot-pink colour that disagreed violently with her red hair. If she'd been born wealthy, she'd have surrounded herself with the feel of Dior and the scent of Shalimar; as it was she spent most nights trussed in a flannel nightgown, propped on yellowed lace pillows her own grandmother had tatted. She hung several cheap plastic leis on the wall for colour, to lend a certain atmosphere to the dreamy dialogues she'd hold with her son.

"What is faith, Mother?" he asked, knowing this was the kind of ingratiating question she liked, and the kind that

Alms

would drive Rosemarie mad should she chance to hear it in the corridor.

In response Teresa would ruffet the air with her tiny painted nails and launch into recitations of extemporaneous poetry, some of which made sense. "Faith is the cool of silver in your palm, Clifford. Faith is the patter of rain on the eaves, the shiver of new leaves in spring. But mostly faith is the sun. Faith warms as it blinds, and what a beautiful blindness it is. What a lovely, lovely infirmity it is."

On a turntable in the corner, Kearney played her favourite records for her: "Sweet Leilani," "Going to the Huki Lau," "Way Down in Hilo Town."

"I wish I could see it, Clifford. The beach with the waves."

"You will, Mother."

"In my mind I see it."

One day she turned to him with a sad look, which worried him. She was usually serene, and though he sensed that all happiness might be nothing more than an idiot's escape from honest despair, it was an idiocy he nonetheless wished on her. "Bad people feel love, Clifford. But only good people practise it. I am a bad person because I could not make real the warmth I felt for others. Breathe out a tune is all I could do and most days not even that. I do not want you to love. I want you to *show* love. Will you do it, Clifford?" He told her he would try, though he never really understood what she was talking about.

Teresa saw him as a kind of Father Damien character, ministering to the lepers on the shores of Molokai. To her, it was not a question of whether he would enter the seminary, but of when. In fact, the local priest became so exasperated

353

at having to come in so often to deliver extreme unction that Clifford memorized the routine and took it over.

There was vomiting and fever, and in the end she could not talk or move. She was taken to St. Michael's and they did what they could. Food poisoning; if she'd been stronger, the doctors said, she could have survived it. To Rosemarie, the death was expected and came as a relief. To her it seemed as if her mother had faded as naturally as a hit song on the radio. Teresa had always been so weak. But Clifford took his mother's death differently. He cried for days, immersing himself in the tinny clang of her ridiculous records.

He wanted to cremate her and scatter her ashes over the palms on a beach made black by crumbled lava, or one thick with the warmest of white sand. But it was out of the question. There was the airfare, for one thing.

His gentle lunatic of a mother. Felled for all time by a simple bowl of split-pea soup.

Martine picked up a broom to sweep up the broken plates. "Did you tell him?" she asked. She tried to wipe surreptitiously at her tears so that Elliott wouldn't see them, but it was useless. You couldn't hide anything from Elliott.

"Nah. Why make it worse for him than you have to? Here, you need this?" He stuck a hand in his pants pocket, took out a wrinkled handkerchief, and held it out to her. His initials were monogrammed in the corner.

"No, thank you," she said. "But you can do me one favour. I don't want to go back to the house on Merseyfield. Will you take me home? To my mom's house?"

"Don't you need your stuff?"

"I don't have any stuff."

What choice did she have: her visa had expired and it was time to return. Indeed, she now saw Moore Park as another country entirely, with its own dialect, mores, and cuisine. When you were born in a country you could not rid yourself of it; you were irretrievably wired to it, even if your blood ran less than blue—and this Martine's did, thinned as it was by the prairie farm taint of her father, but still. She was a Berthiaume born and raised, suckled on soup that bore her esteemed name. Her feet had been moulded by imported leather shoes and could not be reshaped. Her baby's nose was taught the scent of costly perfume. She was not programmed for thrift. You could not unmake a human being.

She looked out the car window and saw in the streetlight that the lawns were still green under a light cover of frost. Hedges out front were still impossibly levelled and squared, and many of them were now suffering under the weight of large and garish Christmas lights. Each grand house was as she had left it, including her own.

When Martine got home, she approached the front door and removed the key from around her neck. She had taken to wearing it this way on a tip from Suleiman, who did the same, with the difference that his front door was thousands of miles away and didn't exist any more.

Martine's house was half lit, but nobody appeared to be home. Certain that her mother was asleep, she padded softly across the carpet so as not to wake and be forced to confront her. But a tentative creep past her bedroom revealed that

Louise wasn't even there. Out for the evening! Could this really be?

Martine was gratified to see that her own room hadn't changed at all. How many times had she thought of taking Flavio Vargas up here, of mussing its department-store-perfect bed with him. He may well have done damage to similar bedding in Carolyn Colterblake's house two streets away, underneath that infernal poster on her wall, the one that featured a Scotch terrier and the legend: A SMILE MAKES MY TAIL WAG. Martine imagined Kearney on the mauve bed, in full uniform, bouncing up and down. Derision would galvanize him; he would bend one of the throw pillows over his head and warble "I Enjoy Being a Girl" at the top of his puny lungs. Neighbours would talk.

She went into the pine chest of drawers and took out a pressed flannel nightgown. It smelled of fabric softener and potpourri. She slid into it, savoured the feel, and remembered that she had left her toothbrush downtown. It didn't matter. Louise always kept ten or twelve unopened in the master bathroom.

When she slid between the cold sheets she felt like an exchange student who had completely forgotten the language she'd just been sent overseas to learn.

The next morning, when Martine descended, Louise was standing over the stove pushing bacon around in a pan. She was happy to see her prodigal daughter, but not overly so. The happiness did not engulf her, cause her to stammer, swell her muscles with the power to hug so hard she inflicted pain. It was more like the happiness she might feel upon coming across a pearl earring long thought lost to shag carpeting. She asked nothing about where Martine had been.

"Come sit," she said brightly, motioning to the dining table in the sunroom.

She looked healthy, too—very healthy; and Martine once again considered that the only thing worse than the troubles of a loved one is the disappearance of those troubles in one's absence. Somewhere, for example, the Gipper must have wept over the fact that they won *without* him.

There were the Scandinavian cutlery and juice glasses on the table, the orange woven tablecloth, and the pot of chrysanthemums in the centre. The butter and jam, on chunky little plates. She still served breakfast like this, even on Emelda's days off.

The younger woman sat down and Louise placed a plate of scrambled eggs in front of her, but didn't, as was her custom, stay there to make sure they were eaten. When they *were* eaten, she didn't seem to care. It was merely the signal that breakfast had ended, not V-E Day or Christmas, though Martine sort of hoped she might see it that way. What was going on here, exactly? Louise continued to express zero-point-zero curiosity about Martine's "trip," or about whether it had in fact ended. A course! That was it, she must have taken a course—like the time she had enrolled in assertiveness training back in the Mack Donovan era, then dropped it when it conflicted with some unspecified need of his. Or maybe she had a guru, or a swami, purring, "Let it go, let it go," on cassette tape in the car.

Louise returned, picked up the empty plate, rinsed it, and placed it in the dishwasher. She wiped her hands, turned brightly around, and said, "Well! What are your plans for the day, then?"

"Mama. I was just remembering something you told me once—about the underdog being that way for a reason. Why did you say that?"

Louise laughed and turned her gaze toward the garden.

"I suppose I didn't want you to get hurt," she said. "Like I have been hurt."

Kindness and forbearance destroyed Louise, drove her to drugs and sleep, almost killed her. She plainly didn't have the taste for them any more.

"But you could have avoided all that hurt, Mama. You could have put your foot down."

Louise's eyes started to mist. She never failed on that score—five miles away from the matter's deepest, blackest heart and she would still start crying. Her upwellings were so regular that the Professor and Martine had dubbed her "Old Faithful," which was a good nickname for her, when you thought about it. And now that she was finally happy, Martine was making her cry. Is this what I've come to? she asked herself. Is this all I'm good for?

But the mist itself was just a trick of the light, and no tears came. "That's very good advice. I wish I'd taken it sooner."

"Well," Martine said, "you weren't so badly off, though, the way you were."

"Oh, yes I was. I was an idiot."

Bandaging *my* knees, pouring *my* cornflakes, driving *me* to lessons, spooning *me* medicine—all the acts of an idiot?

"But you were a *saint,* Mama. Everybody said."

Louise's eyes snapped away from the garden and back into the business of the day, fogged and reluctant to dawn as it was. "Hah. Time for a career change, I guess." She gave a cynical little laugh. "Speaking of which, I have to go in to work today, so . . ."

"Work! But Mama, it's Saturday—and since when do you work?"

Louise blushed. She said that Sharon had lately been doing some fundraising work for the symphony, but since Carolyn was getting married in March—"Oh, did I tell you?"—and there were so many preparations, she was farming out a few hours here and there to her friends.

Martine panicked. "But your volunteering, Mama—your opera, AIDS, all those other things . . ."

Her mother laughed. "Nobody respects you in this world unless you earn an honest buck! You especially, *minou*. You're the one who was always telling me I should get a job."

Martine honestly could not remember this. If it had happened, it was a million years ago. Then she asked, in a voice that aimed for lightness but caved like a failed soufflé, "By the way, who . . . who is Carolyn marrying?"

"Oh, it's that boy from Argentina. He went to St. Joachim's—I'm sure he must have been there at the same time you were . . ."

"Chile," Martine said. A short word, rimed with frost.

"Chile, is it? I always mix those two up. Anyway, Sharon had a hard time with the idea at first, but she seems to have come around. I mean, you don't spend two thousand dollars on a dress six months before the wedding if you haven't come around! But as for the work, it's just a few hours whenever I can spare it."

"Uh-huh."

"Well, Listen, sweetheart. Why don't you take my credit card and let Max give you a haircut? It'll really pick you up and I've already called him—he said he could fit you in around noon. I'd love to see your pretty face again."

Max was Louise's long-time hairdresser, or "hair designer" as he'd recently taken to calling himself. He was a bearded Hanoverian who had been sparring with Martine since her earliest childhood; it was rather a miracle that they hadn't killed each other, though they'd come close one afternoon in 1977: "Don't eefen esk for a Farrah Fozit, Miss Craythorn. Your hair simply von't do it."

"I don't want any stupid ugly Farrah Fawcett."

He picked up a drooping brown skein and shook his head. "If you hed your mother's beautiful netcheral curls, then maybe—but I am thinking for you more a Dorothy Hamill, so."

"Cut it all off."

"Oh, no, Miss Craythorn. No no no no. Your mother vould neffer permit this."

"Look, I can get your Christmas bonus cancelled in two seconds flat, guy. Now cut it off, as short as you can."

Max sighed, took her lightly by the jaw and tilted her head to one side, then the other. He frowned. "But really—forgive me, my dear, but your head is so small! Do you really want a Joey Heatherton, hmm?"

Martine whirled around to face the insubordinate manservant directly. "No, I don't want a Joey Heatherton," she said.

"Or a Dorothy Hamill, or a Suzanne Somers, or any of those other stupid bitches. I want a *Joan of Arc*—that's who I want."

Now it was ten years later. The angry, hacked cap he'd reluctantly given her that day had grown back and then some. Martine fingered the bangs in front of her eyes and said, "I don't really feel like seeing Max today, Mama."

Louise laughed as she tied a beige silk scarf around her neck. "Of course you don't!" she trilled, gay as May. "But you have a great day, whatever you decide to do," she said with a breezy trot toward the door. "Take the credit card anyway, and buy yourself a nice dress."

Martine pocketed the card and took the subway downtown. Downtown as she used to think of it: full of ladies who spritzed you with scent in the department stores, full of teenagers with braces and long futures coiled before them. The windows were tricked out for Christmas, with displays anchored by battery-powered teddy bears thocking out "The Little Drummer Boy" on toy drums. She walked into one of the giant record emporia and started rifling through the albums, as one does if one is young and temporarily at the reins of the familial Brinks truck. Nobody had recorded anything different or interesting in the last two months. It didn't look like anything had really changed culturally since she'd been away, although there appeared to be something of a mania now for flavoured iced tea: I must pick some up, she thought.

She bought three compact discs, though she didn't even want one, and went uptown on foot somewhat comforted by the bag's heft in her hand.

There were miles of streets full of nothing but surging, confident people, people happy on their own, people who never made inappropriate eye contact. It was really a marvellous place, she thought, this city; really something to celebrate. But with whom will I celebrate it? Everyone's gone.

With a little backtracking she was easily pulled west, toward the coffee shop across the street from the Professor's house. Maybe he'll see me from his apartment, she thought. Maybe he'll come down and we'll have tea together.

She sat down at the counter, ordered coffee, and waited. Then she ordered a mille feuille and waited some more. She picked the pastry apart, feuille by feuille, and before long it was gone. But the Professor did not come.

As night came and lampglow spilled across the streets she remembered a story that he'd once told her, on the couch after an Obike date. "Stay," he'd said to her, as she prepared to leave. "Do you have to go?"

Martine was shocked and sat back down: he'd never tried to hold her there before, but there was obviously something he needed to talk about that day.

He told her he'd just come back from a drought-stricken village where many of the adults and most of the children were suffering from malnutrition and its attendant complaints. Bureaucratic bungling prevented any food from getting to them and death came every day. It took every molecule of flesh it could, then plundered hope and breath. You could haul bodies three at a time, like so much cardboard. It was the worst thing he'd ever seen.

His voice was flat and quiet. He wasn't telling her this to educate her, since there was no education to be had from it. He was telling it because he had to keep telling it.

Alms

"And what did you do?" Martine asked him, unable to understand how he could spend even half an hour in such a place. "What did you do to keep yourself from going crazy?"

The Professor stroked his beard and thought about it. "I just kept saying one thing to myself, over and over," he told her. "There was only one thing I could say that made me feel any better at all. And that was: I'm glad it's not me."

Thus do fingers loosen. Thus does one person send another off to sea.

Several days later, as Martine was watering the Boston fern in Louise's sunroom, she noticed an ant crawling round the side of the pot. She remembered that even good, loving St. Francis hated ants, because they stored things for the winter. He much preferred birds, who never saved anything. The truth is they're both annoying, thought Martine, squishing the ant.

She spent the next few days alone, for the most part, accompanied only by the ticking of various grandfather clocks echoing off the walls of faraway rooms. She unearthed her oboe, just to enliven the soundless void. There were even some reeds left from the old days, in relatively good shape, and the sheet music didn't have so many Kool-Aid stains on it that she couldn't read it. She freed "Valse Polonaise" from the bonds of its yellow folder and set about nailing it. In honour of Frost, that most curious and troubled *polonais*. One hour of practice on Wednesday, leading to two hours the next day and three the day after that. By the weekend she was philharmonic-bound: hard work that produced results! But by Monday the glow of mastery had dimmed—the piece was silly and stilted, Chopin by way of Mantovani. And the oboe, no matter how well played, was a minority taste, lacking the authority of the piano or coquettish charms of the flute. "Sounds like a cat farting," Pépère had once remarked after listening to her practise. The instrument's very unpopularity was naturally what had drawn her to it in the first place. She put it away.

When practice time came the next day she watched Phil Donahue instead, followed by twenty-six consecutive rock videos. Having started watching television, she had to keep watching it or else face the fact that she *had* been watching it. While watching she thumbed back issues of *Gourmet* and *Architectural Digest,* to give her fingers, bereft of their oboe keys, something to do. Then, inspired by the Dizzy Gillespie rerun of "Celebrity Cooks," she found herself eating. A lot. Anyone could make Dizzy's recipe for "Harlem Stew," after all: it was only baked beans and bourbon. Searching the cupboards for the former, she realized what a delightful motherlode of sweetened, salted crud her mother's kitchen had become. A can of aerosol cheese here, a bag of gummi worms there. Flavoured iced tea, even. So it was that she ate anything she wanted, and swore she saw her calves thickening with the speed of time-lapse photography: why, she felt like a dreadnought listing through the kitchen, even though she probably hadn't gained that much weight. Still. In the event of an Andean plane crash, someone might even think about taking a fork to her.

There had been a time when this kind of life had held a secret appeal for her, with all its trappings: junk food, booze, drugs, game shows, porn, green eyeshadow, rhinestones, lying in bed until two, photo spreads featuring a sitcom star's new back patio, the saving of the cruellest remarks for the people she most loved. Then, temptation had droned about her like a cloud of midges. But such things had lost their savour now that she gave herself over to them. Her belly was full and her feet were warm, and she felt neither pleasure nor dismay. Each phase of her downtown life had been so bad as to leave her desperately eager for another, which was fine: another was always close at hand. Now there was nothing to look forward to but more okayness—days and days of dreary unbroken okayness. If only she could get her hands on the controls! If only she could find the perfect line between too much and not enough, and pull everyone onto it with her.

On Thursday there was an article in the paper's city section. Martine might not have noticed it, since it was brief and there was no accompanying picture. MAN ARRESTED IN FOOD BANK SCAM was the headline. The article detailed how the police had apprehended a fellow who, over the last several years, had posed as a "Saxon Catholic" priest in order to collect food for charity, which he then sold at a discount to various food wholesalers and distributors. Not so much of a discount, of course, as to leave no profit for himself. In fact, the sum he'd amassed over the few years he'd been doing this was quite impressive; hundreds of thousands, perhaps, though the full accounting was not in. The man's name was Clifford Joseph Kearney. No other names were mentioned.

On Friday afternoon, Louise went antique hunting in the country with Jane Pine. They returned around five o'clock, dappled with sawdust and smelling of woodsmoke. It was all very nineteenth century. They shed their vicuna and leather and wool and decided that mulled wine might be a nice thing, on an awfully cold day like this. "I'll see if I have any cinnamon sticks," said Louise.

Jane Pine entered the den imperially. Her frosted beige hair had grown puffier since Martine had last seen her; the grooves alongside her mouth were deeper. She was all courteous cool, a masterpiece of disdain. "Hello, Martine."

"Hello, Mrs. Pine."

"I haven't seen you in ages! Why don't you give the boys a call?"

"We found cinnamon! Hooray!" Louise shouted from the kitchen. Then, after a plink of spoons, she called, "Elliott's back, did Jane tell you?"

No wonder, then, about the additional yuletide smarm glinting under the good lady's face powder. "And," Louise continued, looming up beside Jane, "you'll never believe what he's doing. Guess."

Any guess she might make would come across as an insult, so Martine shook her head. "I couldn't possibly, Mama. Tell me."

"He's applying to the police academy! Isn't that great?"

Martine had often asked herself why, in childhood, Elliott Pine let himself be thrown down the stairs, time after time. She'd never know, exactly, but he probably had it all thought out even then. Maybe Father Kearney was right: maybe there was no such thing as a loser. Elliott was only ever play-acting, vacationing. Trying on loss for size.

*T*HE DOORBELL RANG while she was sitting in front of "One Life to Live," to which she'd become rather attached. She gathered her housecoat around her and went to see who it was. It was Flavio.

She stood before him, so mystified that she forgot he was standing in frigid winter air. A snowstorm had recently ended and it was surprising to see anyone at the door. When she finally remembered to invite him in she felt immediate shame about the soap opera, the empty chip bag on the floor, the pyjamas at two o'clock, but then she'd never had much of a chance with him anyway.

"I wanted to thank you for the donation," he said gravely. His prideful bulk was increased by the leather bomber jacket he wore. Second-hand, no doubt. At least the ponytail was gone. It had been set loose so that his hair hung in thick black banners. Fashionable—but surely Sharon Colterblake would expect a trim in advance of the wedding? And what's this about a donation?

"It was extremely generous," he continued.

"Oh," Martine blurted, rushing around, cleaning and arranging and smoothing her hair down. "Oh, well. It was nothing." The impulse to lie was bizarrely automatic when it came to Flavio.

"Nothing?" he objected. "I'd hardly call eighteen hundred dollars nothing!"

"Eighteen hundred dollars?" she asked, startled.

He took a cheque out from a white envelope he was carrying and looked at it. "I'm sorry, I should be more precise. Eighteen-hundred and twenty-seven dollars and sixty-four cents. Interesting amount!"

She bade him sit down and noticed there was another piece of paper in the envelope. "Could I see that?" she asked shakily. He handed it to her, a little surprised.

The message was very plain, but it was handwritten. It struck her that in all the time she'd known him she'd never once seen Father Kearney's handwriting. *Please accept . . . To spend in any way you see fit.*

The script was oddly small, with tidy *g*'s and little triangles running off the *f*'s. "Felon's claws," she said.

"Excuse me?"

"Nothing. You're welcome." She folded the paper and handed it back.

"I'm sorry to show up like this," Flavio said, removing his gloves, "but my fiancée gave me your address. Carolyn Colterblake." She noted with nausea that his voice rose when he said her name. "I guess your mothers know each other, is that right? I hope you don't mind my coming by like this."

"Not at all," she said, in a papery imitation of the Colterblake gentility. She heard her voice as if voyaging above it in a balloon; the gay little bell of a voice she was born to, deformed by rising pain. "Could I get you something?" she asked. "Coffee? Cookies?"

He declined with a grace that showed he was more at home in a home like this than she was, which irritated her. She was suddenly angry with him. She wanted to hit him with one of the antique-fireplace implements Louise had bought in the country with Jane Pine. But she flittered like a debutante, too; old habits die hard. "It's been a long time," he said.

"Yes, it has."

"Look, Martine—you're probably pretty busy now"—he said this without even one sarcastic glance at the bare knees jutting from her housecoat—"but I'd like you to know that you're always welcome to come back and work with us, if you have any time to spare. It would be great to see you down at Helping Hands again."

She didn't hear what he said, but she sensed he was proposing something delightful, spectacular, and helpful. A win-win situation. Who could resist that? Was it a garden party he'd asked her to organize? A benefit? Some annual general meeting the purpose of which was the overthrow of everything that wasn't soaked in utter excellence? Whatever it was, it sounded wonderful. "Sure," she said, because she would always say yes to Flavio. Beautiful, perfect Flavio. "Maybe tomorrow afternoon? If the snow isn't too bad."

369

"Absolutely," he replied. "Oh, I should tell you— Helping Hands has moved. We just got a bigger place, right on the subway line. Here, I'll write down the address for you. A lot more space. We've got proper offices, too, and new computers."

Volume volume volume. Location location location.

He scrawled the new address on a business card and handed it to her. After he'd finished, though, he made no move to go. Instead, he stood in the den and looked around, at the waxed mantelpiece with its family pictures framed in silver. His gaze settled on an old photo of Pépère poised to swing a five-iron and rested there for a minute. "Martine, there's something else I wanted to address with you. I'm not sure how to say it."

Damned if he doesn't look uncomfortable, Martine thought, gratified. Flavio winced and crossed the room to sit beside her.

"My fiancée, Carolyn," he began, "she's a psychologist . . ." He looked down at his big hands and started massaging one with the other. "She's very talented."

My God, Martine thought, *he is trying to get out of this marriage and he doesn't know how to do it.* Yes, Carolyn was talented—but what of it? Looks and brains and accomplishments are nothing, if not salted liberally with compassion— compassion being, quite naturally, the thing that drives us, we two, Flavio, keepers of the ancient flame. There aren't many people like us in the world. Go on.

"I'll get to the point," he said. "Carolyn does work with women—girls, really—who . . . have concerns. With eating."

Martine stared at him expectantly, as if he had not said anything at all.

"She's very good at what she does," he continued. "And you know her, of course."

"I know her."

"So, it's just that—if you'd ever like to talk—she's very helpful. And she would see you right away, you wouldn't have to wait."

For months, Martine had been haunted by the woman with the black eye, the one whose boyfriend was just "checking up," the one she hadn't given the shelter number to. The woman came to her in dreams; she'd sincerely thought about going back, trying to find her, but she couldn't remember her name. Marla . . . Darla . . . she conceived the idea of going to Claudia, describing her, but how far would that get her? Blonde Woman with Black Eye, you know the one! The *one*? No, Flavio's approach was the right one. Direct, yet shy and deferential. You covered the bases, but pretended embarrassment at having to cover such bases—such filthy, scuffed, debased bases.

"No, thank you," she said.

"Okay," he said warmly, clearly relieved to have gotten it out of the way. "Oh, I almost forgot. I have a receipt here," he said. "For the donation." His left hand disappeared into the bomber jacket, but Martine stopped him.

"It's all right."

"But—you get a . . ." He shook his head. "I guess I don't understand you, Martine. I'm sorry."

She smiled. At least he had once—up to five minutes ago, at any rate—considered her someone he might understand; not a frightening unmanageable, but a friend. That was flattering. She got up and walked over to the little wooden

Kleenex dispenser she had carved in shop class ten years before. She blew her nose and said, "I don't want a tax receipt. But there is one thing you can do for me."

"What?"

"Wait here a minute."

She ran upstairs to her closet, the one with the Persian carpet that never got used. After some rummaging she emerged with a piece of cardboard and ran downstairs to give it to him.

"Do me a favour. Put this up, beside rules one to five." He stretched his arms before him and beheld it, its pathetically scrawled message chipping, never really legible even in its heyday: LOVE THY NEIGHBOUR AS THYSELF. He accepted it with an uncomfortable frown.

"I can't put this up, I'm sorry. We're not a religious charity."

"But if you're a socialist, you have to be a Christian. You said. Remember?"

"No," he said, handing the pathetic thing back as if he couldn't wait to get rid of it. "It's the other way around."

"Oh, of course. Well, keep it anyway, will you? As a wedding present?"

He took it back unhappily. "Okay." He tried to smile at her but his eyes betrayed him. "Thank you," he said.

She wrapped her housecoat around herself and walked him to the door.

"So, tomorrow afternoon?" he asked.

Martine pursed her lips. "You know what—can I get back to you on that? I'll give you a call, how about?"

"Of course," he said. He seemed relieved.

She watched him march down the bitterly cold walk and into a car that she could just make out as being Mott Colterblake's black Audi. He started it and pressed the gas pedal, but it didn't budge; it was stuck in a drift. She watched him press, and press again. The hysterical engine was sounding ever more operatic and he couldn't move at all.

"Hold on!" Martine yelled. She threw on her cape and ran upstairs to find some sweatpants. Then she hurried downstairs, laced on boots, and ran down the front walk.

Flavio opened the car door, embarrassed. "I'm sorry. It's Carolyn's father's car—the tires aren't great in this."

"Here," Martine told him. "Start the car again, and do a back-and-forth thing while I push."

She got behind the big Audi and heaved against its rump, while Flavio alternated between reversing it and driving it forward. After a few minutes of this they freed it from the drift, and he roared up and out of it.

He rolled the window down. "Thanks!" he called out.

"No problem."

Martine waved him away and watched him drive down Garland Avenue. She was cold, pyjama-clad, and shivering outside in the December dark. She didn't have a penny to call her own either.

But she was glad, as always, to be of assistance.

"Any time," she whispered.

Acknowledgments

Many thanks to my editor, Barbara Berson, for her faith, humour, fine ear, and common sense. To Jennifer Cowan and Margaret Webb, for their friendship and reassurance. And to my wonderful family for all their love and support: my husband Russell Silverstein, my daughters Margot and Rachel, as well as my parents, brothers, and in-laws.

I am particularly indebted to my cherished friend Bernice Eisenstein, whose guidance, kindness, and hard work on my behalf were essential to the completion of this book.